THE KALISTA DIAMOND

A STEELE OPS NOVEL

ERIN MOIRA O'HARA

*This book is dedicated to my husband, my family and
my writing friends, a wonderful group of people
whom I would be lost without.*

The Mission always comes first...

Former SAS Lieutenant Sam Locke is on a mission to locate an underworld figure, missing for fifteen years. New intelligence reveals he is living in the small rural town of Willaroi Downs, biding his time to steal a rare diamond.

Sam arrives in Willaroi Downs to discover not one, but five men who match his target's description. All have secrets that if made public will rock this close-knit community. And then there is Kallie McNeil, the owner of the diamond and far too tempting for her own good and Sam's sanity. Cynical where love is concerned, Sam is staggered by his growing feelings for Kallie, an impulsive and vibrant young woman with close links to all his suspects.

She was seduced the moment she looked into his eyes...

Kallie McNeil's dream is to escape the heat and unforgiving landscape of Willaroi Downs and the men who only want her for her land and precious diamond. Then Sam Locke walks into her life. Within hours of meeting him she's convinced; this tall, rugged stranger is the man she's been waiting for, although it seems he will need a little persuading. Then she discovers he's after her diamond and, along with others she's trusted all her life, has lied to her.

ACKNOWLEDGMENTS

A huge thanks to my critique partners, Susanne Bellamy and S.E. Gilchrist, who have taught me so much.

A special thanks to my beta readers, Michelle Stefani, Mary Bolte, Sandie James, Linda Charles and my dad, Eric. Their desire for the next chapter frequently put a smile on my face.

I must also thank Annie Seaton for her brilliant editing skills. My talented cover designer Fiona, of Fiona Jayde Media. And my excellent formatting team from Author E.M.S.

Particular thanks goes to my friends at the Hunter Romance Writers, for their friendship, advice and encouragement.

Last, and by no means least, I thank my family for their steadfast support and love.

Chapter One

Zero Three Hundred.

Sam Locke lowered his night vision goggles and scanned the lane ahead. Talos, his best mate and one of the team stood behind a dumpster. Sam's gaze lifted to the rooftop where another two of the team waited. Ryan crouched low beside a skylight hub, his Sniper rifle trained on the alley below. Nick leaned against an air conditioning unit, his night vision scope aimed at the entrance to the lane.

"What's your position, Simon?" Sam kept his voice low as he spoke into the coms headset each of them wore.

Simon's reply was instant. "I'm in the van, twenty metres from the entrance. A dark coloured CRV just pulled into the street. I'm too far away to make out the occupants."

Sam's gaze fixed on the roof. "Ryan?"

"I've got a visual. Three males exiting the CRV."

Sam's shoulders tightened. "Nick, is the other vehicle still parked out the front of the warehouse?"

"Yep. Wait—Two males exiting vehicle. They're wearing jackets, beanies and moving towards the front of the warehouse. With the trucks parked there, I won't see if they enter."

"Shit. If anything changes, let me know." Sam pressed against the shadowed wall and waited for the other men to appear in the lane.

What kind of deal is this? Christ, Marzetti must be more important than we've been told. He unclipped his Glock and adjusted the headset.

"Hold your positions. No one enters until I give the word."

Three men came into his line of sight. Two were clearly

identifiable. The third wore a hoodie and was blocked from Sam's view by the first two. They stopped at a doorway halfway along the lane. One unlocked the door while the other two hung back, looking up and down the dark lane.

Keeping them in his sight, Sam whispered. "Simon, do a quick recon. Get their vehicle plates, and watch for other players."

"Already done. There's one male in the driver's seat of the black CRV. I've run the plates. It's a rental from a local company here in Sydney. You want me to take care of him?"

"Negative, just observe," whispered Sam. "We don't want to alert these guys."

A loud creaking echoed through the still air and the three men stepped into the warehouse, leaving the door propped open with a brick.

Now that's odd. Sam pulled out his phone.

His boss, Jarred Steele, answered on the first ring. "Talk to me."

Sam kept his voice low. "We have six males, three inside the warehouse, two out the front, and one driver in the vehicle at the end of the lane. Seems a bit over the top for a minor payoff. Are you sure we got all the intel on…"

A short burst of gunfire rang out and Sam's head snapped up. "What the fuck—"

Simon's voice burst through Sam's earpiece.

"Christ almighty. We have another player with an AK47. He just walked up to the driver and blew his fucking head off. The shooter is moving your way."

Sam stiffened and waited. Nothing happened. *Why aren't the men inside coming out? Everyone within a mile heard those shots.* Barely breathing, Sam scrutinised the man as he approached. A scarf around his neck and a baseball cap pulled low hid his features.

After a quick look around the lane, the man ducked inside the warehouse.

Sam released his breath. *This has underworld written all over it.* He raised the phone to his ear. "Another player just took out the driver with an assault rifle and now he's in the warehouse with the others. I don't like this, Jarred."

"Shit. Watch your step and try not to kill them. They're our best link to Marzetti."

"Over." Sam pocketed his phone. *Why blow the driver away?* He pinched the bridge of his nose. All his special forces training screamed set-up. *Is Marzetti on to us, or is he tying up loose ends?* Sam adjusted the mike on his headset.

"Simon, do a drive by and get the plates of the vehicle out front. Nick and Ryan, stay in position and watch our backs. Talos, come with me." Sam gripped his Glock and kept to the shadows, his heart thudding hard as he ran to the door.

Talos emerged from the behind the dumpster and stationed himself on the other side of the doorway.

"Ready?" Sam gestured to the door with his Glock.

Nodding, Talos adjusted his ski mask and goggles before pulling out his own Glock. Slipping through the door, Sam extended his arms, his finger lightly touching the trigger and his right eye sighted down the barrel as he did a one eighty degree scan. He couldn't even guess how many times he'd done this with Talos during their years in the SASR.

Nothing moved on the ground floor of the warehouse. His neck prickling with unease, Sam glanced up. Bright moonlight from windows high on the wall lit the mezzanine deck.

Their recon the night before suggested they'd find their targets in the warehouse office.

Talos went left so Sam went right, his senses on full alert; there was a man with a semi automatic in here somewhere.

Cardboard boxes packed rows of high, steel shelves. Wooden crates piled on top of each other filled the aisles between the shelves. A soft beam of light shone from under a door at the far end of one aisle, where the low rumble of agitated voices reached them.

Continually scanning his surroundings, Sam worked his way along the aisle and around the crates towards the front of the building.

"You fucking snitch," yelled a male voice. Several shots rang out.

Sam dropped to the ground and rolled, seeking cover behind the crates.

On the other side of the aisle, Talos braced his elbow on a crate and levelled his Glock on the office doorway.

"Wait," whispered Sam into his com-set. "That was a handgun, not the assault rifle." He pointed up to the mezzanine level. "Keep your eyes open."

The door crashed open. A man staggered out holding his shoulder. Blood leached between his fingers and trickled down his arm.

Sam scanned the mezzanine level and froze. The man with the AK47 stood at the edge of the steel grating, his face hidden by deep shadow, his rifle resting on the rail.

Fuck. Sam tightened his grip on the Glock and spoke into the comset. "Hold your positions. If anyone tries to leave, stop them, but don't shoot to kill," he whispered.

Crawling to the corner of the crate, he peered round, thankful for the cover of darkness. The wounded guy was halfway along the aisle when another man strode out of the office holding a handgun.

The man above swung his rifle onto the newcomer and fired a couple of rounds into the back of his head. It was like a melon exploding.

Fuck!

The guy with the shoulder wound fell to the concrete floor, curled into a ball and bawled like a baby.

The shooter leaned on the rail, the rifle held loosely between his hands.

What the fuck is going on? I have to do something before they all kill each other. Sam glanced at Talos, held up his hand and whispered, "I'm going to disarm him, cover me."

Talos nodded and positioned himself.

Pulling his elbows in tightly, Sam took aim. The shot was clean and precise, hitting the rifle within inches of the man's hand. Shock, and the jolt of the bullet's impact sent the rifle flying to the ground. It hit the steel grating with a loud clang, flipped through the rail before dropping to the concrete floor below. The shooter bellowed and grasped his hand to his chest.

Keeping their guns on the shooter, Sam and Talos stepped away from the shelving. They both fired as the man reached inside his jacket and pulled a handgun.

He crashed to the grating, his handgun bouncing over the side and joining the rifle on the concrete floor below. Sam grimaced. This guy wouldn't be answering any questions, not with two bullets lodged in his chest.

He stood over the injured man, scanning the upper level while Talos ran to the office.

"Who do you work for?" Sam asked the man cowering at his feet.

"No one. I don't work for anyone. Who are you?"

Sam raised his Glock. "That's not important. Where is Dominic Marzetti?"

The man inhaled then he blinked. "I've never heard of him."

"You're lying." Sam raised the Glock and moved in closer.

"No, don't shoot." The man's voice trembled.

Talos came out of the office, a small duffel bag in his hand. "There's another body in the office, no I.D." He held the bag out to Sam. "Take a look at this."

Sam looked into the open bag. "Must have been some deal. There's got to be fifty grand in there." The injured man lay at his feet. "If you don't want me to put a bullet through your head, you'll tell me everything you know about Dominic Marzetti."

"Are you cops?" The guy's gaze moved from Sam to Talos and back.

Talos whacked him in the back of the head with his hand. "No, you fucking idiot, but you'll wish we were if you don't start talking."

"Don't shoot me." The guy pointed at the body lying in a pool of blood and brain matter. "That's who we were dealing with. I didn't know Dominic Marzetti was still alive until a couple of nights ago."

Sirens blared, getting louder as the seconds passed. "Who were the others in the office and why did they shoot you?" Sam nudged the man's wounded shoulder and the guy winced.

"It was Marzetti that shot me, but I don't know who the other guy was. I've never seen him before."

Talos stepped in closer. "What were you doing here?"

"We were finishing off a deal when Marzetti and a younger guy came in the front door. They reckoned somebody's been leaking information about Marzetti and they were both staring at the fella I was dealing with. He swore it wasn't him. Then we heard a shot and Marzetti told the other guy to wait in the car."

The sirens were getting closer.

Sam pointed to the dead man on the concrete floor. "And did this guy open his mouth about Marzetti?"

"Yeah, but he swore he only told us. Then he pulled a gun and shot me and my partner."

"And the driver you left in the car?"

"He's with me, but he's just a driver." His voice broke. "If you let me live, I'll tell you everything I know about Marzetti?"

Talos grabbed the guy's jacket and hauled him to his feet. "You're in no position to negotiate. Talk."

"All right, the guy we were dealing with,"—he pointed towards the dead man—"he got pissed a couple of nights ago and started boasting that he'd been told Dominic Marzetti was alive and that he was living in a backwater town under another name."

Underworld—Jesus Christ, I was right. This gets better and better. Sam shook his head and raised his Glock, pointing it at the guy's head. "I already know that, you're no use to me." He pointed the gun at the man's forehead.

Talos looked at Sam, he eyebrow raised.

"Wait." The man's hands shook as he held them up. "The dead guy said Marzetti's been holed up in some backwater town, hiding from police and a bloke he double-crossed. And he's about to steal a diamond that's worth a mint."

Ryan's voice sounded in Sam's earpiece. "You're out of time, Sam. Two patrol cars have arrived and we have a resident pointing them down the lane, over."

Lowering the Glock to the man's kneecap, Sam leaned closer. "Tell me the name of the town and anything you know about the diamond, or I'll put a bullet in your knee then your head."

The man swallowed and licked his lips. "The town is called Willamoi, no wait, Willaloy Downs and"—his voice wavered—"the diamond is called..." He squeezed his eyes shut. "I can't remember, but it sounds like Calipso or Calisto."

Talos stepped forward and made to swipe the man with his Glock. Sam blocked it.

"Wait." Sam blocked him and looked at the man. "What else do you know about the diamond?"

"Nothing, but we heard the owner is a real stunner, and Marzetti's after her too."

Sam narrowed his eyes and stared. "Tell me about the other man with the AK47?"

The man swallowed. "I didn't see anyone except Marzetti and the younger guy who went to wait in the car."

"Fuck, the two guys out the front." Talos ran back to the office.

Ryan's voice erupted in Sam's ear. "Mate, get the fuck out of there, the cops are halfway down the lane."

Sam tapped his fingers against his leg. *Something about this whole thing reeks. God, I hope it's not what I think it is.* "What were you dealing in?"

When there was no answer, Sam stepped closer and aimed his Glock at the man's crotch. "What were you dealing in?"

The man swallowed. "I was the in-between man. I organise the transport and delivery once the packages have arrived. Tonight was the final payment."

Nick's voice was terse in Sam's earpiece. "You need to find a back door pronto. Four cops closing with flashlights and guns drawn, over."

"Roger that. You two get out of there and meet us at point B."

He stared at the man. "I'll only ask this once. What's in the packages?"

The man cleared his throat. "Young Asian girls. They're being imported to work in Marzetti's brothels."

Sam fought his instinct to pull the trigger.

Talos came running back, his goggles on his head. "They've gone and so is the car that was parked out front."

They both glanced up at the same time. The body was gone from the mezzanine grating.

"Fuck, we didn't kill him," yelled Talos picking up the bag of money. "I'll check up above."

Sam holstered his Glock, his gaze fixed on the man's face. "I'm going to let you live, but if I were you, I would stay very quiet."

The man exhaled, his shoulders dropping. "I will."

"If you call out, I'll put a bullet in your head without a second thought. Do you understand?"

The man nodded, cowering against the shelving. A strong whiff of urine hit Sam as he stepped away to follow Talos. *I should do the world a favour and shoot the turd.* He turned back. "Do these girls know they're coming to work in brothels?"

"No," mumbled the man. "They think they're coming as tailors and manicurists."

"You fucking piece of shit." Sam clenched his fingers, wanting to smash his fist into the guy's face, but that wasn't going to help matters. He gripped the man's arm. "That's one shipment that won't be arriving. I'm no saint, but men like you are the scum of the earth. Now move."Ignoring the stench of urine he propelled the man along the dark aisle and up a set of steel stairs.

Talos met them at the top. "He's gone. Must have had a bulletproof vest on and been working with the two men downstairs. I don't understand why he shot one of his own men, unless they were tidying up loose ends." He holstered his Glock, wrinkled his nose, jabbed a thumb towards the injured man. "I assume you're bringing him for a reason?"

"Yeah, he's got a shipment of young Asian girls coming in and we're going to find out when and where. Then the AFP can have him."

The man swayed and both Sam and Talos grabbed him as he collapsed.

"He's fainted." Talos shrugged him over his shoulder.

Happy to oblige, Sam indicated the far wall. "We can get out through that far window."

They both moved as a torch shone through the door at the back of the warehouse. Talos readjusted his load.

Simon's voice came through Sam's earpiece. "Sam, is everything all right?"

"Fine," whispered Sam. "Move the van to Thomas Street then change the plates and meet us at the rendezvous point."

Hastening to the furthest window, Sam climbed up on a packing crate then pushed a hinged window open. He swung his legs over the sill and dropped to the iron roof. Talos lifted their captive though to Sam then followed him through the window, closing it behind him. Between the two of them, they carried the man to the western end of the roof overlooking a loading bay. After a quick scan, Talos lowered himself to the roof of a delivery van then helped Sam get the man down.

Talos hauled the man over his shoulder and ran.

Pulling out his satellite phone, Sam rang Jarred who answered immediately.

"What the hell's going on? I'm intercepting police reports of multiple bodies."

Sam glanced both ways, exited the street and turned right,

keeping to the shadows. He could hear more sirens in the distance and Talos behind him, breathing hard.

"Marzetti and two of his men were here. It seems somebody opened their mouth about Marzetti so he took care of them. There're three dead and one injured. Whoever tipped our client off was very well informed. The wounded guy claims he was told Marzetti is hiding out in a country town called Willamoy or Willaloy Downs. He's using a different name and he's biding his time, waiting to steal some diamond."

"What diamond?"

"It's called something like Calipso or Calisto and named after its owner, who is a young female and who could be at risk. We're bringing in the wounded man. You need to talk to him about a shipment of Asian girls he's importing—hold on a second." Sam stopped at an intersection, looked both ways and sprinted across. He kept a lookout as Talos joined him.

"For a big fella, Talos, you're doing a lot of heavy breathing."

Talos gave Sam the finger and moved past him.

Sam put his phone back to his ear. "Jarred, Marzetti's definitely still active."

Jarred didn't say anything for a couple of seconds and then he exhaled. "I'll get Simon to check out the town and I'll contact our client and see what he's got to say. You and the boys get back here as soon as you can. I'm intrigued by the sound of this diamond. How do you feel about a fishing trip to the country?"

Sam stopped. "Forget the fucking diamond, Jarred. There's a girl out there who could be in danger from Marzetti, especially if she stands in the way of him getting that diamond."

"You're in then?"

"I'm in," muttered Sam.

"Good." Jarred hung up.

Sam pocketed his phone and sprinted to the van, where Talos was offloading his burden. Before closing the sliding door he did a quick perusal of the area. *Nothing moving, no one watching, we were never here. Hang on Calipso or Calisto. We might be trained to kill, but we're all you've got.*

Sam slammed the door. "It's a wrap, boys. Let's get out of here."

Chapter Two

Kallie McNeil lifted her hat and wiped the sweat from her brow. Her eyes stung, her throat burned. Flies swarmed around her face, her plait lay heavy on her back and the heat beat down on her shoulders. Standing in the stirrups, she arched her aching back.

Roy yelled out from the far side of the mob.

Kallie looked towards her guardian and her gaze followed the direction he was pointing. Two steers had split from the mob and were making a mad dash in opposite directions, confusing the cattle.

Damn, not after all our hard work.

Gripping the reins, she dug her heels in and leaned forward. Her horse, Jasper, sprang into action on the hooves of the nearest steer, shouldering him back towards the mob. Catching her breath, Kallie froze as the other steer changed direction and darted across Roy's path. His horse immediately leapt sideways and avoided the animal. Roy regained his seat and Kallie exhaled with relief when the steer rejoined the mob.

Geez, that was close.

Roy galloped ahead, swung the gate open and then cantered to the far side of the mob, cracking his whip. The cattle surged through the gateway.

Kallie held her position at the rear, drew Jasper to a walk and patted his neck affectionately. "Good fella, you must be exhausted. I know I am."

With the last of the cattle through the gate, Roy whistled his dogs, backed his horse up alongside the gate and secured it.

Kallie smiled. *He might be in his fifties, but he's still the best horseman in these parts and a show off with it.*

Roy walked his horse, Watty, across to join her. "That'll do us for the day, bossy. You and Jasper look done in."

"We are. Breakfast seems like hours ago."

"It was, but we need to check those mares of yours. And don't forget you've got that buyer flying in later today."

"No, he cancelled, but I do need to go into town and get some extra feed. The truck from Collie broke down and won't be back on the road for another two days."

Removing his hat, Roy scratched his head. "If you buy much more feed from Ken, he'll start getting suspicious. When are you going to tell everyone what you're up to?"

"As soon as I get legal control of my share of this place. Then we can sell up and you can marry Bunny and go travelling."

Roy grunted. "Is that so? And what are you going to do with your share?"

"Buy Angus a house in Sydney and myself a viable property in the Hunter Valley." She grinned. "You and Bunny could come with me, if you want."

"I'll think about it. God knows what you'd get up to without me to look after you."

"Huh. I might meet the man of my dreams and settle down."

"Poor bloke, he wouldn't know what hit him."

Kallie huffed. "You love having me around, Roy."

"Hmm." He looked into the sky. "Those clouds are building. We're in for heavy rain."

"I hope so, everything's so dry."

They continued walking the horses in companionable silence until they came across a mare running up and down the other side of the fence.

"What's got into her?" asked Kallie.

Dismounting, Roy threw his reins to Kallie and jumped the fence. He called to the mare, crooning in his own special way. The horse trotted to him and calmed beneath his gentle hands.

Kallie frowned. "That's the mare that had the bay colt."

"Hmm, but where is he?" Roy turned and slowly scanned the land around them. "He can't be far. The mare will more than likely lead us to him."

"He must have stepped through this bit of slack wire." Kallie bit her lip. "He's a little beauty. I hope he's all right."

"He won't be far, I'll look for him. You best get into town and pick up that extra molasses mix before we run out, and get some chook pellets."

"Okay, I'll check on the other horses when I get back." Kallie unhooked the lead rope and handed it over the fence.

Roy raised an eyebrow. "You might want to have a wash before you go into town. You're as black as me."

She laughed. "That black, huh? We get more alike every day." Kallie guided Jasper away from the fence, nudged him with her heels and sprang him into a gallop.

All the way home Kallie kept a look out for the young foal but didn't see him. On reaching the barn, she unsaddled Jasper, gave him fresh water, lucerne and a brush down. "There you go buddy. I've got to have a shower. If Roy thinks I'm as black as him then I must really look a sight."

☞☜

An hour later Kallie stood in Macey's Produce Store, talking to Liz Macey while they waited for Liz's husband, Ken, to bring the chook pellets out from the back.

Kallie glanced out the front window. A tall, broad shouldered man stood across from the store with a beautiful German Shepherd sitting at his feet. As she watched, the stranger removed his sunglasses and squatted beside the dog, looking around the street.

Kallie caught her breath.

Wow. "Quick, Liz, pinch me so I know I'm not dreaming."

Liz Macey looked up from her ledger then moved round the counter and joined Kallie at the window.

"What are you looking at, honey?"

Kallie sighed. "The man I've been waiting my whole life for. Look at those shoulders."

"Honey, you'd better pinch *me*. That's one good looking man."

"Do you think he's with the bridge contractors?"

"I doubt it. Check out the back of the black Hilux. He's got fishing rods and a dog. My guess is he's lost."

"And he's probably married."

Liz stepped back from the window. "We'll know soon enough. I think he's coming this way. No wait, he's changed his mind and going into the pub."

They peered through the window as the tall stranger sauntered towards the pub, stopped, gazed up at the faded sign declaring it to be The Royal Hotel then glanced back towards the store. Kallie and Liz jumped to either side of the window, looked at each other and giggled.

Peering cautiously round the window frame, Kallie watched the handsome stranger disappear into the pub, leaving his dog sniffing a tyre.

⚬

Sam came out of the pub and looked about him. *So much for a country welcome, Willaroi Downs is deserted.* A quick movement caught his eye and he focussed on the store across the road. As he watched an older woman looked through the window then turned away. *Not so deserted.* He glanced at the sign above the awning. *Macey's Produce Store and Post Office.*

Within his radius he noted a small school, an old sandstone church and a dilapidated garage with a couple of ancient petrol pumps out front.

"Come on, Ajax." Sam slapped his thigh. "Let's introduce ourselves to the locals."

"You stupid mongrel. You're as useless as tits on a bull," yelled a gruff voice.

Stopping in the middle of the road, Sam turned towards the rundown garage. "Fergie's Auto Repairs." He read the faded sign. *If I'm going to get to know the local men, then Fergie's is as good a place to start as any.*

"G'day," he called as he changed direction. "Anybody home?" Something clanged to the ground and a head appeared around a raised bonnet.

"Jesus bloody Christ, you scared the shit outta me."

Sam laughed. "Sorry, mate. I'm here to do a bit of fishing and need accommodation. I just tried the pub but no one's home. You don't know if there's rooms available, do you?"

Sam studied the grey-haired man wiping oil stained hands on a rag as he ambled towards him. *Right height and build, mid sixties by the looks. A pity he's got a beard.* The man looked up and down the street and then peered at Sam, and scratched his head.

"Don't get many fishermen out here. You sure you got the right place?"

"I'm Sam Locke." Sam grinned and extended his hand. "A mate assured me, Willaroi Downs is the perfect place to do a little quiet fishing."

The old mechanic shook Sam's hand. "Les Ferguson, and yep, it's quiet here. How long you thinking of staying?"

Sam shrugged. "I'm not sure. Depends if I find what I'm looking for."

"Pub's booked out with the bridge contractors." Les rubbed his bearded chin. "Donna Ross would probably take you in, but I wouldn't recommend staying there. You wouldn't get much rest, if you know what I mean?"

Sam's lips twitched when Les winked at him. *Country gossip, this guy could be a gold mine.*

"Maybe not." He glanced at the ancient bowsers. "I need to fill my tank. Do these pumps work?"

Fergie grunted. "They might look a bit old, but they work. Tell you what, you fill your vehicle and I'll wander over to the produce store and see if Liz Macey knows anyone that'll take you."

"Thanks, mate." Sam retraced his steps to the Hilux. His fishing rods protruded over the roof of the cab, adding a nice touch and giving credence to his cover, as did Ajax. Sam pulled out his satellite phone and selected the number he wanted.

"Simon, it's me. I've got a name for you. Les Ferguson, he's the right age and build and runs an auto repair shop." He glanced across at the produce store where Les had gone. Three heads ducked back from the window again. *I bet Les has a captive audience over there, which is exactly what I want. The sooner the locals discover I'm just a fisherman, the better.*

"Sorry, Simon, what was that?"

"Does he have a scar?"

"I've no idea. He has a beard, but there's a good chance Marzetti could have grown a beard to cover his scar. I'll keep looking. Are you set up yet?"

"Yep, we found a spot beside the river with access from the main road. Ryan's out doing some recon now and according to Nick, the pub's the place to be. Locals gather there most nights. He's also raving about a gorgeous young woman, but you know what he's like."

"Okay, mate, I'll catch up with you guys later." Sam climbed into his Hilux and drove to the pumps. He placed the nozzle in the tank and squeezed the trigger, nothing happened. *Okay, what's the trick here?* He flicked a knob on the side of the pump and it came to life so he put the nozzle back in the tank and squeezed.

Nothing.

"For fuck's sake." Sam jumped as a woman appeared beside him and took the nozzle from his hand.

"You don't have to swear." Her voice was soft. "It's temperamental. I'll show you."

Sam leaned back and dropped his gaze to her shapely bottom. She leaned over and his gaze lingered on the strip of bare skin between her jeans and top.

"Go right ahead," he said.

"Fergie loves it when visitors can't work out how to use these old things." The woman's face was hidden by a mass of long auburn hair but her voice was pure honey.

"All you have to do is push the nozzle all the way in, then you..." She swung around and kicked the bowser hard with her boot. "You kick it, where the dent is and...*abracadabra.*"

The diesel began to flow but Sam couldn't take his eyes from the young woman smiling up at him. Her soft brown eyes were almond shaped. She was something else. *This has to be the woman, Nick's been raving about.* "Thank you, Miss...?

"Kallie. Kallie McNeil." She stretched out her free hand.

Sam clasped her hand and he took in the long dark lashes, cute nose and golden skin. *Possibly Italian or Spanish heritage.* His gaze lingered on her full pretty lips.

"Sam Locke. Pleased to meet you, Kelly."

She laughed and a kick of pleasure ran through Sam at the sound.

"Not Kelly. Kallie, it's short for Kalista, but no one calls me that anymore."

"Kalista?" Sam stilled. *The Kalista Diamond just took on a whole new meaning. This must be the girl who owns the diamond.*

"That's a very unusual name." He smiled as he held her eyes with his.

"It means most beautiful. When I was born, my parents thought I was the most beautiful thing they'd ever seen." Her alluring eyes clouded briefly.

Sam had to agree. Kallie was a stunner, one of the most gorgeous women he'd ever laid eyes on. He grinned back at her as she leaned against his Hilux, ankles crossed, one thumb hooked in a belt loop and the other hand on the pump nozzle, and checked him out. She was slim although she filled her shirt in a spectacular fashion.

"So, Kallie, do you live in town?" Sam lifted his gaze back to those beautiful eyes.

"No, but I do work part-time in the Post Office, which is part of Macey's Produce Store."

Sam glanced at her tight-fitting jeans and scuffed riding boots. "And this is how you come to work?"

She laughed. "No, of course not. I only work for the Macey's on Mondays and Fridays. The rest of the week I run my own cattle property. I came into Willaroi today to pick up supplies, and lucky for you that I did."

"Oh, and why is that, Kallie?"

"I was in the store when Fergie came in. He said you're here to do some fishing and need a place to stay?"

"I am and I do." Sam smiled. "Do you know of anyone that will have me, Kallie?"

"I will." A soft pink flushed her delicate skin. "I mean you can stay at my place."

Sam fiddled with his keys as he pretended to consider her offer. She frowned for a second and then her face broke into a smile that had him reeling. He clamped down on his reaction. *I have a job to do and this little honey would be way too distracting.*

"I'll charge you pub prices and throw in breakfast and dinner." She held out her hand.

Sam took it in his. "Kallie McNeil. You have a deal."

She beamed at him then screeched. Sam caught her in his hands as she twisted around, thrusting her lovely backside hard against his thigh.

"Quick, it's spraying everywhere."

It took Sam a couple of seconds to comprehend the diesel gushing from the pump.

"Here give it to me." He took the nozzle out of her hands and slid his other arm around her waist, lifting her out of the pool of diesel. "Flick the knob off."

"Oh." She reached out and turned the knob.

Hooking the nozzle back in its slot, Sam slowly lowered Kallie to the ground. Diesel covered their hands and boots. She stared up at him from enormous eyes and her face had the softest of blushes as the pungent smell surrounded them.

Sam smiled as his mind raced. *I'm going to stay close to you, Kallie McNeil because you are going to lead me to the Kalista Diamond, which will lead me to Marzetti. Operation Locke Down begins.*

She moved between the old pumps to dunk her hands into a bucket of water.

A gruff exclamation heralded Les Ferguson's return. "Crikey, Kallie. How the devil did you make such a mess?"

Kallie glared at him. "It's your stupid, outdated pump, Fergie. It wouldn't turn off. So don't just stand there. Tear off some paper towel so we can clean our boots."

Fergie grunted but did as she asked, and passed Kallie a handful of paper towel.

"Thanks, Fergie. Here Sam. Wipe the diesel off your boots." She dunked the paper towel in the bucket and handed it to Sam before she bent to wipe her own boots.

"Right." Sam reluctantly drew his gaze away from Kallie's bare lower back and did as he was told, then dried off with more paper towel.

As soon as he was done, Kallie took the soggy paper from him and threw it in the bin.

"You pay Fergie and I'll go get my ute. You can follow me home."

"No worries." Sam watched as she jogged lightly across the street to the produce store, Ajax close on her heels. She stopped in the middle of the road to watch a Blackhawk helicopter fly over. Sam ignored it but Les was staring after it, his eyes narrowed.

"Thanks for sending Kallie over, Les. I was starting to think I might have to drive to Collarenabri for some accommodation."

The mechanic's gaze came back to him. "If you're staying round a while you'd better call me Fergie, and I didn't *send* Kallie over. She came on her own after I mentioned you were looking for some place to stay." He shuffled from foot to foot and Sam wondered what was coming. He didn't have to wait long.

"I'll give you a bit of advice, Sam Locke."

"Oh and what's that, Fergie?" Sam stared Les straight in the eyes.

"Watch yourself with that gal. She ain't for fooling round with."

"I'm just here for the fishing." He deliberately shifted his gaze to the rods in the back of the Hilux then returned it to Fergie. "How long have you lived here?"

"About fourteen years. But I ain't no fisherman, so I can't recommend nothing."

Sam couldn't care less about the fish. "So, I'm guessing Kallie lives on a property with her family?"

"Nah, they were killed ten or eleven years ago."

"Killed? How?"

Fergie grunted. "Plane crash. It was real sad round here for a while. Don't know what would have come of little Kallie if it weren't for Roy."

"Roy?"

"Yeah, he's an Aboriginal stockman. Lived with the McNeils all his life. He was one of them stolen generation kids back in the sixties. The McNeils found him in a mission and adopted him."

Sam frowned. "I don't mean to sound judgmental, but isn't it unusual for the authorities to leave a child with a man who isn't related?"

"Nah, Kallie's parents left Roy as her guardian and the child services people did a lot of interviews to make sure he was able to care for Kallie." Fergie chuckled. "Kallie was only twelve but she let them authorities know she wasn't being separated from him. Then a few months later the police tracked down Angus McNeil, Kallie's grandfather. He'd been fossicking in Western Australia for years. They say he was doing pretty well too. He found himself some nice gems. Even a huge one he called the Kal..."

Sam caught the hesitation. "The Kal...?"

Fergie shook his head. "Forget it. I ramble on a bit. What do you owe me?"

Sam pulled out his wallet and handed over a fifty. "Thanks, Fergie, keep the change."

Fergie nodded, took the money and sauntered back into his garage.

Sam climbed into his Hilux. *Let's hope the rest of the locals are as talkative as Fergie. I'll have to watch my step with Kallie McNeil. It seems she's got a few minders.* He started the engine and did a U-turn, stopping in front of the general store where Ajax sat waiting on the step.

഻഻ഺ

Kallie placed her bag on the counter. "Liz, he's so nice. His voice is really deep and he's got the sexiest smile. Oh, and lovely brown eyes, and when he laughs, you want to laugh too. And he's got muscles everywhere and when he picked me up..."

Liz looked up from the ledger. "I saw that. Why'd he pick you up?"

"Fergie's diesel pump sprayed all over me and Sam picked me up with one arm, as if I weighed nothing and moved me out of the way.

Liz raised her eyebrows. "Sam?"

"Yes, his name is Sam Locke and he's even more handsome up close." She gave Liz a dreamy look. "I told you, one day my hero would come and sweep me off my feet. He's here to do some fishing and he's going to stay out at my place."

"What?" Liz came to stand in front of Kallie. "You don't know a thing about him. What's Roy and Angus going to say?"

Kallie shrugged. "I'll handle Roy and Angus. Don't worry, Liz. Sam Locke is a nice guy and I think he likes me."

Liz snorted. "Kallie, you're a beautiful young woman. *All* men like you. But that man doesn't strike me as your run-of-the-mill country lad, so don't go thinking you can handle him. I'd stake the Kalista Diamond on him being a man that's used to doing the handling."

"Liz, I'd seriously think about giving him the diamond if he wanted to handle me." Kallie laughed as she dug through her bag for the keys.

"Kallie McNeil, don't you dare let me hear you talking like that. I think you should...Oh."

Kallie looked up to find Liz staring towards the door. She turned to see Sam Locke standing there with his German Shepherd.

"Oh." Heat flooded her cheeks. *How long has he been there? How much did he hear?*

"This is my dog, Ajax, and we're ready whenever you are, Kallie."

Both women visibly released their breaths. Sam pretended not to notice. The thought of handling any part of Kallie McNeil made him smile. The fact they'd both mentioned the diamond meant it did exist. The older woman looked him up and down as she stepped closer.

"I'm Liz Macey. I own this store. Where are you from, Mister Locke?"

Sam smiled. *Stick to the truth as much as possible. It's easier to remember.* "Call me Sam, and it's nice to meet you Liz. I'm from down the Central Coast."

"The Central Coast! You're a long way from home?"

Sam inclined his head. "Yes, I am."

The rear door of the store swung open and a man carrying two large buckets walked towards them. Sam frowned. *Geez, another man the same build as Marzetti. And like Les Ferguson, this one's got a beard.*

"I've loaded the molasses and here's your chook pellets." He stood the tubs in front of the counter and looked at Sam.

Sam strolled over and offered his hand. "Sam Locke. I'm here to do a bit of fishing."

The older man shook hands. "Ken Macey. We don't get many fishermen out here. What are you hoping to catch?"

Sam shrugged. "I don't care. I've been told to take some time off and I find fishing relaxing, so here I am. The pub's full but Kallie has offered to put me up."

Ken glanced at Kallie with a frown. "You know this fella, Kallie?"

She smiled at Sam. "We met earlier and it's not as if I'm alone out there, Ken."

"No, I suppose not." He turned back to Sam. "Why do you need to take time off?"

"I've got too much leave up my sleeve."

Ken glanced at Kallie. "Where's Roy?"

"He's checking on some stock and I'm supposed to be helping him, so we'd better go. Thanks for loading the molasses and oats, Ken. I was getting a bit low."

Ken's eyes narrowed. "How many horses you got out there now, Kallie?"

"Jasper, Watty and a couple of other nags." Kallie lowered her head and played with a ring on her right hand.

She's hiding something.

Ken snorted. "Molasses and oats are expensive, Kallie. Don't waste it on those nags. And don't give them so much. The way you go through it, anyone would think you had ten horses out there." Ken narrowed his eyes. "You're not back on that idea of breeding horses are you?

"How could I afford to breed horses?"

Sam studied Kallie McNeil with growing interest. She may have answered Ken but she'd kept her eyes averted and continued to twist the ring. Sam's interest grew. *Typical avoidance technique, answering the question by asking another.*

"Bye, Liz, Ken. See you both tomorrow." Kallie turned to Sam and with a smile. "Would you please bring the chook pellets, Sam?"

Sam inclined his head and picked up the tubs. His SAS days had honed his skills. Twisting the ring could mean Kallie was either nervous or she was lying, but why? He followed her out of the store without speaking. Ajax trotted behind Kallie as she walked to her ute.

"Ajax. Heel." Ajax barked and loped back to him. "Good boy."

Sam put the tubs in the rear of his Hilux then held the door open for Ajax. He would follow Kallie out to her property and play his part while he searched for the Kalista Diamond and Dominic Marzetti.

Chapter Three

The McNeil property was further out of town than Sam would have liked, but it might work to his advantage. He pulled up behind Kallie's ute and surveyed the well kept sandstone home. Late 1800s, he guessed, but somebody kept it and the surrounding gardens neat and tidy. Ajax started whining.

"What is it, mate?"

Ajax growled and put his paw up on the dashboard. Sam looked through the windscreen and spotted a ginger cat grooming itself. "I don't think they'd appreciate you eating their cat, boy." He pulled out a leash and clipped it onto Ajax's collar then opened the door.

"Best behaviour, Ajax, and that's an order."

Sam grabbed his duffle bag and guitar then walked to the front steps with Kallie. Two older men sat on the porch, one in a wheelchair. Sam estimated both men to be in their mid-sixties and both had beards. *You've got to be kidding.*

Kallie touched him on the arm. "Let me do the talking, Sam. Liz or Fergie will have already phoned my grandfather, so he knows who you are."

Sam glanced up at the two men. "Fine, as long as you don't expect me to hide behind your skirts."

She laughed. "I don't wear skirts often. There's not much use for them out here."

"Pity, you'd look good in a skirt." Sam's lips twitched when her eyes widened. A soft blush crept into her cheeks as she glanced up at the two men on the porch.

"Ah, Angus, this is Sam Locke. He's here to do some fishing. The pub's full so I've invited him to stay with us." She turned to Sam and smiled.

"Sam, this is my grandfather, Angus McNeil, and this is Bert Chalmers, my grandfather's carer."

Sam stepped closer, held out his hand and shook both men's hands in turn.

"How'd you do, gentlemen? I hope it's not inconvenient for me to be here?"

Angus McNeil looked at his granddaughter before turning back to Sam.

"If Kallie's invited you to stay, then you can stay, but she's got a lot on her plate so don't expect her to be running after you."

Kallie gasped and Sam caught a fleeting glimpse of frustration in her eyes as she turned away from her grandfather and smiled at him.

"I'll show you to your room, then you can get settled. Dinner's at six and"—She looked down at Ajax—"your dog can sleep on the floor but not on the bed, okay?"

Sam inclined his head. "The floor is fine for Ajax, but I won't need dinner tonight. I thought I'd go into town and eat at the pub. Meet some of the locals and find out the best fishing spots." He turned back to the two men. "You two gentlemen can't recommend any good spots, can you?"

Angus McNeil shook his head. "We're not fisherman, the pub would be your best bet."

Strange. Even if Angus isn't a fisherman, he's lived here a good part of his life and should have some idea. Sam gave them a nod and followed Kallie. She'd almost reached the front door when she stopped and he nearly ran into her.

"Roy!" She ran down the steps and across the lawn to an Aboriginal man carrying a young foal. "You found him?"

The man nodded at her but his attention was on Sam. "Who's that, bossy?"

"Roy, don't call me that, he'll think I'm a bossy boots." She stroked the foal's back.

"You are a bossy boots."

Sam dropped his bag and walked down the steps, hiding his smile and pretending he hadn't heard their conversation. "I'm Sam Locke. I'd shake your hand, but I can see that's a bit difficult."

The man stared hard at Sam, then he slowly lowered the foal, holding it still against his bandy legs. Sam noted Kallie was holding her breath, her eyes apprehensive. *Why?*

The man held out his hand.

Roy and Sam shook hands and Kallie appeared to relax.

"Sam, this is Roy Munghara. He helps me run the place and we've been together for"—she smiled at Roy—"forever. If you want to know the best fishing spots, ask Roy."

Kallie watched both men eye each other. Roy was shorter than Sam and lacked his physical stature but as Kallie well knew, looks could be deceiving. Roy had frightened off more fortune hunters than she cared to remember.

Sam looked about him. "How big is the property?"

"Big enough." Roy's reply was curt.

Kallie crossed her fingers when Sam tried again to get Roy to talk.

"How many people have you got working here?"

Roy glanced up to the porch and back to Sam. "Not everyone carries their weight and some of us do more than others."

Kallie glanced quickly at Bert. "Roy, please don't." She looked up at Sam. "We have five thousand acres. Roy and I look after most things on our own but we have a few locals from town who come out to repair fences and help with the heavy stuff. We also get shearing contractors in twice a year for the main shear and crutching."

She glanced back to the porch. "My grandfather was injured in an accident and he's mostly confined to a wheel-chair, and Bert is his carer. I'm going to put some sheets on your bed so if you like, I'll take Ajax and your guitar while you get your bag." She smiled and held out her hands.

After giving Kallie the guitar and lead, Sam turned to Roy who had bent to pick up the foal again. "I would like to talk to you about good fishing spots when you have time."

Roy nodded. "Maybe tomorrow." He looked up at a helicopter flying low in the distance then turned back to Sam. "I got to return this little fella to his mother." He walked off towards the barn.

Sam watched him until Kallie's voice broke into his thoughts.

"Come on, Ajax, I'll find you a nice big bone if you're a good boy."

Sam chuckled. Kallie and Ajax were having a tug of war. He walked over and unclipped the lead.

"Ajax, say hello to Kallie." The show-off sat obediently and held out his paw. Kallie gave a delighted laugh and shook it then they walked side by side up the steps and into the house. Sam's gaze followed Kallie. *Darlin', you wouldn't be so friendly with Ajax if you knew he was a trained killer.*

He climbed the steps and stopped in front of Angus McNeil. "You've got a lovely granddaughter, Mister McNeil."

Bert Chalmers kicked at the porch boards with the toe of his shoe. "Yeah, she's a real diamond, ain't she?"

Sam caught the frown Angus McNeil threw at Bert. *Odd thing to say, this Bert bloke is a sarcastic bastard? And what's he got against Kallie?*

"Look, if it's a problem, me being here, I'll find somewhere else," said Sam.

Bert opened his mouth to speak but Angus placed a hand on his arm before he turned back to Sam.

"Bert's a bit concerned, that's all. We've had a lot of fellas chasing Kallie in the hope of getting their hands on this property and a few little gemstones I gave her."

Sam leaned against a porch post. "I'm not interested in your property or any gemstones and although Kallie seems to be a lovely young woman, I'm just here to catch a big fish."

Sam sensed the disdain in Bert's gaze. *Maybe he really doesn't like strangers or maybe he has a scar under that beard and he's my big fish.* Sam gazed thoughtfully towards the barn. He wondered how much Roy knew.

જ⊶ર

Kallie leaned the guitar against the wall and put fresh sheets on the bed, then she opened the French doors so Sam's dog could come and go as he pleased. After plumping the pillows, she stood back and considered Sam Locke. *I need to find out more about him. No man has ever made my heart skip like it did when he picked me up. That has to mean something.*

Sighing, Kallie smoothed the bed cover and whirled round towards the door, crashing straight into the man she'd been dreaming about.

"Oh."

His duffle bag hit the floor and strong arms locked around her.

"Wow, steady." His voice was deep. "We don't want you injuring yourself."

The warmth of Sam's skin stole through her fingertips where her hands rested against his muscular chest. She could feel his nipples, rock hard beneath his shirt. *Oh, I've got it bad. How can I possibly feel this way when I know nothing about him? For all I know, he's just like the others.*

Sam released her, ignoring his physical response to the soft curves pressed against him. Her rich dark eyes gazed up at him in bemusement. He resisted the lure, tempting him along a path he had no intention of following. Picking up his duffle bag, Sam threw it on the bed.

"I'll unpack and head back into town. Can I leave Ajax here in my room?"

"Um...yes...I..." She looked from him to the duffle bag. "I would prefer you didn't put your bag on the bed. Put it over there on the blanket box."

Sam looked to where she was pointing and grinned. "Right away, Miss Bossy."

Her mouth opened and shut. "I am not a bossy boots. Your bag is probably dirty underneath and that's a clean quilt."

Sam chuckled and moved his duffle bag to the large wooden box. "Is that better?"

"Yes, thank you. I'll leave you to unpack and um...I'll see you later. Angus tends to lock the front and back doors, and we don't have keys, so leave your French doors unlocked or you won't get back in."

"No worries. Thanks, Kallie." Sam held his grin as she backed out of the room and closed the door. *Pity I'm not allowed to mix pleasure with business, because you, Kallie McNeil, would be a real pleasure.*

⚶

Sam angle-parked in front of the general store, surprised to see so many work vehicles parked on both sides of the road. He made a quick call to Simon and asked him to check out Bert Chalmers, then strolled into the crowded pub and up to the bar.

"What'll it be, mate?"

Sam blinked. The barman matched Marzetti's description to a tee. He also sported a beard, which was beginning to give Sam the shits. *Unbelievable.*

"I'll have a Tooheys New, thanks."

"No worries." The barman filled a glass and placed it on the bar. "Are you with the bridge contractors?"

"No, I'm here to do a bit of fishing."

"You the fella that's staying out at the McNeil place?"

"Yes. I'm Sam Locke."

The barman shook his hand. "Bill Murphy. I own this pub. Don't go getting any ideas about young Kallie. She's not one to fool around, if you know what I mean."

Sam raised an eyebrow. "I'm just here to do some fishing." He handed over a twenty. "How long you lived here, Bill?"

After ringing up the beer, Bill handed Sam his change. "Thirteen years, why?"

"Know any good fishing spots?"

"Nope, I'm not a fisherman. The fella you need to ask is Roy. He's the stockman out where you're staying."

"I've met Roy." Sam turned from the bar and scanned the room. The two men he was looking for were on the far side of the room. He was about to head over when a woman stepped in front of him. The first thing Sam noticed was she was very well endowed, her breasts spilling out of a low cut dress. The second thing he noticed was her amber eyes and the blatant invitation gleaming there. He guessed her to be in her mid forties, a little too old for him, but by the way she looked at him, she didn't think so.

She placed a hand on his bicep and ran it lightly down to his wrist. "Hello, handsome and who might you be?"

He took a long, slow swig of his beer. "Sam Locke and you are?" His gaze dropped to her breasts again, now bare inches away. He'd wager they weren't real.

She gave him a sultry, knowing smile.

"Donna Ross, would you like to buy me a drink?"

I enjoy a good romp, sweetheart, but I prefer my women a little less obvious. "Maybe some other time."Sam lifted her hand from his wrist and stepped around her. He headed to the far side of the room where Nick and Talos were deep in conversation.

"Hi, fellas, how's your lodgings?"

Nick muttered under his breath. "Not as good as yours."

Talos leaned forward and lowered his voice. "Nick and I did the reconnaissance and you're the lucky bastard that gets the honeypot."

Swallowing a couple more mouthfuls of beer, Sam looked around the bar. Except for the publican, a couple of old-timers, Fergie and the well-endowed Donna Ross, the rest of the bar was filled with men in high visibility overalls. *Contractors.*

Sam half-listened to the conversation around him as he watched the publican. *Does every local in this town have a fucking beard?* Donna Ross had her eyes fixed on him and as he glanced at her, she gave him another sultry smile, and wriggled her fingers at him. Sam looked away and drained his beer.

"So, where's Ajax?" asked Nick.

"I left him with Kallie McNeil and a ginger cat called Webster. They both have Ajax bloody mesmerised. I've never seen him so besotted. He doesn't realise women and cats aren't to be tangled with."

Talos chuckled. "He'll learn. Do you have anything for us?"

"Not a lot. I'll tell you over dinner. What's the food like here?"

"Great," answered Nick, standing. "But it's wise to get your order in early. Come on."

Sam, Nick and Talos ate in the bar, preferring to be where they could keep an eye on the locals. They were quietly discussing plans when Talos nudged Sam.

"Careful, the mechanic's headed this way."

Sam moved his chair sideways as Fergie grabbed a spare chair and drew it over to their table. "So how did you go out at the McNeil's? Did they send you packing?"

Sam chuckled. "No, but I did get warned to stay away from Kallie, and Angus mentioned the gemstones."

Fergie's eyes flared. "What, he told you about the diamond?"

"Not in specifics, but I got the impression they've had some problems with men chasing Kallie because of some gems and the property."

"I'll be damned. That's a first. Angus isn't normally very forthcoming about the diamond. He must like you."

Sam met Talos and Nick's eyes fleetingly before returning his attention to Fergie. "So, what's happened to make him so wary?"

Fergie lowered his voice. "Over the last five years a few of the locals have thrown themselves, or their sons, at Kallie hoping to make a match. You see Kallie officially inherits half the farm on her twenty-third birthday. Roy owns the other half."

Sam saw Nick raise an eyebrow before engaging Talos in conversation. He lowered his own voice. "Why would Kallie inherit the farm when her grandfather's still alive?"

Fergie snorted. "Not as simple as that. When Angus was a young fella, he had an argument with his father, Kallie's great grandfather, and he left, forfeiting all rights to their property in Queensland. Shortly after, Thomas and Edna McNeil sold up and moved down here to raise their grandson, James, and Roy, an aboriginal boy they'd adopted. Old Thomas changed his will to make both boys his legal heirs."

Sam frowned. "Angus left without his son?"

Fergie shook his head. "Nah, Angus left town without knowing he'd left a local girl pregnant, but his parents took her in and when she took off with some other fella, they raised James themselves."

Sam shook his head. *Apparently I'm not the only one with pathetic parents.* He finished his beer as he absorbed this information. "Okay, but how did Angus find out about the plane crash and how does the Kalista diamond come into it?

Fergie placed his empty glass on the table and signalled for Bill to bring more beers over.

"Angus never knew he had a son or a granddaughter until the authorities tracked him down after the plane crash. The way I heard it, Liz Macey told the authorities about Angus and they did a search. His name came up in a Western Australian newspaper for discovering the Kalista Diamond. It's a rare pink diamond."

Sam's eyes narrowed. "But if he didn't know about Kallie why is the diamond named after her?"

"Ah, I dunno." Fergie scratched his head. "I guess he must have.

Liz reckons Angus was pretty cut up to learn about the crash and he told Liz he would be coming to collect Kallie as soon as possible."

"But something went wrong, didn't it?" asked Sam.

"Yeah. There was a rock fall and Angus got hurt real bad. Roy couldn't leave the farm, so Liz went to visit him in hospital. Angus knew he was in a pretty bad way and asked Liz to get a solicitor so he could make a will. While she was doing that, Angus sent Kallie the diamond, and another few gems and told her to hide them somewhere safe.

"Then a couple of months later, Liz asked Kallie where she'd put the diamond but Kallie couldn't remember. There's lots of theories, but no one knows what really happened to the diamond. Somehow Kallie lost it."

Sam took a swig of his beer. *I doubt that very much. From what I overheard, Kallie McNeil knows exactly where the Kalista diamond is.* He returned his glass to the table.

"So, Angus obviously recovered. How'd he handle the loss of the diamond?"

Fergie shrugged. "He arrived about six months later with Bert. They'd been partners in mine leases on and off for years and they were mates. According to Liz, they all tore the place apart looking for the diamond but they never found it. Did you notice the tension between Angus, Bert and Roy?"

"Actually, I did."

Fergie nodded. "That's because Bert reckons Roy stole the diamond and Roy reckons Bert's a freeloader."

Kallie checked on the new foal, made dinner, cleaned up and folded the washing. Ajax refused to leave the kitchen, preferring to lie there and watch Webster groom himself on top of the fridge. Webster in return ignored Ajax completely. For Kallie, the rest of the evening loomed ahead. *I could do the accounts or I could do the ironing or I could do something totally out of character. I could go to the pub.* Kallie looked into the lounge where Angus lay dozing in front of the television. *He wouldn't even notice I was gone.*

She bit her lip. *Most of the locals don't tend to go to the pub during the week, so Sam won't have anyone to talk to. He'll be lonely and might like some female company. What if Donna Ross goes to the pub? Oh no.* Kallie ran for her bedroom, opened the wardrobe and stared at its contents.

"What can I wear?" Her only good dress was from her Year twelve graduation and was too formal for a small country hotel. She ran to the dresser and yanked a drawer open.

"Something sexy. I don't have anything sexy." She reefed through the contents and finally pulled out a jean skirt and a thin-strapped top her friend Jane had given her. The neckline was lower than she normally wore but at least it looked better than a long-sleeved shirt. She pulled on the skirt, a pair of high-heeled sandals, brushed her hair and applied lipstick.

It normally took her twenty-minutes to drive into Willaroi; Kallie did it in fifteen. She stopped her ute in the middle of the street and groaned. "Damn, I forgot about the bridge contractors."

Parking in the drive beside the pub, Kallie took a deep breath, climbed out of her ute and walked into the hotel. The place was packed. Bill was flat out behind the counter, and Donna Ross was perched on a stool, staring fixedly across the room. Glancing around, Kallie located Sam sitting at a table on the far side with Fergie and a couple of well-built men, exactly where Donna was looking.

"Damn." She gritted her teeth and squeezed through the crowd towards Sam.

"Wow, what have we got here, boys?"

Kallie looked at the man blocking her path. "Excuse me, I need to get through."

"Not so fast, sweetheart. What's your name?"

Kallie swallowed. The man's breath reeked of beer. "My name's Kallie and I'm looking for a man. Can I get through please?"

Another guy came to join the first and took hold of her arm. "Her name's Kelly, boys and she's looking for a man." He laughed. "Well here I am, love, and I'm all yours."

"No, not you, someone else. Please let go of my arm."

Kallie tried to pull her arm free as Bill came round the bar and pushed between the two men creating a space, but her arm was held tight. Kallie glimpsed Fergie looking her way. Beside him sat Sam. Their eyes met briefly before someone stepped into the gap.

Bill put his hand on the man's shoulder. "Come on, mate, leave Kallie alone and have another beer."

Kallie pulled away but the man held on.

"Oh no you don't, love." His friend pushed Bill aside and grabbed her other arm.

"I saw her first."

Kallie saw red. "If you two morons don't let go of me right this instant, I will make you both very sorry."

They both roared with laughter and she'd had enough. Kallie raised her foot and brought it down hard, first on one man's bare instep and then the other. Thongs were no protection against pointy heels. They both howled in pain and released her. One hopped around before falling over backwards; the other swore and raised his hand.

"You little bitch."

Kallie jerked back in an attempt to avoid the impact. It didn't come. Sam blocked the guy's fist, spun him round and jerked his arm up the middle of his back. The man bellowed. The two well-built men who had been talking to Sam appeared on either side of Kallie. One was as tall and broad as Sam, the other was even bigger and they looked anything but happy. *Now I'm really in trouble and so is Sam.* She stared in horror as Sam pushed the drunk into the arms of another couple of men who had risen to their feet.

"Sam," cried Kallie. He gave her a quick glance but didn't seem to notice the two intimidating men either side of her.

Sam glared at the men in front of him. "You are guests in this town so treat the women here with respect or you'll find yourself out on the street with nowhere to stay. Is that clear?"

The contractors looked from him to Talos. There was a little bit of shuffling and some low mutterings before they all went back to their tables. Sam turned to Kallie and his temper flared. *No wonder the contractors are fighting over her. That flimsy top is clinging to her breasts like a second skin.* His gaze dropped to the skirt and her long toned legs. *Holy shit, she should be under lock and key.* Sam dragged his gaze back to her face. She'd lost all colour, her lips were trembling, her breathing hitched and her eyes wide. She kept glancing nervously at Talos as if he might do something to her at any moment.

"Kallie, if you're done, I'll take you home." Sam held out his arm indicating she should precede him.

She nodded but obviously misunderstood and came straight in under his arm, wrapping both her arms around him and sending a jolt of awareness through him. Sam fought not to react as he met the surprised looks on Nick and Talos's faces.

"Thanks, boys," murmured Sam.

The two men stepped aside revealing Fergie and the publican. Both men stood with their arms crossed, blocking his path.

"And where do you think you're going," asked Bill.

"I'm taking Kallie home, Bill. She's had a fright."

Fergie looked at the barman. "What do you think, Bill?"

Bill nodded. "As long as he takes her straight home."

Sam looked down at Kallie. Her head was buried against his chest and she was trembling. He kept an arm around her and headed for the door.

Kallie held her tongue until they were clear of town and she'd gained some control over her scattered wits after being pressed so intimately against his body.

"I'm sorry I ruined your evening, Sam."

He glanced in his rear-view mirror then back at her. "You should be."

Kallie swallowed. "I remembered there'd be no locals at the pub. Well, none except for maybe Donna and I didn't want her..." Kallie bit back the words. *I can't very well tell Sam, I don't want Donna stealing him.* "What I mean is...Donna doesn't fish, so there's no point talking to her, is there?"

Kallie thought she glimpsed a smile but when Sam glanced at her again his lips were compressed together.

"And what about the contractors? Did you forget about them?"

"Yes, I did. That is until I got to town, then I saw all the cars and I thought, I might as well go in as I was there. But that's not the only reason I'm sorry."

He looked in the rear-view mirror again. "So what else are you sorry about?"

Kallie blinked as her eyes watered. "I'm sorry that I could have got you hurt. I thought those two big contractors that came to stand beside me were going to beat you up."

"No, those two fellas were actually protecting you, Kallie."

"Oh."

He shook his head. "I can't believe you walked into a crowded pub dressed like that. Or that your grandfather didn't stop you."

"He was asleep when I left and I don't have a lot of going out clothes."

"Maybe it's time you got some." He looked in the rear-view mirror again.

"Why do you keep looking in the mirror?"

He glanced at the mirror. "I think we're being followed."

Kallie swung around, looked out his rear window and laughed. "Of course we're being followed. That'll be Fergie. He doesn't trust you to take me straight home."

"Oh."

Sam drove up and parked in front of the steps. Kallie's grandfather was on the porch in his wheelchair waiting for them. As Sam climbed out of his truck he caught a movement in the dark shadows and could just make out the shape of a man. *So Roy is here as well.* He climbed the steps beside Kallie. She looked up at him anxiously.

"I'll do the talking, Sam."

"Not this time, Kallie."

She swung around to face him. "What?"

He ignored her and inclined his head at Angus McNeil. "Your granddaughter almost caused a riot at the pub tonight. If I hadn't intervened, a fight would have broken out and Kallie could have been seriously hurt." He turned and headed along the porch to his room, smiling to himself at her outraged gasp. A soft chuckle reached him from the bushes. *It hasn't hurt my image with Angus and Roy either.*

Chapter Four

After a restless night, Kallie woke late to find Sam had already left. She ate quickly, dressed and ran out the front door only to come to a sudden halt.

"Damn. I left my ute in town last night."

"Wondered how long it'd take you to remember."

Kallie looked across the yard to see Roy mounted on Watty. His two faithful kelpies Tess and Jack, sat obediently on the ground, staring up at Roy with adoration.

"Would you please drive me to work, Roy?"

"No need. Your ute's over there," He stabbed his thumb over his shoulder.

Kallie glanced across the lawn and the rose bushes to her battered white ute, parked beside the rusting corrugated water tank. "How?"

"Did a deal with that fella of yours this morning."

"What kind of deal?"

Roy swung down from Watty. "He offered to drop me in town to pick up your ute, if I told him where the best fishing spot was."

"Oh, and did you?"

"Maybe." Roy took off his hat and came towards her.

She chewed her lip. *Oh dear, this can't be good.*

"You be careful round him, Bossy. He's up to something."

Kallie groaned. "You think everyone in Willaroi is up to something or hiding something, Roy."

"That's right. They come here to get away from their past or to get their hands on something that's not theirs and that fella's no different. No one comes here to fish."

Kallie shook her head. "You're a worry-wart, Roy. I'll see you later and thanks for getting my ute. I'll check that fence in Rocky Flat when I get home. We don't want any more foals getting through."

"Suits me." He looked up at the sound of a helicopter and narrowed his eyes. "I won't be here tonight, I'm going to check out what that helicopter's up to."

Kallie waved to acknowledge she'd heard him and ran to her ute. As she started the engine, the ute rocked and she looked in the rear-mirror. Ajax was perched on the back as though he belonged there. Kallie climbed back out. "What are you doing, Ajax. Did Sam go without you?"

Ajax barked, jumped out of the rear tray and straight into the front cabin.

"Oh no, you can't come with me. You'll have to stay here."

Ajax ignored her and looked out the passenger window. Kallie tried to tug him by the collar but he didn't budge. "I'm going to be late, Ajax. Please get out."

Kallie turned to ask Roy for help but he was nowhere to be seen. "Geez." She climbed back in and put the ute into gear.

"Fine, you can come. Why your master left you behind, I have no idea."

Kallie spent the day running the post office and helping out in the store. Ajax laid snoozing at her feet or following her when she left the store to deliver a couple of parcels round town. The dog ignored everyone and only came to life when the two well-built contractors, who Sam insisted had been protecting her in the pub, strolled in. Ajax instantly stood, wagged his tail and trotted round the counter to say hello. Both men gave him a friendly pat and then chatted to Kallie as she helped them with a list of groceries. After they'd paid for their groceries, Ajax escorted them to the door, gave a friendly bark and resumed his position beside Kallie. She patted him, only half paying attention as the contractors climbed into a white van with heavily tinted windows and drove out of town, which didn't make sense. *Why are they buying so many groceries if they're staying at the pub? And if they're not staying at the pub, where are they staying?*

Sam strolled into the kitchen early that evening to find Angus McNeil waiting for him and no sign of Kallie or dinner.

"Two yellow-bellies and a nice cod. Not bad for my first day fishing, Angus. I'll cook these up tonight if Kallie hasn't got anything started. Where is she?"

"I haven't seen her for a few hours, not since she got home from work and went off on her horse with that dog of yours." Angus fidgeted as he looked at Sam.

His internal radar humming, Sam opened his cooler and placed three fish in the sink.

Angus frowned. "I don't know what's keeping her. She should have been back ages ago. I wouldn't worry so much if Roy was with her, but he's gone walkabout and it's late."

Sam looked out the kitchen window at the darkening sky. "Does Kallie carry a mobile?"

"No point, there's no reception out here."

Sam frowned. *I'd better remember that when I'm using my satellite phone or they might get suspicious.* "Does she go off alone very often?"

Angus shrugged his shoulders. "In the daylight, yeah, but she's always back to cook dinner and never stays out after dark, not without Roy anyway."

Sam headed to his room, calling over his shoulder as he went. "I'll get my jacket and a torch. If you had to guess, which way would she go?

"She said something about checking on a northern fence."

"Right, well Ajax is with her so that's something."

"What good is your dog?"

Sam hid his smile. As a retired special ops military dog, Ajax was not your average dog. "You'd be surprised. Do you have a trail bike, Angus?"

"Yeah, I'll show you where it's kept."

Sam followed Angus as he wheeled himself out the kitchen door, down a ramp and across the yard. They'd almost reached the large timber barn when a big dapple-grey horse came trotting into the yard followed by Ajax.

"That's Kallie's horse." Angus yelled. "And your bloody dog. It must have spooked Jasper then chased him home. Kallie's probably lying out in a paddock somewhere."

"Ajax doesn't chase horses, Angus. But he will lead me back to Kallie. Don't worry about the bike; I'll take the horse." He caught the reins of the big horse. "How the hell does a little thing like Kallie handle a brute like this?"

Angus grunted. "It's got nothing to do with size. Roy's taught her how to handle any type of brute, including the human kind."

Kallie hobbled to a large rock and sat. Her ankle throbbed like the billyo. "Stupid idiots, stupid horse, stupid dog." She looked up at the millions of stars strewn across the night sky. *At least it's a clear night. I should be able to hobble home as long as I can walk.*

A loud bark reached her and Kallie twisted to the south. *That's no dingo, it sounds like a domestic dog and Roy's dogs are locked up, so the only dog left is Ajax. Sam won't be happy if I lose his dog.* She balanced on one foot and yelled for Ajax.

Peering into the darkness, she eventually made out the shape of a large horse and rider.

Sam realised he'd found Kallie when Ajax's bark climbed a couple of octaves and he shot off into the darkness. Following slowly, Sam shone the torch over the uneven ground ahead in case of any rabbit holes. As soon as he heard Kallie yelling he relaxed his grip on the reins. At least she was alive. *Not for long when I get my hands on her.*

She was sitting on a rock hugging Ajax.

"You found me. Did Ajax lead you here?" She slid off the rock.

Swinging down from the horse, Sam pulled the reins over its head and shone the torch at Kallie. She squinted as the light passed over her face then smiled as he lowered the torch.

"I didn't know you could ride."

"There are a lot of things you don't know about me, Kallie. One of them is, I don't appreciate idiots who put themselves or their horses in danger by riding about in the dark."

"I didn't. It was light when we came out and I had to check on some horses and fences. I didn't stay out on purpose."

Sam grunted. "So what made your horse throw you?"

"I'll have you know I haven't come off a horse since I was twelve years old. Jasper and I were cantering along normally when a big helicopter flew over and some idiot took a couple of pot shots at us. Jasper spooked, threw me and took off with your dog chasing him. I was following them when my foot went down a rabbit hole."

"I doubt they took pot shots at you, Kallie. It was probably some sort of backfire."

"I know the sound of a rifle shot, smarty-pants. Dirt flew up when one of the bullets hit the ground in front of Jasper. And, I think a bullet hit the saddle, that's why Jasper bucked."

Sinking to his knees, Sam handed Kallie the torch and reins.

"I'll take a look when we get back to the barn. Shine the torch on your ankle so I can see what I'm doing."

Kallie did as she was asked, wincing as Sam slid her boot and sock off. Then his large hands gently manipulated her ankle and she almost dropped the torch. The pain was bearable but it was the touch of his hands that had her twitching. He was so close she could smell his cologne or aftershave or deodorant. It was delicious, just like him.

"It's not broken," he told her. "I'd say you've just stretched the ligaments. It should be fine in a day or two."

Words were beyond Kallie as she watched, mesmerised as he stretched her sock, drew it over her foot, stood and handed her riding boot to her.

"I'm going to put you up on your horse and I want you to slide right up the front so I can get on behind you."

She gasped as Sam lifted her onto the saddle. Drawing in a breath to steady her racing heart, she accepted the reins and met his eyes. "Sam, we both can't ride Jasper. He might be a big horse but with two of us..."

Kallie held on to Jasper's mane as Sam swung up behind her, lifted her a little and pulled her back against him. She'd never been so intimately pressed against a man in her life.

"Kallie, your horse is a Trojan and he can carry us both easily. Now shine the torch ahead and hold onto your boot. I'll hold you and take it slowly."

What little breath Kallie had whooshed out, as one of Sam's arms circled her body, coming to rest under her right breast. *I've died and gone to heaven.* Her heart racing, Kallie forced her body to relax and enjoy the contact while it lasted. How many times had a man like Sam come into her life? *Never.* It was time to get over her suspicion of men and their motives. It was time to take a chance. She sank back and let his chest and arms cradle her. Her mind blanked and it was all she could do to quell the shivers racing down her spine. *Now focus on something else besides his hard muscles and strength. Easier said than done.*

No one was going to believe she came off Jasper because of someone in a helicopter taking pot shots at her. Kallie made a mental note to check the saddle herself. Even if they'd used pellets, they still could have caused serious harm to either her or Jasper. Her lips curved. On a positive note, she was thoroughly enjoying being rescued.

The ride home seemed to take forever and Sam had never felt so uncomfortable. His gut clenched every time Kallie wriggled her arse against his crotch. Ajax raced ahead delighted to be leading the way.

Sam walked Jasper, not daring to risk a rabbit hole in the dark. They arrived back at the house to find Angus McNeil in his wheel chair on the porch.

"You found her. Is she all right?"

Kallie made a sound of disgust. "Jasper got spooked and I twisted my ankle in a rabbit hole while chasing him."

She didn't mention the helicopter or the shooter and Sam could only assume it was because Angus had enough to worry about.

"I see," muttered Angus. "Thanks for finding her. I've had a toasted sandwich, so now you're home, I'm going to bed. Goodnight."

Sam watched Angus wheel himself inside. *Having a granddaughter like Kallie and being confined to a wheelchair, the man must nearly be demented.*

"Poor old guy."

Twisting around, Kallie looked up at him. "Angus might not be able to walk or stand for long and his long-term memory is shot to pieces, but he stays pretty positive."

Sam dismounted and reached for Kallie, gently lifting her down. "You call your grandfather Angus?"

"Yes, because the man I think of as my grandfather was actually my great grandfather and I didn't know Angus existed until I was twelve."

"I see." Sam threw the reins to Ajax who caught them in his teeth and sat. "Stay." Sam picked Kallie up in his arms. *Keeping a close eye on her is going to be a piece of cake.*

Making the most of every second in Sam's strong arms, Kallie directed him through the house to the lounge room, where he lowered her to the couch.

"I'll get you some ice and something for the pain, after which I'll help you into bed."

"I can get myself into bed, thank you, but I need a shower first and I can do that by myself as well."

He smiled at her. "But wouldn't it be more fun if I helped you?"

Kallie opened then shut her mouth. *Liz is right. Sam Locke isn't like the men around here and he's so damn sure of himself.*

He laughed. "It's okay, darlin'. I'm pulling your leg, but call me if you need help."

Kallie nodded as he left the room. What else could she do? *Ask him to wash my back.*

She climbed off the couch, limped to her bedroom, grabbed her pyjamas and limped back to the bathroom.

When she'd showered and dressed, she opened the bathroom door. Sam was leaning against the wall. He smiled, scooped her up in his arms, carried her to her bedroom and gently placed her on the bed.

"Now, let's get some ice on that ankle and I want you to swallow this." He reached for a glass on her bedside table, and handed it and a tablet to her. She swallowed the tablet and water as she watched him take two sealed bags of ice, cocoon them in a tea towel then wrap it securely round her ankle."

"That's very professional. You look like you know what you're doing."

He smiled. "I've had a lot of experience tending injuries."

"Are you a paramedic?"

"No."

"Fergie thinks you're in the army because of the way you stand and walk?"

"Does he?" Sam checked his handiwork. "I'm not."

"Liz Macey thinks you've got a wife and kids back home."

His gaze locked with hers. "I don't have either."

"Good...I mean, it's good that you haven't got responsibilities. That you can go fishing whenever you want."

A hint of a smile appeared on Sam's face as he placed a pillow under her foot.

"Rest that ankle for twenty minutes and I'll rewrap it before you go to bed. I'm going to take Jasper to the barn, brush him down and feed him." He walked to the door and paused.

A tiny slither of uneasiness hit Kallie. "Sam, how do you know so much about horses?"

He grinned. "My best friend had a farm and I spent every spare second there when I was growing up. I'm pretty sure we were riding proficiently before we'd lost all our baby teeth."

"Me, too. My dad..." Kallie didn't finish. For a second she'd forgotten Dad was gone.

Sam came back to the bed, sat down and picked up her hand.

"I know your family died, Kallie, but don't suppress your happy memories. You're lucky to have had a family who adored you. Some kids don't get that."

Kallie searched Sam's face. He had such strong features. His thick eyebrows framed lovely brown eyes, his straight nose had a little bump in the middle, his jawline was rugged and unshaven, and his thick hair looked dishevelled. *He is so handsome and brave and gentle and caring. But best of all he smiles at me like I'm special. I've never met a man I feel so comfortable with and who isn't after my land or the diamond.* She raised her chin.

"My dad used to sit me in front of him on the saddle. When I was older he gave me a pony and took turns with Roy teaching me to ride. Everyone in the district says Roy and my dad were the best stockman ever born."

She smiled. "Roy's brilliant on a horse. When my family...after the plane crash, I withdrew into myself and stubbornly refused to go to school, but Roy decided enough was enough. He gave me Jasper, and then spent all his spare time working on my riding skills. In return I had to go to school and stop being a moody moose."

Sam squeezed her hand. "You've had Jasper a long time then?"

"Yes, he was two when Roy gave him to me and I've had him eleven years."

"So Roy looked after you, but what happened when Angus came back?"

Kallie grimaced. "It was a little uncomfortable for a while. Roy didn't trust Angus because he was afraid he would contest the will or take me away, but Angus had no interest in the farm."

Sam frowned. "Then why come here in the first place?"

"I'm his only family and he needed somewhere to recover. Plus he wanted to get to know me and find out what I did with the…" *Far out, I nearly blew it.* "He wanted to know what I did with myself everyday." Kallie watched Sam carefully but he didn't seem to have noticed her blunder.

"So how long was Angus gone?" he asked.

"You have to understand, Angus never wanted to run a sheep station. He left when he was nineteen without knowing he'd left a local girl pregnant. My great-grandparents took her in expecting Angus to come back, but he didn't. When my dad was two years old his mother signed him over to my great-grandparents and ran off with a shearer. That was the final straw. My great-grandparents changed their wills, sold the sheep station and moved down here."

Sam scowled. "Someone should have told him. I'd be pretty pissed if I discovered I had a child and hadn't been told about him."

"I think he found out. You see when I was about eight a man came to visit. I don't remember much, but there was a lot of yelling. Roy and my dad were away somewhere shearing and I was sent off for a ride on my own, which I was never normally allowed to do. I happened to be near the gate when the man left."

She grinned. "Actually I made sure I was near the gate. The man stopped and asked me my name. I remember him asking me lots of questions then he gave me a pretty rock, which turned out to be an opal." She frowned. "I'm sure it was Angus."

"You didn't ask him after the accident?"

Kallie shook her head. "He'd had a stroke and lost much of his memory."

"It sounds like your great-grandfather was very fond of your father and Roy?"

"Oh yes, the three of them were very close and they all loved horses and working with wood. They made me the most beautiful..." Kallie's eyes darted to the dresser. *Far out, I almost blabbed my biggest secret. What is wrong with me tonight?*

Sam raised an eyebrow. "What did they make you, Kallie?"

She searched his face. *Can I trust him? Roy says I can't trust anyone. Still...*

'They made me beautiful wooden toys and a rocking horse and things like that."

Sam glanced at her jewel box on the dresser. "Did they make that?"

"Yes."

She watched nervously as Sam walked to the chest of drawers, picked up her most treasured possession and examined it. "The carvings are remarkable."

"Yes. They made it for me before the crash, then later Roy told me its...He...ah...he told me each animal's story."

"I see." He replaced it carefully on the dresser. "Okay you rest that ankle and I'll be back as soon as I've taken care of Jasper. I've also got some fish in the oven for dinner so don't go anywhere."

Kallie grinned at him. "Okay."

As Sam left Kallie's bedroom, he fought the impulse to look at the jewel box again. He'd seen something similar years ago and would bet his last dollar it contained a hidden bottom. The weight alone suggested as much. He frowned. *Kallie mentioned something else I meant to verify, but for the life of me, I can't remember what it was.* He stepped off the porch, looked around then pulled out his phone and pressed the number he wanted. It was answered immediately.

"Hey, Sam, it's Simon."

"Is the boss with you?" Sam took Jasper's reins from Ajax.

"Yes, he's right here."

"Good, put him on." He was almost at the barn when Jarred came on.

"I hope you've got something for me, Sam?"

Sam kept his voice low. "I've got another name. It's a long shot but I need you to check out the grandfather, Angus McNeil. He left the McNeil's property in Queensland about thirty-five years ago and is the right age and height, but has a beard like every other fucking man in this town. Could he have moved to Sydney, become Dominic Marzetti, and has now assumed his original identity."

"I think you're clutching at straws," replied Jarred. "The grandfather is in a wheelchair, isn't he? And Marzetti was born and raised in Melbourne."

Sam unsaddled Jasper one-handed. "I did say it was a long shot and I'm not clutching at straws, I'm covering all possibilities. There's something else. Kallie McNeil has an intricately carved jewel box that the Aboriginal stockman gave her shortly after the crash. It's solid and heavy and I'd swear it's got a hidden bottom. She appeared nervous when I examined it, so the diamond may be hidden in it. I'll have a look later."

"Possibly, but you would think the grandfather's already thought of that. Talos told me the mechanic inferred Bert Chalmers thinks the stockman has the diamond."

Sam lowered his voice. "Perhaps. He's had plenty of opportunity and Kallie definitely trusts him. I'll see what I can find out. By the way, she swears someone took a couple of shots at her from a big helicopter."

"It wasn't our boys. Is she sure?"

Sam ran his gaze over the saddle. "I'm just checking the saddle now. She thought a bullet hit it." He ran his fingers over the kneepads, horn and along the back edge of the cantle, where he hit a jagged edge.

"Hang on a second, Jarred." Sam put the phone down and took a closer look. Something was definitely lodged in the edge of the cantle. He pulled out his pocketknife and levered the metal object out. A large, soft-nosed bullet fell to the ground.

"Christ almighty."

Sam picked up his phone. "Jarred, there was a bullet in the rear of the saddle. An inch higher and she'd now be a paraplegic."

"Ryan reported flying over her and the horse rearing, but they definitely didn't shoot at her. Someone else obviously must have though. I'll send the boys out to scout around tomorrow."

Sam slid the bullet into his pocket. "I'll keep closer tabs on her, and see who stands to gain the most if something were to happen to her. Have you got any details on that shipment of Asian girls yet?"

"Yes, our guest wasn't very cooperative to start with, but he soon changed his mind. They're coming in on a freighter. I informed our client about the illegal importation of the girls in exchange for more information on Marzetti. It seems he's wanted for murder, drug trafficking and using illegals for his prostitution rackets. I'll fill you in later, but you were right. This is much bigger than we first thought and I'm alerting someone I know in the AFP. In the meantime, keep your eyes peeled."

"Will do. Anything else I need to know?"

"Yes. Simon and I are joining the team tonight. Ryan's on the way to pick us up."

"Okay, I'll see you later." Sam ended the call and slid the phone into his jacket. *For Jarred and Simon to be coming here, this has to be big.*

He brushed Jasper, checked his feed and water before calling Ajax who was whining at the other end of the barn. Sam hesitated then went to investigate. *What now?*

In the last stall he found the little foal Roy had been carrying and beside it stood a proud looking mare. Sam raised his eyebrows. *This is no nag. So...when Kallie twists that ring, she is skirting the truth. Interesting.*

He left the barn and headed back to the house. Ajax was nowhere to be seen. *No doubt he's already back with Kallie.*

Kallie glared at the big German Shepherd lying on her bed. "If you know what's good for you, you'll get off my bed immediately."

Ajax didn't move.

The side door opened and Sam's footsteps headed for the bathroom. A couple of minutes later she heard him moving about the kitchen and then he appeared, carrying a tray.

"I've taken care of Jasper, so we can eat and then I'll rewrap your ankle."

"Could you get Ajax off my bed? I'm afraid he'll try to get in with me next."

Sam chuckled. "I can't blame him. The thought has crossed my mind once or twice." He looked at Ajax with a stern expression. "Out."

Ajax looked at Kallie forlornly before jumping off the bed and slinking out.

Kallie's face warmed but she couldn't stop the giggle that escaped. *Sam Locke is a wicked man.* They ate their succulent fish then Sam massaged a liniment into her ankle and re-wrapped it. After he'd finished he took away the tray, cleaned up the kitchen and came back. "I've been meaning to ask you where Roy is tonight. Doesn't he live here?"

Kallie fiddled with her ring. "He has a lady friend that he lives with most of the time. But, when he stays here, he uses a cabin on the property. That's where he'll be tonight."

"What about Bert?" Sam pulled the covers up and tucked her in.

"He likes his own space, so he lives in the shearer's quarters."

"I see. You get some sleep and go easy on that ankle tomorrow." He bent and kissed her lightly on her forehead.

"Why did you do that?"

"I couldn't resist." He smiled and left her room, closing the door quietly behind him.

Kallie touched her forehead. *How am I supposed to sleep now?*

CHAPTER FIVE

The rooster's loud crowing woke Kallie. As she stretched, the delicious smell of cooking bacon reached her. She rotated her foot slowly. *A little sore but nowhere near as bad as last night.* Tossing back the covers she sat up and threw her legs over the side of the bed, before gingerly touching her foot to the floor and testing her weight on it. "Not bad."

A light tap sounded and as the door opened, Ajax barked and bounded across the room to her.

"Wow, Ajax, steady boy." She stroked his smooth head and raised her eyes to his master. Sam stood in the doorway, freshly shaven and smiling. The white T-shirt he wore emphasised his big shoulders, muscled arms and powerful chest.

"There's no sign of your grandfather, so I thought you might enjoy breakfast in bed."

Kallie laughed. "Angus doesn't get out of bed until eight-thirty and I would rather get dressed and eat with you, unless you've already eaten?"

"No, not yet. I'll bring your breakfast out to the porch for you. Come on, Ajax."

Kallie sat staring at the closed door. *Not only is Sam handsome, he can cook too. He gets better and better. And, he kissed me last night. Okay, it was only on my forehead, but it's a start.*

Kallie ate breakfast with Sam on the porch while Ajax lay at her feet. She was draining the last of her tea when she looked up at the sky. Heavy purple clouds were gathering in the distance and the air was unnaturally still. She shivered.

Sam looked across at her. "Everything okay?"

"This time of year we get the occasional storm. Most don't last long but every few years we get one that lasts for days and breaks the riverbanks. Willaroi manages to stay above water but some of the surrounding district floods. I'll ask Roy what he thinks when he gets back.

A frown marred Sam's handsome face as he gazed at the clouds in the distance. Kallie figured he was probably thinking about his fishing.

"Don't worry, I'm sure someone told me the fish are more plentiful after a storm."

His lips twitched as he turned back to her. "Kallie, whoever told you that, was pulling your leg."

"You're not thinking of leaving because of a little rain, are you?"

He smiled at her. "No, I'm not thinking of leaving. How's the ankle?"

"It feels much better, thank you. I'm sure I can hobble down to feed the chooks, collect their eggs and feed Jasper. Then I need to catch up on some office work. What are your plans for the day?"

He stood and started gathering up their plates and cups. "I'll feed the chooks and Jasper. You just do your office work and stay off that foot."

Kallie smiled. "Okay, I'll be in the office if you need me." She stood and limped inside, Ajax hot on her heels. *I might have to play on my injury a little, if Sam is going to stay around and keep me company.*

Before feeding the chooks, Sam ducked into Kallie's room and examined the jewel box. He turned it slowly in his hands. A possum, wombat, emu, echidna, kangaroo and goanna had been carved and screwed around the sides of the box. The lid had a koala and kookaburra on it. *These carvings are really something.* Sam tried to open the lid but it was locked. He carefully returned it to the dresser and left Kallie's room. After feeding the chooks and Jasper, Sam went to have a closer look at the mare and foal. All the stalls were empty. Sam frowned and walked back outside to check the stockyards and surrounding paddocks.

"Where'd they go?" He studied the ground for fresh tyre marks. There weren't any, which didn't surprise him. He hadn't heard a vehicle. A quick glance at the shearer's quarters confirmed Bert wasn't up and Roy's ute was nowhere to be seen. "Strange way to run a property." Sam entered the barn and pulled out his phone.

"Ryan, can you take the bird up for a spin? I need you to take a closer look at the McNeil property. I'm looking for a thoroughbred mare and foal. They were here last night and now they're gone. Thanks, mate."

Making sure the phone was on silent, Sam slid it back into his jacket and headed up to the house. Kallie was in the office, sitting in a chair with her back to the desk. She was on the phone and obviously hadn't heard him.

"That's fine, Fred, but I won't take any less. Your buyer's welcome to have another look, but it's a bit hard to arrange at the moment and I think we may be in for a storm. How about next week?" She swivelled in the chair, coming round to face the desk. Her eyes widened when she saw him leaning against the doorframe. "Um, Fred...I have to go. Something's come up. Let me know, okay. Bye."

Leaning over the desk she put the phone back in its cradle, but it fell back out. A faint blush tinged her cheeks as she caught it and tried again. *Why is she nervous and what was that conversation about?* He smiled and stepped into the room. "Sorry, I didn't mean to interrupt you."

She shook her head. "I was just talking to my stock agent. It's not important. What can I do for you?"

Sitting on the edge of her desk, Sam looked away as she twisted the ring on her finger. *Something definitely has her on edge.* He picked up a framed photo of her, Roy and a magnificent bay stallion. Kallie appeared to be holding her breath as she glanced between him and the picture.

"Nice horse." He put it back on the desk and she exhaled. He drummed his fingers on the desk. "I was wondering what time Roy's due back?"

She raised her eyebrows. "Why do you want to see Roy?"

"I want to talk to him about the thoroughbred mare and foal in the barn."

Sam was surprised to see the colour leave her face. She blinked rapidly as he held her gaze. This was getting more and more interesting.

"What about them?" she asked.

"I've lost them," he told her. "They were in the barn last night and I'm sure I latched the stall but when I went to the barn this morning they were gone."

Kallie laughed and all signs of her nervousness vanished. "You didn't lose them, Sam. Roy would have moved them early this morning when he got back."

"No, I was up at six and I certainly didn't hear any vehicles."

"It would have been about five this morning and Roy uses the door at the other end of the barn, plus he would have been on horseback, not in a vehicle."

Sam rubbed his neck. "So, why move them?"

Kallie shrugged but her fingers went straight to the ring. "They don't belong here. The foal got through a broken fence and couldn't get back."

Sam stayed where he was as Kallie stood and limped round the desk. She stopped in front of him and was about to say something else when the sound of a helicopter interrupted her. She whirled round and limped to the window.

"That's the damn helicopter that shot at me and spooked Jasper. It's been flying around here for a couple of days. What are they up to?

"Probably roo shooters." Sam joined her and pulled the curtain aside. Roy was dismounting from a tall chestnut horse. He was watching the helicopter as he looped the reins around a post. Sam dropped the curtain and turned to face Kallie.

"Right, now that Roy's back, I'll head off. I want to do a little fishing before that rain arrives and I need to go into town to get bait." He placed his fingers under her chin and raised it until her eyes met his. "You take it easy and stay off that foot. Okay?"

"Okay," she whispered back.

He winked at her and left. *It's time to have a meeting with the rest of the team.*

Heaving in a deep, contented sigh, Kallie watched Sam jog down the front steps and stop to speak to Roy. After several minutes he called Ajax, climbed into his Hilux and drove away. Kallie stood there daydreaming until Roy appeared in the doorway with a worried frown on his face.

"What's up, Roy?"

"We've got a problem."

Kallie sat. "What sort of problem?"

Roy stepped into the office, his hat in one hand. "I tracked down that helicopter that's been flying around. They've set up camp beside the creek on our western boundary."

Kallie frowned. "On our property?"

"Yeah." He dropped into the chair facing her desk. "I watched them for most of the night. There's five of them and they've got fancy automatic rifles."

Kallie gasped. "Automatic rifles? Do you think they're after kangaroos?"

"No, they're not hunting and I've never seen anything like these fellas. They're fit-looking and disciplined. And they've got one of them big army type helicopters."

Kallie leaned her arms on the desk and bit her thumbnail. "Could they be part of an army exercise or something?"

Roy shook his head. "I don't know. When they're not watching their computers, they're fishing or talking on mobile phones."

"That's odd." Kallie straightened. "Mobile phones don't work out here."

"Theirs do and there's something else."

Swallowing the lump in her throat, Kallie leaned back. "What?"

"I think that fella you brought home could be with them."

"Sam?"

"Yeah. I can't put my finger on it, but he's like those fellas."

"I do think those men with the helicopter need watching, but Sam said he's here to fish and he doesn't strike me as a liar."

Roy stood. "Well, there's one way to find out."

Kallie drew in a deep breath. "How?"

"Give it twenty minutes then ring Liz Macey and see if he's arrived in town. He told me he's going to town to pick up bait. If not, we ride out there and see what they're up to."

Putting her head in her hands, Kallie thought for a minute. "Okay, but you're wrong, Roy. Sam didn't come here looking for me. I'm the one who invited him to stay here."

They discussed farm matters for another twenty minutes then Kallie picked up the phone and punched in Liz's number. After a short conversation Kallie put the phone back in its cradle and looked up at Roy.

"He's not in town." She stood and limped round the desk.

Roy looked down at her bandaged ankle. "What'd you do to your foot?"

"I was checking the horses yesterday and I think someone on that helicopter fired a shot, probably at a kangaroo, but it spooked Jasper and he threw me."

Roy stared at her. "Are you positive?"

"I think it was a gunshot and that helicopter was the only thing I saw at the time. I twisted my ankle chasing after Jasper and I would have sat out there all night if Sam hadn't come looking for me."

"How'd he know where to find you?"

"I'd taken Sam's dog with me and he showed Sam where to find me."

Roy put his hat on and started towards the door. "I'll saddle Jasper and meet you out the front." He stopped and looked over his shoulder at her. "Is Angus or his highness up yet?"

"Not yet. I'll leave them a note to say we're checking stock."

Roy mumbled something she couldn't make out and left the office. Kallie shook her head. *You'd think after all this time Roy and Bert would at least try to get on.* She picked up a pen, scribbled a quick note to Angus and limped to the gun safe. *Not that I intended using the rifle, but better safe than sorry.*

By the time Kallie had her riding boots on and hobbled down the front steps, Roy had saddled Jasper and was leading him towards her. His eyebrows went up at the sight of the rifle.

"You're not thinking of shooting them are you, Bossy?"

Kallie laughed. "No, but it might make them think twice, before shooting us." She put her hat on and clipped the rifle bag to her saddle. "Can you give me a leg up, Roy, so I don't put too much weight on this ankle?"

Hunching, Roy cupped his hands for her boot then threw her up into the saddle. "Use your knees and you won't strain your ankle."

"Okay, let's go." She wheeled Jasper round and he sprang into a gallop, knowing Roy would catch her before she made the first gate.

Sam rubbed his forehead and wondered for the tenth time if they were barking up the wrong tree. He glanced out at the thick purple clouds in the distance and sighed. "I think we're in for a storm."

Talos, Nick and Ryan all glanced up to the sky before looking at Simon, who tapped a few keys on the laptop in front of him and nodded.

"Hmm. It's not looking good. Queensland is being hammered at the moment and if it doesn't let up soon, they'll get flooding, then it will make its way down here. We're also in for some heavy rain in the next week too." He tapped a few more keys.

"To be more precise, if the expected rain comes, the Gwydir River is expected to peak with flooding in the Moree, Mungundi and Collarenabri districts." He grimaced. "We're sitting dead set in the middle."

Ryan snorted and turned to the man coming across the clearing.

"Hey Jarred, it's okay for Sam, he's got proper accommodation, but what about us? I don't fancy getting this equipment drenched. We should move our camp to higher ground, maybe that cabin we found this morning."

Jarred glanced up at the sky. "Hmm, Nick, see what else is in the area. Simon, how much time do we have?"

"There's severe storms expected in Queensland over the next week and the floodwaters should reach here by the following Tuesday. We're also in for some scattered storms."

One of Simon's computers pinged. He swung around to read the message. "That's interesting. A small plane registered to Victor Vassello has just been logged to fly from Bankstown to Mungindi."

Sam turned to Jarred. "Who is Victor Vassello?"

Jarred tapped his fingers against his leg. "Victor Vassello could be after Marzetti as well. It seems they were once business partners and the rumour is Marzetti stole twenty million dollars from Vassello before disappearing. We need to find Marzetti before Vassello finds him."

Sam stood. "What do you want me to do?"

"I need you to stay close to the girl. If Marzetti discovers

Vassello's on his way, he'll grab the money and do whatever he has to, to get that diamond. She's the link."

Sam narrowed his eyes. "What's the likelihood, Marzetti will hurt Kallie to get the diamond? Everyone in town seems pretty fond of her."

"It's very likely," called Talos. "Marzetti was touted as one of our country's most feared underworld criminals. What we've only just discovered is, he got that reputation from the sadistic pleasure he took in extracting information from his victims. So, yes, he will hurt Kallie McNeil and anyone else who gets in his way."

A loud buzzing interrupted him and all six men turned to look at the ultrasonic sensor.

"We've got company," announced Ryan pointing to another screen. They could clearly make out two people on horseback.

Sam sighed. "That's Roy, the Aboriginal stockman and Kallie McNeil. How long have I got before they get here?"

"At the rate they're travelling, ten minutes. The perimeter cameras are two kilometres out." He leaned closer to the screen, frowning. "Ah, Sam. The girl's packing a rifle."

"What?" Sam grabbed the toggle and zoomed in on Kallie. "Something's wrong. That rifle wasn't attached to the saddle last night and when I left, she was planning to rest her ankle."

"They're changing direction," called Simon. "I won't be able to follow them much further, but I think they're skirting us."

Sam grabbed his jacket and the cooler full of fish. "I'll take the Hilux and go further down river. Cover my tracks and keep me informed, but watch the stockman, he's no fool."

Simon rubbed his thumb along the stubble on his chin. "That stockman set the sensors off late yesterday too, but when he didn't show up, I figured he hadn't spotted us."

Nick unbuckled the straps holding up the entrance flap. "If they turn up here, Talos and I should keep out of sight."

"Why?" Jarred asked.

"Because the girl saw us at the pub on Friday night."

"Okay, drop the flap and put on your army fatigues. Talos, you and Nick make sure everything looks normal but stay out of sight. Simon and Ryan, if they do approach, tell them we're on a training exercise for the army."

Kallie and Roy tied their horses to a tree, half a kilometre up river and cautiously made their way towards the men's camp.

Peering through the foliage they could see two men sitting in camp chairs, talking. One was fair, the other dark. Both looked relaxed. There was no other sign of life as Kallie's gaze swept slowly over the entire camp coming to rest on the helicopter.

"You're right, Roy. That's one huge chopper," she whispered.

He crept a little closer then held up his hand. "There are three men missing, yet the chopper and van are still here. Let's check down by the river."

Kallie nodded and followed as quietly as she could. They were almost to the river when a dog's loud bark stopped them. "That's Ajax," whispered Kallie. "What's he doing here?"

Roy's eyebrows lifted. "Just a wild guess, Bossy, but I'd say he's here with his master."

"I know I'm clutching at straws, but maybe there's an explanation."

Ajax came bounding into the clearing from the opposite direction. He came to a skidding halt and sniffed the air then gave another excited bark, and whirled in Kallie and Roy's direction.

"Oh shit," cursed Kallie.

"Watch your language, girl."

The big German Shepherd burst through the foliage, eyed Kallie and jumped up on his hind legs, knocking her back.

"Ssh, fella, quiet."

Roy adjusted his hat. "You stay here with the dog, Bossy and that's an order. I'll wander in and see what they're up to. If there's trouble, you take off. Got it?"

Kallie nodded and took hold of Ajax's collar, patting him to keep him quiet. She peeped through the foliage. The two men had come to their feet and were looking towards Roy as he emerged from the bushes. All seemed to be okay. They weren't reaching for weapons; in fact there weren't any weapons in sight. She watched as the two men shook Roy's hand and offered him a beer and a seat. Roy declined both and pointed at the helicopter then they all walked towards it. The men appeared happy to show Roy their helicopter, inside and out. Kallie caught her breath as another man emerged from behind the white van with heavily tinted windows she'd seen in town. He glanced in her direction before strolling over to join Roy and the other two men. After shaking hands with Roy he pointed towards Kallie's hiding place. She swallowed, but stayed still holding Ajax quietly by her side.

"What are they saying," she whispered. Ajax whined and tried to pull away.

"No, ssh, stay boy."

A shrill whistle resonated through the air and Ajax jerked free of Kallie and took off towards the river, disappearing round the bend.

"Damn you, Ajax." Kallie turned her attention back to the men who were now walking towards the shelter. They appeared to be relaxed, but then Roy removed his hat, ran his hand through his grey hair and dropped his hand to his side, his fingers spread. Kallie nodded. *Okay I get it. You want me to stay put, fine.* She watched them disappear inside the shelter for what seemed way too long.

"Something's wrong." Kallie crept backwards and silently made her way to the horses, using the bush scrub as a screen. She rounded the bend, finding no sign of Ajax or Sam. *The river is running deep and fast so he could be innocently fishing further downstream. That would explain what Ajax is doing here.*

"What should I do?" Kallie bit her lip, unsheathed her rifle and made her way back to the camp. Her heart raced when two big men appeared from the shelter and came in her direction. She unlocked the safety, touched her finger to the trigger and stepped back, right into the middle of a stinging nettle bush.

"Ow." Kallie jumped further back landing awkwardly on her sore ankle, wincing as a sharp pain shot through it. She stumbled backwards and fell over a fallen tree, landing hard and squeezing the trigger as her backside impacted with the ground. The sound of a gunshot echoed loudly.

"Far-out, Kallie." She scrambled to her knees leaving the rifle on the ground and peered over the fallen tree. The two men were now running for cover with handguns drawn. Another two men burst out of a second shelter. These she recognised as the big contractors from the pub that had stood either side of her. They were carrying high-powered rifles.

"Oh shit." She scrambled to her feet and ran as fast as she could towards the river ignoring her sore ankle.

Sam was tying Ajax to the back of his Hilux when a gunshot rent the still air. "What the fuck?"

Ajax began to bark, straining to get loose. Sam yelled at him to stay put and took off towards the camp. He knew the guys were too well trained to fire off a useless shot. He also knew the sound off a twenty two when he heard one, and that meant Kallie or Roy were taking shots at his mates, who would return fire if they were under threat. His legs pumped as he rounded the bend. Kallie was hobbling towards him, whilst darting quick glances behind her.

"Kallie," he yelled.

She stumbled slightly when she saw him then picked up speed.

"Sam, help me," she gasped, sucking in air.

He held out his arms and she ran straight into them. "Kallie, what the hell? Was that a gunshot, I heard?"

She clung to him tightly. "Yes, there's men back there with guns and high-powered rifles and they've got Roy. He thought you were with them?"

"What the hell are you talking about? I've been fishing."

"Oh thank God. I couldn't bear it, if you were one of them." She sagged in his arms.

"Hey."

They both turned to see five men and Roy running round the bend of the river. Kallie yelped. "Sam."

Sam pushed Kallie behind him. "It's okay, Kallie, Roy's with them and he doesn't look like he's in trouble, but stay behind me, just in case."

"Okay," she mumbled against his back, her fingers clutching his shirt on either side. As the six men slowed, Ajax came bounding up and placed himself between them and the approaching men, a low growl resonating from his throat.

Sam sighed. "Ajax, stand down." The damn dog gave him a quizzical look but sat, waiting for his next order. Sam faced the men and put on a questioning look.

"What's going on? Who are you and why do you have guns?"

Roy bent over at the waist, leaning against a tree as he tried to catch his breath. The other men glanced quickly at each other.

Jarred stepped forward. "That girl took a shot at us."

"No, I didn't," cried Kallie poking her head around him. "I tripped and the gun went off. I didn't mean to shoot at you."

Jarred raised an eyebrow. "Why were you spying on us?"

Sam pulled Kallie around in front of him, but kept his arm around her.

"Kallie, what's going on?"

She looked up at him and bit her lip. "I was waiting for Roy to see what they were doing on our property and when he didn't come out I got worried, then those two,"—she pointed at Ryan and Simon— "they came towards me and I switched the safety off, then I stepped back on a nettle bush, which made me jump and hurt my sore ankle, and then I fell over a tree stump and the gun went off."

She pointed at Talos and Nick. "Then those two came out with high-powered rifles and I recognised them from the pub. They're not contractors, Sam."

Sam squeezed her tightly and looked back at the men.

"Okay, and what's your excuse for carrying guns and being on Kallie's property?"

Jarred's lips twitched. "We're on an army exercise. I'm sorry if we gave your girlfriend a scare, but we generally keep a low profile."

Sam looked towards Roy, who was still breathing hard by the tree. Kallie relaxed against his side.

"You should have asked permission to camp here, then this wouldn't have happened," she declared, waving her hands around. "And while I think of it, did one of you fire a rifle from the helicopter yesterday?"

"No," said Jarred. "We saw you out riding but my men do not fire weapons around civilians." He looked across to Roy then back at Kallie and Sam.

"As I was just telling Roy, it's hard to tell who owns the land. We're thinking of moving to higher ground. We noticed a cottage with stables, a helipad and a dozen thoroughbred mares and foals in paddocks close by, but nobody in residence. You don't know who owns that place, do you?"

Kallie stiffened beside Sam and he looked down to see her

twisting her ring again. She looked across at Roy who gave her a nod.

"I do." She glanced at Sam. "I'm branching into pure bred stock horses and my buyers often come in by helicopter."

Sam frowned. "That's what all the extra horse feed is for, isn't it?" He rubbed his chin. "I remember you telling the Macey's it was for a couple of nags."

She looked up at him and nodded. "I usually get it delivered from the Collarenabri produce market but their truck broke down. The reason I haven't told Liz and Ken is they worry about Roy and I. They think we have enough to do running this place."

Sam had to agree with the Maceys, but then again the mare and foal he'd seen were up there with the finest horses he'd ever come across.

"Okay, now that that's sorted out, I should get you home and have another look at that ankle." He turned to Roy. "Can you bring the horses back Roy? I'll take Kallie in the Hilux."

Roy nodded and turned to the other men. "You better move that chopper. This land here will be under water in a couple of days." He looked at Kallie. "You reckon they can stay at the cabin, Bossy?"

"Yes, that'll be fine, it's got a couple of bedrooms and a fully equipped kitchen. Just don't go near the stallion, he's a little temperamental."

Jarred gave her a smile that usually made women swoon. Sam was pleased to see it had no effect on Kallie. He nodded at the other men then swept Kallie up into his arms and walked back down river towards his Hilux. "Ajax."

Growling deep in his throat, Ajax came to his feet and fell into step beside them.

Sam smiled. *Ajax has certainly developed a crush on Kallie. He's becoming obsessed with her.* Sam frowned. *Maybe we both are.*

Chapter Six

Kallie, Sam and Ajax arrived back at the homestead to find Liz Macey sitting on the porch having morning tea with Angus and Bert. Liz stood when Sam opened Kallie's door and lifted her in his arms.

"What's she done now?" called Bert gruffly.

"I haven't done anything. It's still my sore ankle." Kallie looked up at Sam and lowered her voice. "I would prefer we didn't mention my slip up with the rifle, if you don't mind, or those army men."

"Suits me, but how are you going to explain what happened to Jasper?"

Kallie laughed. "Angus wasn't even awake when we left so he won't click."

Liz came to the top of the steps. "Hello, you two. I came out to see if you need anything. It's a good thing Sam was there to rescue you last night. How's the ankle?"

Kallie grinned as Sam lowered her to the porch floor. "Sore but getting better. I brushed up against some nettles a while ago and I swear that's worse than twisting my ankle."

Liz laughed and looked up at Sam. "How's the fishing?"

Sam held up a finger then jogged back to his Hilux, lifted the cooler out of the rear and came back up the steps. He opened the lid, displaying a large catch of fish.

"Help yourself, Liz," he told her. "There's more than enough for all of us."

Liz raised an eyebrow. "You have been busy. If you don't mind, I might get some on the way back. I'm here to take Kallie into Collarenabri to do some shopping."

Kallie looked up in surprise. "Shopping, what do I need in Collie?"

Tutting, Liz took hold of Kallie's arm. "I heard about the pub incident through the local grapevine and when I rang earlier, Angus told me about your ankle. As you can't do much, it's the perfect opportunity to go into Collie and buy new clothes that actually fit you. You're not fifteen anymore."

Kallie felt her cheeks heat and glanced at Sam.

He raised an eyebrow but said nothing, which was just as bad.

"Fine, but I'll need a shower first, I'm hot and bothered from...helping Roy."

She left the four of them on the porch and limped into her room, grabbed some clean jeans, a shirt and underwear then she limped down the hall to the bathroom. *The last thing I want to do is go clothes shopping, but I really do need something other than jeans.*

Coming back out onto the porch, Kallie paused when she saw Sam had showered and wore fresh jeans and a white T-shirt. She looked askance at Liz.

'Sam's never been to Collarenabri so he's coming too. You don't mind, do you, love?"

"No." Kallie shrugged. "It's not that exciting."

"No time to waste," called Liz hurrying down the steps.

Sam stepped closer, a wicked gleam in his eyes. "I don't normally like shopping but Liz thought I might be helpful in getting you into a dress." He lowered his voice. "Personally, I'd much prefer getting you out of it."

Gulping, Kallie glanced quickly at Liz to see if she'd heard. Liz was busy settling herself in the back seat of Sam's Hilux. Kallie narrowed her eyes. *What is Liz up to?* She glanced around for Ajax. He lay further along the porch outside Sam's room, his snout on his paws. He'd obviously been told to stay and wasn't happy about it.

"Bye, Ajax. Be a good boy."

The hour it took to get to Collarenabri was taken up mostly with Liz questioning Sam about every aspect of his life. Kallie tried to introduce a different subject but Liz wouldn't be swayed. Every time Sam sidestepped a question, Liz would come at it from a different angle. Kallie discovered Sam was thirty years old, he was an only child and he'd spent eleven years in the army. On hearing this, Kallie turned and frowned at him.

"When I told you, Fergie thought you might be in the army, you denied it?"

Sam smiled at her. "I'm not in the army, anymore."

"But you were?"

"Yes."

"A technicality," Liz said. "I'll have to tell Fergie."

"I'd prefer you didn't, Liz. I don't like reminiscing about my army days."

Kallie wanted to ask him about those army guys camped by the river but if they were on an exercise they probably didn't want the whole town knowing they were there.

"What do you do now?" asked Liz, "and where on the Central Coast do you live?"

Sam smiled across at Kallie. "She's like a hound dog, isn't she?"

"Sorry," Kallie apologised. *I'm not really, this is interesting.*

Sam winked at her. "It's fine. I have a bit of land in the Yarramalong Valley. It's quiet and surrounded by mountains."

"Then why did you come here?" asked Kallie. "Your valley sounds much nicer than Willaroi Downs?"

"I felt like a change and there's that big fish I need to catch."

Kallie nodded but Liz wasn't finished yet.

"You didn't say what you do for a living, Sam?

"I work for a security company. It's not very exciting, but I get sent all over the place. How many years have you and Ken lived in Willaroi, Liz?"

"I moved here with my first husband twenty-five years ago. I have a daughter, Jane, who is Kallie's best friend, but she's married now and lives in Sydney. My first husband died with Kallie's family in a plane crash."

Sam glanced at Kallie but she looked away.

Liz sighed. "Then eight years ago Ken came to Willaroi. And after a whirlwind romance, we were married. The rest is history."

Sam parked the Hilux outside the boutique Liz wanted to go into and left them to do some browsing. He headed for the café on the opposite side of the street where he ordered a coffee, sat near a window that gave him a clear view of the boutique and pulled out his mobile phone.

"Simon, it's Sam. Les Ferguson and Kallie McNeil said something the other day that bothered me but I couldn't put my finger on it. I just discovered what it was. After her family died, Roy looked after Kallie with the help of Liz Macey. I assumed Liz's husband helped, but he's only been in the town eight years, so you'd better check him out too. Get the boys to meet me at the pub tonight with any info you've found on him or the others. I'm in Collarenabri at the moment keeping an eye on Kallie McNeil—wait a second."

Sam smiled at the waitress as she set his coffee down in front of him. As soon as she moved away, he put the mobile back to his ear.

"Did the boys check out that spot where Kallie came off the horse?"

"Sure did. They found an area of flattened grass and cigarette butts on a rise about four hundred metres away. The shooter was hidden from above by a couple of gum trees. No wonder she thought it was us doing the shooting, but it's possible he was shooting kangaroos and a couple of shots went wide."

"Possible but unlikely." Sam took a sip of coffee. "Any news on Victor Vassello's movements?"

"Yeah, his plane landed and three guys disembarked. They hired a car and asked for directions to Willaroi Downs."

The door of the boutique opened and Liz emerged ahead of Kallie waving her hands about as she talked. They turned left, Kallie's limp hardly noticeable as she laughed at whatever Liz was saying. A couple of young men turned to watch Kallie as she passed them and Sam's gut clenched.

Wake up, Locke. You're here to do a job and Kallie McNeil wants a lot more than a quick romp in the hay. You can't give her what she wants so leave her alone.

Sam stood and drained his coffee. "Got to go, Simon, our little bird is on the move." He slid the phone into his jacket and left the café.

Kallie stood in the cubicle in her underwear while Liz and the shop assistant searched out every dress or skirt they thought she'd like and passed them in to her.

"Liz, I don't have time to try on everything in the shop. Roy and I have to move three hundred head of cattle to higher ground today."

"Don't be ridiculous, Kallie, you can do that tomorrow. It's your birthday soon and you need something nice to wear to the party I'm planning."

Kallie sagged against the wall. "I don't want a party, Liz. You know how I feel about celebrating my birthday."

Liz snorted on the other side of the door. "Kallie McNeil, you will be twenty-three soon and you will officially inherit that farm of yours and have control of the insurance payout. It's time you seriously thought about your future. Ken and I will be moving to the South Coast soon and what about Roy?"

"What about him?"

"He's getting too old to be doing all the work he does. You need to either take on more people or sell the place. Roy could retire and you could move to Sydney, closer to Jane."

"I can't leave Roy. He's my family."

"Oh for goodness sake, Kallie. Roy deserves to take it easy in his old age. He and Bunny can go off travelling or he can buy a small place of his own. You need to get away from here and meet people your own age and for once celebrate your damn birthday."

A sob caught in Kallie's throat and she slid to the floor.

Liz knocked on the door. "Kallie, I'm sorry honey, but your family is gone and you need to get over the fact they died on your birthday. They would hate the fact you haven't had a birthday since the crash."

Kallie buried her head in her arms and cried.

Having heard enough, Sam pushed past Liz and knocked on the change room door. "Kallie, it's Sam, open the door." He heard another broken-hearted sob.

"Come on, darlin', open the door."

"Please go away, Sam, and take Liz with you. I want to be alone."

Sam gritted his teeth and turned to Liz. "Why don't you go and have a cuppa and let me talk to Kallie?"

Liz hesitated. "Well, it can't hurt." She picked up her bag and left. The shop assistant was hovering in the background, unsure of what to do. Sam glanced at her. "I need to open this door."

She nodded and reached behind the counter. "We use this when children lock themselves in." She handed him a nail file.

"Thanks, but I have something better." Sam pulled out his keys and separated a thin disk. He glanced at the shop assistant's nametag.

"Jenny, I'll call you if I need you."

"Oh, right. I'll be at the front counter." She backed away, her gaze slowly sweeping him from head to foot.

Sam waited until she was out of sight and turned back to the door. "Kallie, I'm going to open the door, okay?"

"No," sobbed Kallie. "Leave me alone."

Sam inserted the metal disc and turned it to the right. The door unlocked and swung out revealing Kallie on the floor facing him, her arms wrapped around her legs and her head resting on her knees. For a second he thought she was naked and his gut clenched, then he realised she was wearing light coloured underwear.

Sam locked the door, sat beside her and put his arms around her. "Come here, darlin'."

She turned her face into his chest and clung to his T-shirt. "How can I celebrate my birthday when it's the day they died? Yet every year, Liz pressures me into having a party."

Sam rocked her gently, stroking her bare back. "I take it, she doesn't succeed?"

"No, I usually spend the day doing stock work. This year I was planning on leaving the night before and coming back the day after."

"That'll do it." Sam chuckled and brushed some loose hair and tucked it behind her ear. "I can't even begin to know what it was like to lose your whole family. I'm not close to my parents and I never even knew my grandparents."

Looking up, Kallie's eyes filled with tears. "They were going to a property auction in the Hunter Valley. They said the land was fertile and too high to flood. They said I would love it, because it was ideal for breeding horses. We had breakfast together and were going to celebrate my birthday that night when they got home." Another sob escaped.

Sam stroked her silky, thick hair. "Then let's change your birthday. Let's make it the week before. I'll take you out to dinner at the pub and I'll even sing you a song. How does that sound?"

Kallie wiped the tears away. "But I'll still be celebrating my birthday."

"Yes, but not on the day your family died." His gaze dropped to her luscious breasts partially covered by a plain bra.

"You'd better get dressed before I do something reckless."

"Like what?" asked Kallie, sniffling.

Sam put a finger under her chin and raised it then he lowered his head and gently touched his lips to her pretty lips. "Kiss you."

"That *is* reckless."

Sam gazed into her beautiful dark eyes. "Will you come out with me?"

"Yes." She wiped her cheeks. "But please don't sing happy birthday to me."

"Deal. Now try on these clothes before I do something that *will* get me arrested."

Sniffing, Kallie climbed to her feet. "I don't think I could tempt you to do that."

Sam stood, ran his finger down her face, across her shoulder and down her arm, smiling when she quivered under his touch.

"Oh yes, Kallie, you could."

Kallie's eyes widened and a soft blush crept into her cheeks. "I could?"

"Yes, now stop fishing for compliments and start trying on these clothes so we can get back. I'll help you and Roy move the stock if you hurry." He opened the door.

"Really?—Okay."

The next half hour flew by as she tried on dresses, skirts and tops. By the time Liz came back Kallie had decided on three dresses, two skirts and four tops. She also bought five matching sets of lingerie and two pairs of shoes. Sam was more than ready to escort the two ladies to the café for lunch.

When Kallie informed Liz of their dinner date, Liz gave Sam an appreciative glance and spent the rest of lunch texting on her mobile. Sam hoped she wasn't up to anything sneaky, but he had serious misgivings.

As soon as they arrived back at the farm, Liz collected a few fish and drove off home. Kallie and Sam changed, collected Ajax and headed for the barn where Roy was waiting. When Kallie told Roy that Sam was going to help move the stock he stared long and hard at Sam, then nodded.

"Righto. You can take the trail bike. We'd better move, it's going to rain."

Kallie grinned at Sam and moved to Jasper's left side. She'd put her left foot in the stirrup when large firm hands grasped her hips and she found herself being tossed up into the saddle. With heated cheeks she glanced down at Sam's smiling face. He winked at her.

"Be careful of that ankle."

"Okay." She glanced at Roy who was now on his horse. A frown marred his face as he stared at Sam's departing back. *Oh, please don't spoil this, Roy.*

They both walked the horses out of the barn and waited as Sam sent Ajax back to the house and went to get the trail bike.

Roy shook his head. "Something's not right. I got a bad feeling we're going to have trouble, and that fella's mixed up in it." He glanced at Kallie. "You get in a bad situation, you do what I taught you."

"I will, but Sam's a good guy. He's taking me to the pub for dinner in a couple of weeks to celebrate my birthday early. Do you want to come? Liz, Ken and Fergie will be there."

Narrowing his eyes, Roy looked off into the distance. "So he plans on staying a while."

"It looks like it." Kallie beamed at him. "Are you eating with us tonight?

"Nah, I want to keep an eye on those fellas with the chopper."

"But they're here with the army," insisted Kallie.

"I know that's what they said, but my gut tells me different and your fella's not what he seems either."

"Oh, Roy. You're being over-protective. I have a good feeling about Sam."

Roy grunted and called up his dogs.

By late afternoon all the cattle were grazing in the highest paddocks and the black clouds still hung low and oppressive. The stillness was eerie and not a bird could be heard anywhere. Roy insisted on detouring via the stables to check on the horses and the men staying in the cabin. When they mentioned they'd be heading into the pub for dinner, Roy changed his mind and told Kallie he'd see them in there.

❧

Over the next two weeks, Kallie laughed more than she had ever and she was happy. Each afternoon, Sam arrived home with a several nice sized fish. The freezer was full. He would spend the evening helping Kallie with her chores. They'd cook dinner together, share the meal with Angus and sit on the porch talking. Occasionally they'd go into Willaroi to the pub for dinner and Kallie would introduce him to other locals. Fergie and Bill usually ambled over to have a chat while they were there.

The days Kallie didn't work at the post office, they'd saddle up Jasper and another horse, and ride out to the cabin to check the mares and foals, or boundary fences and stock. They sometimes stopped at the cabin and chatted to a couple of the army men, and even though Sam hadn't made a move on her, Kallie was in seventh heaven.

On the evening of her pretend birthday, Kallie, Sam and Roy arrived back at the barn as heavy drops of rain began falling. By the time they'd stabled, brushed and fed the horses there was a steady downpour of rain.

Sam stood at the barn entrance looking out through the heavy rain. *Bloody hell, this looks serious.* He glanced over his shoulder. "Are you sure you're high enough here?"

Roy and Kallie came to stand on either side of him. Removing his hat, Roy scratched his head. "I reckon we'll be all right, but once the river peaks, don't go driving around or you'll get washed away. Too often people underestimate the power of flood water." He left them and climbed the steps at the back of the barn, disappearing into the loft.

Sam held out his hand. "Let's make a run for it."

Kallie gave him her hand and they raced across the yard to the house, arriving at the back door completely drenched, and laughing. Ajax met them, wagging his tail.

"How's that ankle?" asked Sam, pulling her through the door.

"Completely healed." She smiled. "It should be fine to dance on."

"Who's dancing tonight?" asked Bert gruffly from the laundry doorway.

Kallie tensed. She didn't want Bert to say something sarcastic and ruin her night.

Sam squeezed her hand and met Bert's gaze. "I'm taking Kallie to the pub for dinner. You're welcome to join us if you'd like."

Kallie pulled her hand free. "That's if you want to, Bert. Fergie, Roy and Ken will be there." She glanced back at Sam and smiled. "I'm going to grab a quick shower and then I'll ask Angus if he wants to come."

Sam nodded at Bert and followed her through the kitchen. He caught her at the bedroom door. "Why do I get the impression that was a backhanded invitation you gave Bert?"

Kallie shrugged. "Bert doesn't like Fergie, so he might not come. Angus might not either, but I'll ask him. Now go have a shower or I'll go without you."

Reaching out, Sam smacked her backside as she entered her bedroom. She scooted forward giggling and closed the door.

Sam smiled. *Kallie McNeil, you're a tempting little minx.* Ajax pushed into the bedroom as soon as Sam opened his own door. He came to an abrupt stop, a low growl coming from his throat. Sam ran a critical eye over the room. To the layman it might look exactly as he'd left it, but to Sam there were numerous differences. The drawers lined up perfectly when they shouldn't. The pillows were at a slightly different angle and his tackle box had been moved forward an inch on the chair. Someone had been in here and gone through his stuff. He crossed the room to the straight-backed chair, lifted his tackle box to the ground and tipped the chair upside down. Kneeling beside the box he opened the lid and lifted the top tray out. Underneath was a box of colourful sinkers and hooks. He removed its lid and lifted the display tray out, revealing his switchblade. *So far, so good.* He used the switchblade to lever out several tacks from the underlining of the chair and pulled it back far enough to slip his hand inside. He withdrew his Glock and re-tacked the upholstery, then wrapped the gun and switchblade in a towel and put them on the bed. Standing, he picked up the chair, repacked his tackle box and sat it back on the chair. He went to the dresser and pulled out clean clothes. Sam looked around the room again before he picked up the bundled towel and paced into his bathroom, his earlier good mood gone.

Angus and Bert might think they have Kallie's best interests at heart, but that doesn't give them the right to go through my stuff. He locked the door, dumped his things on the vanity cabinet, turned on the shower and picked up his mobile phone.

"Simon, I need you to find out everything you can on Kallie McNeil. She turns twenty-three next Monday and stands to inherit half this property and a large amount of money from her parents' deaths. I want to know how she's been able to afford those horses and keep this place running. And let Jarred know I'm taking her into Willaroi tonight for dinner. Our bearded locals will be there, so if Vassello turns up we need to be ready."

"No worries. Jarred wanted you to know our client passed on some interesting information."

"Oh, and what's that," asked Sam as he bent and pulled off his socks.

"The police matched fingerprints from the AK47 and the handgun found in the warehouse. They belong to a man by the name of Gus Bowen. He used to be Dominic Marzetti's henchman back in the day. He supposedly died in a fire around the time Marzetti disappeared. The general feeling is if he's alive, he could be running things for Marzetti."

"Okay. Any news on Vassello?"

"Yes," replied Simon. "He lodged another flight plan for Mungindi airport and arrived there this afternoon with two men. Ryan made sure he was hanging around when they arrived. He saw them showing a photo around before they hired a white Land Cruiser."

Sam rubbed his forehead. "Talos said the contractors have packed up and won't be back until the flood threat is over. It might be a good idea if the boys book into the pub for a few nights. Victor Vassello is one of the few men who will recognise Dominic Marzetti and when that happens, we may need all hands on deck."

"Good thinking, I'll pass it on."

Sam finished his call, stripped and stepped into the shower.

Fifteen minutes later he pulled on a black T-shirt and jeans, slid his switchblade inside his right boot and the Glock into the back of his jeans. After shaving, he pulled on his leather jacket and zipped it up a couple of inches. A quick look in the mirror assured him that the gun was well hidden. He strolled into the lounge to wait for Kallie. Angus was sitting in an armchair.

"Evening, Angus. Did Kallie tell you I'm taking her into town for dinner tonight?"

"She did, and that Roy, Fergie, Liz and Ken will be there."

"That's right," confirmed Sam. "Kallie told me she doesn't celebrate her birthday because it's the day her parents died, so I talked her into dinner tonight instead. Would you like to come?"

"No thanks, I'm not really one for crowds." He leaned back and linked his fingers across his stomach. "Don't mess with Kallie, Sam. I don't want her hurt when you leave."

"I have no intention of hurting Kallie, Angus. I'm just taking her out to dinner. I'll leave Ajax in my room so he doesn't chase after us."

CHAPTER SEVEN

Kallie couldn't contain her happiness as she showered and washed her hair.

Perhaps with him around, my birthday won't be so bad this year. She smiled at the thought of spending the whole evening with him. *I hope he kisses me properly tonight.* She turned off the water and towelled herself dry then spent ten minutes styling her hair.

Wrapped in her towel she scooted along the hall to her room, shut the door and pulled all her new clothes out.

Now, which one of these will make Sam want to kiss me? She chose the colourful fitted dress with its flaring skirt, slipped on her new silver high-heeled sandals and hoped for the best.

When Sam stopped speaking mid-sentence, Kallie figured she'd achieved her goal and by the smouldering look in his eyes, she knew he'd definitely be kissing her later. A thrill of excitement ran through her. Tossing her hair behind her shoulders, she pranced into the lounge.

"What do you think?" She twirled, the short skirt of her new shoestring-strapped dress rising to show even more of her legs. She smoothed down the jersey fabric. "Do I look all right? It's such a colourful dress, I couldn't resist it."

"You'll do." A slow smile spread across Sam's face as his gaze swept her again. "But you might want to wear a coat and gumboots. It's pouring outside and you wouldn't want to ruin those shoes."

Kallie looked down at her silver heels. "Hmm, good idea. I'll put these in a bag and get my raincoat and umbrella. She glanced at Angus who was staring at her with a strange expression on his face.

"Are you sure you don't want to come with us, Angus? You might enjoy yourself."

"No, I can't hear when there's too many people talking at once." He shook his head and leaned forward in his recliner.

"Where did that come from Kallie?" He was staring at her pendant.

Her face heated and Kallie swallowed, glancing first at Sam and then back to Angus. "I've had it for years. It's the black opal you gave me when I was eight. At least I think it was you. I had it polished and set a few months ago when Liz and Jane went to Sydney."

Her grandfather's gaze lifted to her diamond stud earrings. "And those?"

"They were my mother's."

Her grandfather studied the pendant again. "Where have you been keeping them? I've never seen them before."

Kallie glanced at Sam who was watching with interest. *Heavens he must think this is a very odd conversation.* She shrugged. "They were in a safety deposit box at the bank in Collie with a few other things my parents left me." She glanced at Sam. "We should get going or the kitchen will be closed."

"Certainly." Sam nodded at Angus and trailed her out to the back porch where she shrugged into a raincoat and pulled a pair of gumboots off the shelf. Sam took them from her, returned them to the shelf and lifted her up in his arms.

"I was joking about the gumboots, Kallie. You cover us with an umbrella and I'll carry you to the Hilux."

Kallie smiled as her heart raced. "Deal." She reached for the golf umbrella and opened it as Sam stepped out into the heavy rain.

The drive into Willaroi was slow and precarious, taking a lot longer than usual, but Sam didn't want to take any unnecessary risks. The rain was so heavy, his headlights could barely pick up the road ahead and being dirt, there was a real chance of sliding into a ditch.

Sam pulled up in front of the pub and dashed around to Kallie's door. He leaned in and scooped her out, not bothering to wait for her to open the umbrella then he lowered her to her feet under the pub awning. She stood looking about the street, frowning.

"What is it, Kallie?"

She pointed at all the cars and Utes lined up on either side of the road. "There must be something on here tonight."

Sam shrugged. "I've no idea." He took her hand and led her into the pub.

They were barely over the threshold when a roar went up and people surrounded them, smiling and laughing as they wished Kallie happy birthday. Sam held Kallie close when she recoiled and shrank against him, her eyes widening as she stared around the packed bar. Sam had to admit it was a surprise to him. When Liz said she'd invite a few friends, he didn't expect the whole district to turn up, especially in this weather.

A very pregnant, pretty brunette with sparkling green eyes pushed through the crowd and beamed at Kallie. "Hello, stranger."

Kallie gasped. "Jane, what are you doing here?" She stepped away from Sam as the woman laughed and hugged her.

"You didn't think I'd miss this, did you? When Mum sent me a message saying you'd agreed to a birthday party, Andrew suggested we fly up, and let me tell you, it's a long trip when you've got a baby pressing on your bladder."

"I didn't agree to a party," Kallie muttered, reaching out to gently touch her friend's large bump. "Just dinner."

Jane grinned. "Too late now." She glanced shrewdly at Sam, "So this must be the handsome stranger Mum's been talking about. You going to introduce us, Kallie?"

Kallie smiled at him, a soft pink seeping into her cheeks.

"This is Jane. Liz's daughter and my best friend." Kallie turned back to the brunette. "Jane, meet Sam Locke, who's here to do some fishing."

Jane smiled and shook his hand. "Nice to meet you, Sam. What are you hoping to catch?" Her gaze slid to Kallie then back to him.

Sam's lips twitched. "Something rather special, Jane?"

She chuckled. "Don't tell the locals what you're after. They can be very protective of their...fish." She chuckled. "Can I borrow Kallie for a little while?"

"Of course." He winked at Kallie and headed to the bar.

Kallie shook her head. "Jane, that wasn't very subtle."

"I know." She laughed and caught Kallie's hand. "You look fabulous. That dress really shows off your figure. I don't have a waist anymore. Come and sit down, I want to hear all about that hunk of a man."

"Jane." Kallie glared at her. "Keep your voice down."

They sat at a table with Jane's husband, Andrew, and over the next hour caught up with each other and numerous other locals. It humbled Kallie that so many had braved the rain to be here and that Liz had gone to so much trouble.

Bill was busy working the bar and coordinating the finger food. Conversation and beer flowed throughout the room. Jane's husband, Andrew, stood and excused himself to catch up with Ken.

Kallie's gaze fell on Sam, deep in conversation with three of the helicopter guys. Jane noticed and leaned closer. "They all have the same look about them, don't they? They're all tall, well-built and attractive. I take it they're here with Sam?"

Kallie shook her head. "No, those guys are part of an army exercise. Sam doesn't know them."

Jane frowned. "They sure look like they know each other. Check out their body language. They are very comfortable with each other, and check out the big guy. Wow, now that's what I call an exciting man."

Kallie studied Sam and the three men standing at the far end of the bar, deep in conversation. Every now and then they'd all glance around the room and a couple of times she caught the huge guy looking at her and Jane. The door opened and in walked a glamorously dressed woman.

"Oh no, Donna's here." Kallie bit her lip. "And she looks like she's on the prowl."

They both watched the busty redhead sashay through the crowd, stopping to talk to Ken and Andrew, her husky laugh sounding above the buzz of conversation. Andrew's lips thinned and he took a step back from her.

Jane snorted. "You'd think she owns the place, wouldn't you? Look at the way she keeps touching Andrew's arm. It's pathetic."

Kallie nudged her friend. "She might flirt with every male but by the look on Andrew's face, you don't have any worries."

Donna Ross's gaze settled on the four large men at the end of the bar. A smile spread across her face and she headed in their direction.

"No, don't go over there," whispered Kallie, clenching her fists in her lap.

Donna stopped by Sam and ran her fingers all the way from his shoulder to his wrist before leaning against him, one breast pushing into his arm.

Jane choked. "Has she no shame? He's got to be fifteen years younger than her."

Kallie swallowed, not taking her eyes from Sam.

He glanced across the room and met Kallie's gaze, then leaned down to say something near Donna's ear. She laughed her husky laugh, and leaned closer.

"Far out," whispered Jane. "He's flirting with her."

Kallie stood. "I should have known he was too good to be true. I'm going to talk to the ladies in the kitchen for a while."

"Oh no, you're not!" Jane grabbed Kallie's hand. "Think about this."

"What is there to think about? He obviously prefers women like Donna. I'm not going to make a fool of myself over any man."

Jane pulled her back onto the chair. "Kallie, you are so much hotter than Donna and Sam's been throwing you smouldering looks for the past hour. Mum told me what happened in Collie and we all saw the way he protected you when you arrived tonight. That guy is into you, but maybe he's playing it cool because the pub's full of locals. I bet they've all warned him off you, plus Donna's got him hemmed in. Go over there and stake your claim. Donna might be more experienced, but you're young and beautiful and vibrant and warm—everything she's not. Sam doesn't strike me as an idiot."

Kallie glanced at Sam. *He does look a little hemmed in.* "You really think I should?"

"Yes. You've never lacked for backbone, now go use it."

Drawing in a deep breath, Kallie stood and before she lost her nerve, she strode to the end of the bar, excused herself and squeezed between two of the big rescue guys.

Don't lose your nerve. Just do it, stake your claim. God, how do I do that? She stopped in front of Sam and looked up into his face.

He raised an eyebrow. "Is everything okay, Kallie?"

"Yes." *Damn it Kallie, do it. He's the man you want. Stake—your—claim.* "Everything's fine. I just wanted to do this." She stretched up on her toes, placed her hands on his shoulders and kissed him, bang-smack on the lips.

Sam was stunned by Kallie's boldness. A hush fell over the room then his senses took over. He reeled at the soft touch of her lips, her firm breasts pressed against his chest. Unable to help himself, Sam placed his hands on her hips and pulled her closer, deepening the kiss. *To hell with her reputation, I need this.*

A female screech brought him to his senses. Liz Macey marched over and glared at him. "Playing the field is one thing, but I will not have you leading Kallie on and then breaking her heart." She took Kallie's hand. "Come away this minute, love."

Kallie looked at him with glazed eyes, her pink lips softly swollen and a faint blush tinting her cheeks. He tucked a stray curl behind her ear. "You're beautiful."

"Stop it," Liz said. "She's not in your league."

Kallie smiled at him and Liz let out a sound of frustration then dragged her to the other side of the room. Sam turned back to his friends, who were all looking at him questioningly.

"What?" he asked.

Donna Ross, who only moments ago had been all over him, gave him a cold, piercing stare and stalked away, disappearing into the crowd. *It's no skin off my back, lady. I only flirted with you to protect Kallie and look where that got me.*

Ryan raised an eyebrow. "What was that all about?"

Sam's lips twitched. "It seems I've developed a conscience where Kallie is concerned. I wanted her to see my true colours before getting involved with me."

"Well, it backfired." Ryan shook his head. "Spectacularly."

"Hmm." Sam glanced at Kallie. *Hell, the moment she kissed me I forgot everything else.*

"You're not serious, are you, mate?" Talos asked. "She's the type of girl who will want marriage and kids."

Sam grunted. "There isn't a woman alive who could tempt me into marriage."

Talos gave him a dubious look. "That one would have to come close?"

Sam drained his beer and placed the glass on the bar. "Won't happen. There is no way in hell I will put a child through what I went through, not even for a beautiful girl like that." His gaze settled on Kallie. *I wish it was different, but I don't believe in fairy tales.*

Talos paid for another round of beers and they moved to a table in the corner, positioning their chairs so they all had a good view of the room. Conversation was flowing again, but a few locals threw Sam curious glances. He paid special attention to men in their sixties, dismissing them if they were too tall or too short, but other than Ken, Fergie and Bill, no one else stood out as a possible match.

He glanced at Nick who was holding his phone up, pretending to look for coverage. "Make sure you get facial photos of everyone in the room. Then we can run them through Simon's Identiscan and see if we get any hits."

"Almost done." Nick casually looked around the room. "I checked out that black opal Kallie's wearing."

"And?" asked Sam.

"It's worth a lot of money. Black opals are extremely valuable and when they have red colour in them, like that one, it increases their worth substantially. That opal is up there with the best."

"Really?" Sam glanced across at Kallie. "I haven't located the key to her jewel box yet. Did you get round to making me one?"

Nick dug three skeleton keys out of his pocket. "I made these up for you. One of them should fit."

A ping had Talos reaching for his phone. He read the message and lowered his voice. "Simon's sent the info we've been waiting on."

"Tell us," said Sam.

Keeping his phone below the table out of view, Talos read, "The mechanic, Les Ferguson, sixty-two years old, ex-soldier in the standard army. He did four overseas tours. The last one in Afghanistan where he suffered a breakdown after insurgents massacred a village full of woman and children. He came home; started drinking, his marriage failed and he was discharged. Then he completely disappeared."

Nick grunted. "Marzetti could have topped the real Les Ferguson and assumed his identity."

Talos raised an eyebrow. "The publican, Bill Murphy, sixty-five years old, ex-bikie, did two years for possession of an illegal firearm and is known to be a crack shot. After his release from prison he worked as a barman in Kings Cross for several years, then disappeared until he bought this pub twelve years ago."

Ryan rubbed his forehead. "Again, Marzetti could have topped him. They may have known each other in Kings Cross."

Sam glanced at the publican. He was leaning on the bar, deep in conversation with Ken Macey. Both men turned to look their way.

Sam gave them a casual nod and turned back to Talos. "Go on."

Talos clicked on the next message. "Ken Macey, fifty-six, ex..." He glanced across at Ken Macey.

"Ex what?" Sam asked.

"Ex-cop with the Australian Federal Police. Last based with the Drug Enforcement Unit in Sydney. Suspicions were raised when his partner was shot in a drug bust. The stress got to him and he resigned after twenty-four years on the force. He was cleared due to insubstantial evidence, but by then his wife had left him and he'd severed ties with all known family and friends. He moved here eight years ago as a farm hand and he married Liz Hughes a few months later."

They all glanced at Ken Macey as he strolled across the room, spoke to his wife and they both went through the door to the dining room.

Sam sighed. "He looks older than fifty-six. What about Bert Chalmers? What's Simon got on him?"

Talos looked down at his phone. "Bert Chalmers is sixty years old according to his license, not a lot known about him. Lived in Western Australian for many years, owned various mining leases on his own, and with Angus McNeil. Born in Queensland and arrested once twenty years ago for drunkenness along with Angus McNeil and several others. No charges were laid. Hasn't lodged a tax statement in years."

Nick shook his head. "How does Simon get all this information?"

Sam grinned. "There isn't a computer system Simon can't hack into, and his sources are amazing."

"What about Angus McNeil?" Sam said. "Did Simon find anything else on him?"

"Yep." Talos murmured scrolling to the next message.

"Angus McNeil, born in 1947 in Eromanga, Queensland. The taxation department has him down as a shearer, labourer, jackaroo and fossicker. He's registered as owning a couple of mine leases on his own and with Bert Chalmers and a fella called Wallace King.

"Angus was hurt in a rock fall near Kununurra ten years ago and taken to hospital with head and spinal injuries." Talos raised an eyebrow.

"He spent months in rehab learning to walk again, but according to his medical discharge, Angus McNeil was expected to spend the majority of his days in a wheelchair."

Sam shrugged. "Yeah, that's him."

The door from the dining room opened and a grey-headed man with a bushy beard, stooped shoulders and a weather-beaten face ambled in. He headed for the bar.

"Who's that?" asked Nick.

Sam frowned. "I've no idea, but he's the right height and age."

Talos raised his phone and while pretending to look for coverage, took the shot.

The door to the hotel's foyer opened and Roy walked in. Gone were his dusty boots, faded shirt and stained jeans. In their place were clean moleskin jeans, a pale-checked dress shirt and shiny brown riding boots. He moved through the crowd, nodding to some and stopping briefly to have a quick word with others.

Sam turned to Nick. "Don't bother taking Roy's photo. We can rule him out for obvious reasons. I'll get the next round of beers and check out that beardy bloke. Upload those photos to Simon as soon as you can."

On the way to the bar Sam paused behind Kallie and her friend. Jane's voice rose slightly. "You can't just walk up to a guy like that and plant one on him."

Kallie placed both hands on her hips. "You said to stake my claim, so that's what I did."

Jane groaned. "I didn't mean you should plaster yourself to him and kiss him in front of everyone. I meant, go over there and talk to him." She sighed. "And why didn't you stop him when he started kissing you like there was no tomorrow?"

"Because it was incredible."

Jane threw her hands up in the air. "If you let him kiss you like that, you'll end up…" She saw Sam and gasped.

Kallie swung round and inhaled deeply. "Sam." Her eyes widened and a rosy blush crept into her cheeks.

Sam focused on Jane. "If Kallie lets me kiss her like that again, it definitely won't stop with a kiss." He winked at Kallie and grinned when both their mouths dropped open.

As Sam reached the bar, a freckly-faced kid was asking the newcomer what he'd like.

"A schooner of Toohey's Old, thanks, mate."

The young barman poured the beer, passed it across and took the ten-dollar note offered. As he rang up the beer, the man gulped down a couple of mouthfuls before wiping the back of his hand across his mouth.

Sam slid onto the stool beside the man and nodded. "G'day, I haven't seen you here before. Are you just passing through?"

"Sure am. I'm on my way to Queensland to visit family and thought I'd stop by and look up an old mate. His name's Angus McNeil."

Sam hid a grin as Bill stopped in front of the stranger. "What do you want with Angus, if you don't mind me asking?"

"We used to be mates. He's not here tonight, is he?"

Sam shook his head. "Nope, but that's his granddaughter over there with her back to you. The one with the long dark hair sitting with the pregnant lady."

"Is it really?" The man swung round and looked where Sam pointed. "I'll be damned. Thanks mate." He took his beer and started towards Kallie.

Sam watched the man weave his way through the crowd.

Bill leaned across the bar, his gaze flicking between the stranger and Sam. "Do me a favour, Sam, and keep an eye on that fella. He might be who he says he is, and he might not."

"No worries," replied Sam. "Can you get the young bloke to deliver those beers to the three men at that table?" He pointed at the table Ryan, Talos and Nick were at. "They're with Emergency Services."

Bill glanced across. "I've seen two of them before. I thought they were with the bridge contractors?"

"Yeah, everyone did." Sam's gaze followed the prospector.

Kallie and Jane were still evaluating Sam's departing remark when a grey-haired stranger with a bushy beard stopped beside them. He looked straight at Kallie with twinkling blue eyes.

"Kalista McNeil?" he declared loudly.

"Ah, yes." Kallie looked up at the old man and smiled. "Do I know you?"

He brought his palm down on the table loudly. Kallie and Jane both jumped. All those in close proximity who hadn't noticed the newcomer before, now turned to see what was happening. The man snatched hold of Kallie's hand. "So you're the little lady the Kalista diamond's named after?" He glanced at her pendant and a big smile appeared on his face. "I was with Angus when he discovered that opal you're wearing. We were out near Lightning Ridge. And a few years later your grandpa discovered the Kalista Diamond." He stared off into space. "I ain't never seen anything like it." His smile widened. "Your grandpa told me he was calling it after you and swore he'd give it to you personally. He was pretty cut up to hear about the plane crash."

Kallie blinked and pulled her hand away. "I'm sorry, I don't..."

The old timer sobered and sank into the empty chair on her right. "Angus was shattered about losing the son he didn't get a chance to know. But when he heard you hadn't been on the plane, he decided he was going to get to know you and be a proper grandpa."

Kallie didn't know what to say, the old man had a faraway look on his face and the whole room had fallen silent. Sam appeared behind her and put his hands on her shoulders. The tension left and Kallie smiled up at him.

Sam squeezed gently then lifted his right hand and offered it to the bearded stranger.

"Sam Locke, I'm staying out at the McNeil's. Do you have any proof you're who you say you are? It's just that Kallie gets pestered over this fabled diamond."

Sam observed Kallie blinking rapidly as she twisted the ring on her right hand.

The old fella stood to shake hands. "The name's Wally King. I'm a prospector and I've known Angus on and off for years, before his accident that is. He'll tell you who I am? And it's no fable; I can describe the Kalista diamond perfectly. It's not very big but it's flawless and although it's called a pink diamond, once it's polished it will be the prettiest shade of…"

Kallie twisted towards the prospector and interrupted. "Angus isn't here tonight, Mister King. He doesn't hear very well and he hates crowds."

Wally King grunted. "So he hasn't changed then. If you give me directions, I'd like to pay my respects and I wouldn't mind another look at that diamond either."

Sam narrowed his eyes. *I bet you would.*

The prospector looked at him. "It ain't no fable, son. I got a photo of it in my wallet."

A deafening crack of thunder boomed and Sam flinched.

Fergie made a strangled noise, threw himself to the floor and curled up in the foetal position, hands covering his ears.

Sam's gaze followed Talos who went to help Fergie up. Sam focussed on his own breathing. *I know exactly how you feel, Fergie. Only a man who has been under attack from heavy artillery fire reacts like that, unless he's been desensitised.*

The downpour grew heavier and Sam noticed he wasn't the only person looking up and listening.

Wally opened his wallet and pulled out a couple of battered photos. He handed them to Kallie. Jane and Liz leaned forward for a closer look. Bill, Ken, and a clean-cut, fair-haired guy, ambled over from the bar to have a look.

Leaning closer to Roy, Sam asked. "Who's the young bloke with the goatee?"

"Jane's husband, Andrew Rossini. He works in Sydney for some mob that buy up businesses and attempt to bring life back into small towns."

Sam watched as Kallie laid the two photos out on the table in front of her. He leaned over. One was of three men in saggy, broad-brimmed hats with corks hanging from the edges. They all had beards, rolled down socks, dusty boots and navy shorts. None of them wore a shirt and their faces were hidden partly hidden by shadow. The other photo was definitely Wally without his hat. He was smiling and holding out his hand, displaying something small.

"That's me, Angus, and another mate called Bert Chalmers," stated Wally pointing at one photo. "And that's me holding the Kalista Diamond. Course it's not polished, but the colour was there. Never seen anything like it."

"And you never will again," called Fergie, dusting himself off. "There wasn't a pink diamond amongst the gems Kallie received from Angus."

Wally shook his head. "Nah, that can't be right. I spoke to Angus at the hospital before his stroke and he told me he'd sent the diamond to Kalista for safekeeping."

Sam glanced down at Kallie who was studying the photos carefully and frowning. She looked at Roy then pushed the photos over so he could have a better look. Sam watched Roy carefully. *Something is going on here. What?*

Roy looked at the photos then at Kallie. Sam sensed she was trying to send Roy a message.

She turned to Wally. "And this is definitely you, Bert and Angus? With those beards it could be anyone?"

"Yep, but getting back to the diamond. Angus told me he sent it to you for safekeeping, and he planned to sell it and take you travelling, but he didn't think he was going to make it."

Sam looked down at Kallie. Her hands were clenched in her lap and she was staring at the photos. Every person in the bar was focused on her. She cleared her throat.

"That's true. Angus and I talked on the phone before his stroke and he said he was going to take me around the world. He told me he was sending me some precious stones and to keep them safe until I was old enough to control my own future. So I did. Then Angus had the stroke and needed intensive therapy and the child welfare people turned up saying I couldn't live with Roy. There was a lot of confusion and I don't know what happened to the Kalista Diamond. I thought I had it but the gem I thought it was turned out to be too small."

"And you have no idea where it is now?" asked Wally, his face ashen.

Sam watched Kallie keenly. Her eyes briefly met Roy's before sweeping the room. She shrugged.

No real answer. Sam wasn't surprised to see her twisting the ring. He turned to the prospector. "Did anyone else know Angus sent the diamond to Kallie or was there anyone else interested in its whereabouts?"

Wally's shoulders sagged. "Lots of people. After Angus discovered the diamond we made the papers and our camp was torn apart several times, but they never got it. Then after the stroke, Bert and I visited Angus. We thought he was going to die so we went to the pub and got plastered. It's possible we mentioned it."

Sam glanced at Kallie again. She slid to the edge of her seat and smiled at Wally.

"Bert is here too. He looks after Angus."

Wally brightened instantly. "Bert's here? I'll be damned. The three of us used to be as thick as thieves before the accident."

"Are you staying here at the pub?" asked Sam.

"Nah, I've got one of them little motorhomes parked outside the school."

Kallie picked up a coaster. "I'll give you our phone number and some directions, but don't try to drive out there tonight. The rain is too heavy and unless you know the roads well, they can be dangerous."

Jane rummaged through her bag and handed Kallie a pen. The noise level increased again as people lost interest and returned to their conversations. Kallie wrote down her number, drew a map and handed the coaster to Wally.

"Come for lunch tomorrow." She pushed back her chair. "You should give Angus a call tonight, but don't be disappointed if he doesn't remember you. His memory is patchy."

The prospector nodded. "I might do that. Thanks, Kalista, I'll see you tomorrow." He picked up his photos, nodded at Sam and made his way to the foyer. Roy followed.

Kallie stood, drew in a deep breath and turned to Sam. "I'm hungry, let's go and eat."

Sam stepped back and let Kallie and Jane precede him to the dining room. Ken and Bill were staring after Wally and Roy. *It could be either of you.* Sam strolled across to his three mates, picked up his beer and casually perused the room then he sculled the beer and placed the glass back on the table.

"Do a check on Wally King and a deeper check on Bert Chalmers. He knew Angus sent the diamond to Kallie and he did come over with Angus. The fact that he's still here means he hasn't got it yet, if indeed he's after it. Bert's a nasty sort of fellow, so he could be Marzetti."

Talos frowned. "But Angus McNeil would know?"

"Maybe not. After the brain haemorrhage he did lose his long-term memory. I'll watch him. You keep an eye out for Vassello and his two companions."

Talos and Ryan nodded. Sam held out his hand and made a point of shaking each of their hands. "I don't know you fellas, remember. We need to keep up pretences." He left the bar and headed for the dining room.

Chapter Eight

Walking into the dining room, Kallie was surprised by the number of people there, especially on such a horrid night. People she'd gone to school with, farming families from outlying districts who were customers, and locals who'd known her all her life. Everyone was smiling and waving at her. There was a big, round table in the middle of the room set for nine with an arrangement of crimson gerberas in the centre. Kallie followed Jane to the round table. *I had no idea all these people thought so much of me.* She drew in a deep breath and forced a smile, returning a wave here and there as she sat beside Jane and looked around the room.

Andrew, Jane's husband slid into the seat beside his wife and leaned across the table towards Fergie.

"Bill was just telling me, he's calling a flood meeting later, seeing as there's so many folks in town tonight and we might need those army guys' help. Apparently they're camped out at Kallie's place."

Jane frowned at Kallie. "Why are they at your place?"

"They are on an exercise, but if it does flood we may need their helicopter to get people out." She set her purse down on the empty seat beside her.

Ken and Liz left the people they were chatting with and came over to the table. Ken looked down at Kallie's purse, hesitated then moved further round the table. Liz glanced down, picked up the purse, put it on the table and sat. She shook out her serviette and leaned closer to Kallie.

"You should never make things too easy, Kallie. Play hard to get. You'd be surprised how well it works."

Kallie glanced at Jane who was biting her lip, trying not to laugh. Kallie crossed her eyes at Jane and turned back to Liz.

"Whatever you think is best, Liz. You know I always listen to everything you say."

Jane choked and Andrew turned round and thumped her on the back. She waved him away. "I'm fine."

"You were choking," he argued.

"No, I wasn't." She looked round the table. "Okay, maybe I was, but Kallie shouldn't make statements like that when I have a mouth full of water." Everyone at the table laughed.

Opening her eyes wide, Kallie asked. "Like what?"

"You may listen to Mum's advice, but when have you ever taken it? You, Kallie McNeil always do whatever you think is best, no matter what anyone else tells you."

Kallie huffed and looked across the room as Sam strolled in, his broad shoulders filling the doorway. He surveyed the room's occupants, his gaze coming to rest on her. He smiled and began to make his way around the tables.

Jane leaned closer and whispered. "Gees, Kallie, he's a real hunk, but a bit too intimidating for me. I don't know if I could control someone like him." She smiled, "or his big friend. I bet they know how to excite a woman though."

"Ssh," whispered Kallie. She glanced quickly at Andrew. *Thank goodness, he's talking to Fergie and didn't hear.* She turned back to Jane.

"For me to find out about Sam's sexual prowess, he would have to actually make a move on me, and for some reason he hasn't. I don't know what else I can do."

"Be yourself. He can't take his eyes off you and from what Mum was saying earlier, he likes spending time with you."

"Oh God, I hope you're right. I couldn't stand it if he was just after the diamond."

"Well, he knows about it now. Let's see if he starts pestering you about it."

"Hmm."

Jane sighed. "I bet that big guy looks fantastic without a shirt."

"Ssh." Kallie nudged Jane with her elbow.

Sam pulled out a chair between Fergie and Ken, sat and glanced round the table. Fergie and Andrew were deep in conversation, discussing the odds of Willaroi flooding. Kallie and Jane had their heads together speaking quietly. Liz was frowning at Kallie and Ken was reading his menu. Sam waited until Liz glanced across at him.

"It's a great turnout, Liz. How'd you arrange everything so fast?"

Before Liz could say a word, Ken spoke. "She's been on the phone all afternoon. Had me running here, there and everywhere. Bill had to get in extra supplies from Collie and call in more staff. Fergie had to drive into Mungindi for flowers and she had Andrew fly Jane up from Sydney. You'd think it was a bloody wedding."

Everyone laughed and Liz swiped Ken with her menu.

"Don't be a drama queen, Ken. This is the first time since the plane crash that Kallie's let us give her a birthday. I had to make the most of it."

Sam glanced at Kallie. She had her head down studying the menu. *Damn it, Liz. Let Kallie enjoy the night and stop reminding her of the past.* His gaze shifted to Jane who was openly glaring at her mother. He picked up his own menu.

"So, what should I order? I tried the Cottage Pie a couple of nights ago and that was pretty good. What's the Lamb Casserole like?"

Everyone offered their opinion on what Sam should order and Kallie visibly relaxed. Roy and his girlfriend, Bunny came into the dining room, made their way to the table and sat between Andrew and Fergie. Over the next two hours Sam got a glimpse into Kallie's life as a number of people got up to recite amusing stories of her as a mischievous child, a persuasive teenager and a determined hardworking young woman. Sam couldn't remember laughing so hard. Kallie laughed, blushed, and cringed with each story. Sam discovered she could be righteous, stubborn, indignant and obstinate. She was also kind, compassionate, generous and loving. She'd been a defender and saviour of creatures big, small, domestic, human, native and feral. Mostly native and feral to the horror of locals who recounted stories of Kallie standing between them and wombats that had destroyed fences, or foxes who'd stolen chickens to feed their pups. And woe betide anyone who lied to Kallie or intentionally deceived her.

A twinge of guilt hit Sam. *How's Kallie going to feel when she discovers I'm a gun for hire, using her to get the diamond and Marzetti? Do I even care?*

He glanced across the table at Kallie holding her face in her hands, laughing and wiping tears away as three young men retold stories of their unfortunate encounters with Kallie. At sixteen, she pushed one into a patch of blackberries after he kissed her. Another was pushed into a dam for the same misdemeanour when Kallie was eighteen, and the third received a punch in the eye, which knocked him to the ground. Kallie, then twenty-one, had stood over him and said, "when I want a man to kiss me, I'll tell him." With that she jumped on Jasper, and left the guy eating her dust.

Everybody roared with laughter and someone yelled out, "She certainly let that big bloke in the bar know she wanted him to kiss her."

Kallie's gaze flew to Sam; she blushed again and collapsed on the table hiding her face in her arms. "Oh God, I'm never going to live that down."

There was more laughter and people turned to look at Sam. He smiled but said nothing. *Yes, I care what she thinks.*

After the dessert plates were cleared everyone filed back into the bar for the flood meeting. Sam stayed out of it and was glad to see Talos, Nick and Ryan did too. Ryan told the locals they couldn't comment as they were waiting for the latest report and all their orders came from higher up. The locals accepted this and started making contingency plans in case Willaroi did flood.

Roy was heading for the bar, so Sam strolled over, ordered a beer and stood next to him. "What do you think, Roy? Will it flood?

Roy gave a light shrug. "Signs are all there. The Gwydir River is rising, birds have disappeared and the cattle are grouping." He glanced across the room to where the local farmers were arguing with Ken. Roy turned back to the bar and shook his head.

"What they should be doing is moving their stock to higher ground and bringing in extra supplies. If it don't flood, it don't flood, but if it does then they're ready."

Sam looked across to Kallie. She was standing with hands on hips and a scowl on her face. She tried to speak a couple of times but the farmers and Ken talked over the top of her.

Sam glanced at Roy. "The meteorology centre is predicting rain for two more days. Shouldn't you be over there helping Kallie convince them to move their stock?"

"Wouldn't do any good. We've had plenty of storms and warnings before." He turned back to his beer.

"But what do you think?" asked Sam.

Roy narrowed his eyes and stared at Sam. "We're surrounded by three major river systems and they're all full. When the water from the Queensland floods reaches here, a lot of farms will go under and Willaroi will be completely cut off."

"I see." Sam turned back to watch Kallie. She was rolling her eyes and appeared frustrated. Sam glanced at several young men standing near Kallie. They were the three that had kissed her. At the moment, their gazes were locked on her. They looked fascinated.

He grimaced and swivelled back to Roy. "Why does Kallie think the local men are only after her for her farm and the diamond? Anyone with half a brain can see those three are besotted with her?"

Roy glanced around to Kallie and her admirers. He grunted and turned back to the bar. "There's been a few older locals putting the hard word on Angus for Kallie's hand in marriage, to either them or their sons. Angus got rid of them pretty quick. Those three boys behind you aren't so bad. Their mistake wasn't kissing Kallie; it was what they said after they kissed her."

"After?" Sam looked at Roy.

"Yeah, after they kissed her, they started making plans for the future. How they'd either sell her half of the property or combine it with their own and sell the diamond to finance improvements." He chuckled. "Bossy blew her top. You see, since she lost her family, I've made a point of asking her opinion, so she feels important and has something else to think about. Those fellas just assumed she'd let them take everything and make all the decisions."

Sam nodded. "I can understand that. She likes to be included in the decision making."

"You bet she does," agreed Roy. "They're nice young fellas but they're not equipped to handle a high-spirited girl like Bossy. She needs someone with backbone, who isn't out to deceive her. Someone that respects her intelligence and ability to make decisions but doesn't take no shit from her." He sighed. "She's got a lot of her dad in her. She has a real way with horses, but she's more like her mum. Mariana was stubborn, impulsive and passionate about everything. Her family back in Italy wanted her to marry some Italian millionaire, but she was determined to marry young James, and when she did, her family never spoke to her again."

Sam glanced back to Kallie. *Stubborn, impulsive and passionate. You forgot beautiful, fascinating, desirable and mine.* He put his elbow on the bar and rubbed his forehead. *Not mine. I'm the wrong guy for Kallie. Shit, she's probably a virgin and thinks marriage is the be all and end all.* The thought brought him up straight. He looked at Roy.

"Why are you telling me this, Roy? Aren't you worried I'll make a play for Kallie or... is that your intention?"

"I'm telling you"—Roy pointed a callused finger—"cause she's infatuated with you, and I've seen the way you look at her. It's a hard life out here and if her family was alive, she'd be living an easier life down in the Hunter Valley. She needs to be taken care of properly by someone strong-minded, who values her opinions and can satisfy her passionate nature. I don't know if that's you or not."

He picked up his beer and looked Sam in the eye. "Don't deceive her or you'll lose her. And don't hurt her or I'll come after you." He skulled the beer then gave Sam a nod and walked out of the bar.

Sam's gaze followed him. *I bet you would, but you have no idea who I am or what I'm capable of. Fuck, what am I thinking? It's Roy's job to protect Kallie. My job is to get that diamond and Marzetti.*

Sam put his hand up and signalled Bill. "Is it all right with you if I get my guitar and play a few songs? I promised Kallie I'd sing a song for her."

Bill's eyes widened then he grinned. "No worries. I think she'd like that and it might calm things down. They're getting a bit hot-tempered over there." He nodded across the room.

Sam walked towards the door, passing Kallie on the way. She looked up, her eyes meeting his then she frowned and ran after him, standing between him and the door.

"Sam, please don't go. The meeting's winding up and we can play something from the Jukebox. It's only nine-thirty."

Sam looked down into her pleading eyes and smiled. "I'm just getting something out of the Hilux, sweetheart. I'll be back in a minute." He placed his hands on her upper arms, moved her to the side and strolled out the door.

Kallie watched him disappear into the foyer and smiled. *He called me sweetheart. Oh heart, be still.* Jane came up behind her.

"Where's he going, Kallie?"

"To get something out of his car." She grinned. "Earlier he told me I was beautiful."

"Have you slept with him yet?"

"Not yet."

Jane's eyebrow rose. "Please tell me you're not still abiding by that, *I'm not having sex until I'm in love* crap."

"It's not crap, Jane. I need to desire a man before I sleep with him."

"It's probably a good thing." Jane worried her bottom lip. "There are a lot of men who take what they want and then move on, and you're left with a broken heart."

"You slept with Andrew before you were married."

"That's different," Jane snapped. "He chased me for months and I thought he was head over heels in love with me."

Narrowing her eyes, Kallie stared her friend. "You *thought* he was in love with you? Jane, is everything okay between you and Andrew?"

Twisting her serviette, Jane's gaze dropped to her lap. "Why wouldn't it be? I'm pregnant with his baby, aren't I?"

"Something is wrong. Tell me or I won't let up until you do."

Looking up with glassy eyes, Jane bit her lip. "He hasn't touched me since I told him I was pregnant. Unbeknown to me, Andrew never wanted kids and whenever we're alone, he gives me the cold shoulder or looks at me with disgust."

"Hang on a second. You were barely back from Vietnam when you found out you were pregnant. Are you saying he hasn't touched you since the honeymoon?"

"Yes." Jane closed her eyes and took a deep breath. "Sometimes I wish Ken had never introduced Andrew to us."

Kallie reached for Jane's hand. "You need to talk to him. Sort this out."

"Don't you think I've tried? I think Andrew's having an affair."

"No." Kallie gasped. "You need to find out for sure."

"Let's not talk about that now." Jane squeezed Kallie's hand. "You've always been able to read people well, and if you think Sam's a decent guy then go for it, but he won't be a pushover." She chuckled. "What am I saying? You have a way with obstinate brutes."

Kallie gaped. *'I have a way with horses, not men, and I've never met a man like Sam. I don't know the first thing about attracting him. I need your help."*

Jane moved sideways as Sam re-entered the room carrying a guitar, winked at them and strolled over to an empty chair. She smiled.

"Actually, I think you're doing fine. Just think twice before falling in love with him." She turned and waddled away.

Oh, Jane. What can I do to help you? How could Andrew be so stupid? Kallie glanced at Sam who was tuning his guitar. A lot of people were leaving, some looked at Sam curiously and slid back into their chairs. Roy had disappeared. *Probably gone home.* Kallie glanced around the bar. Ken, Liz, Jane and Andrew were sitting at a table in the corner, talking. Fergie was at a table on his own, so Kallie decided to join him.

"Hi Fergie, how's it going."

"Not bad. I see Sam's going to play us a song."

Kallie glanced at Sam. He started strumming his guitar and looked across to her. Her cheeks heated as others in the room also glanced at her.

Sam strummed the guitar. "This is a song for Kallie and it's called, 'Wonderful Tonight', by Eric Clapton, and I think you'll all agree, she does look wonderful tonight."

Kallie couldn't tear her eyes from him as he sang the lovely song, his voice clear and deep, his gaze on her the whole time. Each verse seemed to have been written just for her.

She blinked when he finished and everyone clapped. Flustered, she glanced at Fergie. He was watching her with one eyebrow raised. Kallie's face grew hotter, warmth radiated through her body, her legs shook and her heart soared. *Far out, I don't know where to look. He sang that song to me.*

Someone yelled out a request for "Stairway to Heaven'. Sam laughed and obliged.

"He's got a good voice, I'll give him that much," murmured Fergie. "I'm more a country and western fan myself."

Not wanting to be overheard, Kallie leaned closer. "You were right, Fergie. Sam told me he was in the army, but he doesn't like talking about it."

"Yeah," agreed Fergie, "Special Forces—you can tell them a mile away. Him and his mates are probably all in the same unit."

"Pardon?" Kallie stared at him. "What mates?"

Fergie finished his beer and covered a burp. "The ones saying they're on an army exercise. I've seen their chopper flying around the last few days. That's a Black Hawk, the real thing. I reckon they're here on a Special Force training mission. All hush hush, if you know what I mean."

Kallie looked to Sam. "But he's not with them."

"He's with them all right, Kallie. No one comes here to fish and it's too much of a coincidence to have six Special Forces fellas in town at once, don't you think?"

Fergie stood. "I'm heading home, Kallie. It's been a good night. You take care, and watch that fella. I think he might be keen on you."

Kallie half-smiled. "Goodnight, Fergie." She watched him leave. *Sam isn't with them. He didn't even know them the day they chased me. He wouldn't make up a lie like that.*

She straightened her shoulders and turned back to Sam.

He finished "Stairway To Heaven" and everyone cheered. Then he put down his guitar, wandered over to the jukebox and selected a song.

Excited shivers ran through her when he strolled over and held out his hand.

"Care to dance, Kallie?"

She drew in a shaky breath and gave him her hand. *Who are you?*

Sam drew her into his arms as the first notes of "Unchained Melody" rang out. Kallie closed her eyes and laid her head against his chest. It was one of her favourite songs. One of Sam's hands encased hers, the other rested low on her back, sending quivers racing through her body. The sound of his heartbeat against her ear calmed her own racing heart as they moved slowly with the music. As the chorus began, Sam lowered his head and sang softly.

Kallie opened her eyes and their gazes met. "Thank you, Sam. I'm having a lovely night and I'm really glad you came to Willaroi."

A smile slowly spread over his face. "So am I, Kallie."

Ken pushed a table closer to the wall then he and Liz joined them on the dance floor. When a few more couples decided to dance, Bill stacked chairs and carried them through to the dining room. The music ended and someone selected another slow song. Several more couples strolled onto the dance floor and began dancing.

Slow dancing with Sam was the most romantic thing Kallie had ever done. She linked her hands behind his neck and had moved in a little closer when the barroom door opened and Sam stiffened, stopped dancing and stared at something behind Kallie. She glanced over her shoulder to see three men she didn't know.

"What is it, Sam?"

Sam dragged his gaze from the men back to her. "Nothing."

He drew her close and began dancing again, but his gaze followed the men to an empty table. Kallie leaned her cheek against his chest again and peeped at the newcomers. Two were big men, in their late thirties to early forties and staring around the room as if they were looking for someone in particular. The other man was older, perhaps mid-fifties. He wore a grey suit and pale blue shirt, open at the neck. His black and grey peppered hair was caught at the base of his neck in a band and he looked self-confident, wealthy and out of place in Willaroi Downs.

The door opened again and three of the army guys walked in, glanced around the room and headed for the bar.

"I've never seen this place so full," Kallie murmured. "And on such a terrible night."

"Hmm." Sam eased her away. "I think it might be a good idea to head home before it gets any worse." He took her hand and led her across the room to the end of the bar just as Bill came in from the dining room.

"Hey, Sam, I think you've started a new trend. The locals don't normally dance in my pub." Bill laughed, his gaze skimming the crowd as he went to wipe down the counter. His hand suddenly froze in mid-air, the smile vanishing from his face as he stared across the room at the three newcomers.

"Holy shit."

"What?" Kallie asked. "Do you know those men?"

Bill glanced at Kallie, his face ashen. "Ah, no, no I don't." He looked at Sam. "You might want to take Kallie home. The weather's getting worse and it isn't a good night to be hanging around here."

Sam met Bill's gaze then moved his body to block the three men's view of Bill. "I'll get Ken and Liz to take Kallie home with them, but I might stay around in case those fellas give you any trouble." *If you're Marzetti, I'm not losing you now.*

Bill nodded. "Maybe your army friends might stick around as well."

Kallie looked from one to the other. "What trouble? I don't want to go home." She turned to Bill. "And they're not Sam's friends, he doesn't know them."

Sam took Kallie's elbow. "Come on, Kallie. You go home with Ken and Liz. I won't be long." He looked back at Bill. "I suggest you let the kid run the bar and make yourself scarce. You're just the sort of bloke those two big thugs would pick a fight with."

Sam guided Kallie over to Liz and Jane who were putting raincoats on. When they saw Kallie's scowl they both stopped.

"What's wrong?" asked Jane.

"Sam's sending me home with you." Kallie muttered crossing her arms. "He reckons those men who just arrived might make trouble."

Both women looked across the room, then Liz glanced up at Sam.

"Why can't you take Kallie home?"

"I'm going to stick around in case Bill needs help. Where's Ken and Andrew?"

Jane picked up her bag. "Andrew's gone to get the car. As for Ken, I have no idea where he went. He disappeared a few minutes ago."

Liz frowned at the three men. "I think Ken recognised those men. He almost choked when they came in, and then he told me to get Jane and go straight home." She put her hand on her chest. "I hope he didn't go home to get his rifle. Oh, dear God."

"He'll be fine, Liz." Sam guided the three women out into the foyer where Andrew was shaking his raincoat. Kallie hung back and peeked into the bar.

"Oh good, there you are," called Andrew, dripping water all over the carpet. "Come on, I think there's a break in the rain."

Liz hesitated, "Maybe I should stay and wait for Ken?"

Sam shook his head. "Just go home, Liz, and stay there. I'll take care of those three." He unzipped his jacket and felt for his Glock.

Gripping Jane's hand, Liz towed her towards Andrew. "Come on, Kallie," she called over her shoulder. "Let's go."

Kallie stepped from behind Sam, her eyes narrowed. "What's going on, Sam? Who are those men and why is there a gun in the back of your jeans?"

Sam rubbed his forehead and glanced towards the door where Jane was trying to extricate her hand from her mother's. "I can't tell you at the moment, Kallie. You are going to have to trust me and say nothing to anybody, and I mean anybody. Your life depends on it."

Kallie's eyes widened and she swallowed. "Who are you?"

CHAPTER NINE

Sam grabbed Kallie's arm and moved her towards the pub's entrance. "I told you. I work for a security firm."

She shrugged her arm loose. "Don't lie to me, Sam. No security guard carries a gun when he's away on holidays. I want the truth," she whispered.

"Come on, Kallie, hurry up," Liz called, pushing a reluctant Jane ahead of her.

Sam stared at Kallie. *Fuck, she's going to blow everything.* "Kallie, I promise to explain later. Please trust me?"

She backed away. "You didn't come here to catch fish, did you?"

"I did, Kallie." *Jesus, I need to give her something or Marzetti is going to get away.* He rubbed his forehead. "The fish I'm after is human and very dangerous. He's been hiding here in Willaroi for years and if he knows I'm onto him, he's likely to kill anyone who gets in his way. My uncovering his identity depends on you keeping quiet."

Kallie straightened her shoulders and drew in a deep breath. "Are you an undercover police officer?"

"I don't have time to explain, Kallie, you will have to trust me."

"I'll think about it." She opened the outer door and ran into the dark, wet night.

"Do you want me to go after her?" Talos stood behind him.

"No, I want you to wait here for Ken Macey, in case he comes back armed."

"Okay, but you better do something about Kallie McNeil or Jarred will."

Sam clenched his fists. "I'll think of something to pacify her." He looked towards the bar's half-open door. "I'm betting that's Victor Vassello in the suit. Both Ken and Bill recognised him, but which one of them is Dominic Marzetti?"

Talos nodded. "We'll know soon enough. Marzetti will either make a run for it, or confront Vassello, and with those two bodyguards, I don't like Marzetti's chances."

Sam shrugged. "Possibly, but Victor Vassello won't shoot Dominic Marzetti, at least not until he gets his money back." Sam sighed, "There's something else that's been bugging me. Why would the guy with the AK47 kill his own people?"

Talos narrowed his dark eyes. "Maybe his job was to take out the snitch, collect the money and leave no witnesses. It's a shame we couldn't identify those bodies in the warehouse. It might have given us a lead."

Sam pushed the bar door wide. "Keep your eyes open. I'm pretty sure the bodyguards are packing. Shout if you have any trouble with Ken."

"You got it." Talos turned back to the pub's entrance.

❦

Kallie sat in Liz's kitchen drinking hot chocolate, her mind whirling as she drummed her fingers on the table. *Why does Sam have a gun and who is the dangerous man he's after?* She put her cup down and chewed her nail. *Is Fergie right? Does Sam know those men and are they all highly trained Special Forces soldiers on a secret mission? No, that can't be right. Sam wouldn't be allowed to stay with me if he was on an army exercise, plus he said he's not in the army anymore. But is he lying.* She put her head in her hands. *How can I find out?*

"Hey, what's wrong?" asked Liz, coming into the kitchen.

"Nothing." Kallie forced a smile onto her face. "It's good to see Jane. She's going to make a great mother and you and Ken will make super grandparents."

"Yes." Liz smiled. "I'm looking forward to the baby and I can't wait to move closer to them." She reached across the table and squeezed Kallie's hand. "I'm sorry we had to sell the store, Kallie, but Ken is getting too old to be lifting heavy sacks and I do miss Jane."

"I do, too." Kallie squeezed back. "You've made the right decision.

Jane's going to need you when the baby's born, but I'll miss you."

"I'll miss you too, love." Liz stood. "You can always sell up and move to the south coast too. I'm sure Roy wouldn't object. In fact, it might make him marry Bunny and take her on that trip she's always on about."

"We'll see. Thank you for organising dinner tonight, Liz. It was lovely and I was having a great time until those men came in and ruined everything."

Liz tightened the cord on her dressing gown. "Don't worry, love, there'll be plenty of other nights. If Sam thought those men were trouble, then he did the right thing sending us home. I just hope they can talk Ken out of doing something silly."

"You're right." Kallie's gaze dropped to her cup. *I don't want anything to happen to Jane or the baby.* She smiled at Liz.

"How long is Jane staying?"

"A couple of days. Andrew's decided to wait out the storm." She walked to the linen press and pulled out a light blanket. "You might as well bunk down in the lounge room for now." She handed the blanket to Kallie. "Curl up on the chair in front of the fire."

"Thanks." Kallie hugged the blanket to her chest. "Liz, do you think Sam's interested in me? It's like he's sending mixed signals. One minute I get the feeling he likes me, then the next minute he's pushing me away and...I'm afraid he's not who he says he is." *And he carries a gun. Don't forget about that.*

Liz drew in a deep breath and exhaled. "Some men act a certain way because they believe they're protecting us. It's up to us women to take charge and point them in the right direction. If it helps, Ken thinks Sam and those other fellas might be working an undercover operation of some sort." She kissed Kallie's forehead. "Get some sleep, love, it might be a while before he comes to take you home."

Nodding, Kallie stood and headed for the lounge room. The fire was dying, but heat still radiated from it. She sat in the armchair and covered herself. *This isn't exactly how I envisaged ending my night.* Staring into the flames relaxed her and it wasn't long before her eyelids became heavy.

❧❧

Sam walked back into the bar and casually glanced about the room. The young barman was serving a couple of old timers sitting at the counter. The man in the suit and his two friends were deep in conversation. Nick and Ryan were playing pool and Fergie sat alone at a table in the corner, a woolly hat pulled down over his ears. Sam crossed to the bar, ordered two beers then strolled over to join him. He placed a beer in front of Fergie and pulled out a chair.

Fergie picked up the beer. "Thanks, mate." He took a couple of mouthfuls then placed the glass back on the table. "I thought you took Kallie home?"

"No, she's gone with Liz and Jane. I thought I'd stay a bit longer and then pick her up on my way through." His mobile vibrated in his pocket. Sam checked the message. It was from Simon. *Identiscan has verified newcomer is Victor Vassello.*

Sam glanced across the room. Victor Vassello and his two friends were sipping their beers, speaking in lowered tones and watching the other patrons. The two men with Victor had their eyes on Nick and Ryan. Victor was staring straight at Fergie.

Sam frowned. *Could we be wrong? Is Fergie Dominic Marzetti?* Sam slid the mobile back in his jacket.

"Is that one of them fancy satellite phones?" asked Fergie.

Shit. Sam shook his head. "No, just a top of the range mobile."

Fergie raised an eyebrow. "I didn't come down in the last shower of rain, Sam. Mobile phones don't work out here and I know you're with them fellas playing pool, so cut the bullshit. What's really going on here? You're SAS, aren't you?"

Christ. Sam considered Fergie leaning back in his chair, his arms crossed.

"I been around long enough to recognise elite ones when I see them," Fergie said.

Tapping his fingers on the table, Sam thought about lying. He glanced at Fergie who was waiting patiently. *No, lying's not going to work. I'll have to tell him part of the truth. But first I need to check he's who he's supposed to be.*

"I saw how you reacted to that loud crack of thunder, Fergie. Before I tell you anything, I need to know why, and then I'll decide if I can trust you."

Fergie rubbed his hand over his bristly beard and then sniffed loudly.

"Fair enough. I was in the standard army for thirty years and did a few tours to East Timor and Afghanistan. That's how I know a Black Hawk when I see it." He cleared his throat. "On the last tour in Afghanistan my unit made a routine visit to a village under our jurisdiction. We arrived to find the whole village had been massacred." Fergie closed his eyes and swallowed.

"The village was made up of old men, women and children. We were searching for survivors when militants hit us with a heavy mortar attack. I got out with minor injuries, but psychologically, I was a mess. I couldn't get the images out of my head and it destroyed my military career and my life."

Sam nodded in understanding. "I've done a few tours myself and I often wake up in a sweat when there's thunder about." He glanced around the room, relaxing a little when Talos came back into the bar. *Obviously Ken's been taken care of.* Sam raised his glass and drained the contents.

"Okay, Fergie. What I'm about to tell you, goes no further. That is non-negotiable and every person in this town's life could depend on it."

Fergie's eyes widened. "That serious, ay?"

"Yes, Fergie, it's that serious," agreed Sam.

"Fair enough. You have my word."

"You're right, I do know those fellas." He nodded in the direction of Nick, Talos and Ryan standing around the pool table. "We're searching for a man who disappeared some years ago and could be living here under a new identity."

Fergie sat back, interlocked his fingers over his belly and frowned. "Who?"

"We don't know his new identity and I'm not at liberty to tell you his real name, but we do know he was involved in underworld activities. We have a general description but the only photo we have isn't clear. We also believe he intends to steal the Kalista Diamond."

Sam glanced towards Victor Vassello and his two mates. "Those three fellas at the table over there are also after this man, for reasons of their own."

Fergie looked across the room then back to Sam. "An underworld figure, you say?"

Sam nodded.

"Would this person have anything to do with Ken and Bill?"

"Why would you ask that?" asked Sam tilting his head to the side.

"Bill used to run pretty wild in his younger days and he disappeared pretty quick tonight when those three arrived. I've never known him to leave young Brendan running the bar. As for Ken—I saw his reaction when those three walked in. I reckon he recognised them too." Fergie rubbed his chin. "But I can't see Bill or Ken as underworld figures." He stiffened and stared at Sam.

"You say this person's after Kallie's diamond."

"Yes, that's why I'm staying out at Kallie's place. We think this person is about to steal the diamond and disappear."

"But Kallie doesn't know where it is." Fergie's voice was adamant.

"I think she does," Sam said. "And from what we've learned, this underworld figure doesn't leave witnesses alive to testify against him. That's why I'm pretending to be on a fishing holiday and the boys are masquerading as army personnel. It's also why I must stay close to Kallie."

"Fair enough. Do you realise she's head over heels for you?"

Sam sighed. "It's only a crush, Fergie. She'll get over me when I'm gone."

Fergie looked doubtful but shrugged. "I guess you know best, just don't take advantage of her infatuation." He pushed his chair back and stood. "I'm heading home. If you need me, yell. I'm still pretty handy with a rifle."

"Thanks." Sam stood and watched as Fergie called out a farewell to the two old men at the bar then ambled out. Sam exhaled. *I hope he can keep his mouth shut.*

"Sam," Ryan called over to him. "You up for a game of pool?"

Lips twitching, Sam strolled over. "You fellas staying at the pub tonight?"

Nick burped. "Sure are. Beats tackling that road in this weather."

Keeping his back to the room, Sam picked up a cue. "I just got a text from Simon. That's Victor Vassello in the suit."

Ryan's eyes narrowed. "I'd love to know how he found out that Marzetti's here."

Sam looked across at Nick and Ryan. "Watch Vassello. We don't want him snatching Marzetti from under our noses.

They took up positions around the table, making sure at least two of them had a clear view of Vassello and his two friends. Sam moved beside Talos.

"What happened with Ken Macey?"

Talos chalked his cue. "You were right. He came back with a rifle. I pointed out he'd had a few beers and three against one wasn't good odds and he'd pretty much end up dead."

Sam huffed. "What did Ken do?"

Talos blew the chalk off his cue. "He said something about I didn't know who I was dealing with and that one of those fellas was the bastard who ruined his life. Then he tried to push past me, so I disarmed him and helped him home."

Ryan chuckled. "Is that what you call it?"

A fleeting smile crossed Talos's face. "I may have used a little force, but he did say something rather interesting."

"What?"

"That he had a score to settle with that bastard."

Nick shrugged. "Ken could be referring to the drug raid where his partner was killed and he was accused of tipping off the dealer. Or, he could be Dominic Marzetti masquerading as Ken Macey and wants to settle some other score with Vassello."

"Maybe," Talos said quietly. "I saw the old prospector taking a leak outside a motorhome earlier so I took down the plates and Simon is checking them out."

"Good thinking."

They played one game of pool and were starting another when one of the bodyguards walked to the bar and called Brendan over. After a brief conversation the young barman slipped out the back.

"What's that all about?" asked Ryan.

Sam narrowed his eyes. "Don't know, but we'd better find out." He placed his cue on the rack and strolled to the bar. Talos followed.

"Where's the barman?" Sam slurred his words and looked around the bar. "A man could die of thirst here."

"He won't be long," someone called out. "He's gone to ask Bill what rooms are empty."

"Thanks." Sam turned to look at the heavily-muscled man beside him.

"G'day, I haven't seen you round here before."

The man eyed Sam up and down. "Just passing through."

Sam made pretence of swaying unsteadily then burped. "Scuze me."

The man's lip curled and his fist clenched, but he remained silent as Brendan came back looking a little confused.

"Ah, sorry mister, we're booked out tonight."

A big, solid arm reached across the bar and grabbed Brendan by the shirt. Sam tensed, as the young man was half-dragged across the bar to within inches of the thug's face. "You just told me you weren't full, so go back and check again."

Talos grabbed the man's wrist in what Sam knew would be a vice-like grip and squeezed until the man released his hold. Brendan lurched back, his eyes wide.

Talos leaned in. "You were told there's no rooms available, so I suggest you drive to Collarenabri and book into a hotel there." He dropped the man's wrist and half-turned away.

The thug went for his gun and Sam moved fast, grabbing the man's arm and twisting it behind his back, then he lashed out with his steel-capped boot, kicking hard behind one of the man's knees. As the man's leg gave out, Talos grasped the back of his head and slammed the guy's face into the bar. He crumpled to the floor like a rag doll.

Talos dragged him towards the door, leaving a trail of blood droplets across the floorboards. Sam's gaze went to Nick and Ryan who both stood ready if needed.

Victor Vassello sat calmly in his chair watching. He slowly stood and directed his gaze at Sam and Talos. "I must apologise for my friend's behaviour." He looked at the bloodied man and shook his head. "We won't take up any more of your time." He started towards the door then paused. "Perhaps you would be good enough to help Ivan to the car?"

Sam gave a slight nod then he and Talos dragged the guy after Vassello. The other bodyguard fell in behind, followed by Nick and Ryan.

As Sam glanced back towards the bar, he couldn't help but grin at the open mouths of Brendan and the two old-timers.

After shoving Ivan onto the back seat of Vassello's Land Cruiser, Sam slammed the door and stepped back under the pub's awning.

Nick, Ryan and Talos stood alongside until the lights had disappeared into the thick curtain of rain.

"How are we going to explain this to the locals?" asked Nick, shoving his Glock in the back of his jeans.

Talos snorted. "Forget the locals. How are we going to explain it to Jarred?"

"Thanks," Bill called from the doorway.

"Who were they?" Ryan asked, feigning ignorance.

Bill stepped out under the awning. "I don't know the two thugs, but the other fella is Victor Vassello and he's into some heavy stuff. He runs a few nightclubs and strip joints in Sydney." Bill looked at Sam. "Thanks for taking care of things. I'd rather not come face to face with Victor. He might remember me and I'd rather he didn't."

"No worries, Bill." Sam shrugged and looked out at the rain. "I might call it a night. Where exactly do Ken and Liz live?"

Bill pointed down the street. "Second house after the school."

"Thanks. Night all." Sam zipped his jacket and ran to his Hilux. He noted the old prospector's motorhome. The flicker of a television could be seen through the window.

Sam knocked lightly at the Macey's front door, and when no one answered he turned the handle and pushed the door open. A lamp came on in the nearest doorway and Liz stepped out, wrapping her dressing gown around her. She smiled at Sam, held her finger to her lips and disappeared into her bedroom again. When she came back she held out a pair of men's pyjamas to him.

"You're drenched and it's too wild to be driving home tonight. Have a hot shower and put those on, I'll stick your clothes in the dryer." She pointed into a room off the hall. Kallie was asleep in a recliner by the glowing fire.

Liz whispered. "You can sleep on the couch. I've thrown a blanket there for you." She tiptoed off again and stopped at another door. "Bathroom's in here. Pass your clothes out and I'll put them in the dryer."

"You don't have to do that, Liz."

"No, I insist. Go on." She pushed him through the door.

Sam undressed, picked up a neatly folded towel and wrapped it round his waist. He opened the door and handed out his clothes, keeping his leather jacket, shoes, mobile, knife and gun discreetly hidden behind the door.

"Thanks, Liz." He closed the door, turned on the taps and stepped in under the shower rose. Hot water began to warm his frozen body instantly.

Ken's pyjama pants were too big round the waist and too short in the legs but at least Sam could pull the cord to tighten them. He didn't bother putting the pyjama shirt on; instead, he wrapped his knife, gun and mobile in it then picked up his jacket. When he reached the lounge he stood for a couple of minutes watching Kallie sleep. Her thick, black eyelashes lay feathered against golden skin, her pretty, full lips pouting softly, her long dark hair fanning over the blanket like silken threads. *You really are beautiful, Kallie, and as if that's not enough, you have a lovely disposition and a body that's driving me crazy. I wish there was such a thing as happy ever after, because if there were I would choose you in a flash.*

He bent and covered her bare toes with the blanket and then turned to the large couch beside her. He hung his leather jacket on the chair, placed his bundle beside the couch and climbed in under the wool blanket.

❧

Kallie woke chilled to the bone and shivering. She glanced at the fire. *Damn, it's gone out. I should have put another log on earlier.* She climbed off the chair and crouched in front of the fire. The wood box was empty. *It's so cold in here; I'll freeze to death if I don't get warm.* Standing, she glanced around for something warmer to wrap herself in. Her heart quickened when her gaze fell to the couch. *Sam!*

Shuffling over to the couch, she stood and stared down at him. *He looks so warm lying there on that big comfortable couch, under that thick blanket.* Another shiver racked her body and her teeth began to chatter. *I need warmth.* She stared at his handsome face, his huge chest rising and falling with his steady breathing. Liz's words came back to her. *Most men act a certain way because they believe they're protecting us. It's up to us women to take charge and point them in the right direction.*

It was time to take charge. Kallie picked up a corner of the blanket covering Sam and peeled it back. Her pulse quickened when she revealed his naked chest. *He does look fantastic without a shirt.* Her eyes skimmed the muscled contours as she lowered her bottom to the couch, lifted her freezing feet and squirmed in under the blanket. The heat of his body sent more shivers racing through her. She wiggled a little closer, inching her toes as close as she dared.

He's like a furnace. Her foot touched his warm leg and she felt him jerk against her. *No, please don't wake.* Twenty seconds passed and he didn't stir. Kallie released her breath and wiggled as close as she dared. His heat gradually seeped into her cold body and warmed her. Kallie laid her hand gently on his chest and closed her eyes.

Sam dared not move or react even though he ached to take her in his arms. He waited until Kallie's breathing slowed then opened his eyes and studied her. His hand involuntarily moved to cover hers. His gaze lowered to the swell of her breasts, rising and falling evenly. He squirmed, fighting the urge to slide her dress down and take possession of her beautiful body. *It wouldn't be hard to seduce her.* He clenched his teeth, hating his newfound conscience. *I can't do it. I like her too much and she deserves someone who will stick by her.*

Being careful not to wake her, Sam raised his leg slightly and moved it to cover her cold toes tucked in under his calf muscle. *A man could get used to this.*

His mobile vibrated. He checked the screen then pressed talk.

"Jarred?" his voice was a whisper.

"I need to know where we stand with the girl, Sam. Is she a threat?"

Sam glanced down at Kallie sleeping deeply, curled against his side. "No, I have the situation under control."

"The boys and I are worried, Sam. She's side tracking you. Maybe I should pull you out and let Nick get close to her."

Sam stiffened. "Keep Nick the fuck away from her," he warned, his voice rising. Kallie stirred, mumbled something and cuddled closer. Sam tensed, but she didn't wake.

He lowered his voice again. "I said I have the situation under control, Jarred. You wanted me to get close to her. That's what I'm doing." His lips twitched. *I can't get much closer than I am at the moment.*

"All right. Stay close and watch she doesn't fuck this up for us."

Sam ended the call and slid his mobile back under the pillow. He looked down at Kallie. *No fucking way is Nick getting near you. Who the fuck cares if I've developed an attachment? It's none of their fucking business.* He released Kallie's hand and turned on his side, pressing back against the lounge to give her more room. She immediately responded to the loss of heat by pressing closer to him.

"No you don't, darlin'." Sam gently rolled her onto her back and covered her again. The room temperature was rapidly dropping. He glanced at the fire. *No wonder, it's gone out.* Kallie shivered beside him and tried to turn on her side, seeking his warmth again. Sam's teeth clenched as he considered the obvious solution. *No, I need another option.* He grimaced, climbed over her then lifted her into his position.

She stirred and opened her eyes, blinking in confusion. "Sam?"

"Shush, I'm trying to keep you warm." He eased her onto her side against the back of the couch and tucked the blanket around her. "Now, go back to sleep," he ordered laying his hand on her hip.

She snuggled closer, sliding her arm around his waist. "I like this," she mumbled drowsily.

So do I, darlin'. Sam closed his eyes, willing his body to ignore the fragrance of her perfume, the soft fullness of her breasts, pressed intimately against his chest, the feel of her hip under his hand, the silkiness of her foot against his shin. All his blood was rushing to one particular organ. *Fuck. This is what I was trying to avoid.*

CHAPTER TEN

Kallie woke, as cosy as toast, and cocooned against a lovely warm body. Peeping out from beneath her eyelashes, she spied her own hand resting in the middle of Sam's magnificent naked chest. Her gaze flitted to his massive bicep and then followed his arm down to where it disappeared under the blanket. A tingling started low in her core as she realised the weight on her bare thigh was his hand. Barely able to breathe, she swiftly glanced down at her chest and exhaled. She still wore her dress.

Her other hand lay curled amid the folds of her dress, bunched up between their bodies. *Keep it together, Kallie and don't move or you'll wake him.* She closed her eyes again and savoured the feel of his steady heartbeat under her hand, the heat of his body and the delicious sensation of his hand on her skin. *Now this is how I envisaged ending my night.*

The next time Kallie opened her eyes, she was alone. *Damn. Where'd he go?* Throwing back the blanket, she scooted off the couch, picked up the light throw and flung it round her shoulders. *You're not getting away without an explanation. Trust me, I'll explain later. Huh.*

As she bent to slip her shoes on, a low humming sound caught her attention. She felt in the pocket of Sam's jacket and pulled out a phone. The humming stopped when she picked it up. She frowned. *To work out here, it must be a satellite phone.* She jumped as it started vibrating. Pressing the talk button she held it to her ear. "Hello—hello, can you hear me?"

No one answered and it kept vibrating. *Idiot, it's a text message.* She fiddled until a text message popped up from someone named Ryan.

Has she told you where the diamond is yet?

A sharp pain pierced Kallie's heart. She clenched her teeth and flicked to the previous message, from someone called Simon.

Jarred doesn't want the girl to know Marzetti's after the diamond or that she's in serious danger. We need to keep a lid on this.

Kallie gasped and flicked to a message from someone named Nick. *If you're having a moral dilemma, I'm happy to swap places and do the job for you.*

Kallie's hands shook as cold fury spread through her body. "Like hell."

The next message was from a Talos. *I see your truck's still in town. Come join us for breakfast, we need to talk.*

"I'll say we do." Kallie muttered.

A door closed and Jane and Sam's voices reached her. She shoved the phone back in the jacket and dived under the blanket pretending to be asleep. She heard him enter the lounge, a bit of rustling then his footsteps as he strode down the hall and left the house.

As soon as the front door closed, Kallie threw back the blanket and strode through to the kitchen. Jane stood at the bench buttering toast. She glanced quickly over her shoulder.

"Good morning, you little hussy."

"What?" Kallie dug her fingernails into her palms. *I can't upset Jane. She's got enough on her mind with Andrew and the baby.* "What are you talking about?"

Jane chuckled. "I'm eight months pregnant, Kallie, that means I'm up half a dozen times a night peeing." She picked up her toast and came over to the table.

"I peeped into the lounge about four o'clock this morning and I saw you on the couch. Sam didn't have a shirt on." She sighed. "God, what a sight."

Kallie said nothing.

Jane frowned. "Are you all right?"

"I'm fine, why do you think I'm a hussy?"

Jane raised an eyebrow. "Kallie, you were both cuddled up together on the lounge. It doesn't take a genius to work out something's happened."

Shaking her head, Kallie bit her lip, fighting to hold back tears.

"Nothing happened and nothing's going to happen. He doesn't want me."

"What are you talking about? I saw the way he looked at you in the pub. We all did."

Kallie shook her head again, wiped her eyes and sank onto a chair. "His mobile made a noise so I checked it and read some messages."

Jane frowned. "What are you talking about? Mobiles don't work out here."

"His does." She told Jane what each message said.

"S'truth. Oh God, Kallie, I'm so sorry."

"It doesn't make sense. I invited Sam out to my place and he never asked about the diamond. Not even after Wally King mentioned it last night."

Jane stared at her. "Who are Ryan, Jarred, Nick, Talos and Simon?"

"I guess they're the men pretending to be army personnel."

"I'm telling Mum and Ken." Jane whirled around.

"No." Kallie cried, grabbing Jane's arm. "Let me handle this my way."

Jane's fist clenched and she opened her mouth to argue.

"Please, Jane. There might be a good explanation. Something is going on in town at the moment and those men are involved." She closed her eyes. *Jane is my best friend and she knows all my secrets. If I can't tell her then who can I tell?* Kallie opened her eyes and inhaled.

"Sam told me a very dangerous man has been hiding in Willaroi for years and if he thinks people are onto him, he'd likely kill them. Sam said uncovering this person's identity depends on me keeping quiet and that those three strangers who arrived late last night are after this person as well."

"Who is it?" asked Jane, her eyes wide.

"I don't know, but Bill was acting strange last night and he recognised those men."

"So was Ken," whispered Jane. She pulled out a chair and sat. "After that gorgeous big man brought Ken home last night, I heard Mum and Ken arguing. Ken knew those men and he's been in Willaroi for eight years. And something bad happened before he came here."

Kallie frowned. "Bill's been here twelve years and he was pretty scary when he first arrived. He could be this person."

Jane nodded. "Fergie's been here about twelve or thirteen years and he was downright strange when he came."

Their eyes met and widened. Jane grabbed Kallie's wrist. "What do Ken, Fergie and Bill have in common?"

Kallie shrugged. "Lots of things—height, build, similar age and they all have grey hair and beards." Her hand flew to her mouth. "Last night, Sam and a couple of those army guys or whoever they are, were watching Fergie, Ken and Bill."

"So they suspect one of them is this man," Jane whispered.

"They must." Kallie stiffened. "Who else in town matches that description?"

Jane looked to the ceiling for a minute and shrugged. "No one, unless you count Bert and Angus, but we know who they are."

"Do we?" asked Kallie. "Angus has no memory of anything before his stroke. What if Bert is impersonating another man? He came here ten and a half years ago and neither of us has ever liked him. What do we really know of his past?"

"We might not like Bert, but that doesn't make him a killer. If this Marzetti person *is* after the diamond, or Sam and those other men are crooks, then we need to set a trap." Jane paced back and forth.

"No, *we* don't," Kallie snapped. "You have a baby to think of. How would I ever face your mother if something happened to you and the baby?"

"But..."

"No, Jane. I will handle this my way. But you're right. I need to set a trap or..." Kallie smiled. "Drop a bomb."

"What are you going to do?"

"We need to get all our suspects in the same room, plus Sam and his friends."

"How?"

"What time is it now and where are your mum and Ken?"

Jane glanced at the clock. "It's seven-thirty and Mum and Ken are having breakfast at the pub. They're organising a contingency plan in case we're cut off by floods."

"Excellent. I have an idea, but I need to borrow some clothes."

"Okay." Jane looked dubious. "I'm sure I've got some jeans and things here that will fit you, but first tell me your plan."

"If I tell you, you'll try to stop me, but you're welcome to come along."

Jane's eyes narrowed and she stared at Kallie for a couple of seconds. "Fine, wait right there." She disappeared into the hall and Kallie heard a door open and shut.

A couple of minutes later, Jane came back into the kitchen with an armful of clothes. "These are the only skinny clothes I have here."

"Thanks." Kallie took them to the bathroom. The jeans and runners were a good fit, but the jumper was a little on the tight side. She gave herself a quick once-over in the mirror as she raked her fingers through her hair. *Crikey, I look like I'm fourteen.* Her gaze dropped to her breasts and the figure-hugging jumper. *Maybe not fourteen. Still, it's better than my wrinkled dress.* She rubbed some toothpaste on her teeth with her finger, rinsed her mouth and ran back to the kitchen.

"Right, let's go."

Jane's eyes widened and she opened her mouth but Kallie didn't wait to hear. She turned and walked out the front door leaving Jane to follow. They strode up the street, careful to avoid puddles from last night's downpour.

Wally's motorhome was gone. *He must be on his way to see Angus.*

The pub's dining room was busy and Kallie hesitated, almost changing her mind.

Jane groaned beside her. "I don't know what you're planning to do, but there's a lot of people here."

"Yes, there are." Kallie located Sam sitting with his back to her at a table with the five supposed army men.

Jane nudged her. "That's the sexiest bunch of men I've ever seen in my life."

Kallie might have agreed yesterday, but today they were a bunch of lowlife liars. She glanced at the other diners. Ken, Liz and Fergie sat at a table in the corner, deep in conversation. Two large groups of local farmers and their wives took up the dining room's centre tables and most of the noise was coming from them. *They must all be here for the sandbagging.* Her gaze settled on Roy at a table with Bunny. *I would have rather done this without them here.* Donna Ross and Bert were eating breakfast together at a table in the corner and Bert was scowling.

Bill walked past carrying a tray of plates laden with food. "Morning, Kallie, Jane. Take a seat and I'll take your order shortly."

"Thanks, Bill but we're not staying. I just popped in to have a word with those guys at the back."

Bill stopped and looked towards Sam's table. "Oh, okay."

Kallie straightened her shoulders. "Let's do this, Jane."

"What exactly are we doing?" croaked Jane.

Kallie didn't reply, instead she began zigzagging her way around the tables, keeping her gaze on Sam's back. One of the men noticed her approaching and spoke to the others. Sam stood and waited for her.

"Kallie?"

His smiling welcome nearly undid Kallie, but she managed to hold it together and refocused on what she had to do. "Sam." She dug her nails into her palms to stop herself punching him.

"What's happened?" He reached for her hand.

She ignored him and walked around the table, stopping beside the big broad-shouldered man with dark eyes, short hair and an olive complexion.

"We haven't been introduced. I'm Kallie McNeil.

The man glanced at Sam then back to her. "James Talarico."

"Ah, Talos." Kallie smiled coolly. "I hope your serious talk with Sam went well."

He frowned at her with a quick glance at Sam.

She turned to another handsome man with blue eyes and sandy hair. "And you are?"

"Ryan Dutch, ma'am."

"It's nice to meet you, Ryan, and no, I didn't tell Sam where the Kalista Diamond is. In fact, now that I've found it, I have no intention of telling him or anyone where it is." Kallie heard a gasp from a nearby table and the room quietened. *Good now I have all their attention.*

She looked across the table to a man with chestnut brown hair and green eyes. He didn't look as rigid as the others. "And who are you?"

'Simon Hawke, ma'am."

"Thanks for the info, Simon. Forewarned is forearmed, and if some idiot is stupid enough to threaten me or try to steal my diamond then he deserves everything he gets."

She looked at the two remaining men. One stared at her from steely grey, narrowed eyes and she swallowed as her confidence faded. The other man had an amused grin spread across his face. *And you'll be Nick.*

Kallie focused all her attention on him as anger rushed through her. The whole room was now deadly silent. "As to your offer, Nick—there is no need to swap places with Sam. I wouldn't let you near me with a ten foot pole."

That wiped the grin off his face.

She glanced around the room. Roy, Ken, Bill, Fergie and Liz were standing.

"Oh shit, now you've done it," Jane whispered from her other side.

Sam rounded the table. "What the hell's going on, Kallie? What did Nick say to you?"

"Don't blame Nick, Sam. It's your phone."

The man with the steely eyes rose to his feet and stepped alongside Sam. "This is not the place to air your grievances." He lowered his voice. "Sort it out with Sam in private."

"You must be Jarred," declared Kallie, forcing herself not to look in Sam's direction. The broad-shouldered man locked gazes with her. He held very still, his cold eyes drilling right through her. A chill ran down her spine as she acknowledged both his physical presence and an underlying lethal dominance. She tore her eyes away and glanced round the table. *Actually they all have it, but this one doesn't bother concealing it.* Kallie swallowed, straightened her shoulders and returned her gaze to the man who was staring at her.

"Yes, I'm Jarred Steele," he said in a voice devoid of emotion.

The promise of retribution hung between them as he continued to hold her gaze. Kallie cleared her throat. You're the boss of these...army guys?" Kallie waved her hand to indicate the men around the table.

His eyes narrowed. "I'm in charge, yes."

Sam stepped around Jarred and caught her elbow. "Kallie, I don't know what this is about, but let me take you home." He tried to move her away from the table. Kallie shrugged him off and stared at the two men. Sam still appeared confused, his dark chocolate eyes searching her face.

Jarred crossed his arms, one eyebrow raised. "You have something you want to say to me, Miss McNeil?"

"Yes, I do." Kallie glared at him. "You have three hours to get your men and your helicopter off my land. If you're not gone in that time, I'll have you arrested for trespassing."

"Kallie." Sam's voice was terse. "Tell me what happened?"

She ignored him and turned on her heel. In other circumstances, Kallie would have laughed at all the open mouths in the room, but the urge to cry was far greater. She'd made it to the pub's foyer before Roy caught up with her.

"Bossy, what happened last night? Did Sam do something to hurt you?"

Kallie nodded. "Yes, Roy, he lied to me. You were right, Sam's not what he seems." Tears rolled down her cheek. "He's after the diamond, not me."

Roy frowned. "You'd better tell me everything."

"Not now, Roy. I need time to calm down and work a few things out. Go back to Bunny and finish your breakfast. I'll get Jane to drive me home later—when they've gone."

He hesitated. "All right, suit yourself. I'll make sure he's gone by the time you get home." He studied her face. "Why didn't you tell me you found the diamond?"

Warmth rose in Kallie's cheeks. She bit her lip, feeling contrite. "I didn't find it, Roy. I just said that...in temper."

Roy nodded. "All right. I'll talk to you later." He shook his head and returned to the dining room, passing Jane in the doorway.

She touched Kallie's arm. "What just happened in there?"

Wiping tears away, Kallie shrugged. "I set the cat amongst the pigeons."

"You could have told me you found the diamond and I don't understand why you announced it to the whole room?"

Kallie grabbed Jane's arm and urged her out of the pub as a crowd of diners walked out of the dining room. "If there really is some bad guy intending to steal my diamond, then it's up to me to draw him out, before he hurts someone I care about."

Jane gawked at her. "But we don't know who he is. If that text message is right, then *you're* the one in danger. You should have just left things as they were. What if he gets you alone and threatens to hurt you unless you hand over the diamond?"

Biting her lip, Kallie glanced back towards the pub. "Then I have a problem."

"I'll say you do." Jane took off, dragging Kallie along with her. "Holy shit, Kallie, you need to find that diamond."

"Don't worry, Jane. I'll think of something."

"You told those army guys to get off your land, but you didn't blow their cover and as far as the locals know, Sam isn't with them."

Kallie glanced back towards the pub. "I didn't want to expose them until I know who they're after. I need to figure out if it's Ken, Bill, Fergie, Bert or someone else in the district." Tears filled her eyes. "And I couldn't bring myself to expose Sam." She sniffed and angrily wiped the tears away. "I really liked him, Jane. I've never felt such a strong attraction or connection like that in my life and I would have sworn it was mutual."

Jane blinked away her own tears as she hugged Kallie. "At least he didn't take advantage of you. That's something in his favour. Maybe you should give him the chance to explain? After all, he did seem pretty mad when he thought Nick had propositioned you."

Jane didn't give Kallie a chance to argue.

"If Ken's right and they're undercover cops, then Sam wouldn't have been allowed to tell you the truth, not without blowing his cover, and it's not like he's personally after the diamond, is it? It's a means to an end."

"What do you mean?" Kallie stepped back, her tummy suddenly queasy.

"Let's think about this. We now know Sam is with those men, and they're chasing someone who is willing to hurt you to get the diamond, right." Jane frowned as she spoke.

Kallie nodded, the tightening in her tummy intensifying. "Go on."

"Sam didn't ask you if he could stay at your place, you asked him. But *if* he's an undercover cop, it's the perfect place to be. He can wait for the bad guy to come get the diamond and protect you at the same time."

"Shit, I probably just blew their whole operation. Sam should have told me the truth. And why pretend to like me? I would have helped him."

Jane shrugged. "Maybe he wasn't pretending, Kallie. I saw the way he watched you and that kiss looked pretty real to me. It would explain why he was so angry at Nick."

Kallie closed her eyes. *He did seem genuine when I twisted my ankle.* Her mind raced back to the shooting incident. *He was pretty convincing, pretending not to know those guys, but as an undercover cop, he wouldn't have any other choice. And in Collie, he was so understanding and kind. Shit, what if Jane's right. That kiss was real and he did promise to explain everything, but I didn't give him the chance.*

Kallie opened her eyes. "What if I've blown everything? What if he never wants to speak to me again?"

"He will. Come on, let's go in the house and have some breakfast. Everything will seem better on a full stomach."

"I hope so." Deep in thought, Kallie led the way up the garden path of Liz's house and almost ran into Andrew standing on the porch.

He smoothed his goatee. "Where is everyone? I woke up and the house was deserted."

Kallie and Jane exchanged quick looks as they followed him back towards the kitchen.

"Flood meeting at the pub," Jane said. "Mum and Ken are having breakfast there, but we thought we'd come home to eat with you."

Andrew shook his head. "You country folk get up too early."

Kallie raised an eyebrow at Jane. *It has to be eight o'clock. Most country folk would have been up before six.*

Jane started on an omelette while Kallie put the kettle on and set the table.

"I've no idea what's going on." Ken's voice came down the hall. "Sometimes I wonder what gets into that girl, she's always on some crusade. God knows what it is this time."

"It will be important to her," answered Liz. "She doesn't get a bee in her bonnet over nothing. Still, I'm a little hurt she never told us she'd found the diamond."

Andrew's head shot up. "You found the diamond?"

"Shush," Jane whispered.

Liz's voice was weary. "I can't believe she ordered those army men off her place. What's got into her?"

Kallie almost dropped a glass as Sam's chuckle resonated down the hall. "It's him," she whispered."

Andrew looked up. "Who?"

"Shush," Jane hissed. They all turned to the door and listened.

"Kallie had good reason to do what she did." Sam's voice was getting closer. "She read a couple of texts those fellas sent me. I was pretty angry myself when I read them.

"How does your phone even work out here when we don't get mobile reception?" asked Liz. "And why were those men texting you in the first place?"

"They've got satellite phones and so do I." Sam said. "They were texting me because we know each other. That's what I wanted to talk to you about."

The kitchen door swung open. Ken and Liz came, in closely followed by Sam. Kallie tightened her fingers round the glass as they stared at her.

"What's happened? Who's on a crusade?" Andrew looked from her to Sam to Ken and Liz and back again.

Sam's gaze held Kallie's as he crossed the room, prised the glass out of her hands and put it on the sink. He took her hands in his and gently squeezed.

"I intended to explain things last night, Kallie, but you were asleep. I'm sorry you saw those texts. They weren't meant for your eyes and if you'll let me take you home, I'll explain everything on the way?"

"I'd certainly like to know how you know those men?" Jane demanded.

Sam winked at Kallie before he turned to face the others.

"I know them because we used to be in the army together. When I heard the boys were being sent up this way, I thought I'd kill two birds with one stone, so to speak. Do some fishing and catch up with them." Sam squeezed Kallie's hand.

Meeting his gaze, Kallie nodded to show him she understood. *He wants everyone to believe the others are part of an army exercise, but really they're all undercover cops after the man who wants my diamond.*

"I see," replied Liz. "Well, I'm glad that's sorted." She glanced at Kallie. "As for your outburst this morning, young lady, I can't think what got into you. And why didn't you tell us you'd found the diamond?"

Kallie glanced to Jane for support, but Jane shrugged helplessly and turned back to her omelette. *I can't tell them I lied, Ken is here and he's a suspect.* Kallie cleared her throat. "I hadn't intended on telling anyone as the diamond just stirs up trouble, but I was so angry this morning that it slipped out."

Ken nodded. "Fair enough, but when are we going to get a look at this precious diamond? I, for one, am keen to see it and Angus will be very relieved."

"We can talk about that another time." Jane said. "Andrew, Kallie and I haven't had breakfast and this omelette is ready." She looked at Kallie. "You and Sam should get going straight after breakfast, it looks like it's going to start raining again."

Thank you, Jane.

CHAPTER ELEVEN

Sam slid into his seat, buckled the seatbelt and glanced across at Kallie. She was already belted in and watching him carefully.

"Thanks for not blowing my cover."

Kallie raised an eyebrow. "Which cover story are we talking about? The one where you're here on a fishing holiday, or the one where those friends of yours are pretending to be on an army exercise, or the one about you hunting a dangerous man after my diamond?"

Sam couldn't help smiling. *Avoidance tactics needed here.* "I'm sorry I couldn't tell you who we were or why we came here. I honestly did intend telling you some of it last night. It's just that by the time those three fellas left last night, it was very late."

Kallie shrugged her shoulders. "I understand all that, but now that we are on our own, I want to know everything and I want the truth."

Christ, I don't even know everything. As for the truth, I don't have the authority to tell you. Sam pushed the gearstick into first gear, released the handbrake and did a U-turn. He didn't speak until they were clear of town.

"Kallie, it's hard to know where to begin. There are some things I'm not authorised to tell you and some could result in us losing the man we're after."

"Let's start with something simple," she suggested. "I know you're with those men and I know you're not part of the army. So who are you really?"

Sam kept his eyes on the road. *Stick as close to the truth as possible.* "You're right. We're not straight out army, but we are part of a unit and we are here to track down a man wanted for murder, drug trafficking and the importing of Asian girls for use in illegal brothels. I can't tell you any more than that."

"I see. Jane told me that Ken thinks you're part of an undercover police team."

Sam made no comment.

"Okay, what about this man you're after? How long has he been on the run?

"Fifteen years."

"I see. And I take it he resembles Ken, Fergie, Bill, Bert and my grandfather, or could even be one of them?

Sam's head shot round so fast he nearly gave himself whiplash. "Whatever gave you that idea?" he asked before returning his attention to the road ahead.

"I've got eyes and ears, Sam. I saw you watching them and I saw Bill and Ken's reaction in the pub. They both recognised those men and made a hasty retreat, which leads me to believe Ken and Bill are hiding something. But to be fair, they're not the only men to have arrived in town in the last fifteen years. That's why you're also watching Fergie, Bert and Angus, isn't it?"

Sam sighed. "Now you can see why I couldn't say anything."

"Yes," she turned to him. "We need to eliminate them, one by one."

"Oh no, Kallie. There is no *we* in this. You will be staying right out of it."

"But I can help you. All your suspects know me and wouldn't suspect a thing. I can get much closer than you. I'm surprised you haven't used your police contacts to have background checks done on them. I'm sure that would help eliminate our innocent suspects."

Sam held his tongue. *If she wants to believe we're police then so be it, but I have to make it clear she is to stay out of this.*

The town's only bridge appeared ahead and Sam pulled off the road into a wide clearing. He killed the engine and turned to her.

"Kallie, we *have* done background searches, and all our suspects check out."

She undid her seatbelt and faced him. "Then why are you still watching them? It's my diamond and I have a right to know who I'm dealing with."

Sam grabbed her by both arms and hauled her across the cab to within inches of his face. "*You're* not dealing with anyone Kallie. *You're* to stay out of this and *you* don't need to know anything about this man."

Her eyes widened then she pushed against his chest, using her knees to gain leverage as she strained to put some distance between them.

I've frightened her. Good. Suddenly the tension left her body and she relaxed against him. Sam narrowed his eyes. *What is she up to now?*

She cleared her throat. "You mean Marzetti."

"Shit, those bloody text messages." *This is not going as I planned.*

"Who is Marzetti?" she asked. "You may as well tell me because if you don't, I'll just Google him or do my own investigation."

Shit, shit, shit. Sam released her arms, closed his eyes and inhaled deeply. Her scent surrounded him. The same scent that had kept him in torment all night. *That and her glorious body.*

Sam placed his hands on her waist and lifted Kallie back to her seat. "Fine, but this stays between us. You are not to tell anyone. Is that understood?"

She nodded. "You have my word."

"Dominic Marzetti used to be an underworld crime boss. Besides the illegal brothels, drug trafficking and extortion, he is also wanted for several murders and has a reputation for torturing people." He kept his voice hard, hoping she would leave it at that.

Kallie stared back at him, her eyes wide. After a minute she bit her lip. "Why didn't the police arrest him? Why did they let him get away?"

"They could never get close enough to arrest him. He is a master at staying one step ahead of the police."

"Why would he come here? No wait." She shook her head. "There is no one like that in Willaroi Downs." Kallie wrapped her arms around herself and stared through the front window. After a minute she turned back to him. "You said all the background searches came back clear?"

"Yes, they did. But we suspect Dominic Marzetti has assumed one of those identities."

Her eyes widened. "But that would mean..."

Sam nodded. "Yes, Kallie. That would mean Marzetti murdered someone and took over their life."

"That's terrible," whispered Kallie, placing her hands over her nose and mouth. "That's..." She blinked and then sat up straight. "That's a motorhome."

"What?"

Kallie pointed over his shoulder. "A motorhome." She scrambled to open her door. "We have to help them."

Sam looked over his shoulder through the window. His gaze fell on the old bridge covered in scaffolding, the fast flowing river beneath it, and a large white object wedged against rocks in the middle of the river. He looked closer. *Christ, it is a motorhome.*

Sam wrenched the door open and leapt out of his truck. Kallie was already sliding down the bank.

"Kallie, wait," he yelled. His feet shot from under him and he slid down the rest of the bank on his backside behind her. At the bottom Sam launched himself into the river after Kallie, who was already waist deep in water and struggling to stay on her feet.

"Jesus, Kallie. Stop, it's too dangerous."

Sam lunged as she hesitated, grasping her wrist as her legs were swept from under her.

"Sam," she screamed then disappeared beneath the surface. Sam fought to hang on. "Little idiot." He hauled her out of the water, spluttering. "What the fuck were you thinking, Kallie?" he dug his heels into the mud as he fought to stay upright and get them out of the cold water and onto the bank.

Kallie coughed and gulped in air. "Sorry."

"Sorry," Sam roared. "When I tell you to fucking wait, you fucking wait. You could have drowned."

She clung to him. "Stop swearing, I get the message."

"Do you?" He pushed her onto the bank and climbed up after her. "What the hell got into you, Kallie?"

She looked towards the motorhome. "I'm pretty sure that's Wally King's motorhome. He said he was coming out to see Angus and Bert today. I was just trying to save him."

Sam pulled her onto his lap and glanced at the motorhome. "It would take more than a little thing like you to save him. How the hell did he end up in the river?"

"I don't know, but we have to do something, Sam. He might still be alive."

Sam nodded and pulled out his phone. "That's a very slim chance, Kallie, but we'll try." He hit Ryan's number.

"Sam, what's happening mate? You sweet talked her round yet?"

Glancing at Kallie, Sam ignored Ryan's jibe. "Are you still in town, mate?"

"Yeah, just about to leave."

"Grab Jarred and the boys and get in the air. I'm on the side of the road about ten kilometres north of Willaroi. There's a motorhome on its side in the river and it could be the old prospector, Wally King."

"Fuck, you're joking?"

"No, mate. Get here as quick as you can and let some of the locals know. We'll need some extra manpower and ropes."

"No worries, we're on it."

Sam ended the call and returned the phone to his jacket pocket. "They'll be here in a couple of minutes."

"But how will they get Wally out?"

Sam wished he could reassure her but the odds weren't good. "It all comes down to safety. Ryan and Nick are excellent pilots and we've done plenty of water retrievals before, but we have to consider the weather conditions, the current and vehicle movement."

"If he's inside, he could still be alive?" Kallie shivered.

Sam glanced at the motorhome lying on its side. "Maybe, there could be an airlock." Sam kept his arms around Kallie, giving her as much heat as he could while they waited for the chopper. He felt a great sense of relief when, a couple of minutes later, the chopper came zooming in low over the trees.

"Here they are," Kallie cried jumping up off his lap. She started waving her arms in the air and jumping up and down. "We're here, over here."

Sam's gaze was drawn to the transparent jumper clinging to Kallie's perfect breasts. *Shit.* He leapt up and dragged her into his arms. "Kallie, if the boys get a look at you like that, they're likely to crash the chopper."

"Like what?" she asked through chattering teeth.

Sam's gaze dropped to her breasts again. "Your jumper's transparent."

Kallie glanced down, gasped and slammed into his chest. "Oh my God."

"Here, put this on." He shrugged out of his jacket, held it out for her to put her arms in and then zipped it up. "It's a bit big, but better than nothing." *And better than distracting every man who sets eyes on you.*

"Thank you, Sam." She huddled closer to him, still shivering as the chopper landed at the edge of road.

Sam looked up. "At least it's stopped raining." He watched his team run towards them.

"How'd he get in there?" Talos stared across the river.

Sam pointed at the bank. "There are tread marks over there. It looks like he came round the bend, stopped and then drove straight into the river."

Jarred turned towards Sam. "If Ryan hovers over the top, you and Talos could abseil onto that side. It's risky with the river running so fast, especially if the motorhome shifts."

"Hmm." Sam glanced across the river to the opposite bank. "We'll need to run a dragline between the banks. Good thing there's a bridge there." He turned to Simon. "There's a nylon line in the chopper. If you get that set up and keep an eye out for debris, Talos and I can check out the motorhome."

"What's the old fella's chances?" Simon asked.

Sam glanced at Kallie. "If he's in the cab, not great."

"Right then," announced Jarred. "Do what you can, but don't take any unnecessary risks. I'll handle the locals and keep them out of your way." He turned to Kallie. "Miss McNeil, you stay with me. Nick, there should be a blanket in the chopper, please give it to Miss McNeil in case she's tempted to take Sam's jacket off."

Sam glanced at Kallie who was blushing. *So I didn't cover her up in time.* He winked at her and headed after the boys with the image of her breasts etched into his brain. As he climbed aboard the chopper, Talos grinned.

"What's so funny?" Sam asked, kicking off his wet boots and socks.

Talos handed him his wetsuit and dive boots. "Do you know what Kalista means in Greek, my friend?"

"Yes, as a matter of fact, I do," replied Sam, opening a hatch under the back row of seats. He pulled out a blanket and handed it to Nick. "It means most beautiful."

Talos nodded, opened another hatch and pulled out a coiled nylon rope, which he handed to Simon.

"Most beautiful, and from what we saw last night, she's also crazy about you."

"Do you know what Samuel means?" called Nick from the cockpit.

Sam pulled off his shirt. "I shudder to think."

"Bloody idiot, that's what," answered Nick. "You're being handed a gorgeous woman on a platter and you go and develop a conscience."

"Who would've guessed?" agreed Talos, shedding his own clothes.

Sam pulled on his wetsuit, zipped it up and looked at Talos. "You of all people know how it is. How I feel about serious relationships, especially with women like Kallie who've been sheltered all their lives. She's living in a romantic dream and has no idea what we are. Christ, she thinks we're undercover cops. If she knew the truth, she'd run for her life.

Talos raised an eyebrow. "What if you're wrong? What if she's still willing to take you on, even knowing the truth?

"Then I'll tell her I don't believe in happy ever afters and have no intention of ever marrying or having kids. End of story."

Talos pulled on his dive boots. "Mate, if you can resist a woman like that, then you're a stronger man than me." He opened another panel under the rear seats, pulled out their harnesses and began sorting them.

Ryan chuckled from the cockpit. "And me. Here comes Simon, you guys ready?"

"Ready," called Talos.

"Ready," called Sam, slamming the cargo door harder than necessary.

"Nick pulled his door shut and swung round. "All clear, let's go."

Kallie wrapped the blanket round her shoulders, shivering as the helicopter lifted off and flew over their heads to hover above the river, where the motorhome was still wedged. Simon had tied the rope around a tree on the opposite bank. He ran back across the bridge holding the other end.

"I've never seen a helicopter like that. What is it?" asked Kallie turning to Jarred.

"It's a UH-Sixty Black Hawk and I'm not surprised you haven't seen one. They're primarily military helicopters."

Kallie bit her lip. She cleared her throat. "Jarred, about this morning."

"You have every right to be angry, Miss McNeil. I can only apologise for the way you found out about our operation. As soon as we check the motorhome, I shall move all my men off your property and we won't bother you again."

All your men! Kallie's gaze flew to the helicopter. *No, that's a bad idea.* She glanced back to Jarred to find him watching her. "I was a bit hasty, Jarred. You don't have to leave the cabin and anyway, where else are you going to stay?"

He smiled. "Your concern is touching, Miss McNeil, but I have secured rooms at the pub so we no longer require your cabin."

"But, what about Sam? He should stay at my place, so he can keep an eye on Bert. After all, isn't he one of your suspects?"

Jarred looked down on her with his steely eyes. "I will not discuss any aspect of this operation with you, Miss McNeil."

Kallie held his gaze. *You really are a cool customer.* She shrugged. "Very well, I guess I will have to keep an eye on Bert myself. I hope I don't give anything away, accidentally."

His eyes narrowed and Kallie almost baulked at the warning in them. She turned away to watch two figures in wetsuits getting ready to descend from the helicopter.

"The river is running so fast, I hope they don't get washed away." She glanced round to make sure Simon had fastened the rope this side of the river. He was standing on the bank watching Sam and Talos.

"They know what they're doing," replied Jarred. "They've done plenty of rescues in much worse situations."

"But what if something goes wrong and they don't catch the rope."

"Then they let the current take them. The worst thing a person can do is use valuable energy fighting a current. It's the same as a rip in the ocean. Keep your head and eventually you'll wash up on a bank or beach." He pointed to a bloated sheep carcass moving swiftly towards them. "See how the current is sweeping the sheep this way?"

"Yes."

"If that were a person, as soon as they were within a metre of the bank they would be wise to strike out for the bank, but if they left it too long they'd be swept away again."

Kallie watched as the carcass swept in close to the bank, slowed momentarily then zoomed back out to the middle and away under the bridge.

Nodding, Kallie kept her gaze on Sam and Talos as they descended onto the side of the motorhome and unhooked their harnesses. The helicopter hovered a moment longer before flying over Sam's vehicle and landing.

Talos pulled the side door of the motor home open and Sam ducked his head and shoulders into the van. Kallie held her breath and waited.

A couple of minutes went by then Sam hauled himself out, looked their way and shook his head.

"He's not in the rear of the van," Kallie murmured. She watched Sam and Talos make their way towards the cab. "So if Wally got swept into the river, he might have a chance, as long as he doesn't panic or waste energy?" she asked.

"Yes," replied Jarred. "As long as he hasn't been knocked out by debris."

"That's why Simon's watching the river, isn't it?"

"Yes, he'll yell out a warning if something is going to hit them."

Kallie and Jarred turned towards the road as a convoy of four-wheel drives came round the corner. They stopped side by side on the bank. Doors opened and people ran towards the river, carrying ropes, flotation devices and blankets. Ken ran to the back of his Toyota and unhitched a boat trailer. Men in orange overalls were already donning helmets and life jackets. Bill, Fergie and Roy helped Ken push a small runabout to the edge of the river.

Kallie smiled at Jarred. "These guys make up our Emergency Services team. How do you plan on keeping them out of the way?" She was rewarded with an answering smile.

"You, Miss McNeil are a pain in the arse. I will agree to let Sam stay at your place on the condition you stay out of my operation and keep your mouth shut."

"Thank you, Jarred." She hid her smile and turned back to the river. Kallie focused on Sam and Talos who were on all fours and struggling to balance on the side of the cab.

"What are they doing?" she asked, through chattering teeth.

Jarred kept his gaze on Sam and Talos. "They're attempting to verify whether there is a body in the cab. It will be harder to see if the cab is full of water."

"Oh, let's hope there isn't. Wally King seems like such a nice man and he knew my grandfather and Bert before they came here. We need him to identify them."

"Miss McNeil, I think we can safely rule out your grandfather and—"

"I'm not worried about Angus, Jarred," interrupted Kallie. "I'm more concerned about Bert. He's unfriendly, mean, rude and obnoxious."

Jarred laughed. "So are a lot of people, Miss McNeil. That doesn't make them killers."

"No, but what if Marzetti knew about the diamond, discovered Angus had lost his memory in the accident and was headed back to a quiet country town to recuperate. He could have killed the real Bert Chalmers then waited for Angus to be released from hospital and turned up pretending to be Bert."

Jarred shook his head. "I've checked with the hospital. Bert was a regular visitor at both the hospital and the rehabilitation clinic. And when Angus was released, it was into the care of Bert Chalmers. The only reason either of them came under my radar is because of their age, general appearance and time they've lived here."

Kallie crossed her arms and glared at Jarred. "Fine, but of all your suspects, Bert is the one I'd put my money on. The others are all nice—he isn't."

Jarred's lips thinned. "A word of warning, Miss McNeil. Any man can be nice when he wants something or until he's crossed."

Kallie scowled and glanced to the river as Sam and Talos jumped in, caught the drag rope and pulled themselves to the bank.

Kallie sighed. "Wally isn't in the cab."

"No." Jarred stared across the river, his arms folded across his chest.

Chapter Twelve

"That water is fucking cold." Talos shivered as he peeled off his wetsuit.

Sam chuckled and threw him a towel. "At least we had wetsuits on. Before you got here, Kallie jumped in the river and I had to jump in after her fully-clothed. That wasn't nice."

Nick stuck his head between the pilot's seats. "Dry yourselves and get dressed. Jarred and the girl are on their way over."

Talos smirked at Sam. "If she offers to warm me up, I won't say no."

"She won't." Sam towelled his body, dragged on jocks and dry overalls then unlocked the cargo door. After checking Talos was decent, Sam slid the door wide, his gaze sweeping Kallie as she ran to keep up with Jarred. *Shit, she's still in wet clothes.*

"I take it there's no body in the vehicle?" Jarred locked eyes with him.

"No," answered Sam pulling on dry socks. "But the keys are in the ignition, the handbrake is off and the shift lever in drive. He either drove into the river, managed to get out and was swept away, or he left the vehicle in drive, got out to relieve himself and it rolled into the river. He could have tried to stop the vehicle and ended up in the river."

Kallie stepped around Jarred. "That doesn't make sense. There are plenty of flat spots to pull over safely. Why would he do such a stupid thing?"

"I have no idea why people do idiotic things, Miss McNeil. Why did you jump in the river?" Jarred's expression was grim.

Sam hid his amusement as Kallie put her hands on her hips and stepped closer to Jarred.

"That is completely different." She caught the blanket as it slipped and shrugged it back onto her shoulders. "I was attempting to save Wally's life. I suggest you do the same and get this helicopter up in the air, Jarred."

Sam glanced at Talos, Nick and Ryan who were attempting to hide their grins and failing miserably. Jarred caught Sam's eye and raised an eyebrow.

"As Miss McNeil is so keen to run things, perhaps she should join us. An extra spotter is always welcome, although it would be a terrible shame if she was to fall out of the chopper." Jarred held out his hand indicating she should climb aboard.

Kallie paled, stepped away from the chopper and shook her head. "No, I'm not getting in that thing. I'll help with the ground search." She sneezed.

Sam opened a hatch and pulled out a spare pair of boots. "I've got my truck so I'll help with the ground search." He pulled his boots on and scanned the river. "It looks like the locals have started without us."

Kallie sneezed again.

"Very well," agreed Jarred. "I'll go with the boys. You should get Miss McNeil home before she catches pneumonia."

"My name is Kallie," she grinned. "But thank you for your concern, Jarred."

Grunting in response, Jarred climbed aboard the helicopter. Sam tied his laces and jumped out. "Let's go, Kallie, you're freezing."

"I'm okay," she replied, her teeth chattering.

They walked to Sam's Hilux, arriving as Liz and Jane pulled up.

"My God, Kallie, what happened to you." Liz ran over to her.

"I'm fine. Wally's not in his motorhome so we're going to check along the river."

Liz turned to Sam. "Kallie needs dry clothes. She's shivering."

"I'm taking her home now."

Kallie sneezed. "I'm fine. What are you two doing?"

Waddling round the front of the bonnet, Jane gave a strained smile. "We've got hot tea, coffee and sandwiches." She ran her gaze over Kallie. "You really should go home and have a hot shower, Kallie. Also, you might want to be the one to tell Angus about Wally. We saw Bert in town and Mum told him."

"What did he say?"

"He had no idea Wally was in town and doesn't know if Wally rang Angus or not. Apparently Bert spent the night in town with Donna Ross."

Kallie's mouth dropped open. "How do you know that?"

Leaning closer, Jane whispered. "Ken reckons Bert's car was in Donna's driveway all night and he's seen it there before."

"Really. I saw them having breakfast together at the pub, but I had no idea they've been seeing each other."

"No one did. When Mum told Bert about Wally's motorhome, he seemed genuinely concerned about how Angus would take the news."

Sam cleared his throat. "Kallie you need to get out of those wet clothes and into a hot shower. If Bert hasn't told Angus, we'll do it."

"Okay, we can keep an eye out for Wally on the road."

Sam turned into the driveway as Bert drove out. He stopped alongside Sam.

Looking across, Sam noted Angus, sitting stiffly in the passenger seat. "G'day, Bert, Angus. You know about Wally King then?"

"Yeah, Bert told me. We're going in to see if they've found him yet."

Kallie undid her seatbelt and leaned across Sam, her teeth chattering. "Angus, are you all right. I'll come with you if you want me to?"

Angus's eyes widened. "What happened to you?"

"Sam and I found the motorhome." She shook as another shiver wracked her. "I was trying to see if Wally was in it and I lost my footing. Sam saved me from being swept away."

Angus looked at Sam. "You seem to be making a habit of rescuing Kallie. He glanced back to Kallie. "I hear you made a bit of a scene at the pub this morning. I'd like to know what you thought you were doing?"

Bert grunted. "I'd like to know where she spent the night?" He stared at Sam. "Although I can guess."

Kallie spluttered. "You're such a jerk, Bert. Liz let us stay with her because of the storm."

Easing Kallie back into her seat, Sam put his truck into gear. "We won't hold you fellas up any longer. I hope Wally turns up safe and sound."

Angus nodded, "Yeah, let's hope so."

Scowling, Bert put his window up and drove off. Sam shook his head. *What a prick.*

"Sometimes I really detest that man." Kallie wrapped the blanket tightly round her. "Are you sure he isn't Marzetti?"

Sam drove through the gate. "I doubt it. From what I've heard, Marzetti has an explosive nature. Calling him a jerk would likely get you shot in the head."

She clutched the blanket with shaking hands. "Then he's definitely not Marzetti. When I was fifteen, I called him a lazy bludger and he went to hit me. Angus flipped and told Bert I was right and he'd better start earning his keep by tending the gardens."

Sam examined the neat lawn as he cut the engine. "He's doing a good job."

"So he should. It's all he does, besides keeping Angus company."

Her hands were shaking as she attempted to undo the seatbelt. When Sam came round to her side he placed his fingers under her chin.

"Look at me, Kallie."

"Huh."

Sam narrowed his eyes. Her healthy glow had disappeared; her lips were blue and her breathing shallow. "Shit, Kallie, we need to get you warm." He released the belt and scooped her into his arms. "You're showing signs of hypothermia."

"I am?"

Sam ran up the steps, opened the front door and strode down the hall to the bathroom. Standing Kallie on the tiles, he flicked the faucet on full and pulled the blanket from her shoulders. "Let's get you out of these wet clothes." He peeled his jacket off her.

She nodded, her fingers fumbling with the button on her jeans.

"Here, let me do it." Sam pushed her hands out of the way, undid the button, pulled her shoes and socks off and dragged her jeans down. Her long slim legs were covered in goose bumps. His gaze skimmed her black bikini briefs as he rose.

"Now for the jumper, arms up."

She complied without argument. He hurled the jumper aside, his eyes coming to rest on her black lace bra and the bounty within as she stood shivering violently, making no move to cover her glorious body.

"Step into the shower, Kallie." He tested the water. "It's nice and warm."

"I'm so cold I ca...n't mooove." Her teeth chattered.

"Shit." Sam untied his laces, kicked off his boots and socks and then stripped off his overalls, leaving only his jocks.

"Come on, darlin, we've got to get you warm before you get hypothermia." He lifted her over the hob and into the shower, drawing an unsteady breath as his gaze lingered on her smooth belly and exquisite breasts. He repressed the rush of desire spiralling through him and raised his gaze to her face. Her eyes were closed, but her lips parted in a smile of pure bliss as she absorbed the warmth on her upturned face.

Sam stared spellbound. *She really is gorgeous.* He had an overwhelming urge to kiss her pretty lips. *Idiot, that's the worst thing you can do.* Instead he turned her and reached for the shampoo, squeezed a blob into his palm then began lathering her hair.

"That...feels... wonderful," she whispered, leaning forward to give him better access.

Sam's gaze dropped to her backside. He shuddered, squashing the impulse to strip off her bra and pants. He glanced down at his erection. *Get a grip man. If she sees that, she'll know exactly what you're thinking.*

Moving her under the water spray, Sam soaped her legs and arms, rubbing briskly to get the circulation going. He resisted the temptation to soap her delicate neck, knowing the moment he did, he'd be lost. Instead, he concentrated on her back and shoulders.

Kallie moaned, arching her back. Sam's gaze fastened on the generous swell of her breasts. His erection strained against his jocks, the need to touch her becoming unbearable. He closed his eyes and groaned. *God help me. Resisting Kallie is the hardest thing I've ever done in my life. He* opened his eyes to find her facing him with her arms crossed under her breasts, lips parted and a soft blush in her cheeks. Their eyes locked.

A tremor ran through Sam as he fought an overwhelming desire to take her in his arms, kiss every inch of her and sate the hunger growing inside him. "How do you feel?"

"Alive," she whispered, her sparkling eyes never leaving his. "I've never had a shower with a man before." She swayed towards him.

Oh no you don't. Sam turned the tap off, stepped out of the shower and grabbed a towel. "Here, dry yourself before you get cold again." He tossed the towel at her, determinedly keeping his eyes averted. "Once you're dressed, we'll go back to the river." He picked up his stuff and left the bathroom, closing the door firmly.

And while we're at the river, I'll get Simon to check out that jewel box. Pulling out his satellite phone, Sam headed for the barn to let Ajax out.

Kallie clutched the towel to her chest. *What just happened? I thought he was going to kiss me. I wanted him to kiss me.* A shiver brought her to her senses. She stripped off her undies and bra, threw them in the washing basket and dried herself.

Kallie swaddled her hair in the towel, pulled another from under the vanity and wrapped it round her. *He could have taken advantage of me but he didn't.*

Opening the door, she peeped out. No tall, handsome man awaited her. Disappointed, she slipped into the hall intent on reaching her room, changing and joining the search.

Loud barking and claws scrabbling on wooden boards alerted her to Ajax's imminent arrival and the possibility of being covered in muddy paws.

"Oh no."

Sam stepped out of his room and she slammed into his chest, the towel on her head unravelling. "Argh."

Sam's arms encircled her and he twisted, shielding her from his excited dog.

"Down, Ajax. Get down," he ordered. The dog whimpered and sat.

Wrapped within Sam's strong arms, Kallie's heart raced and from where her hand rested on his chest, she knew his was too. She leaned around him and winked at Ajax. "Good boy."

Clutching her towel, Kallie wriggled out of Sam's arms and backed away, her gaze never leaving his. He kept eye contact, but didn't say a word. Kallie opened her door, slipped through, closed it and leaned there smiling. *He is definitely interested.*

Kallie dressed warmly, dried her hair and joined Sam in the kitchen. He had a cup of warm chocolate milk waiting.

"Here, drink this and we'll head back to the river."

"Thanks." Kallie took the cup and leaned against the table. "Jarred told me you've done lots of rescues in worse conditions. Was that in the army or police?"

Sam lowered his cup. "Army."

"Was that here or overseas?"

"Overseas."

Kallie bit her lip. "Were you involved in front line stuff or mainly rescue operations?"

"Front line."

Geez, this is like pulling teeth. "Where were you sent?"

"Wherever we were needed. Our unit was more of a problem-solving force."

"Problem solving? What kind of soldier were you?"

He sighed. "I was with a squadron in the SAS, but I can't talk about that, Kallie."

SAS, that's...Oh my God. She straightened. "I saw something on television about SAS recruitment. It was called, The Search for Warriors. They put one hundred and thirty men through hell for three weeks and in the end only about thirty made it."

"It's a very gruelling three weeks."

Kallie stared at him. "You were one of those soldiers?"

"Yes." He drained his cup and rinsed it.

Kallie blinked. "Talos and the others, they were SAS soldiers too?"

"Yes, but again, it's something we can't discuss."

"What does SAS stand for?"

He sighed. "Enough questions. Let's go." He called Ajax and left the kitchen.

Kallie rinsed the cup and left it on the drainer. *If Sam won't tell me about the SAS, I'll find out for myself.* She padded out to the back porch, pulled on her boots and ran to join Sam and Ajax. *I am going to make it my mission in life to find out everything there is to know about you, Sam Locke.*

Kallie climbed into the front passenger seat, aware of Sam's gaze. Ajax sat in the middle of the back seat, his tail wagging madly. *At least someone is delighted to see me.* Giving him a quick pat and another wink, Kallie pulled her seat belt on.

"Ready whenever you are." She smiled as innocently as she could. His eyes narrowed.

"What? Let's go," she said, settling more comfortably.

"Hmm." Sam released the handbrake.

By the time they arrived back at the river, more people had arrived, among them Roy and Bunny. Everyone was watching a tractor drag the motor home to the edge of the river with a steel cable.

Sam joined his friends so Kallie and Ajax headed to an open sided marquee where Fergie had steaks, sausages and onions cooking on a portable barbecue and Liz, Jane and Bunny were buttering bread and making tea and coffee for the men standing around. Something they'd all done many times during floods, bushfires and emergencies.

"Hi ladies, what can I do to help?" Kallie asked.

"Oh good, you're back, Kallie." Liz looked at her. "You can help Jane and Bunny. I need to go back into town for more meat and bread."

"Okay." Kallie squeezed between a tent pole and the table. Ajax followed.

Jane gave her a quick hug. "You look one hundred percent better than you did earlier. I was actually quite worried about you. Did Sam come back with you?"

"Yes, but I need to ask your advice about something." She glanced across to Fergie who was slipping a sausage to Ajax. "When we're alone," she whispered.

Jane's eyebrows rose. "Ah, Fergie, would you please get me another jerry can of water, we're a bit low."

Fergie straightened. "Huh, yeah sure, Janey. I'll get right on it."

Kallie smiled at Jane. "You are so good at manipulating people."

Jane laughed. "Everyone but you and I suspect those men." She glanced up as the helicopter flew over.

Biting her lip, Kallie checked no one was within hearing. "I need some advice."

Eyes wide, Jane stared at her. "Why, what's happened?"

"Nothing, I want to know how to entice Sam."

Jane huffed. "He already is. I told you, anyone with eyes could see that."

"No, I think he sees me as too young or too inexperienced for him."

"Not by the way he kissed you in the pub he doesn't." Jane scoffed. "If I were you, I'd be very careful. If you give him an inch, he'll take a mile."

Kallie sighed in frustration. "No, he won't. We were both almost naked in the shower and I thought he was going to kiss me, but he didn't."

Jane's eyes nearly popped out of her head. "You had a shower with Sam?"

"It wasn't like that." Kallie took a deep breath and told Jane everything.

"And he didn't kiss you?"

"No."

Looking at the sky, Jane rubbed her neck. "He can't be gay, because no gay guy kisses a woman the way he kissed you in the pub. He might be married."

"No, he told me he wasn't," argued Kallie.

"Men will tell a woman anything to get them into bed."

"But he didn't try to get me into bed."

"Hmm." Jane glanced across the clearing to where Sam stood talking to Roy. "If he's not married then there has to be another reason."

Kallie leaned against the portable table and crossed her arms. "I need to be more like Donna Ross. She's so confident and sassy."

"Sassy." Jane shook her head. "S'truth, Kallie, you have more sassiness in your little finger than Donna has in her whole body. After you left this morning, I saw her bail Andrew up outside the shop. He wasn't very civil. He really can't stand the woman."

A couple of men strolled over, so Kallie dropped it. Then Fergie ambled back.

"Here you go, Janey. Anything else you need?"

"Yes, actually there is," replied Jane. "Could you take this steak sandwich to Roy and while you're at it, take that dog before he steals any more sausages."

"No worries." Fergie accepted the serviette-wrapped sandwich, whistled to Ajax and the two of them ambled away.

"Right," Jane turned to Kallie. "You have to touch Sam."

"Touch him how, where?"

Jane pulled her further back into the shelter. "Touch his arm when you ask him a question, bump into him, brush past him, stop suddenly in front of him. Just touch him."

"Why?"

"Because"—Jane exhaled—"if he reacts, he's interested. It might be that he stops talking mid sentence, or he loses his train of thought, or he stares at you, or kisses you. But if Sam steps away, he's either gay, married or there is something majorly wrong with him, because my dear friend, only an idiot would reject you."

Kallie hugged Jane. "You are such a confidence booster." She considered Jane's words. *He did stop talking and stare at me the other night. I should test Jane's theory.* She picked up a coffee. "Okay, I'll give it a go."

"Not here." Jane shook her head. "Somewhere private."

Smiling, Kallie ignored her and walked off. "No time like the present," she called. "He's busy talking, let's see if I can distract him."

Jane shook her head and went back to buttering bread.

Walking up to the group of men, Kallie handed Roy a coffee then squeezed past Sam to look at the motor home now standing on the bank. His arm brushed her breast sending a tingle to her very core. Sam's breath hitched as he moved to give her more room.

Hmmm. Kallie glanced at the even ground. *Not really what I need, but it does look a little slippery.* She pretended to lose her footing, falling against Sam. He grabbed her round the waist steadying her.

"Are you all right, Kallie?"

She smiled, his biceps rippled under her fingers. "I am now. Thank you, Sam."

He released her and took a step back. Kallie glanced at Roy who was studying the ground.

"What did you trip over, Bossy?"

They all looked at the smooth ground. "My boot slipped. I'm such a klutz sometimes."

Roy's gaze fixed on her. "Since when?"

"Since..." Kallie heard the helicopter coming in low. She reached out and touched Sam's forearm. It quivered beneath her fingers. "Look, they're back. Maybe they have some good news." As Roy glanced up at the helicopter, Kallie ran her fingers down Sam's arm as she'd seen Donna do.

His eyes narrowed and locked with hers. "We should find out." He caught her hand and pulled her along to where the helicopter was coming down.

Sneaking a peek at Jane, Kallie noticed her shaking her head. *I'm doing what you suggested.*

They were almost to the helicopter when Sam stopped. Kallie made sure she ran into him. His hands gripped her shoulders. "I know what you're doing, Kallie—don't."

Opening her eyes wide, Kallie stared at him. "I don't know what you're talking about, Sam. Oh look, you've got a smudge of dirt on your face." She raised her free hand to his right cheek and smoothed the non-existent smudge away. His jaw clenched under her fingers.

"There is no dirt on my face, Kallie." His voice sounded raspy.

"Yes, there is, but don't worry, I'll get it." She smoothed her fingers down the left side of his face. His eyes flashed.

"All gone," she whispered.

He scowled. "You're playing with fire, Kallie. Stop it or you'll get burnt."

"I have no idea what you're talking about, Sam." She pulled her hand free and flounced off towards the helicopter, her heart thundering in her chest. *Keep walking, Kallie, you're doing fine.* She could hear him striding in her wake. *What did Jane say about stopping in front of him? Ah yes, I remember.* Kallie looked at the ground. *There's no flower to stop and pick. No amazing thing to study. No shoelace to tie.*

Her eyes fell on a black wallet half buried in the soft earth. Without thinking she bent to pull it free. Sam collided with her backside, his arms enfolding her as his momentum took them forward. They both crashed to the ground.

"Bloody hell, Kallie. What the devil are you up to?" He rolled off her, stood and dragged her to her feet. "You don't just stop in front of a person."

Kallie stared at the open wallet in her hand. Wally's picture stared back at her from his driver's license. She swallowed and looked up at Sam. "It's Wally's wallet."

"What?" Sam's gaze dropped to the wallet and license. "What's it doing here?"

"I don't know, it was almost buried." She looked down. "There's a tyre mark going right over where it was." Kallie pointed at the tyre marks leading all the way to the river. "He must have dropped the wallet, before his motor home ran over it."

Kallie flicked through the wallet. "Money, cards." Her eyes met his. "No photos."

"Let me look," asked Sam taking the wallet. "Odd, maybe they're in the motorhome.

"Maybe."

"Hey, Sam." Talos called.

They both looked across to see Talos standing with Jarred and Ryan beside the now silent helicopter. A body shrouded in a blanket lay on the floor of the helicopter.

"Oh no," whispered Kallie, sagging against Sam. "I was so hoping he'd be all right."

Sam's arms came round her. "So was I."

CHAPTER THIRTEEN

"It doesn't make sense. Why would he drive into the river?" Kallie chewed her nail.

"Ssh, Kallie." Sam stroked her back. "The police will sort it out." He looked across to where Angus was sitting, shoulders slumped, staring at the helicopter.

Jarred glanced across at Sam, said something to Talos and then strode across the wet grass. "I've got more bad news. The riverbanks are breaking and the State Emergency Service has predicted this whole district will be under water by tomorrow morning." He looked at the crowd of locals. "Willaroi Downs is going to be completely cut off."

Still cocooned in Sam's arms with her cheek against his chest, Kallie looked up at Jarred. "Can you pass that on to the others please? Families on low-lying farms will have to evacuate into Collie and the rest will need to get in supplies." She eased away a little. "I need to go into town and get a few things then go home to check on my horses."

Roy and a pleasant faced, grey-haired woman joined them. Roy took in Sam's arms around Kallie. "I'll take care of the horses, Bossy," he offered. "You'll be needed in town. His eyes met Sam's and then moved to Jarred. "You fellas should move into town and take Kallie with you." He glanced towards Bert and Angus. "Just in case."

Bunny smiled at Sam. "We haven't met, but I'm Bunny Morgan. Roy's been telling me about you and your friends." She glanced at Jarred. "It's a good thing you're here in town, we're going to need all the help we can get." She turned to Sam. "I'll get a few supplies in for Angus and Bert if you take Kallie home to pack."

Sam nodded and released Kallie, watching her for signs of delayed shock.

She gave him a thin smile. "I'm fine now."

"Okay, can you look after Ajax? I want to check on something. Meet me at my truck."

Kallie looked across to where Liz and Jane were packing their car. "I just want to say goodbye to Jane. Andrew will want to leave town as soon as he hears about the flood."

"I'll come with you," Bunny said.

Waiting until Kallie and Bunny were out of earshot, Sam turned to Roy. "Is there something else we should know, Roy?"

The stockman rubbed his chin. "I've got a knack for reading people and I'm rarely wrong. I also know when I'm being hoodwinked. I reckon you fellas are okay or I wouldn't be letting any of you near Kallie, but you're not being straight with us." He glanced across to the group of men bunched around Bert and Angus.

"There are a few others in town who haven't been honest with us either, and I figure you fellas are interested in one, or all of them." He regarded Jarred then Sam.

"I don't give a tinker's arse who you are, or what you're after, as long as it's not Kallie or her diamond. She gets hurt in any way, I'll come after you."

Sam narrowed his eyes. "Why do you want Kallie in town with us?"

"Because I reckon now that she's announced she's found the diamond, she's going to need protecting and I reckon you might be the fella to do that."

"You obviously don't think we're after the diamond?"

Pursing his lips, Roy shrugged. "No, but I think you might be after someone who is."

Jarred stared at him. "We can't discuss why we're here, Roy, but we'll do our best to keep Kallie safe. Having said that, if there's something you do know then please speak up."

Turning to Sam, Roy narrowed his eyes. "I want your word you won't let Kallie out of your sight, not for a second?"

Sam raised his eyes to the grey sky. *Fuck, if I spend every second of the day and night with Kallie without touching her, I'll go mad.* He drew in a deep breath, raised both arms, linked his fingers behind his head and exhaled. He lowered his gaze to Roy.

"I swear I'll do my best to protect her, but spending every second with her is impossible. She'll be at the Macey's house during the night?"

"No, I don't want her there. She's better off staying at the pub with you, where there'll be lots of people. It's only for a couple of nights. Sleep on the floor."

Jarred stirred. "What about Liz Macey, she'll object surely?"

Snorting, Roy glared at Jarred. "It's going to be chaos at the pub for the next few days and I'm sure Sam's an expert at slipping in and out of places unobserved. I bet you all are."

Sam lowered his arms and pinched the bridge of his nose. *It's only a couple of nights. You've been in much worse predicaments.* He looked across to where Kallie was talking with the other women. His gaze tracking her every movement, the soft curve of her face as she smiled at Jane, the tilt of her head as she considered something Bunny said, the contour of her breasts as she straightened, hands on hips to argue with Liz.

Fuck, how am I going to keep my hands off her? He clenched his fists. *Wake up, Sam, it's not as if she knows what she's doing to you.* He frowned, remembering her earlier attempt at flirting. *Nah, you've got this covered. Kallie is an innocent.*

"All right, you have my word. I won't let Kallie out of my sight."

"Good," replied Roy. "That's all I ask."

Jarred shifted impatiently. "Now that's sorted. What is it you want to tell us?"

"Kallie hasn't found the diamond."

Sam frowned, recalling Kallie's outburst this morning. Was Roy lying, trying to protect the diamond or attempting to malign Kallie. "But she said..."

"I know what she said." Roy interrupted him. "But it's not true."

"Go on." Jarred stared at him.

"You've met Bert, Bill, Ken and Fergie. They're all running from something and don't like to talk about themselves or where they came from. When they first arrived in Willaroi, I didn't trust any of them as far as I could throw them, but some of them have grown on me over the years.

"That one..." He looked to Bert who had moved away from the group and stood by the river smoking a cigarette. "He's a snake in the grass and I reckon the only reason he sticks around is because he's hoping to get his hands on the diamond. Greed can change a person and where that diamond's concerned, I don't trust any of them."

"What makes you think Kallie hasn't found the diamond?" asked Sam.

"She told me, and I'm afraid she only said she had found it to draw out the person you're after." He gave them a nod and ambled off.

Sam spotted Bert pushing Angus in the wheelchair towards their vehicle. He met Jarred's gaze. "Did you drop Simon off at the farm?"

"And Nick. Between the two of them, they should've been able to search the house, barn and Bert's quarters. We'll pick them up now, drop the body into Collarenabri and then come back and pack up the cabin."

Sam frowned. "The police in Collarenabri will ask questions?"

"I have a letter from our client that will satisfy the police."

"And if they do ask questions, you'll have all the answers."

"Exactly. What are you going to do?"

"I'm taking Kallie back to the farm so she can pack, then I'm going to send her and Ajax into town in my truck and disable her ute."

Jarred's brow wrinkled. "You obviously have a reason for doing that?"

"I'm hoping Bert will give me a lift into town. It'll give me a chance to interrogate him." Sam pulled out the wallet and handed it to Jarred.

"What's this?"

"Wally King's wallet. Kallie found it on the ground."

Opening it, Jarred looked inside. "He wasn't robbed."

"No, but it's odd that the two photos he was showing around last night are missing. I'm going to have a quick look in the motorhome before it's towed into town."

"They might have been in his jacket. The old guy only had a light shirt and pants on."

Sam shrugged. "A heavy jacket would drag him under, he might have got rid of it. Any sign of foul play?"

"He's got a nasty gash on his head, but that could've come from a debris in the river."

"Hmm." Sam scanned the crowd. "It wouldn't hurt to do a search of Ken, Bill and Fergie's places tonight. With the whole team in town, it shouldn't be a problem."

Jarred nodded. "I presume our targets will all be at the pub tonight?"

"You would have to think so." Sam watched Bert and Angus drive off.

Jarred slid Wally King's wallet into his shirt pocket. "I'll see you in town." He turned and strode towards the helicopter.

Drawing a deep breath, Sam headed for the motorhome. *I have a bad feeling.* He darted a quick glance at Kallie. She stood talking to Jane, but her gaze was on him.

Kallie observed Sam striding to the motorhome. "Sam told me I'm playing with fire and if I don't back off, I'll get burnt."

Jane's eyes widened. "Really? That's interesting."

Kallie glanced across to the helicopter as its engine surged to life. A white Land Cruiser crossed the bridge and stopped, its path blocked by the helicopter.

"Who's that?" asked Jane.

Kallie scrutinised the occupants as they peered out the windows. "It's those three men from last night." *I need to keep an eye on them too.*

The helicopter lifted, hovered for a moment then dipped and flew west.

"I wonder where they'll take Wally's body," Jane said.

"Collarenabri." Kallie watched the Land Cruiser.

"Then why are they flying west? They should be going north."

Kallie shrugged. "Maybe they're going to pack up their stuff, in case they're delayed in Collie and it's dark when they get back."

The Land Cruiser crept forward, the older man in the front seat wound down his window and moved his gaze through the crowd, his eyes intent as the car moved slowly forward.

Kallie glanced at Sam. He'd left the motorhome and was now on his way towards her although his attention was on the Land Cruiser. She stared at him as he strode purposely towards her. The confident tilt of his head, broad shoulders and solid chest, tapered hips and flat stomach, muscled thighs, long legs. A strong yearning took hold deep in Kallie's core, a yearning to know Sam intimately. She raised her eyes and they locked with his dark, smouldering gaze.

"There you are."

His eyes held hers. "Yes, here I am."

Jane looked from one to the other. "Right then, I'll um, leave you two to…"

Kallie tore her eyes away from Sam and glanced at Jane. "Take care and ring me when you get back to Sydney."

"Sure." Jane hugged her and smiled at Sam. "Bye."

Sam gave her a nod, but kept his eyes on Kallie. "Shall we go?"

"Yes, of course." She glanced around for Ajax. "Come on, boy, let's go."

Ajax barked and trotted after her.

"What were you doing in Wally's motorhome," Kallie said as they reached Sam's Hilux.

"I was looking for this." He pulled a photo out of his shirt pocket and handed it to her. "Everything else is soggy and strewn all over the place. That photo survived because it was under a magnet on the fridge." He opened the door for her.

Slipping into her seat, Kallie studied the photo. It was the one with three shirtless men in baggy shorts and cork rimmed hats. She glanced up at Sam. "You can't tell who is who with those beards and hats, can you?"

"No, the tattoos are a giveaway though. Match those up to Angus, Bert and Wally and you'll know who is who."

Kallie looked closer. "You're right."

Neither of them spoke during the short drive to the farm. Sam shot an occasional glance at Kallie, but she appeared content to gaze out her window, deep in thought. When he pulled up in front of the house, Kallie looked up at him as he reached across and touched her arm.

"Before we go in there's something we need to talk about."

"Oh, and what's that?"

Sam rubbed his chin. "Roy wants you to stay at the pub and he's asked me to keep an eye on you…night and day."

Kallie's eyes widened. "Really, why?"

"I think Roy sees a lot more than others and he's figured we're after someone who might pose a threat to you."

Kallie frowned, her hand covering his on her arm. He willed

himself not to react to the light touch of her fingers, instead biting his tongue.

"I swear, I didn't say a word to him." Her voice was firm.

"You didn't have to. He guessed."

"How does Roy expect you to keep an eye on me at night?"

A quiver of excitement ran through Sam. He looked through the front windscreen to avoid meeting her eyes. "He wants us to share a room at the pub." He glanced at Kallie to find her mouth hanging open.

"Roy asked you to share a room with me?"

"Yes, and I've given him my word that I will keep you safe twenty-four hours a day and that includes safe from me. I'll be sleeping on the floor."

She stared at him. "That's a brilliant idea."

"What?" Sam's eyes narrowed. "Kallie, it's a terrible idea. Sharing a room is the last thing we should be doing. It may well lead to..."

"Yes, it may." She grinned.

"Kallie, let's get one thing straight. I'm only here for a short time and I'm not after a meaningful relationship nor do I have any desire to get married and have children."

"What, never?" asked Kallie.

"Never," reiterated Sam.

"Why?"

"Because I don't believe in happy ever afters." He opened his door. "As I said earlier—don't play with fire or you'll get burnt." He climbed from the truck, opened the rear door and Ajax jumped out.

Kallie walked round to join them, a smile playing on her lips. "I can handle a little singeing." She turned on her heel and ran up the steps, Ajax hot on her heels.

Shit. Sam's gaze dropped to her shapely arse. An image of her full rounded breasts flashed before his eyes, and his erection stirred. He clenched his fists and called after her. "Pack enough for a week and bring anything sentimental or valuable. In case this place goes under as well."

Kallie kicked off her boots and disappeared through the front door with Ajax.

Sam examined the house. Nothing moved. *Right.* Bert's four-wheel drive was parked outside the shearer's quarters a couple of hundred metres away. Kallie's ute had been parked in the barn, nicely hidden from view. Sam strolled into the barn, opened the driver's door and released the bonnet. Within seconds he had the cap off and the middle ignition coil disconnected. He grinned, shut the bonnet and pulled out his phone. "Nick, it's Sam. How'd the search go? Did you find anything?"

"Not much," answered Nick. "The jewel box is solid, but I couldn't find any secret compartments. We did find the key hidden in a vase of fake flowers, but there's only dress jewellery in the top of the box."

Sam frowned. "You didn't see the opal necklace or diamond earrings?"

"Nope. We did find an office safe and the combination stuck to the bottom of a drawer. They're not in there either, but there are several accounts journals. She's getting top dollar for those foals she's breeding."

"Hm. What about the rest of the house and Bert's place?"

"Nothing. Clean as a whistle."

"Okay, thanks. I told Kallie to bring anything valuable with her, so I assume she'll bring the box. I'll have a closer look later. Also while everyone's in the pub, we should take the opportunity to search Fergie and Ken's places. Bill should be busy serving, so his rooms will be easy enough."

"Okay, we're just putting down in Collarenabri now. I'll see you later."

"Yep, later." Sam ended the call and headed for the house.

CHAPTER FOURTEEN

Kallie examined her bed and scowled. Almost every item of clothing she owned lay there, as did her photo albums, account books, jewel box and two-treasured photos of her parents and great-grandparents. The total wouldn't even fill a suitcase. That was the problem. Kallie patted Ajax who'd perched himself beside her belongings to watch the proceedings.

"What's wrong?"

Kallie looked up to see Sam studying her from the doorway. "I'm trying to think what I can put this stuff in?"

Sam's lips twitched. "I hesitate to suggest this, Kallie, but haven't you ever heard of a suitcase."

Rolling her eyes, Kallie shooed Ajax off the bed. "Very funny. I don't have a suitcase."

Sam looked taken back. "Then what do you use when you travel?"

Kallie shrugged. "I've never been anywhere—well not since I was little and even then, my mum packed my things in her case."

Sam frowned. "You've never been anywhere, not even Sydney or Brisbane?"

"When I was about eight years old. We caught a train, spent a whole day at the Royal Easter Show, took a ferry across the harbour and spent another day at the zoo, then we caught a train home."

Sam looked at her in disbelief. "That's it?"

Kallie shuffled from foot to foot. "I would have gone to Canberra on a school excursion in year six, but that was round the time of the plane crash."

Kallie drew in a breath and looked at the mess on her bed. "And there was the time Liz and Jane wanted me to go to New Zealand with them, but since...since the crash, I'm too scared to fly, so I didn't go." She shrugged. "I wanted to, but I couldn't."

Sam came round the bed and picked up her hands. Instant tingles shot up her arms. He drew her gently forward, released her hands and wrapped his arms round her. Kallie closed her eyes and sank against his solid chest and thighs. Hot desire shot throughout her body as her heart began a rapid tattoo inside her chest. Her breasts grew heavy and her nipples sensitive. Kallie shifted closer, enthralled by the unfamiliar sensations assailing her.

Sam stiffened and Kallie looked up into hungry, dark-chocolate eyes. *He does want me.* Her hands moved up over his magnificent chest and around his neck. Her lips parted as the elation spread, but before her smile could fully form, Sam's mouth descended in a kiss that stole her breath, then he forced her lips apart and his tongue entered her mouth.

Kallie's legs trembled and his arms tightened, crushing her against him. She fought for breath, as his hands glided down her back, cupped her backside firmly and lifted her hard against him. Kallie's pubic bone slammed into his hard erection. She gasped, her senses soaring.

Ajax growled and Sam thrust her away from him. She landed on the bed amongst her clothes. "What?"

"Ssh," whispered Sam, breathing hard. "Listen."

Confusion enveloped Kallie. Her lips were throbbing, her body screamed for his touch. Her breath ragged, she blinked, fighting for composure as she swept her gaze over Sam. His chest rose and fell as rapidly as hers, his erection an impressive bulge in his jeans and his eyes... Kallie shivered. His eyes were feverish, frantic, furious. His fists clenched, and she swallowed.

"What's wrong," she whispered, sliding further back.

Ajax growled again and ran to the open doorway. Kallie heard footsteps and Angus's wheel chair on the back porch.

"It's Angus and Bert," she whispered.

Sam's gaze swept over her, he moved closer, his nostrils flaring, his hands still fisted. Kallie wasn't sure what to think. He was scaring her. As if sensing her fear, he stepped away and drew in a deep breath.

"I suggest you put a cold compress on your lips before Bert or

Angus see you," His voice was low and controlled. It did nothing to ease Kallie's fear as she scrambled off the bed. Sam walked to the door and turned.

"I'll see if I can find a cardboard box and a couple of garbage bags for your stuff." He hesitated, a tightness appearing around his mouth. "That shouldn't have happened."

Biting her lip, Kallie met his eyes. "I don't understand why you're so angry. You're the one who hugged me."

He stiffened. "I was only offering comfort. I didn't intend for it to be anything else."

"Comfort." Kallie crossed her arms under her breasts and raised her chin. "You wanted to kiss me as much as I wanted to kiss you."

His eyes narrowed. "Wanting and doing are two separate things, Kallie. You were lucky we were interrupted." He turned on his heel and strode down the hall. Kallie heard his bedroom door open and close.

She glanced at her reflection in the mirror. Her eyes were huge, her lips swollen, her cheeks flushed. "Maybe I don't want to be lucky," she whispered.

Ajax whined and padded across to her. Kallie rubbed his ears, but her eyes remained fixed on the doorway.

"Maybe I want you to make love to me." *I like being in his arms and I like him kissing me.* She closed the door. *Damn you, Sam Locke.*

Kallie heard Sam's shower burst to life next door. "Geez, how many showers does that man need a day?"

She did a final check of her bare wardrobe and drawers then glanced at the bed. *Except for my horses, I don't have a lot to show for twenty-three years of life, do I?*

Kallie shook her forlorn thoughts away and glared at her reflection. "If you're not happy with your life, then do something about it. If you want him bad enough, then get off your backside and grasp him with both hands." She giggled at the thought of grasping a particular part of Sam Locke.

Ajax gave an excited bark and wagged his tail. Kallie grinned.

"Exactly my friend." She rubbed Ajax's ears. "So how do I go about grabbing your master and convincing him, we belong together?"

The squeak of Angus's wheelchair coming down the hall propelled Kallie into action. She ran to the door and leaned on it. A couple of seconds later a discreet knock sounded.

"Kallie, you in there?"

"Yes, Angus. "I'm just changing."

"What, again?"

Kallie silently slapped her forehead. *Idiot.* "Yes, I've decided to stay in town for a few days. I'll be more use in there."

Silence. She waited.

"What about me? Who's going to cook my meals?"

Kallie bit her lip. "It's only for a couple of days, Angus, and Bunny is bringing you more supplies and there's plenty of things in the freezer that can be heated."

"What about your horse? I can't feed it and Bert won't go near the beast."

"Don't worry about Jasper. Roy will look after him."

"I don't see why you've got to go into town. There's a lot of strangers about at the moment and I'd feel better with you here."

"I'll be fine, Angus. Sam promised Roy he'd keep an eye on me."

"That's what I'm worried about," called Angus. "There's something about Sam and those friends of his that has me worried. The very fact they didn't tell us who they were from the beginning troubles me."

Kallie heard the shower turn off. "I'll be fine, Angus."

"Hmm, all right. I suppose you're safe enough at Liz's." His wheelchair squeaked back down the hall.

Far out, that was close. Kallie waited until she was sure the coast was clear then hurried to the bathroom, washed her face in cool water and pressed a cold washer to her lips. *Men are so controlling. When are they going to learn, I am old enough to make my own decisions? If I want to stay at the pub, I will, and if I want to kiss Sam, I will.* A prickle of fear struck as she remembered Sam's controlled fury, then she thought about how thoughtful, gentle and protective he'd been towards her.

Sam's just afraid of his feelings for me and is trying to scare me away. I need to find out what happened to make him this way.

Kallie dried her face, opened the door and hurried into the kitchen. The television blared in the lounge and Angus and Bert were trying to talk over it. Opening the freezer, Kallie pulled out a frozen casserole and placed it on the bench. *That takes care of Angus tonight.* She opened the cupboard under the sink and pulled out a roll of garbage bags. *My clothes can go in a couple of these.*

"Now, what am I going to put my albums and account ledgers in?"

"Have you got a cooler?" Sam strolled into the kitchen.

"Um." She searched his face and eyes for any sign of his earlier anger but his expression was calm. "Yes, there's one on the porch." Kallie grabbed a note pad. "I'm just leaving a note for Bunny to take Webster with her."

Sam glanced up at the cat. "I have a better idea. Why don't you bring him into town? Roy and Bunny are going to be busy enough with the horses. In fact, you can take my Hilux. I noticed you have a tyre that's a bit low. I'll pump it up and come in later."

Straightening, Kallie grinned. "You trust me with your Hilux? It looks pretty new."

"It is, but I'm sure you'll look after it."

"Oh, I will."

"Good, I'll shout you a late lunch at the pub. I'm hungry enough to eat a horse."

Kallie glanced at the clock. "Oh my goodness, it's past two o'clock. I'll be ready to go in ten minutes." Kallie snatched the garbage bags and cooler and ran down the hall.

Sam smiled. *That was easy. Let's hope it's as easy to avoid kissing her again.* He cursed, annoyed to be reminded of the kiss. The way her body moulded to his, the feel of her tight arse in his hands and firm breasts and hard nipples rubbing against his chest. His hard on cradled against her... *Fuck, if I keep having cold showers, I'll run their tanks dry.*

He swore again. *That last shower only just took the edge off, now I'm right back where I started.* Sam scooped the cat off the fridge and picked up his bag from the hallway. *I'd make Nick or Ryan guard her, only I don't trust them. Shit, I don't trust myself.* He strode out to his Hilux, threw his duffle bag in the back, opened the rear door and dropped the cat in.

"Stay there, cat," he ordered closing the door. Sam took a couple of calming breaths before returning to the house. No woman had ever affected him as Kallie did.

He met her in the hall, dragging two bags and lugging the cooler.

"Here let me." He took the cooler and one bag then poked his head into the lounge.

"We're off into town, Angus. Hopefully we'll run into each other again before I leave town."

Bert barely looked away from the television. *Ignorant bastard.* Sam's glance moved to Angus. "Thanks for putting me up, I'll get some money out in town and fix Kallie up."

Angus raised a hand. "No worries. Thanks for your help at the river today." He glanced at Kallie then back at Sam. "The sooner the water goes down the sooner things can go back to normal."

Sam got the message. *The sooner the water goes down, the sooner I leave town and Kallie.* A tightness gripped Sam's chest. The thought of never seeing Kallie again didn't sit well. *What the hell is wrong with me?*

"Let's go, Sam," murmured Kallie touching his arm. A bolt of awareness shot up his arm. He clenched his jaw as he struggled not to snatch his arm away and draw the attention of the other two men. "Oh, by the way, Bert, I've left a couple of nice yellow bellies and a cod in the freezer for you and Angus."

Surprise showed in Bert's eyes. "Ah, thanks. Thanks a lot."

"No, worries. See you round."

Sam smiled, deeply satisfied with the way things were working out.

After stowing Kallie's gear, Sam opened the driver's door for her. The cat sat on the passenger seat with one leg up over its head as he licked his tummy. Kallie climbed in and buckled her belt. Ajax whined beside Sam and placed a paw on Kallie's thigh.

"Can't he ride in the back tray?" Kallie asked. "Then you can come with us."

Damn. He thought quickly. "I want to have a word with Bert and your flat tyre gives me the perfect opportunity but Ajax can go with you."

"Thank you."

"Hmm, you're turning my dog into a mummy's boy."

Ajax gave an excited bark and jumped into the back tray of the Hilux. Sam secured him and handed his keys to Kallie.

"Take it easy and keep Ajax with you. I'll see you in town."

"Okay, my keys are in the ignition." Kallie started the engine, gave him a wave and drove off.

Sam exhaled. "Now for Bert." He ambled over to the barn, climbed into Kallie's ute and spent the next couple of minutes attempting to start the engine while keeping an eye on the side mirror. He'd almost given up when he observed Bert entering the barn. Sam hid his smile and slammed his hand on the steering wheel.

"Fucking piece of shit, why won't you start?"

"Trouble?" Bert leaned in the window.

"Yeah, blasted thing won't start and I let Kallie take my Hilux." He scratched his chin. "You don't know anything about cars do you, Bert?"

Bert shook his head. "Naa, but I guess I could give you a lift."

Sam pretended to sigh with relief. "That would be great. Thanks."

"I'll just tell Angus what I'm doing." He left the barn and Sam strolled across the yard to Bert's four-wheel drive.

A couple of minutes later Bert reappeared on the back porch and sauntered over. "Petrol's expensive you know. I'm not doing this for nothing."

Sam reached for his wallet. *Tight arse.* He pulled out a twenty. "It's all I've got until I get to an ATM."

"It'll do." Bert snatched the note, shoved it in his jeans and walked around to his side of the vehicle. Sam shook his head. *This guy really needs to work on his people skills.*

Sam waited until they'd cleared the front gate then glanced at Bert. "Shame about Wally, isn't it."

Bert grunted. "He should've been more careful."

Sam glanced out the window in an attempt to hide his anger at Bert's insensitivity. "Where did you all meet?" he asked casually.

"I can't say for sure. It was a lot of years ago."

Sam turned to study Bert. "It was good of you to come here and look after Angus."

Bert shrugged. "I had nowhere else to go and we've been together a long time."

"You must find it hard though, not being a farmer?"

"Yeah, but Angus and me go to Brisbane fairly often, so it ain't so bad."

"What's in Brisbane?"

Bert sneered. "Bloody more than what's here, that's for sure." He snickered before shooting a quick glance at Sam. "Every few months Angus has some physio and sees his doctor, so we go for a week or two."

"Why stay here, if you hate it so much?" asked Sam.

"We can't leave, can we?"

"Why not? Kallie can look after herself and she's got Roy to help her with the farm."

Bert snorted. "Because Angus ain't ready to go yet." He smiled. "But that's about to change, now that Kallie's found the diamond."

"I'm not with you," Sam probed.

"Well, she'll give it back to Angus, so he can see out the rest of his days in comfort, some place nice."

Sam shrugged. "Or she could sell the diamond and keep the money. It is her diamond after all."

Bert shot him a look of irritation. "Angus only gave it to her for safekeeping while he was laid up in hospital."

"What if Kallie doesn't want to give it to Angus?"

"She will."

Sam's eyes narrowed. "You seem very confident."

Bert sniggered. "I am. She don't care about the diamond, never has. As soon as Angus asks, she'll give it to him without a second thought. Kallie only cares about Roy and Jane and that horse of hers."

"And the farm," Sam added.

"Nah, I heard her on the phone not long ago. She's thinking of selling the farm and starting a horse stud. Hah, what does she know about breeding horses?"

"Hmm." Sam glanced out his window. *Kallie's right. Bert is an ungrateful bludger, but he and Angus are in for a shock when they discover Kallie hasn't found the diamond.*

"We're here. Where do you want me to drop you?"

Sam focused. "The pub will be fine."

"No worries."

Two minutes later Bert did a U-turn in front of the pub and braked. "There you go."

"Thanks, I appreciate it." As Bert drove off, Sam scanned the street. His Hilux was angle-parked on the other side of the road.

A loud excited bark came from above. Sam glanced up to see Ajax peering through the railings of the pub's second floor porch.

"What are you doing up there, buddy?"

Ajax barked again and disappeared. Sam smiled. *He's probably gone to tell his mistress I've arrived.* Sam froze. *Kallie's not his mistress and never will be.* Shaking his head, Sam wandered into the pub.

In the foyer, Sam ran into Talos and Ryan. They both grinned and Talos punched him lightly in the shoulder.

"You lucky bastard. Why don't things like this happen to me?"

"What the hell is lucky about having to share a room with a gorgeous single woman and not being allowed to touch her? It's going to drive me insane."

Ryan raised an eyebrow. "Why exactly can't you touch her?"

"Because she's a bloody innocent with stars in her eyes and living a romantic fantasy."

"So give her a little romance," Talos said. "If that's all she wants."

Sam glared at him. "It's not. She wants it all. Marriage, kids and my bloody dog."

Talos and Ryan looked at each other then Ryan turned to Sam.

"She said that?"

"No," grumbled Sam. "But I know she does. Kallie sees everything through rose-coloured glasses and I'm not going to be the one to disillusion her."

Talos and Ryan glanced at each other again.

"And neither are you," warned Sam. "What room am I in?"

Talos grinned. "You mean what room are *we* in. You're sharing with a gorgeous woman you can't touch, remember." The two of them burst into laughter.

"Just tell me the fucking room number."

Ryan pointed up the stairs. "Turn left at the top and it's the last room on the left. You're overlooking the street. Oh, and it's got a double bed. That should make things interesting."

"You're a real comedian, Ryan," Sam muttered, taking the stairs two at a time.

Their laughter followed him up the stairs and along the hall.

Christ, getting through the next few days without touching her is going to be damn near impossible, but someone did take a shot at her and for what it's worth, she's safer here in town with me than out on the farm.

CHAPTER FIFTEEN

After stowing her gear in the hotel room and leaving Ajax with Talos, Kallie raced over to Liz's house, which had always been like a second home to her. With the house all to herself, Kallie sat in front of the computer, reading the information she'd downloaded.

"You've got to be joking," Jane whispered over her shoulder.

"Jane!" Kallie spun round so fast Webster fell off her knee. "I thought you'd gone back to Sydney?" She quickly minimised the computer screen.

"I decided to stay, now open that up again."

"It's nothing," declared Kallie. "I'm just checking something."

"It's too late, Kallie. I saw what you were reading. Open it."

Sighing Kallie enlarged the article. "It's Dominic Marzetti."

Jane peered at the grainy newspaper shot of a man in sunglasses, his hand up blocking most of his lower face. "How did you find out his first name?"

"Sam told me, just before we discovered Wally's motorhome in the river. Sam said Dominic Marzetti is a dangerous man and he's wanted for murder and all sorts of things. This article verifies everything Sam said."

Jane's eyes narrowed as she looked at the picture more closely. "You can't really make out his features, can you?"

"No," Kallie agreed. "Plus this photo was taken just before he disappeared, fifteen years ago. I was hoping I'd be able to identify him."

"Hmm, what else have you discovered?"

"Nothing about him, but I want to check out the SAS." Kallie brought up a search engine and typed in Australian SAS.

Jane dragged a chair over. "What's SAS?"

"That's what we're going to find out." She clicked on the first reference and read the heading. "Special Air Service Regiment."

Jane's eyes widened. "Why are you interested in the SAS?"

"Because Sam told me he used to be an SAS soldier, but he wouldn't elaborate."

"You're kidding." Jane stared at Kallie.

"No, I'm not."

"What else does it say?" Jane grabbed the mouse off Kallie and scrolled down. "The SASR is a special unit with unique capabilities." She looked at Kallie. "What sort of unique capabilities?"

Kallie shrugged and took control of the mouse again. "Operating under the motto 'Who Dares Wins' the SAS is a unit of the Australian Special Operations Command. Soldiers are specially selected and trained for situations that have national and strategic consequences. They are required to work in small teams for extended periods without support."

Jane gasped. "Sam was one of them?"

"Apparently, and so are those other guys who are pretending to be normal army personnel." She turned back to the screen. "It says here, special ops soldiers have served in major conflicts in Afghanistan and Iraq and provide support to peace enforcements. They are also trained to handle domestic and offshore counter-terrorism."

Jane's stunned eyes met Kallie's. "So they're like America's Navy Seals?"

"I guess so. I saw an army documentary not long ago called Search for Warriors and I think it might be about these guys." Kallie began typing again.

"There," pointed Jane. "It's a You-Tube video."

Kallie double clicked on it and they spent the next hour watching it. When it ended Jane put her hand on Kallie's arm.

"No wonder those guys are intimidating. They're the best of the best. The fittest of the fit, the strongest, the fiercest, the toughest, the—"

"I get the message, Jane. That's why Sam said he can't talk about it. They must be sworn to secrecy even though they're not in the SAS anymore."

"Say's who? Ken thought they might be undercover cops, but I bet they're still in the SAS and they're on a secret mission to catch this Marzetti guy."

Kallie frowned. "Maybe...but that means Sam's lied to me, again."

"If they're sworn to secrecy, he can't tell you."

Kallie's tummy rumbled and she glanced at her watch. "Holy cow, it's nearly four o'clock. I was supposed to have lunch at the pub with Sam."

One of Jane's eyebrows rose. "You know Mum thinks of you as a daughter, and if she finds out you're staying at the pub with all those SAS guys, she's going to have a pink fit. Especially since Andrew's gone home and you could have shared my bed."

Kallie's mouth dropped. "Andrew's gone home without you?"

"Yes, I told him our marriage is over and that I'd raise the baby on my own."

"He didn't argue with you?" Kallie was incredulous.

"No. If anything, he seemed relieved. I think he's happy to be rid of me so he can run off with his mistress." Jane stood up. "And I really don't care. How are you getting on with Sam?"

Kallie closed the computer and hurried after Jane to the kitchen. "Did you ask Andrew if he has a mistress?"

"I didn't get a chance. He was in too much of a hurry to get away. Do you want me to make you a sandwich, seeing as you missed lunch?"

"What?" Kallie stared at her. "You're very calm for someone that's just announced her marriage is over?"

"It's been over a long time, Kallie. I have no feelings for him anymore. Now tell me why you're really staying at the pub and not here?"

"Roy made Sam promise he wouldn't let me out of his sight. In fact he suggested Sam and I share a room at the pub as a way of keeping me safe from this unidentified Marzetti."

"You're joking?"

"No, I'm not," Kallie said, pacing back and forth. "Sam has agreed to sleep on the floor, but he's not happy about sharing a room with me. He even gave me this spiel about only being here for a short time and that he doesn't want a long-term relationship because he doesn't believe in happy ever afters."

"Oh." Jane began buttering bread. "I think you should forget him, Kallie. A guy like Sam Locke doesn't give warnings lightly. Maybe you should stay here tonight."

"No, that's a terrible idea. Sam is a good guy and he's the only man I've ever felt this way about. If it doesn't work out, then so be it."

Jane came around the table and clasped Kallie's hands. "But what if he never wants to see you again. It will break your heart."

"Maybe, but I'd rather risk that for a chance at happiness than not try at all."

"The odds are in your favour. At least he's attracted to you."

"Yes, he is." Kallie opened the fridge and handed Jane the ham and cheese. "I think I'll wear one of my new dresses tonight."

"And put your hair up. I read somewhere that men like bare necks. It looks sexy." Jane finished making the sandwiches and handed one on a plate to Kallie. "Eat, you can't win a battle on an empty stomach."

Kallie grinned. "Yes, General." She bit into the sandwich.

Jane grinned back. "Go get him, girlfriend."

"I will, and in the meantime I need to find out if Fergie, Bill, Ken or Bert is Marzetti."

"Ken's got some boxes of stuff in the office. I'll talk Mum and him into going to the pub for dinner and then I'll search through the boxes while they're out. If he's Marzetti then maybe there is something amongst his stuff that will give him away."

"Great. As I'm staying at the pub and Bill will be busy serving, I'll check out his office later this evening." Kallie frowned. "I'll pretend I'm going to bed early, otherwise Sam won't let me out of his sight."

Jane nodded. "And we can check out Fergie's place tomorrow when everyone's busy filling sandbags."

"Good thinking." Kallie finished the sandwich, hugged Jane and grabbed her jacket. "I'll check in with you later. Be careful, and if you need to talk or a shoulder to cry on, give me a call. I'll come straight over."

Jane waved her off. "I did all my crying months ago. You can leave Webster here, I'll look after him. Good luck with Sam."

Kallie grinned. "Who dares wins."

As Kallie jogged up the street, she ticked off all the local vehicles that were parked there, Sam's Hilux and the white van with tinted windows that belonged to his friends. She slowed to a walk when she saw the white Land Cruiser. *That belongs to those other men looking for Dominic Marzetti.* Kallie casually made a detour between the vehicles. She leaned against the Land Cruiser and peeped in.

"Where the hell have you been?"

Kallie squealed, her heart in her mouth when Sam grabbed her shoulder and spun her round. "You scared the living daylights out of me and you're hurting my..." She looked up into his face and blanked. His features could have been carved from rock, his eyes were glacial, his lips a thin, hard line. Rage emanated from every cell in his body. Kallie tried to pull back, but his fingers held her hard and fast.

She shivered. "What's wrong?"

His jaw clenched. "I asked you a question first."

Clearing her throat, Kallie lifted her chin. "I have no idea why you're being such a bully, but you're scaring me."

"I'm scaring you?" His eyes narrowed. "Do you have any idea how scared I've been for the last hour?"

Kallie shook her head. "Why would you be scared?"

He released her, clenched his hands and then scrubbed his face. Kallie had the distinct impression he was trying not to strangle her. She jumped again as his hands landed hard against the Land Cruiser, either side of her.

"I promised Roy I wouldn't let you out of my sight. I asked you to keep Ajax with you and I expected you to be in the pub waiting for me. I have been all over town looking for you and I've been worried sick that Marzetti got to you."

"You were worried about me?" Her fear evaporated to be replaced by hope. "I was at Liz's doing some...research."

Sam groaned. "I didn't look there because Ken and Liz were in the pub." His eyes narrowed. "What research?"

"I found an old newspaper article on Dominic Marzetti. I also discovered some very interesting things about the SAS and what they do, and before you scared the daylights out of me, I was checking out this Land Cruiser because it belongs to those three men."

Glancing round, Sam grabbed her hand, dragged her round the side of the pub. "For Christ's sake, Kallie, I don't want you doing any research or investigating. These are dangerous men and you are already in enough danger without locking horns with them." He spun away and paced a few steps, turned and came back. "I want your word you will stay out of this, Kallie?"

"But I'm in a perfect position to help you."

"No, Kallie, I want your word," Sam demanded, leaning over her.

That is so unreasonable. Kallie opened her mouth to voice that very thought when the three men from the pub rounded the corner of the building. "Those men are coming this way," she whispered.

"Play along." Sam hauled her against him and kissed her hard.

Kallie's lips opened to welcome him. She slid her hands up his chest and round his neck, pressing closer against the hard planes of his body and felt him still. The tenor of the kiss changed, his lips softened, and his tongue began a gentle exploration of her mouth. Kallie moaned and pressed closer, her fingers creeping into his hair.

A sound impinged on Kallie's subconscious, but she ignored it, too caught up in the pleasure of Sam's kiss. A man cleared his throat and Sam's fingers tightened on her waist. He pulled back slightly and looked at the men.

"Can I help you?" he asked sounding none too pleased at being interrupted.

Kallie hid her smile and glanced at the men.

The older man stepped forward. "I'm looking for a young lady by the name of Kalista?"

Kallie stiffened, her gaze lifting to Sam's face. His fingers briefly tensed on her waist.

"Why?" Sam's gaze pinned the man who'd asked the question.

The man's eyes shifted to Sam. "I have a proposition I'd like to make her, regarding a valuable diamond she owns." The man's gaze moved back to Kallie. "I'm prepared to make the young lady a very generous offer."

"How generous?" Kallie leaned round Sam's arm.

Sam cursed softly and glared at her. "I was handling this," he muttered.

"I assume you're Kalista McNeil," the man said as the two men behind him took up a stance on either side of him.

Sam gripped Kallie's upper arm and steered her towards the back door of the pub. "We're not interested." His voice was cold.

Kallie tried to peek at the man, but Sam pushed her through the door and closed it.

She stood her ground. "What was that all about?"

"I don't want Victor Vassello anywhere near you."

"I meant the kiss. You warn me off, then kiss me like you're can't get enough of me."

Sam rubbed his forehead. "I kissed you for two reasons. Firstly it was the only thing I could think of to hide you from Victor Vassello and secondly, he's less likely to approach you, knowing someone like me is in your corner." He exhaled slowly. "I'm assuming Vassello discovered Marzetti's whereabouts the same way we did, but someone must have tipped Vassello off about your diamond."

Kallie grimaced. "What do we do now?"

"You don't do anything." Sam guided her along the hallway. "We're going upstairs so you can unpack, and then we're coming down for dinner. I'm not letting you out of my sight, but if I don't eat something soon, I'll keel over."

Kallie led the way up the stairs, chewing her lip. *How am I going to search Bill's office if Sam doesn't let me out of his sight? I could suggest he take Ajax out to do his business.* She swivelled round to do just that and caught Sam's eyes on her bottom. His gaze slowly rose and Kallie's mouth went dry. His eyes had the look of a hungry predator—a very hungry predator and he made no attempt to hide it. She blinked, warmth creeping into her cheeks.

"I'm sure I'm not that tasty."

A slow smile spread over his face. "One taste of you, darlin" and I fear that would be the end of me."

Kallie placed her hands on her hips. "Are you saying I'm poisonous, Samuel Locke?

One eyebrow rose. "Not poisonous—lethal. And don't call me Samuel," he ordered as he moved past her.

Kallie followed, staring at his broad shoulders. "That's the most uncomplimentary thing anybody's ever said to me...Samuel," she pronounced loudly.

Sam stopped, turned and waited until she halted in front of him. She crossed her arms under her shapely breasts and raised her chin defiantly. "Don't you have anything to say?"

He stepped closer, his gaze on her full sensual lips. *They're the first things I'll taste then I'll...* He refocused. "Call me Samuel again, darlin" and I'll tan that pretty arse of yours." He raised his hand and slowly traced his thumb over her lips. They quivered beneath his touch.

"When I said tasting you would be lethal, I meant, one taste wouldn't be enough. I would end up devouring every inch of you."

Kallie's arms dropped to her sides. "Then why didn't you devour me earlier?"

Sam unlocked their door and pushed it wide. "Because I'm not prepared to have a cheap fling with you, because you're... special."

Kallie stepped past him, sat on the bed and stared at him.

Picking up his bedroll, Sam unclipped it and spread it on the floor alongside the bed before rummaging through his duffle bag, conscious that her eyes followed his every move. He frowned. *How has someone as gorgeous and vibrant as Kallie stayed so innocent?*

Sam pulled out his wet jeans and anything else in need of a wash and stuffed them into a plastic bag. He considered Kallie's untutored but eager responses to his kisses. Heat spread, his gut clenched. *She has such a passionate nature. She would be amazing with a little experience.* His world tilted. *I could be her tutor. Christ, what am I thinking?* Sam stamped on the idea and glanced over his shoulder.

"Bill said I could use the laundry, so I'll put a load on and feed Ajax. I want you to stay here and unpack then we'll go get some dinner."

She blinked. "I left him with your friend Talos."

Sam picked up the bag. "I know, which reminds me. Why did you go off without Ajax? If Marzetti or Vassello had tried something, you would have been defenceless."

She shrugged. "What could Ajax have done, he's a dog and they'd more than likely have a gun?"

Sam sighed. "Ajax is a retired military dog, trained in personal protection. He's very intelligent and has decided you're the love of his life, so please take him with you."

"I knew he had good taste." She stood. "I'll change and meet you in the dining room."

Sam opened his mouth to argue then hesitated. *She should be safe enough. I can always get Talos and Ryan to watch the door.* "All right." He glanced at his watch. "If you're not down in half an hour, I'll come looking for you."

"That should be plenty of time." She declared picking up one of her garbage bags and emptying it over the bed.

Plenty of time for what? Sam's gaze followed her as she put clothes in the wardrobe and her carved jewel box on the chest of drawers. He turned to the door.

"Half an hour. Don't make me come looking for you."

"I won't," she called after him.

Sam closed the door and lightly knocked on Talos and Ryan's door. He heard Ajax whine on the other side.

"Who is it?" came Ryan's voice.

"It's me, Sam."

Ryan opened the door. "Did you find Kallie?" he asked pulling the door wide.

"Yes," Sam strolled into the room. "She was over at Liz Macey's house using a computer." He refrained from mentioning what she'd been researching, knowing it would only cause problems. Sam glanced down at Talos who was doing stomach crunches.

Ajax head-butted Sam's thigh.

"G'day mate." Sam gave Ajax a rub then glanced at Ryan and Talos. They were both dressed in black. "I see you two are ready to do a little snooping tonight."

"We're doing it in shifts," called Talos, breathing through crunches. "Jarred doesn't want us all missing at once, so while he, Simon and Nick are having dinner, I'll go through Ken Macey's place and Ryan will go through Les Ferguson's."

"That's assuming Ken, Liz and Fergie are in the pub tonight," interrupted Ryan.

"Yes," agreed Talos. "Then Ryan and I will have dinner while Nick and Simon go through Bill's rooms. We'll leave Bill's office until the early hours of the morning when everyone should be asleep."

"What about you?" Ryan grinned. "Anything special happening tonight?"

Talos chuckled. "Like a midnight rendezvous between the sheets with your roomy."

"No," replied Sam, shutting the door. "I promised Roy I would sleep on the floor and keep Kallie safe and that's exactly what I intend doing." He opened the door. "She's unpacking at the moment, so can you keep watch while I put my washing on and feed Ajax?"

"No worries." Talos said getting to his feet. "Leave the door open. If anyone comes down the hall, we'll see them."

Sam nodded. "Thanks. Come on, Ajax, let's go, buddy."

Ajax bounded out the door and stopped to sniff at Kallie's door.

"No, mate, this way," Sam called heading for the stairs. Ajax gave the door another sniff, pawed at it then came trotting back to Sam.

"You've developed a real thing for her, haven't you?" Sam frowned. *We both have.*

Chapter Sixteen

Leaning into the wardrobe mirror, Kallie applied her lip-gloss and stepped back to study her reflection. As she normally only wore sunblock and moisturiser during the day, she'd decided to go all out tonight. She liked how the soft shade of brown shadow and mascara made her eyes stand out. Kallie's gaze dropped to her new three-quarter sleeved top of vibrant blues and greens. It clung provocatively to her breasts, drawing her eye to the black opal hanging there. Kallie ran a critical eye over her short black skirt, tights and long boots.

"If this outfit doesn't make Sam sit up and take notice, nothing will." Her gaze lifted to her hair, twisted in a French roll and secured with her mother's diamanté clip. The overall effect pleased Kallie and gave her a boost of courage. She placed the lip-gloss on the dresser, picked up her perfume and sprayed a little behind her ears, before walking across the room and opening the door. *I hope this works.*

Kallie was almost to the stairs when she heard a noise behind her, and she glanced back. Talos and Ryan stood together, both dressed in black, and staring at her. Neither spoke, although if the expression on their faces was anything to go by, Kallie had achieved her objective. *Now, if I could just get Sam to react like that.*

"I'm off to join Sam for dinner. It will be busy tonight, so don't leave it too long or you'll miss out," she warned with a smile.

They both gave a nod, but remained silent so Kallie continued to the stairs, grinning with anticipation.

Drumming his fingers on the table, Sam speculated on what could be keeping Kallie. *How long does it take to change?* He glanced around the noisy dining room. Every table was occupied. Jarred, Simon and Nick were sitting with Fergie near the door. Victor Vassello and his two friends sat a couple of tables away. The young bar tender was running back and forth and had already been over twice to see if he was ready to order. He glanced at his watch impatiently. *I'll give her another two minutes.*

As he raised his glass the noise level fell. Sam glanced around to see Kallie standing in the doorway, her olive complexion glowing, her expressive eyes sparkling, her tempting lips smiling. Sam's lungs seized, every muscle locked. He lowered his glass and stood, uncaring that every set of eyes was moving between him and Kallie.

Hauling in a deep breath and slowly exhaling, he willed his body to relax. She started towards him. Sam's gaze flitted to her breasts, encased in a clinging creation of colour that drew his eye to her cleavage. His appetite went from hungry to ravenous, heat spreading to his loins. As she cleared the last of the tables obstructing her path, his focus dropped to her short skirt, stockings and boots, directing his full attention to her long slender legs. His brain seized, his mouth dried and his world tilted.

Kallie stopped in front of him, smiled and reached up to kiss him lightly on the cheek. "I hope I didn't keep you waiting too long."

Jaw clenching, Sam pulled out her chair and leaned close. "I know what you're up to, Kallie and it's not going to work." He drew a deep breath and froze as her soft fragrance assaulted his senses. *Delicate yet intoxicating, just like her.* Aware the other diners were still watching, he exhaled slowly.

As she sank onto the chair, his gaze settled on her shining dark hair, twisted and held up by a fancy clip. He held still, his eyes dropping to her delicate ear and slender neck.

"I'm going to strangle you when I get you upstairs," he whispered gruffly.

Softly blushing, she met his gaze as he returned to his seat. "I'd prefer you kissed me."

Sam blinked, unable to believe her audacity. *Little fool.* He glanced around, relieved to see the nearest diners had returned their attention to their meals.

Focusing on Kallie he leaned across the table. "This is not a game, Kallie. You don't want to get mixed up with me."

"Yes, I do." She calmly picked up her menu.

Sam growled. "Kallie, if we take this any further, you're going to get hurt when we have to end it."

"Why do we have to end it, Sam? It's obvious we're attracted to each other, so why can't we see where it takes us."

Sam shook his head. "Because, it's not going to take us anywhere. I don't believe in happy endings, Kallie. I've told you that already."

"I do." She reached out and softly touched his hand.

He fought not to react and instead softened his voice. "I don't want to hurt you."

She smiled. "Then don't."

Sam grimaced as the young bartender appeared, along with Liz. Her gaze ran over Kallie then shot to him, one eyebrow raised. She pulled out a chair and sat. Sam inwardly groaned. *There goes any chance of reasoning with Kallie.* He reminded himself that he'd successfully evaded women with far more experience than Kallie. *I will just keep her at arm's length.*

Liz glanced around. "They're closing the bridge in the morning so most of these people are only here to learn of any updates for the expected flood, then they'll be leaving." Her attention turned to Kallie. "You might be better off staying at my place, love, otherwise you'll be stuck out at the farm."

Kallie lifted her shoulders in a non-committal shrug.

Sam frowned. *So Liz doesn't know Kallie's staying at the pub.*

The bartender cleared his throat. "Can I take your orders?"

They each gave their order then Liz's gaze settled on Sam.

"Bill asked me to let you know three men booked in to the pub while we were all at the river." She glanced across to Vassello's table. "Bill also said he'd give you free accommodation if you'd consider staying a few extra days, and your helicopter would certainly come in handy in an emergency."

Sam shot a look across the room. Vassello's gaze was trained on Kallie, keen interest evident in the way his eyes didn't leave her. *Over my dead body.*

"That shouldn't be a problem," Sam kept his voice even and his expression calm, although he felt anything but. *I can't risk putting*

Kallie in a room on her own, not with Vassello here. "Where are Bill and Ken? I haven't seen them tonight?"

Liz met Sam's gaze. "With this crowd they're a little short-staffed, so Ken and Bill thought it better they stay in the kitchen and help out."

Sam glanced towards the kitchen. *How convenient. This would have been a great opportunity for Vassello to identify Marzetti for us.* He looked across at Vassello who had turned his attention to Jarred's table, or was it Fergie who sat with his back to Vassello and wore his old woollen hat. *That's twice now I've caught Vassello staring at Fergie.* A small part of Sam relaxed. *I'd rather he stared at Fergie than Kallie.*

Kallie smiled across the table. "It looks like we'll all get to know each other a lot better over the next few days."

"Yes," agreed Liz, her eyes narrowing. "That generally happens when a flood hits."

Sam levelled a cautionary glare at Kallie who chose to ignore it. She chatted idly with Liz about the wonderful friendships that came out of disasters. Sam bore it all silently as he planned his revenge.

He was tucking into homemade apple-pie when Kallie excused herself and stood.

"I'll be back in a moment, I just need to check in with Roy and Angus." She twisted the ring on her finger. "I'll see if they need anything."

Sam narrowed his eyes and watched her glide out of the dining room. He glanced across the room and noted Jarred, the boys, Victor and his goons, plus a fair few locals watching her as well. *That woman ought to be locked up for her own safety.*

Kallie stepped into the kitchen, called out a greeting to Maud and Lil, the two women who ran the hotel's bistro. Ken stood at a sink scrubbing saucepans. Kallie walked round the back of the counter where Bill was frying chips.

"There you are, Bill."

He looked up, his forehead covered in sweat. "What can I do for you, Kallie?"

"Can I please use your phone to call Roy and your computer to check my emails?"

"Sure. The computer is on—take as long as you like."

"Thanks, Bill."

Kallie hurried to Bill's office and closed the door behind her. Her gaze skimmed the room. *For a rough looking guy, Bill keeps his office very tidy.* She sat on the swivel chair and pulled out each of the four drawers, checking the contents as quickly and carefully as she could. Then she turned her attention to the bookcase under the window. *Nothing that points to Bill being Marzetti.*

Approaching footsteps sent her in scurrying back to the computer. She brought up her web browser and was typing in her email account when the door opened. Bill came in and closed the door.

"Sorry to interrupt, Kallie, but I've been thinking."

"Oh?" Kallie looked up, her heart racing.

"Now that you've found the diamond, I think it would be wise to put it somewhere secure and there's no better place than in the safe here." He indicated a picture on the wall.

Kallie raised an eyebrow. "Are you telling me there's a safe behind that picture?"

"Yes, and it needs both a key and combination to open it."

"I see." Kallie leaned back in the chair. "That's very kind of you, Bill, but I don't have the diamond with me."

He scratched his beard. "What if the farm floods?"

"There's not much I can do now."

He shrugged. "I can drive you out there tonight or early in the morning before they close the bridge, then we'll come back and chuck the diamond in the safe."

Kallie pretended to consider Bill's offer. She looked at the picture. "Can you show me how secure your safe is?"

"Sure." Bill eagerly lifted the picture off the wall and pulled out a set of keys.

Kallie came round the desk as he inserted a key then turned the dial. *Right three revolutions, stop on 50, left two revolutions, stop on 10, right one revolution, stop on 70.*

The door popped open.

"I suppose it's a good idea to keep it somewhere secure." She reached up and closed it as the office door swung open and Brendan, the young bartender, burst in.

"Bill, come quick, there's a huge dog in the kitchen and he's got Maud bailed up."

Bill dashed out of the office. "Good boy, Ajax." Kallie quickly opened the safe and peered in. Aside from a bag of coins there were several banded bundles of fifty-dollar and hundred dollar notes. She lifted them aside and slid out a large envelope "Hmm, let's see what we have here?"

"What the hell are you doing?" Kallie jumped as Sam's angry voice interrupted her.

Kallie whirled round, dropping the envelope. "Far out, Sam. You scared the living daylights out of me, again."

He strode across the office, picked up the envelope and handed it to her. "Put that back exactly how you found it."

"But, it could be evidence proving Bill is Marzetti."

"Christ, Kallie." He ran his hand through his hair. "Just put it back."

Kallie snatched the envelope and slid it back under the bundled notes. "Happy?"

"No. What do you think you're doing?" he demanded, closing the safe.

Kallie rolled her eyes. "I'm proving Bill is Marzetti."

"No…you're…not." He took the key out, picked up the picture and rehung it, then tossed the keys to her.

Kallie opened her mouth to argue when heavy footsteps came hurrying down the hall. "Quick, look natural." She dived for the chair, dropped the keys on the desk and clicked on her email account. Sam glowered at her and sat on the corner of the desk.

The door swung open and Bill entered, breathing hard. Kallie had to admit, Sam looked completely relaxed, as if he'd sought her out for a friendly chat. Only his eyes as they met hers indicated his simmering temper.

Bill's panicked eyes looked from Kallie to the picture then Sam who slowly stood.

"I hope you don't mind me popping in to see Kallie? I saw one of Vassello's men leave the dining room and wanted to check he hadn't followed her."

Bill visibly relaxed. "No, not at all." He crossed to the desk and picked up his keys. "Don't forget my suggestion, Kallie. Better safe than sorry," he called as he left the office.

As soon as Bill's footsteps faded, Sam turned to Kallie. "What suggestion?"

"Bill wants me to get the diamond and put it in his safe." She rolled her eyes. "It doesn't take a genius to figure out he plans to steal it."

Sam's eyes narrowed. "Maybe, maybe not. Still it's better not to be alone with him or Ken for the time being. Come on, the meeting is about to start."

"But what about that envelope? I've got the combination."

"Not your problem, Kallie. Leave it to us." He walked to the door. "Coming?"

"You go. I need to call Jane."

Sam hesitated. "All right, meet me in the foyer in five minutes."

"Okay, I'll come and find you as soon as I'm done."

He nodded and left. Kallie waited until she was sure he wasn't coming back and reached for the phone. After three rings, Jane answered.

"Hello, Jane speaking."

"It's me," Kallie whispered. "How's the search going?"

"Kallie! I thought it was Mum. I'm glad you called."

"Why?"

"I think Ken is Marzetti."

"What?"

"I found a huge file on a man named Victor Vassello and two hand guns and bullets. They were all in a sealed cardboard box."

"Wow," exclaimed Kallie. "That's the man who was in the pub last night."

"Yes, I know. There's a photo of him in the file. I'm about to read the notes."

"Be careful, you don't want Ken to catch you," Kallie warned.

"He won't. I've turned all the main lights out and I've got the file in my bedroom. They'll think I'm asleep and won't bother me, but tell me, how are things going with Sam?"

Kallie made a sound of disgust. "They're not. He was really angry earlier because he couldn't find me and I hadn't kept Ajax with me. He said I had him worried sick."

"So he does cares. What else?"

"When he found out I'd been researching the SAS and Marzetti, he ordered me to stay out of it. Then Victor Vassello turned up with his two sidekicks and Sam kissed me, apparently to show Victor we're together."

"What did Victor Vassello want?"

Kallie expelled a breath. "To make me an offer for the diamond."

"I think Sam's making excuses to kiss you."

"Hm."

"Kallie, anyone can see he likes you, but something is holding him back."

"Maybe his heart's been broken and he's too scared to risk it again."

"Sam Locke doesn't strike me as a man who's scared of anything. This goes much deeper."

"So what do I do?" Kallie asked.

"You could always ignore him and flirt with his friends," Jane said. "If Sam cares half as much as I think he does, then he won't want anyone else to have you and it might..."

"Might what," asked Kallie.

"Shush, I hear something," Jane whispered. "Crap, someone's at the front door. Mum and Ken must be back."

"Okay, hide the file under your bed and turn the light out. I'll talk to you in the morning." Kallie hung up, logged out of her email account and left the office. As she walked past the kitchen she glanced in and froze. Ken stood at the sink scouring a pan and Liz stood beside him, drying a saucepan. *If Ken and Liz are here, then who is....*

Kallie ran, almost colliding with Sam as he stepped off the stairs into her path. Her brain registered the odd fact that he'd changed and now wore a black skivvy and black jeans like Talos and Ryan, but she didn't have time to wonder why.

"Jane's in trouble, I have to go."

His hand shot out and shackled her wrist. "Jane! I thought she went back to Sydney with her husband."

"No, she stayed here to help me catch Marzetti and..." Kallie bit her lip. "Please, Sam, let me go. Someone is at her house." Kallie tried freeing her wrist. Sam's fingers tightened.

"Fuck, Kallie. I told you to stay out of this. Now I find out Jane's helping you?"

"Yes, and once she figures out it's not Ken or Liz at the door, she might confront the intruder with a gun."

"Fuck."

"Will you please stop saying that word and help me?" Kallie tugged at her hand. "Jane could be in trouble. We have to help her."

"You stay here." Sam released her wrist. "You've done enough damage for one night."

Kallie wanted to argue, but one look at his granite-like face, clenched jaw and cold eyes had her balking. *He's really angry.* She crossed her fingers and nodded.

"Get Ajax. He's tied up on the back porch, and then go straight to our room," he dropped their room key in her hand, turned and ran.

Kallie's gaze dropped to the key. *I am not going to stay here while my best friend is in danger.* She ran through the foyer and peeped out the front entrance. Sam was halfway down the street. She ran along the porch using the cars as a shield in case he glanced back.

Kallie growled with frustration. "I may have it bad for you, Sam, but Jane's like a sister to me and I would do anything for her." She shrieked as Donna Ross stepped from the shadows at the side of the pub, a cigarette held high between her fingers.

"Anything?" Donna asked in a sarcastic voice. "Even give up your precious bloody diamond. Would you do that, Kalista?" she slurred.

Kallie took a step back. "Donna. Are you drunk?"

Donna gave an unpleasant laugh. "Drunk, well hell yes. What else is there to do in this God forsaken place?" She turned unsteadily and wandered down the porch.

Kallie dismissed Donna's ranting and ran as fast as her heeled boots would allow. On reaching Jane's house, she unzipped her boots, pulled them off and tossed them on one of the cushioned porch chairs. *Where is Sam?* Glancing around for a weapon, she spied Ken's golf umbrella and grabbed it. The front door opened silently and Kallie stepped into the darkened hall. *Why is it so quiet?* She swallowed and tiptoed along the carpet, past Liz and Ken's closed door, her heart pounding. Kallie stopped at the open lounge room door and bit her lip as she peered around the doorjamb, searching for movement. *Nothing, where are they?* Inhaling a shaky breath, she crept past the lounge and stopped at Jane's door, reached for the handle and slowly turned it.

A squeaking floorboard in Liz's bedroom propelled her through Jane's door without a second thought. She wheeled, her breathing way too loud and closed the door. Sliding sideways, Kallie slammed into Jane's chest of drawers.

"Oomph." She gasped rubbing her elbow.

"Kallie—Is that you?"

Kallie exhaled, relief flooding her. She peered around the dark room. "Where are you?"

"Under the bed."

"Gee whiz, Jane, that's the first place he'll look. Quick, come out and hide behind the door. We need to take him by surprise."

Kallie crept forward, hands outstretched, using a ribbon of light from the window to guide her. Jane's darker shape slid awkwardly from under the bed.

"Here, let me help you." Kallie reached for Jane's arm and heaved her to her feet.

"What are you doing here?" whispered Jane, her voice shaking.

"I saw Ken and Liz at the pub." Kallie pressed Jane against the wall behind the door. "We just have to stay quiet while Sam deals with the intruder."

"Sam's here too?" whispered Jane.

"Yes. He must have gone around the back. I heard someone in the kitchen and I think the intruder was in your Mum's room."

"Shit, Kallie. I could have shot you or Sam."

"What!"

Jane thrust a gun into Kallie's hand and took the umbrella. "I loaded it when I saw a shadow and realised it wasn't Mum or Ken at the door.

The door handle turned. Jane pulled Kallie against the wall as the door slowly opened. A torch beam roved over the room. Kallie's heart thundered, she could hear Jane's heavy breathing, or was it her own. Swallowing, she started to raise the gun. Suddenly the door flew away exposing them to two very big black hulks. Jane screamed and swung the umbrella, catching one of the hulks on the shoulder. He didn't move.

Kallie raised the gun and fired into the ceiling. "Leave us alone," she screamed.

Strong hands tore the gun out of her hands, then an arm of steel clasped her around her waist and she was lifted off the ground. Kallie kicked out violently, punching into her captor with both fists. He caught her arms and crushed her against his chest.

Jane cried out and Kallie saw red. She tried slamming her head into her captor's forehead, but he was too tall. She tried digging her nails into his chest, but couldn't get enough leverage. She opened her mouth wide and bit into his shoulder. He swore, dumped her on the bed and landed on top of her, securing both hands above her head.

"Be still," he roared.

Kallie stilled, the light went on and she blinked in confusion. "Sam?"

"I really am going to tan your backside," he thundered, releasing her hands.

"Sam." Kallie wrapped her arms around his shoulders and hugged him. "I thought you were the intruder."

He pulled her arms away and stared at her with cold, emotionless eyes. Kallie flinched.

"I was just trying to help," she whispered.

His jaw clenched. "I don't need your help, Kallie."

"I—"

"I told you to stay at the pub." He glared at her. "You could have shot someone or been killed."

"But I—"

He pressed a finger to her lips. "Talos and I are trained to react swiftly and effectively to any threat." His voice had dropped to a low growl. "I could have killed you, Kallie."

Kallie shivered. "What about the intruder?"

Sam leapt off the bed. "That was Talos. We thought Jane had left town with her husband. With Ken and Liz at the pub, it seemed a good opportunity to search the house."

Kallie sat up. "And you didn't tell me?"

"No." Sam looked across the room.

Kallie followed his gaze and gasped. Talos had Jane imprisoned within one arm and had his hand over her mouth. Jane's eyes were wide with fear.

"Let her go," Kallie demanded, jumping off the bed. Talos stared at her unmoving.

"I said, let her go." Kallie stalked over and pulled his hand and arm away. Jane gave a cry and clung to Kallie.

"How dare you scare her," yelled Kallie. "Get out."

Talos looked towards Sam. "We can't jeopardise our investigation. We need to remove these two."

Kallie and Jane both gasped then Jane clutched her tummy and bent over double.

"Oh no."

"What," exclaimed Kallie. "Is it the baby?"

"Yes, I'm having a contraction."

Kallie glared at Talos. "Now look what you've done."

"When's it due?" Talos demanded.

"Four weeks," Jane cried, her voice shaking.

Talos came forward, took Jane's arm and gently steered her to the bed. "Lie down, keep your feet up and breathe slowly. It might be a false alarm."

Kallie hovered, not sure what to do. "Maybe I should get Liz," she offered.

"No," The three of them spoke at the same time.

Kallie looked doubtfully at Jane. "Why not?"

"It could be a Braxton Hicks contraction. I've been getting a few lately."

"What the hell are they?" Sam's voice was cold.

Jane rubbed her belly. "Hardening and softening of the uterus. For some reason mine are starting to get painful."

Kallie turned to Sam and Talos. "We won't jeopardise your investigation. We want Marzetti caught as much as you do."

Liz's voice sounded in the hall. "I don't understand why the front door is open and all the lights are out."

Sam and Talos moved so fast, Kallie's head spun. They had the window open and were through as a light knock sounded at the door.

"Jane, love, is everything all right." The handle turned as the window slid shut.

Liz stuck her head in, Ken stood behind her. "Kallie, I thought you'd gone home." Liz looked at Jane. "Sweetheart, what's wrong, you're both flushed?"

Jane waved her hand aimlessly. "I just had a couple of Braxton Hicks contractions and they scared us."

Liz came into the room. "They're very common towards the end of a pregnancy. You just take it easy, love."

A loud knock sounded at the front door. "I'll get it," called Ken.

As Liz fussed over Jane, Kallie stepped onto small bits of ceiling plaster and prayed Liz wouldn't look up. Sam's voice came clearly down the hall. "I came to collect Kallie. Is she ready to go?"

Kallie's eyes locked with Jane's. Jane smiled. "Who dares wins, Kallie. I'll be fine."

Nodding, Kallie walked out of the room, her gaze briefly connecting with Sam's.

"I'm ready."

"Drive carefully," called Liz.

Sam gripped Kallie's elbow and guided her down the hall.

Ken opened the door. "Don't forget they're closing the bridge to everything but four wheel drives in the morning, so if you want to stay in town, you'll have to get back early."

"Okay, see you tomorrow." Kallie ran out to the porch and pulled on her boots. "Ready," she called as she joined Sam at the gate.

He nodded and started towards the pub. Kallie had to run to keep up. "You really should have told me Talos was at Jane's house. It would have saved a lot of trouble."

He stopped. "Kallie, I don't need to tell you anything, because you are not part of my team and we are not in a relationship." He stalked off ahead of her.

Kallie frowned and slowly followed. *I know he's attracted to me, but why is he so determined to fight it? What happened to him? Maybe I should take Jane's advice.*

CHAPTER SEVENTEEN

Waiting for Kallie to catch up, Sam was surprised to see a crowd of people leaving the hotel. He looked at his watch as Les Ferguson stepped out onto the porch. "Evening, Fergie. What's happening, it looks like a mass evacuation?"

Fergie ambled over. "The State Emergency are closing the bridge in half an hour, so if you're not planning on staying in town, you better get going now."

Sam glanced down at Kallie as she stopped by his side. She smiled at Fergie.

"Will they open it again in the morning, Fergie or leave it closed?" she asked.

Rubbing his beard, Fergie shrugged. "Have to wait and see, Kallie. We'll have another look early tomorrow." His gaze dropped to Kallie's boots then tracked back up to her face.

"Crikey, Kallie. I've never seen you looking like this before. Poor Liz nearly had a heart attack when she saw you come in the dining room and she ain't the only one."

"Why?" Kallie asked.

"Because you look the spitting image of your mother. She was a real beauty too and always dressed real nice. I can remember a lot of us idolised her, but she only had eyes for your dad, and he felt the same about her." He gave Kallie a sad smile. "Such a shame. I ain't never seen two people so in love."

Kallie's chin dropped and her gaze became fixed on her boots. Sam silently cursed and put his hand on her back intending to steer her forward. Her head came up and tear-filled, beautiful brown eyes locked with his. She drew a shaky breath and smiled. Sam's heart lurched. He felt an overwhelming need to put his arms around her and hold her.

"Fergie's right," she whispered. "My parents adored each other and they adored me."

A cold vice clamped around Sam's heart, his jaw clenched. "Then you were extremely lucky, Kallie. A lot of married couples make each other's lives a living hell and couldn't care less where their children are or what they're doing."

Kallie frowned. "Are you talking from personal experience, Sam, or is this just an observation of yours?"

Sam manoeuvred Kallie aside as another group of locals came out of the hotel. "Both."

Fergie began to move off then turned back, his gaze on Sam. "We'll be filling sandbags first thing in the morning and could do with some extra muscle, if you and your mates got nothing better to do?"

Sam glanced at the mountain of sand he'd seen dumped by the pub earlier. It now had a tarp covering it. "Shouldn't be a problem."

Fergie gave a nod. "In that case, you better stay at the pub tonight. Kallie knows the way home."

Sam's lips twitched. "I'll get right on to it."

Fergie gave a wave and headed off down the street.

A chuckle had Sam glancing at Kallie. She showed no sign of her earlier distress.

"I may be barking up the wrong tree here, but I think the whole town has conspired to keep you and your friends in town so they can put you to work."

"Hm, I think you're right." Sam dropped his hand an inch and lightly guided Kallie up the steps and into the hotel's foyer.

As they walked towards the bar, Vassello and his two sidekicks came out and headed for the stairs. Vassello hesitated then glanced at Sam and appeared to reconsider. Sam steered Kallie past them.

Kallie entered the bar and glanced around. Except for Brendan, who stood on the other side of the bar chatting to Jarred, there were no locals left there. Talos and Ryan were playing a game of pool and had replaced their black clothing with jeans and white T-shirts. Kallie's eyes narrowed. *That's why they were dressed completely in black. Talos must have been sent to search Ken's house while Ryan searched Fergie's.* Her eyes skimmed the room again. *Where are the other two?*

Swiftly turning to Sam, she caught his gaze locked on her. Kallie's breath hitched and instantly the shutters came down over his eyes. He smiled, his face devoid of emotion. *He does want me, but why hide it? What do I have to do to get him to admit he has feelings for me?* Jane's advice rang in her ears. *Who Dares Wins.*

"Where are Simon and Nick tonight?" she asked.

"In their room, I assume," he drawled. "It's been a long day."

"Really—I'm surprised they're not searching Bill's rooms while he's in the kitchen."

One of Sam's eyebrows rose. Kallie gave him her sweetest smile. "We should discuss our plan of attack. I can tell you what Jane and I have learned and you can tell me what you and your team have learned."

Sam groaned then guided her across the bar to a far table and pulled out a chair for her. "What exactly have you learned, Kallie?"

"Well," Kallie slid down onto the chair. "Ken has a thick file on Victor Vassello and a couple of guns. Jane's got the file under her bed, but I can get it for you."

Sam's eyes narrowed. He stood over her. "Kallie, I don't need your help, nor do I want you putting yourself or Jane at risk. I will get the folder."

"But I'm the best..."

"No." He leaned closer, his voice a low rumble. "The man I'm after is a very dangerous individual who won't think twice about killing you or anyone who gets in his way."

"Fine, but what about us?"

"There is no us. You have a romantic view of the world. I don't and I'm not into starry-eyed virgins. Once this job is over, I'm out of here and you would do well to remember that."

He's still pushing me away. Kallie's chin came up. "I'm not starry-eyed. I know what I feel and I know what I want.

Sam's lips twitched. "But you are a virgin and I definitely avoid those."

"Very well." Kallie stood. "In that case you won't mind if I go and mingle. Perhaps I can find someone who isn't frightened of virgins. Perhaps one of your friends."

"Kallie."

Ignoring the warning in his voice, Kallie stepped round Sam and headed for the other side of the room where Talos and Ryan were playing pool. *I'm not giving up on you yet, Sam Locke.*

"Hi, may I join you?" She smiled at each of them.

Both men shot glances across the bar to where Sam was standing.

"Don't worry about him," Kallie scoffed. "He just told me he has no romantic interest in me whatsoever, and it's too early to go to bed yet."

Ryan glanced at Talos and shrugged. "I'm game."

"Sure, why not," replied Talos, handing her a cue.

Kallie walked round the table where she could keep an eye on Sam who had moved to a bar stool beside Jarred and sat scowling at her.

Good.

They played a couple of games then Nick and Simon appeared. Suddenly Kallie found herself surrounded by four very tall, very overpowering, handsome men, who seemed set on making her laugh as they tried to outdo each other. Each time she glanced Sam's way he was glaring, not at her, but his friends. She noticed they all occasionally looked his way too, but other than appearing a little stiff, he didn't show any sign of interfering, so eventually they ignored him and concentrated on her.

He is so frustrating. What do I have to do to get a reaction?

Kallie let Nick buy her a couple of glasses of sparkling wine, the first one making her giggle when the bubbles went up her nose. Sam's eyes narrowed but he made no attempt to intercede or join her. Kallie huffed. *Fine, if he wants to be a dog in the manger, so be it. I'm going to enjoy myself.*

After another hour of harmless fun they wound up their game. Talos, Ryan and Simon wandered over to the bar for another drink. Kallie found herself alone with Nick, who had a distinctive gleam in his eye. Deciding her plan sucked and she needed to rethink her strategy, Kallie pulled out her room key.

"Goodnight, Nick. Thanks for your company and a very entertaining evening."

He smiled. "It doesn't have to end yet, Kallie." He winked and Kallie dropped the key. Nick bent, picked it up and handed it to her, his hand closing round hers.

"I can easily take Sam's place and...keep an eye on you tonight." He squeezed her hand and Kallie almost choked. Sam came to his feet, his eyes narrowed. *Finally I get a reaction.* Kallie swallowed and pulled her hand free.

"No, need. I'm happy sharing with Sam, plus I have to be up early tomorrow." She backed away. "I'll see you later...I mean tomorrow." Kallie turned quickly on her heel and fled, her cheeks burning.

In her room she sagged against the door. *So much for making Sam jealous, he barely cared that Nick propositioned me. Far out, that was awkward.*

A firm knock vibrated against the middle of her back. Kallie squealed and jumped away. *Holy crap it's Nick. What am I going to do?* She chewed her nail, staring at the door. *I have to get rid of him.* Another firm knock sounded.

"Just a minute," she called. *I'll just open the door and calmly tell him I'm not interested and then I'll tell him I'm sorry if he got that impression and I'll...*

Another knock sounded, louder and firmer. "Okay, I'm coming." Taking a deep breath, Kallie opened the door. "Look..." Her eyes widened.

"Sam?"

Kallie gasped and stepped back, away from the fury radiating from Sam. He advanced towards her, his eyes glowering, his fists clenched. She baulked when he slammed the door and locked it. Kallie swallowed. "Um, I thought you were, Nick."

Sam's first instinct was to grab Kallie, throw her on the bed and sate his hunger. Show her exactly what her little experiment had done to him. Maybe when she was flat on her back naked, and he was deep inside her she might realise exactly how vulnerable she was. Or maybe he should give her a good hiding for putting herself in such a precarious situation. He dismissed that thought instantly. *I could never lay a finger on her in anger.* The thought of what could have happened if she'd flirted with someone other than his mates still infuriated him. *I should stash her in a secure room with an impregnable lock.* His control hung by a thread.

She backed all the way to the bed. He followed, staring hard at her. Her cheeks were delicately flushed. His gaze dropped to the slender column of her throat, the firm, full swells of her breasts, rapidly rising and falling, her narrow waist and long, slender legs. Without thought his body responded and he stepped closer, closing his fingers round her upper arms, trapping her between him and the bed, their bodies touching from thighs to chests. Her breath hitched and she shuddered, but the eyes looking into his showed awareness not fear.

Sam pulled back on his desire, determined not to give in. *Perhaps if I give her a taste of what I'm feeling, it might scare her off.* He hesitated. *But will I be able to stop?* He lowered his head, brushing her lips once, twice, three times. Her lashes fluttered and a soft moan escaped as she stretched up to meet him with her own light kisses. Sam's wits scrambled, he covered her lips and deepened the kiss. Her instant response beckoned and his hardened senses reeled. He angled his head, deepening the kiss. When her lips parted, he claimed her mouth, sliding his hands down to cup the globes of her bottom and draw her hard against his erection. She gasped before melting against him, her fingers clenching the sides of his shirt as she touched her tongue against his.

Rocking into her, Sam sent them both tumbling onto the softness of the mattress. Kallie squeaked and stilled, her eyes blinking rapidly at him. Sam slid his hand over her hip to her rib cage watching her closely. Her eyes grew wider but she didn't stop him.

"Do you have any idea how close Nick came to taking up your invitation? I had to stop him following you up here."

Kallie inhaled a shaky breath. "I didn't invite him up and I had no intention of sleeping with him. I only want you." She swallowed. "I've only ever wanted you." She stared at him from bright eyes, her face flushing. "I was trying to make you notice me."

"Bloody hell, Kallie, I've done nothing but notice you since I first set eyes on you."

She smiled. "Really?" Not waiting for his answer, she wrapped her arms around his neck and whispered. "Please kiss me again, Sam?"

Sam groaned and took possession of her mouth again, slowly and thoroughly, his hand closing over her breast. She arched into his palm, her arms tightening. Sam kneaded gently, deepening the kiss. Under his hand her nipple hardened through the soft fabric. Sam drew up her skirt, pushed her thighs wide and eased into the junction at the top of her legs. She stilled. It didn't ease his need. His hand firmed over her breast and he thrust harder against her.

She gasped, pulling her head away. Wide eyes blinked at him. *Now I've got your attention.* Sam rubbed his thumb roughly over her nipple and thrust again.

"Is this what you want, Kallie? A night of sex, no strings, no commitment, because that's all I can offer you?" Sam forced his body to still and waited.

Confusion clouded her eyes. She cleared her throat. "I want to get to know you, Sam. I don't want sex; I want you to make love to me. I want a relationship with you."

"No. I told you. I'm not into relationships."

She squirmed beneath him, sending another wave of desire crashing through his body. "Why? What made you this way? She gently touched his cheek.

Sighing in frustration, Sam rolled onto his back, bringing her with him to rest against his side. He was reluctant to lose the contact just yet, but she did deserve an explanation.

"I've seen too many marriages, including my own parents, fall apart and the kids are the losers. They're used as tools by their parents to hurt each other or ignored altogether. I would never subject a child to a life with two parents who hate and despise each other. Believe me, it's devastating to see your parents screaming at each other and blaming you for all their problems."

Kallie rose on one elbow and stared at him, her eyes incredulous. "Your parents did that to you?"

"Yes."

"But it doesn't have to be that way. My parents had a wonderful marriage and even though they were only able to have one child, I was the centre of their world."

He shrugged. "You were extremely lucky. Given time, that may have changed."

"No, they were truly in love." She frowned. "Why did your parents treat you like that?"

Sam closed his eyes. He hated recalling his childhood, *but how else am I going to make her see sense? How else am I going to get her to back off before I hurt her?* Opening his eyes he sighed. "My parents had a volatile relationship. When my mother caught my father cheating, she did the same. It resulted in an unwanted pregnancy. My mother knew my father desperately wanted a child so she passed me off as his."

"When I was about five they had a huge argument and my father decided to take me and leave. My mother never wanted me, but took great pleasure in announcing I wasn't his but the result of a one-night stand with a soldier by the name of Eric Locke. They made up again, but from that day forward neither my mother nor my father wanted me. Do you have any idea what that's like? I would have ended up on the streets except for Talos and his father."

A tear ran down Kallie's cheek. Sam raised his thumb and wiped it away. "Now you know," he whispered.

Kallie swallowed, her heart aching for Sam and the child he'd been. "So you changed your name to Locke."

"Yes. When I was old enough I went searching for my real father and discovered he'd been an SAS soldier. He's a nice guy, but we don't see much of each other, plus he lives in Western Australia."

"I would never do that to a child and I would never be unfaithful to the man I marry." She gently traced the side of his face. He tensed under her fingers. "Your parents were weak-minded and selfish and they didn't deserve you."

Repositioning herself, Kallie straddled Sam and cupped his face. "Neither of us is weak minded and I know we have something special." Leaning down, Kallie caught his face in both hands and kissed him lightly. "Please give us a chance, Sam."

She saw the struggle in his eyes. She also knew the moment he made his decision and disappointment flooded her. Sam lifted her off him and climbed off the bed.

"I've told you what I can give you and what I can't. I'm going for a run and when I get back I expect you to be in bed, asleep." He picked up the key and strode from the room, slamming the door behind him.

Crossing her arms, Kallie glared at the door. *I'm not a child.* She shook her head and took two deep breaths. "I will go to bed when I want to go to bed." She climbed off the bed, unzipped her boots and hurled them at the door.

'Stubborn, pig-headed mule. She stripped off her skirt and top and flung them towards the chest of drawers. *Why won't you let me love you? I'm not like your mother.* She shivered. *No man looks at a woman like that or touches her like that unless he wants her, and you want me, Sam Locke.*

"Aarrghh." Kallie walked to the dresser and wrenched the top-drawer open, messing up her neat piles as she searched for her new silky pyjamas. Her eyes fell on the soft lilac nightie she'd also bought in Collie. Her hand hovered between it and her pyjamas. *Do I dare?* A slow smile spread across her face. *Who Dares Wins.* Stripping off her stockings and underwear, Kallie donned the nightie, brushed out her hair and added a touch of perfume. Then she picked up her discarded clothes, turned down Sam's side of the bed and climbed in to wait.

Opening the door soundlessly, Sam peered in, surprised and more than a little disappointed to find no temptress lying in wait for him. The only light came from a lamp in the far corner, saturating the room in a soft glow. His gaze swept the room, finding her curled up on the far side of the bed, sleeping soundly. A deep disappointment invaded his soul. After an hour of soul searching, he'd finally accepted the fact his life was about to change. He might not believe in happy endings but for the life of him, he wanted Kallie and damn the consequences. So here he was, only to find she'd listened for once.

So why do I feel cheated. His eyes fell on the near side of the bed, where the bed covers were neatly turned down in silent invitation. A smile touched his lips at her naivety. *If I were to accept that invitation, honey, you wouldn't be sleeping for long.*

Holding his wet runners he stepped into the room, swearing silently when his big toe connected with a long black boot. He glanced down to see another boot. *So she does have a temper.* As quietly as he could, he closed the door and tiptoed across the room towards the bathroom, only to come to a shuddering halt at the end of the bed. The blanket lay loosely around Kallie's waist leaving her upper body uncovered. The temperature of the room had dropped.

He came round the bed and stopped. His chest expanded, his hands clenched by his sides. Her hair lay spread in silken folds over the pillow, her beautiful face cradled on one hand, the other tucked beneath the pillow. Her long thick lashes lay feathered against creamy cheeks, her full lips curved in the hint of a smile. His gaze skimmed over her golden shoulders to her breasts, clearly defined under the sheer material of whatever she was wearing. It wasn't much and only held by tiny straps on her shoulders. Sam's gut spasmed, his erection jerked, as his body screamed with need.

He switched the lamp off and backed away in disgust. *An hour of hard running and I'm right back where I started.* He tore his gaze away from Kallie and headed for the bathroom and another cold shower. *If that doesn't work, I'll resort to a couple of hundred push-ups. That's guaranteed to kill any lustful thoughts.*

CHAPTER EIGHTEEN

Kallie awakened to the sound of the shower. Blinking, she sat then stared towards the bathroom. *He's back.* A quick glance at the illuminated face of the clock radio told her he'd been gone over an hour. *No wonder I fell asleep.* From the edge of the blind a small slither of light fell across the room. Kallie pursed her lips, narrowed her eyes and planned. *I want him to kiss me, but only if he wants too, and if he really isn't into me, then I have to accept that.*

The shower turned off and Kallie scrambled under the covers, faking sleep but peeping from under her lashes. A minute ticked by before the bathroom door opened and he stepped into the room. Kallie observed the towel slung low on his hips, displaying a huge expanse of bare skin over toned muscle. She held her breath, trying not to react as her eyes feasted. Sam hesitated at the foot of the bed and she waited, hardly daring to breath. Her gaze skimmed the breadth of his muscled shoulders and upper arms, the sculptured planes of his powerful chest, lightly dusted with dark hair, his ridged abdomen. *Oh. My. God.*

Thunder crashed overhead startling them both. Kallie's eyes flew open, locking with his. She quelled a shiver at the lust she saw in his eyes, the reined-in power she sensed. He turned away and Kallie released her breath, closed her eyes, thankful for a minute's reprieve. Keeping her eyes tightly shut, she tracked his movements until she heard slight grunts and heavy breathing. *What's he doing now?*

Lowering the covers, she opened her eyes and peered round the room. *Where is he?* The grunts were coming from the floor at the end of the bed. Curiosity getting the better of her, Kallie sat and peered over the end of the bed, her eyes widening when she found him on the floor doing the fastest set of push-ups she'd ever seen. The strength and power in his arms and shoulders transfixed her as muscles rippled across his broad back and shoulders.

Sliding from between the sheets, Kallie stole round the bed and stopped, her toes in front of his face as he pushed himself away from the carpet. His arms locked, fully extended and his head lifted. Kallie's heart thundered as his gaze rose, travelling slowly up her bare legs, stopping briefly at the hem of her nightie. She swallowed. *What's he going to do?*

Suddenly he was standing, his naked chest inches away. A droplet of water fell from his still wet hair, landed on his massive chest and started a slow descent down his chest, ribs and stomach, disappearing into his navel.

Her eyes lowered further to his boxers hanging low on his hips and an erection that had her blinking. Her gaze shot to his face and she gasped at the blatant lust in his eyes. Awareness blasted through her. *I can't decide what's more fascinating; his chest, his erection or his eyes.* Her heart racing, Kallie cleared her throat and licked her lips. His jaw clenched. *Why is he fighting this?*

She stepped closer, her silk clad breasts brushing his chest. She caught her breath at the sensual contact. His eyes took on a ruthless intensity that immobilised Kallie. Heat invaded her limbs and for the first time, a sense of her feminine power settled within her. *Now, that's more like it.* Raising her hands, she caressed his huge shoulders. Muscles bunched but he didn't attempt to stop her. Unable to tear her gaze from his eyes, Kallie brushed her fingertips down over the hard planes of his magnificent chest, exulting when his breath hitched. Her confidence grew.

"I take it, you like me doing this?"

"Yes," he rasped. "You know I do, but you're a virgin for Christ's sake, Kallie, and that doesn't bode well for what I'm feeling at the moment."

Kallie beamed. "So you do want me?"

He groaned, his hands rising to grip her waist. "Of course I want you, Kallie. I've been in a state of sexual frustration since I met you, but this is a big step and your first time. It should be special and taken slowly. I really don't know if I can do that."

Kallie stretched up and kissed him lightly on his lips. "I trust you, Sam. Show me."

Sam moved one hand to the base of her spine, the other lifted to grip her chin then he traced her lips with his thumb, sending tiny quivers racing through her body.

"If we do this, Kallie, there's no turning back. For better or worse, we see where this... relationship takes us, but I haven't changed my mind about marriage or kids."

Kallie nodded, relief surging. *If he's willing to consider a long-term relationship then he must care, and if that's the case then maybe one day, he'll change his mind about the rest.*

"Fine, now will you please kiss me, Sam?"

"Sweetheart, I'm going to do a lot more than kiss you."

Kallie licked her lips. "Are you going to taste me?"

Sam groaned. *Bloody hell, I'm trying to take this slow and she's out of the barrier and running.* "One step at a time, okay?" He lowered his head and brushed her full soft lips. Any lingering thought of denying either of them fled when her eyelids fluttered and she stretched up into the kiss. He moved his fingers, angling her head to deepen the kiss, coaxing her lips apart so he could plunder and explore. Her pulse leapt beneath his thumb, her eyes flared with awareness and Sam's tight control almost slipped. *One step at a time.*

Ignoring his need, Sam fought to dampen down his desire. *If I'm going to do this, then I'm going to do it properly.* He lowered his hands to circle her waist, intending to slow things down, when she raised her arms, slid her hands round his neck and pressed her glorious breasts into his chest, and her belly against his erection.

Christ almighty.

He squeezed her waist, before spreading his fingers and sliding his hands round to cup and knead her backside. It wasn't enough. He lifted her against his erection.

Stepping closer to the bed, Sam lowered her onto the mattress and followed her down. His hand slid down over the soft material, found the lower edge and slid it above her waist, sliding his hand over her silken thigh, hip, ribs, closing over her breast.

Kallie gasped through the kiss. She'd never imagined making love could be so intoxicating. She sank her hands into his hair, holding him to her, prolonging the kiss as long as she could, consumed by the pleasure invading her senses. His hand left her breast, stroked down her ribs and tummy. He pulled away, rose to his knees and stared down at her.

"You're beautiful." He gripped her lacy underwear and dragged them down.

"Oh." Kallie covered herself with her hands.

"No, don't." Sam drew both her hands away, lowered his body beside her and kissed her again. His hand moved to splay across her belly before sliding slowly down over her curls to cup her. Gasping, she pulled away and his gaze fell to her enticing breasts. He lowered his head, licking one nipple through the material of her nightie. Kallie moaned, arching into his mouth. He chuckled before swirling his tongue over her peaked nipple and sucked. Kallie cried out. He transferred his attention to her other breast and she moaned again. Her body quivered with anticipation.

Sam pressed his leg between her thighs, forcing them apart, then found the flesh he sought, slick and swollen. He parted her folds, pressed one finger inside her and stroked. Kallie's moan filled him with pleasure. This was her first time and he was going to make sure she remembered it forever. He withdrew his finger and thrust it back in again, working his finger within her, revelling in her soft cries.

Holding his control by a thread, Sam pressed a second finger inside her tight sheath, stroking and stretching, pleasuring her before he found her nub and circled. His nerves tightened as she quivered beneath his fingers.

Kallie sucked in her breath, her senses splintered. Sam's mouth closed over her nipple and he sucked. Kallie stiffened and bucked, crying out as ripple after ripple of pure pleasure tore through her. When the final waves of her orgasm ended she drifted back to earth and opened her eyes. He hovered over her, holding himself still.

"It's not too late to change your mind."

"Yes, it is." She met his gaze. "I want it all."

"I was hoping you'd say that." He left her to rummage through his duffle bag, pulled out a condom and then dropped his boxers.

Kallie's gaze lowered to his nice—taut—butt. *We're really going to do this.* She raised her eyes as he turned and settled back on the bed beside her.

"I'll go as slow as I can." He drew her nightie up over her head, tossed it aside and kissed her as he pressed her legs wide. He shifted and lifted over her, sinking between her thighs, trapping her beneath his muscled body.

The hard length of his erection pressed against her. His crinkly chest hair brushed her already sensitive breasts. One of his knees eased her leg wider and a thrill of ecstasy shot through her body.

He gently nudged into her an inch, stretching her. It was uncomfortable, alien. He withdrew and pressed in again. Coiled tension showed in each muscle as he held back and repeated the action again and again, stretching her as his hard length eased in a little further each time. It was overpowering. His hands clamped her hips, holding her as he withdrew all the way. Kallie locked gazes with him. His eyes were almost black, his forehead covered in moisture.

She swallowed. "Do it."

He surged into her, filling her completely. Kallie cried out and stiffened at the sharp, stinging sensation. He stilled, his breathing heavy. "I'm sorry, darlin'."

He slowly withdrew and eased in again. Pulled out and eased in again. Raw desire engulfed her. Kallie moved her hips and met his next thrust. Her body came alive with exhilaration. The stinging disappeared. Her inner muscles contracted like a tightly wound spring about to explode.

He closed his mouth over her nipple, suckling hard. Kallie cried out and dug her fingernails into his arms. His mouth left her breast and he took her without restraint, thrusting faster and deeper. Then he touched her where they were joined, she stiffened, cried out and shattered as wave after wave of sensation swept over her for a second time. He made a guttural sound and collapsed on top of her.

Dragging in a ragged breath, Kallie raised her hands and stroked his hair. "That was incredible. Thank you."

Breathing just as hard he kissed her neck. "It was my pleasure."

As the minutes passed, Kallie lay in a state of sensual wonder, sapped of all energy, content to absorb his weight while she floated back to earth. Eventually he lifted off her and, without saying a word, left the bed and entered the bathroom. Unsure of the protocol in situations like this, Kallie bit her lip and studied his magnificent body as he grabbed the hand towel and soaked it under the hot tap. *What's he doing?"* He turned the tap off and twisted the hand towel tightly then came back to the bed.

"Allow me." He knelt beside her and began sponging between her thighs with slow deliberate strokes. His touch and the delicious warmth of the cloth sent erotic quivers shooting through her again.

Leaning down, Sam kissed her lightly. "That should feel better." He hurled the towel towards the bathroom and sank onto the mattress beside her. For a second, Kallie thought he was going to roll away, but he wrapped his arms around her and drew her against his chest. Kallie's heart filled with joy. She sighed and drifted off, cocooned in the warmth of his arms.

Sam was oddly disorientated and more than a little uneasy as he watched Kallie sleep, curled against him. *I can't ever recall being this affected by a woman.* He considered his past conquests. None had sparked the awareness or the chemistry he felt with Kallie. He searched for any sign of panic. It didn't come. *Another surprise.* He sighed and closed his eyes. *Life is full of surprises.*

Thunder woke Sam in the early hours. He flinched and then relaxed as he registered Kallie's soft body spooned against his. His arm rested on her waist, his hand splayed over one ripe breast and her delectable backside pressed against his groin. He kissed her naked shoulder and closed his eyes again as he considered how he'd wake her in a couple of hours.

Chapter Nineteen

The next time Sam woke he found himself alone and the room bathed in weak sunlight. He frowned and looked towards the bathroom where he could hear the shower running. *Damned woman, I was looking forward to waking her.* He considered joining her in the shower only to dismiss it. Not only was the shower cubicle too small, it also backed onto the wall of Jarred's room and Sam didn't want him hearing Kallie if she cried out. That was for his ears only. Sighing, Sam checked the time and climbed out of bed. *There's always tonight.*

He was dressed and ready to shave by the time Kallie came out of the bathroom. His gaze roved over her neat blouse and jeans. She'd tied her hair back in a band and had a healthy glow in her cheeks. He smiled. "You could have dressed in here. I wouldn't have minded."

"I thought about it, but decided if you woke, I'd never get to work."

Sam smiled. "And I thought it was because you were shy."

"Not at all." She crossed to him, stretched up and kissed him lightly. "I would have loved to have breakfast with you, but I'm late for work, and Liz will be run off her feet in the store today." She pulled on some sandals and placed the key in his hand. "You might as well take the key, but leave the French doors unlocked in case I need to get back in."

Sam smiled and opened the door for her. "I'll watch you from the balcony until you're inside the store, and I'll be over to check on you after I've had breakfast."

Kallie gave him another kiss. "I love you, Sam."

He opened his mouth to say something but closed it again as Victor Vassello strolled past their room and down the hall.

Kallie grimaced. "At least he isn't a local, so our secret is safe for now."

Sam's gaze returned to hers. "Let's take one day at a time, Kallie. I'm still coming to terms with what I'm feeling." He caught a fleeting look of disappointment on her face before she straightened and smiled.

"Okay, one day at a time. Now I really must go. Have a good day." Kallie hurried along the hall and down the stairs, passing Victor Vassello as he stepped into the dining room.

When she reached the store, Liz was just leaving. "Oh, there you are, love. I have a parcel for Bill, but now that you're here, maybe you could take it to him." Liz handed Kallie the package. "By the way, you've lost an earring."

Kallie touched her ears. "Oh, thanks, I'll go look for it after I grab some breakfast. I was running a bit late this morning and haven't had any."

"No problem, Jane's here too, she wanted to talk to you. I'm just running home to check on Ken, he wasn't well this morning."

"Okay." Kallie put her purse under the counter and walked through to the back office. "Hi, Janey, what's up?"

"Hi, you're looking bright and happy. I take it things have improved with Sam?"

"You could say that. How are you feeling?"

"A bit odd, but I haven't had any more contractions. Talos came back last night."

"Why?" Kallie put her hands on her hips. "He didn't try to intimidate you, did he?"

"No. He wanted to apologise for scaring me and take the file I found. He's actually a very nice guy."

"Hmm." Kallie grimaced. "I would have liked to have had a look at that file before you gave it to them. Never mind." She looked at her watch. "I'd better deliver this parcel and find my missing earring. You take it easy today."

"Okay, I'm just going to help Mum out with sorting the mail." Jane waved her off.

Kallie hurried back to the pub, gave the parcel to Brendan who was sweeping the front path then ran round the side of the building. *Best not to advertise the fact, I'm staying here.* Slipping off her muddy sandals, Kallie ran up the outside stairs to the upper porch without meeting anyone. She could hear the rumble of male voices in the next room as she opened her French doors. Her gaze fell on the dresser. *Where's my jewel box?*

In a panic she ran to the dresser and hunted through the drawers and then the wardrobe. It wasn't anywhere. *I shouldn't have asked Sam to leave the door unlocked.* She hurried back through the doors and along the porch. As she neared the next room, she heard the word jewel box and stopped. *That's Sam's voice.*

"From the weight of it, I was sure it had hidden compartments, but I've had no luck."

Kallie flattened herself against the wall. *They've got it, but why?*

"Did you use the skeleton key, I gave you?" One of his friends asked.

Kallie frowned. *Skeleton key?"*

"Yes," Sam said. "She's got some earrings and trinkets, but no sign of the black opal or the Kalista diamond. That's another reason I was sure this box had secret compartments."

Kallie's fingernails dug into her palms, and her stomach roiled. *They want my opal and diamond. I can't believe Sam tricked me.*

Talos's voice made her jump. "Forget the jewel box. We have more important things to discuss. If this flood gets any worse, they'll send in the army and we can't afford to blow our cover or Marzetti will get away."

Sam's voice came from deeper within the room. "Most of the locals are confused as to who we are. Some think we're army personnel and some think we're undercover cops. We should be safe for now."

"What about Kallie? Does she suspect we're guns for hire?" Another of the men asked.

Kallie held her breath. *Guns for hire?*

"No, she thinks we're undercover cops."

A knock sounded and Kallie bit her lip as she waited to see who had arrived.

"Ah, Simon. It's about time you showed up." She recognised Talos's voice. "Did Identiscan reveal anything?"

"Yes." I hacked into the police personnel files. Ken Macey is exactly who he claims to be. I couldn't get into Fergie's file. It's locked."

Kallie released her breath. *At least Jane can relax. But who is Sam? Guns for hire?*

'So what about Bill Murphy?" asked Sam.

"He checks out too. I downloaded his rap sheet and got a facial match. But he did live and work in King's Cross during Marzetti's time there. In fact, he was working in one of Marzetti's clubs when he was arrested for drug and firearm possession."

Kallie blinked. *Bill's been in jail?*

'So he could be protecting Marzetti?" Sam said.

"So could Ken Macey," said Talos. "It was Vassello's warehouse the police were raiding when Ken's partner got killed. Ken wasn't where he was supposed to be and his partner paid the price."

Kallie clamped her hand over her mouth to hold in her gasp. *Shit.*

"So, that leaves Bert Chalmers," said Talos. "He must be Marzetti."

"Oh, that reminds me." It was Simon speaking. "That bullet you pulled out of Kallie's saddle belongs to a 303 rifle and Bert Chalmers has one in his quarters. He also rolls his own cigarettes and they match the ones we found out where Kallie came off her horse."

Kallie's legs began to shake. *So there was a bullet in my saddle and Sam didn't tell me. Far out, Bert was trying to kill me.*

She slid down the wall and put her head between her knees as her head spun. *Stay calm, Kallie, you need to hear this.*

Sam "s voice continued. "When I searched the McNeil place, I came across Kallie's Will in the safe. She's left the farm, lock stock and barrel to Roy."

He searched my home. He lied to me. He used me to get to the diamond. He made love to me. A tear ran down her face.

He betrayed me. Pain lanced through her heart, smashing it into a million pieces. She wanted to march into that room, punch him in the eye, grab her jewel box and tell them all to stick it. But the energy needed to move had deserted her. Kallie wiped her running nose with the back of her hand. They were still talking, but Kallie couldn't hear for the pounding in her ears. *Sam doesn't want me. He wants the diamond.* She rolled onto her hands and knees then stood and padded to the stairs. *I'm not going to let them get away with this and I'll be damned if I'll let Sam know how much he's hurt me.*

She descended the stairs, slipped her sandals on and stumbled across the road to the Store. *I have to warn Jane and then I need to get out of town, away from him.*

As Kallie opened the store's door she was met with raised voices coming from the office. Frowning she walked round the counter. The voices belonged to Jane and Liz and were getting louder. Kallie pulled her purse from under the counter and was about to knock on the office door when Jane's voice stopped her.

"You're moving now, but why couldn't we move after the plane crash?"

"Because Kallie needed me," Liz said. "And I felt obliged to look out for her."

"I needed you," Jane cried. "Why do you think I wanted to go to boarding school?"

"I assumed it was because you wanted to meet other girls and get a good education."

"No. It was to get away from here and my memories of Dad."

"I'm sorry, Janey. You seemed to be fine, whereas Kallie was inconsolable."

"I was hurting just as much as Kallie. At least she still had Roy."

"She nearly didn't. I had to bully him into staying. He wanted to up and leave. It was only the fact he found out he'd been left half the property that he stayed."

Kallie shrank against the counter, clasping her hand over her mouth. *I don't believe this.*

She heard Liz sigh. "I'm so sorry, Janey. I was trying to stay strong for everyone. You should have said something."

"Like what? I hate Kallie for taking you away from me."

"Jane!"

Kallie dropped her purse and backed away as she struggled to process what she'd overheard. The one person in the world she thought she could tell anything, her best friend, hated her. And Liz, who had helped her through the worst year of her life, had only done it out of a misplaced sense of obligation, while discounting her own daughter's needs. And Roy. *No, it can't be true.* Could this day get any worse?

I have to get out of here.

Kallie stumbled out of the store and ran into Fergie.

"Watch where you're going, Kallie. You nearly knocked me flying."

"Sorry." Keeping her head down, Kallie made to slip around him and nearly ran into Victor Vassello and his two minders. One of the men had tape across his nose and blackened eyes.

"What's up?" Fergie said. "You're shaking like a leaf and you're as pale as a sheet."

Struggling to keep it together, Kallie pulled away from him. "Headache. Liz and Jane are in the office, they'll help you."

Fergie hesitated, looked at Victor Vassello then held the door wide. "After you, gents."

Victor Vassello blocked Kallie's escape route as he stared at Fergie for a couple of seconds. He glanced at Kallie. "Actually, it's this young lady, I was looking for." He pulled a photo out of his pocket and held it in front of her. "I was hoping you might recognise this man. He's a friend of mine."

Having no choice but to look at the photo, Kallie glanced down at a woman and a man. The woman's face was obscured by Victor Vassello's thumb. The man she guessed to be in his mid-thirties. He wore sunglasses, had a moustache and scruffy fair hair. A cigarette hung out of the corner of his mouth and a nasty jagged scar ran along the lower edge of one cheek.

"No, he's not from around here."

"Have another look. It's an old photo. He's about sixty-five now and more than likely has a beard."

Wanting nothing more than to find a place she could lick her wounds, Kallie begrudgingly studied the photo again. *So this is Dominic Marzetti.* She shook her head. "It's a pity he's wearing sunglasses. It could be anyone. What do you think, Fergie?"

"Huh?

"Do you recognise the man in the photo?"

After a quick glance, Fergie shook his head. "No, can't say I do."

Kallie frowned at Fergie. *For the biggest sticky beak in town he's not showing much interest. Maybe Fergie's protecting Dominic Marzetti. Geez, I can't handle this.*

"What about the woman?" Victor Vassello said.

I just want to go home. Drawing in a deep breath, Kallie looked at the woman and did a double take. *Holy cow, that's Donna Ross.* Her gaze met his. "Who is she?"

Victor Vassello's eyes narrowed. "Her name is Donatella Rossini. Do you know her?"

Donatella Rossini? Kallie blinked. *What the hell's going on here?* "Um, no."

Victor stared. "You're sure? It's extremely important that I find these two."

"I'm sure."

The door suddenly swung wide and Liz exclaimed. "Good heavens, what are you all doing out here? Kallie, did you get some breakfast?"

Not meeting Liz's gaze, Kallie backed around Victor Vassello and his two muscle men. "I'm not staying. Excuse me." She turned on her heel and hurried down the street.

"Kallie, what's the matter?" Liz called after her. "Where are you off to?"

Not stopping, Kallie broke into a jog. *I might not like Donna, but once those men show that photo round the pub, someone will tell them where she lives and I need to ask her if Bert is Marzetti before they come knocking. Far out, Angus could be in danger.*

Sam called out from the pub's second floor terrace, where he stood with three men. *Go to hell.* She fastened her pace and cut through the church grounds to the street behind.

Donna's house was an old two-bedroom weatherboard building in desperate need of painting. Kallie ran up the path and hammered on the front door. After waiting a minute, she hammered again.

"Donna, open up, it's Kallie McNeil and I need to talk to you urgently."

Movement sounded on the other side of the door as a safety chain was undone. The door opened and a bleary-eyed Donna stared out at her.

"What the hell's all the banging about? You'll wake the bloody dead."

"Donna, I need to talk to you. There's a man called Victor Vassello in town and he's got a photo of you and a man with a scar. I think it's Dominic Marzetti."

Donna's eyes widened, she stepped out and checked the street before grabbing Kallie's arm and dragging her through the front door and slamming it shut. "Are you sure?"

"Yes, he was just at the store, asking if I recognised either of you."

Donna grasped her neck. "What did you tell him?"

"Nothing, I said I didn't know either of you. But he didn't look convinced and he has two nasty looking thugs with him."

"Shit." Donna ran down the hall and disappeared through a doorway.

Kallie followed. *Oh my God, she does know them.* Kallie found Donna in a bedroom pulling a suitcase from under the bed.

"Donna, is Bert's real name Dominic Marzetti?"

"What?" Donna dragged a drawer open and began throwing clothing into the suitcase.

"I want to know who Marzetti is?" asked Kallie.

"No, believe me, you don't." Donna ran to the wardrobe and pulled a couple of dresses off hangers and grabbed some shoes. "Did Victor see you come this way?"

"I don't think so. But if you're afraid to talk to him, we can take a four-wheel drive across the bridge and go to my place."

Laughing, Donna emptied another drawer into the suitcase. "I'm not afraid to talk to Victor." She zipped up the suitcase and dragged it out of the bedroom.

Kallie followed her to the bathroom, where Donna began rifling through the vanity. "Then why are you packing?"

Donna filled a toiletry bag. "Because I'm afraid of what Dominic will do to me if he finds out I talked to Victor."

"You have to tell me the truth, Donna. Is Dominic Marzetti, Bert Chalmers?"

"I'm not telling you anything. I value my life too much." She brushed past Kallie, grabbed the handle of her suitcase and wheeled it through the kitchen and out the back door, still wearing her dressing gown and slippers.

"Wait, Donna. Is your last name really Rossini." Kallie gripped the suitcase handle.

"Get out of my way." Donna snapped.

"It can't be a coincidence. You must be related to Andrew? Should we ring the police before Marzetti hurts someone."

"I don't want him arrested." Donna opened the CRV's rear door, lifted the suitcase in and slammed the door. "Not now when I'm about to reap the benefits of all the years I've spent running after him." She opened the front car door, climbed in and started the engine.

"But..." Kallie sagged against the house as Donna reversed out of the drive, crunched her gears before speeding off down the road. *Has everyone gone mad? Nobody is who I thought they were. Everyone has been lying to me.*

Straightening, Kallie pulled herself together and turned the corner of the house. Sam stood at the end of the driveway with his hands on his hips. *Shit, I can't talk to him.* She turned and ran back around the house.

"Kallie, wait. What's wrong?"

Sam sprinted down the driveway after Kallie.

What the hell is going on?

"Kallie, wait." She was climbing a side fence. *Why is she running from me?* Sam doubled back, ran down the drive, across the front lawn, jumped the small fence and caught Kallie as she came hurtling out of the neighbouring driveway.

"Kallie, what's wrong?"

"Let go of me." She lashed out at him with her hands and Sam caught them.

"I hate you." She kicked him in the shin.

"Christ, Kallie, stop it." He locked his arms around her and held her immobile. "Talk to me, let me help you."

She tried to wriggle out of his hold. "I don't need you or anyone else in this town. Let me go."

"No. Not until you tell me what's wrong. What did Victor Vassello say to you?"

"I'm not telling you anything. The only person I can trust is myself."

Sam cursed as a white Land Cruiser pulled into the driveway behind them. Victor Vassello and his two henchmen climbed out, their gazes fixed on Sam and Kallie.

"Who owns this house?" asked Sam, keeping his voice low.

"Donna Ross, now please let me go."

"Not until you tell me what you're doing here and what's upset you?"

"Fine." Kallie glared at him. "I came to warn Donna, that Victor Vassello has a photo of her and Dominic Marzetti, and to ask her which of our bearded locals is Marzetti. Happy?"

"No. You should have come to me. It's a pretty good bet Donna's gone to warn Marzetti."

"I don't care, but I'm going to scream if you don't let me go." She wiggled again.

Sam tightened his hold. "Scream and I'll pick you up and carry you out of here." He watched as Vassello approached Donna's front door. The other two went round the back.

"Did you recognise Marzetti?"

"No, just Donna," she snapped.

"Then you'd better tell me where she's gone, because her life is now in danger."

"Go to hell."

Donna's front door opened and Vassello entered. Kallie tried to prize Sam's arms apart.

"Damn it, Kallie, what the hell is wrong?"

"I'm never going to speak to you again," she yelled.

"Well, you're going to have to." Sam picked her up and threw her over his shoulder. She gasped and then thumped her fists into his back. Sam ignored her and ran across the street, through the church grounds and onto the main street. A group of people had gathered in front of the store.

"Christ, that's all I need." Sam ducked back behind a thick shrub, lowered Kallie to the ground and pulled her hard against him. "I can't fix this unless you tell me what's wrong?"

"You betrayed me. You lied to me."

"Shush." Sam clamped his hand over her mouth and sneaked another look down the street. The team's white van with tinted windows pulled out from in front of the pub and accelerated in their direction.

"About time." Sam's hold tightened as Kallie struggled harder. *She's found out something about us, but what?*

The van stopped and the side door slid open. Sam picked Kallie up and threw her into Talos's arms. "Get her out of here and keep her safe. She knows something. I'll see if I can find out what happened and catch up with you later."

"No worries, you might want to get Ajax too, I've locked him in my room."

Kallie punched Talos in the shoulder and screamed. He grabbed her hands, Simon covered her mouth, Sam slammed the door shut and Nick drove off.

Sam jogged to the store.

"What's going on, Sam?" Liz looked down the road. "Is Kallie all right?"

"Something's upset her. Did you hear what Vassello said to her?"

"Yeah, I did," Fergie offered. "He showed us a photo of a man and woman and asked if we knew them. Don't know the man, but the woman was Donna Ross. That ain't what upset Kallie though. She came out of the store upset.

"Oh no." Liz cried. "Kallie must have heard us arguing."

Sam glanced at Jane. She was pale and had her hand over her mouth. She met his gaze. "Please tell me she didn't hear that. I was eleven years old. I didn't mean it."

Sam advanced on Jane. "What did she overhear?"

Clearly upset, Liz and Jane told him what Kallie might have overheard. Sam clenched his fists. "That explains a lot, but not why she's mad at me."

"She wasn't mad at you when she came into the store earlier, but then she went back to the hotel to deliver a parcel and find her missing earring."

Sam closed his eyes and silently cursed. *Now I understand. She must have heard the boys and I talking. Fuck, I'm screwed.* All morning he'd been reliving his night with her. Savouring each little moan as he explored her delicious body, her cries of ecstasy as he thrust into her. The powerful thrill of being inside her when she came.

"Where did your friends take her?" asked Jane.

Sam opened his eyes. *Only Fergie knows the truth, so what do I tell the others?* He drew in a deep breath. "I didn't like the way those strangers were looking at Kallie and she was extremely upset, so I asked the boys to take her somewhere safe. If the bridge is open, they may even take her home." It was the best thing he could think of for now.

Ken cleared his throat. "I think we should get back to safeguarding the town against the flood first." He glanced at Liz and Jane. "Then you two can explain yourselves to Kallie when she's had a chance to calm down."

Sam was about to leave when Liz gripped his arm. "Please go after Kallie. She'll be devastated if she heard any of what we said. Please tell her we love her and that Roy didn't think he had a choice in the beginning. He thought the authorities would kick him off the property and never give him custody of Kallie. That's why he was going to leave, but he intended on taking Kallie with him, no matter the consequences. She needs to know that."

Jane wiped tears from her face and blocked his path. "And I didn't mean what I said. I was just saying what I felt at the time and it didn't last long. I missed Kallie too much, so I convinced Roy to send her to boarding school with me."

Relief surged through Sam. "I'm sure once you talk to her, all will be fine." *I may not be so lucky.* "I'll go after her now."

Sam strode out the door and crossed the street to where his truck was parked beside the pub. Pulling out his phone, he rang Ryan.

"Hey, buddy. I need you up in the air. Donna Ross knows Marzetti's identity and she's taken off in a silver CRV. My guess is she's already over the bridge and on her way to alert Marzetti. And keep an eye out for Vassello, he's on Donna's trail."

"Any clues as to who Marzetti is?"

"It might be Bert Chalmers, but if it is, and he thinks we're on to Donna, she will be a liability to him. Angus McNeil could also be in danger."

"All right. The boss is with me, so we'll take a look."

"Thanks. I'll get Ajax and meet up with you as soon as I can."

Chapter Twenty

Refusing to let them intimidate her, Kallie sat on the bench seat, crossed her arms mutinously, and glared at Talos and Simon.

Everything I believed in is a lie. She bit her lip. *Angus is the only person who hasn't lied to me. He openly admits to hating the farm and wanting the diamond so he can get away.* She glanced through to the front cab where Nick sat at the wheel, driving. The only time he'd spoken was to inform Talos, he'd put the child safety lock on so she couldn't get out the sliding door. *Bastards.*

Kallie glanced around the van. The roof was high enough that she could have stood without bumping her head. A narrow counter ran down one side with three computers secured to it. All the windows were heavily tinted. Three chairs with seatbelts fronted the counter, and as Kallie had witnessed, they could swivel, move backwards and forwards or be locked in position. At the moment Talos and Simon were using two of them and tapping away on keyboards.

"What is this, some sort of command centre?"

Simon's lips twitched. "Something like that."

The van slowed and Nick looked over his shoulder. "Looks like Donna Ross must have gone across. The road blocks are smashed."

"Is the van high enough to go through?" Talos looked ahead at the road.

"We'll have to get out and check." Nick called and braked.

Talos stood, hunching to avoid hitting his head and moved to the side door. Kallie feigned disinterest as she heard the safety lock snap off. Talos opened the door, jumped out and closed it behind him.

Damn.

"Keep an eye on our guest," Nick called as he got out the front.

Kallie's gaze met Simon's. "It's not as if I can go anywhere. It's raining, we're surrounded by floodwater and we're miles from town."

Simon turned back to his screen. Kallie dropped her hand to the seatbelt buckle and pressed the release with a soft click. Simon didn't notice as he tapped the keys on his computer. Kallie edged around and glanced into the front cab. The keys were still in the ignition. Talos and Nick were on the bridge, knee deep in water. Kallie chewed her nail as she thought. *The current must be strong; they're struggling to stay on their feet.*

"Oh, no. Nick just got swept off the bridge."

"What?" Simon unbuckled himself and bounded out of his chair.

Kallie stood, blocking his path and view as she looked out the front window.

"No, don't Talos." She clapped her hands to her mouth. "He's gone over too."

Simon grabbed the handle, slid the door open and jumped out. The door slid shut and Kallie locked it, scrambled through to the front and locked the driver's door. As she reached for the keys, she saw Simon come to a grinding halt. Talos and Nick were on their way back to the van. Simon swivelled, astonishment spread across his face as he noticed Kallie in the driver's seat.

"That will teach you." Kallie pushed the gear stick into drive and hit the accelerator.

"No, Kallie, don't," Simon yelled, grabbing for her door handle.

"Huh. You don't think I'd leave it open, do you?"

Talos and Nick were running towards her. "Get out of my way."

They didn't.

She pressed the accelerator down and swerved at the last minute. Talos roared and flung himself out of the way.

Kallie eased off the accelerator as she came to the bridge. The van was heavy, but it still drifted sideways. Swallowing, Kallie gripped the steering wheel and fought to keep the van in the middle of the bridge. Looking in the side mirrors, she saw Talos, Nick and Simon hanging onto the railing as they dragged themselves after her.

"No, go back."

They kept coming.

Kallie drove off the bridge and several metres up the road before she braked and waited until all three men cleared the bridge, cursing when she saw Talos pull out his phone.

"I bet he's calling in that damn helicopter." She increased her speed to fifty kilometres. In every direction, all she could see was water. Kallie's heart thundered as she kept to the middle of the road and peered out through the downpour.

After what seemed like hours, Kallie pulled up in front of her house, surprised to have made it home without sighting the helicopter. Donna's CRV was parked outside Bert's quarters. Rivers of muddy water ran around the tyres. Kallie got out of the van and sloshed up to the path. *At least the house is on high ground.*

Running up the steps, Kallie ignored the front door and headed round the porch to her bedroom. The rain pelted down, blocking out all else. Kallie ran across to her bedroom and cracked the door opened. There was no sign of anyone. Grabbing her dressing gown, she dried her face and arms. *I need to warn Angus and find somewhere safe for us to hide out while I decide what to do.*

She ran to the drawers, pulled out dry clothes, stripped and redressed. Then opening her door, she tiptoed down the hall, past the lounge to the kitchen.

Where's Angus? She retraced her steps, knocked lightly on his bedroom door and entered. It was empty. Frowning, Kallie sat on the bed. *I wonder if they went into town.* Her gaze fell on a photo beside the bed. It was the one Wally had shown her of him, Angus and Bert. They all wore baggy shorts, work boots and hats. Beards covered their faces and numerous tattoos covered their arms.

All I have to do is match up the tattoos. I bet Bert killed Wally so he wouldn't blow his cover. She chewed her lip. *The night Wally arrived, Bert was in town and he stayed at Donna's house. It has to be him.*

Kallie left Angus's bedroom and went to the kitchen. Glancing out the window, she gasped. Bert was dragging Donna towards the house and he had a gun in his hand.

"Shit."

Jumping out of sight, Kallie searched for something she could use as a weapon.

"I thought you were staying in town?"

Kallie whirled. "Angus."

"If it's not droughts, it's bloody floods. This place gives me the shits."

Running across the kitchen, Kallie grabbed the handles of the wheel chair. "We have to hide. Bert is some underworld boss and he's got a gun."

"What the hell are you talking about, girl?"

Kallie swung the chair round and rushed Angus down the hall and into the office, closing the door behind them.

"A man by the name of Victor Vassello is in Willaroi and he's looking for a criminal named Dominic Marzetti. He's showing photos round town of Donna Ross and this Marzetti guy. Angus, Donna's real name is Donatella Rossini. What do you make of that?"

"Huh?"

The kitchen door slammed and Kallie jumped. She lowered her voice. "I'm pretty sure, Bert is Dominic Marzetti and I think Donna is related to Jane's husband."

He blinked a couple of times. "Don't be ridiculous, if Donna and Andrew were related then Jane would have told you and I've known Bert for years."

"Angus, you lost your memory and Marzetti needed somewhere to hide. I think he tricked you into believing he was Bert Chalmers."

"That's nonsense."

"Sam and those army guys are after Marzetti as well."

Angus scoffed. "Have you been smoking something?"

"I'm not on drugs, Angus. Donna told me she was about to reap the benefits of years spent running after Marzetti and then she took off and came here."

Something smashed in the kitchen and a female scream resonated through the house. Kallie bit her lip and reached for the phone.

"See! We have to get help."

"You're barking up the wrong tree. Bert's no underworld boss."

"Ssh. I can't get a dial tone."

"The lines must be down. What else has happened?"

"I found out some horrible things today. Nobody is who I thought they were."

Heavy footsteps came down the hall. Kallie pushed Angus into the corner and stood in front of him as the door swung open.

Bert's eyes widened when he saw her. "What are you doing here?"

Kallie shuddered. *What's happened to Donna?* She crossed her arms under her breasts to hide her shaking hands. "I came out to get a few more things and to see if Angus wanted to come into town."

"Did you?" Bert leaned sideways to check out Angus.

Kallie blocked him. "Yes and we have to get back before the water rises."

Bert put his hand behind him and drew the gun out of his jeans. "I don't think so."

"What's going on, Bert?" Angus tried to push Kallie aside.

"Stay there, Angus." Kallie batted his hands away and turned to Bert. "We haven't done anything to you. Please, just go before Vassello or those other guys get here."

"What other guys?"

"Sam and his friends. They're after you too."

Bert's gaze went from her to Angus. "I'll leave, but not without the diamond."

"I don't know where—"

"Don't give me that bullshit. I heard you'd found it, so hand it over."

A choking noise came from behind her. "The bloody hell she will."

I knew this would come back to bite me. Kallie held Angus back. "I'll deal with this, Angus." *Think, Kallie, think.* She reached into the top drawer and retrieved a key. "Will you promise to let us go, if I give you the diamond?"

"Yeah, I might not like you much, but I got no gripe with Angus and he needs someone to look after him."

"Thank you." Kallie took a step towards the safe. "I need to get a key out of the safe."

"All right." He stepped back.

Angus wheeled forward. "If you think, I'm going to sit here and just let you walk off with my diamond..."

Kallie jumped back in front of Angus as Bert raised the gun. "I won't give you the diamond if you shoot Angus."

Bert lowered the gun and narrowed his eye. "All right, where is it?"

Thankfully Angus remained silent while Kallie moved to the safe, inserted the key and turned the dial right, left and right again. The safe clicked and she pulled the door open, reached in and removed a small silver key.

"There's a moveable floorboard in my bedroom. It's under the bed. You'll find a security box there and this is the key to open it. The diamond is in the box."

Bert snatched the key. "It better be. Wait here while I check." He left the office.

Kallie grabbed Angus's wheelchair. "Let's get out of here, before he comes back."

"No, let's wait. Bert won't hurt us."

"Angus, I'm going for help."

"You do what I tell you. Bert's fed up with living here and I reckon he's having a breakdown." He wheeled through the door. "That's all."

Kallie shook her head and followed Angus through the kitchen. A casserole dish and its contents lay smashed on the floor. There was no sign of Donna. Ignoring the mess, Kallie grabbed the handles of the wheelchair and pushed Angus onto the porch and into the laundry.

"Stay here and keep quiet. I'll go and get help."

"Kallie."

In the distance, the sound of a large helicopter reached her. *Thank goodness. They can deal with Bert.* She smiled reassurance at Angus.

"It's Sam. He won't hurt you, Angus. He just wants Marzetti."

Grabbing her riding boots, Kallie dragged them on and jumped off the porch. She sprinted for the barn, almost losing her footing in the slippery mud. Heart racing, she pounded through the barn, unhooked Jasper's bridle and opened the door to his stall.

"Sorry, fella. I need your help."

"Argh." Kallie slammed against Jasper's side as the wind was knocked out of her. A woman's arm came round her and a knife blade pressed sharply against her neck.

"Not so fast, my dear."

"Donna, what are you doing? I'm trying to rescue us."

"I don't need rescuing. I need the diamond. Where is it?"

"You've got to be kidding me. Forget the diamond and get out of here. You're a loose end and Bert's going to kill you."

Donna laughed. "You and that interfering friend of yours are the only loose ends."

"Sam's not my friend."

"Not him. Jane."

"Jane?"

"Yes. Poor Andrew can't wait to be rid of her. It was you he was supposed to marry."

"What?"

"Andrew is my son. We hatched the perfect plan to get our hands on your diamond, only you wouldn't play along. You rejected him."

Kallie shivered. "Your son?" *Oh my God, I rejected Andrew because I knew Jane had a crush on him.*

Donna pressed the blade closer. "So we went with plan B. He married your best friend, hoping she'd tell him where the diamond was. But it turns out she didn't know."

"I can't believe Andrew is *your* son."

"And Dominic's."

Kallie closed her eyes and tried to calm herself. A warm droplet slid down her neck. "But Jane's having your grandchild."

"Oh don't worry. We plan on keeping the kid, it's Jane who'll disappear."

This can't be happening. Kallie stared at Donna, her chest constricting. "Was Wally's death an accident or did you have something to do with that?"

"Not me personally, but we couldn't allow him to expose us, could we?"

Bile rose in Kallie's throat. "If you kill me, the police will hunt you down."

"I'm not going to kill you. Dom has other plans for you, once he has the diamond."

A low, vicious growl erupted behind them.

"Christ." Donna pulled Kallie round to face their attacker.

Ajax hunkered ready to leap. His upper lip curled, exposing lethal incisors. His hackles were raised, his tail stiff and his ears pricked. Kallie's heart hammered. *Shit, it doesn't even look like the same dog. I'm done either way, the knife or him.*

Jasper whinnied and moved, jolting them forward. Ajax sprang forward a couple of inches, his snarl turning to a savage barking.

Jasper swung round. His head went down and he pawed the ground. Kallie pushed back against Donna, to get out of the way of his hooves and Ajax's teeth. Between them and the pounding rain, the noise was horrific. Kallie had never seen Jasper in such a state.

"Christ, what sort of animals do you breed here?" Donna yelled.

I have to save Jane and stop Andrew. Why hasn't Ajax attacked? What's he waiting for. An idea formed.

"Ajax will stop if you throw the knife down. He'll kill you if you don't."

Donna threw the knife and shoved Kallie towards Ajax. He leapt sideways and resumed his position, snarling at Donna as she cowered in a corner.

Jasper ceased his squealing and backed out of the stall.

Kallie ran to the barn door and peered out through the heavy downpour. She spied the helicopter setting down on the front lawn. Four men dressed from head to foot in black and carrying high-powered rifles were moving stealthily towards the house. *Sam's team.* The laundry door stood wide. Angus had disappeared.

No, Angus, I told you to stay put. Shit, I need to save Jane. Jasper nudged her shoulder. Kallie caught his reins and ran him to the rear doors.

"Where are you going?" Donna cried. "Don't leave me with this vicious creature."

"Don't move. Help is coming."

Kallie pushed the door wide, climbed onto a drum and mounted Jasper bareback. Digging in her heels, and gripping him with her knees, she urged him into a gallop. A shot rang out from inside the house followed by a round of gunfire. Kallie flinched and looked over her shoulder. *Oh, please don't let Angus be dead.* Two men in black were running back towards the helicopter. *Shit, they saw me.*

She leaned in close to Jasper's neck and spurred him on. "Come on, boy. We can't let them catch us." Kallie held on tightly as Jasper galloped over the sodden earth.

The helicopter followed her, coming in low on the right and Jasper shied. A black clad figure leaned out and waved at her to stop. She couldn't tell if it was Sam or one of the others.

"No way." She pulled Jasper left.

The helicopter lifted and came in low on her other side. Jasper pig-rooted and almost wrenched the reins from Kallie's hands. She cursed and held on to his mane. Out on her right side, she could see a motorbike coming through the rain towards her. The rider had a woolly hat on, but he wasn't dressed in black. *Who is it?*

'Oh no you don't." She pointed Jasper to a lower pasture and glanced over her shoulder. The bike had stopped.

Her breath caught as he lifted a rifle. "Crap." She flattened herself against Jasper.

Two shots rang out, followed by a blast of gunfire from the helicopter. Jasper reared and Kallie lost her grip, plummeting to the soggy earth. As she jumped to her feet, she noticed the bike rider was also on the ground. She glanced up at the chopper. The black-clad figure in the open doorway had a high-powered rifle in his hands.

They shot him. Fear enveloped her. *Why is everyone shooting?*

The helicopter began descending.

"No. I'm not giving in." Kallie ran in the opposite direction, towards the fallen man. She saw his rifle lying on the ground and picked it up, casting a quick glance at his face.

"Bill?"

Kallie's legs gave out and she fell to her knees. Faintness threatened to engulf her and bile rose in her throat. His chest was covered in blood.

She vomited.

Running feet and voices brought Kallie back to her senses. *Run or shoot?* She swung around with the rifle and fired. The bullet hit the helicopter, but not the big man coming at her like a bat out of hell. She swung the rifle towards him. He leapt sideways as she fired.

Missed again.

Another man in black launched himself out of the chopper as it hovered just off the ground and sprinted towards her.

Kallie threw the rifle and ran as hard as she could. *Why are they after me?*

The two men were gaining on her. Kallie searched ahead. *I have to make the river.*

'Stop, Kallie. We're not going to hurt you," Talos yelled.

Her legs pumped harder. "Leave me alone. Go and save Jane."

The river was running fast. Two shots rang out behind her. She twisted to see Talos and the other man hit the ground.

Now who's shooting?

Kallie kept running.

A bullet smashed into the tree beside her and pieces of bark flew out and hit her arm and face. Kallie dived to the ground. *Ouch, that hurt.*

Another bullet hit the ground near her. *I'm a sitting duck if I stay here.*

A blast of heavy machine fire sounded.

Kallie struggled to her feet and ran the last few feet to the river. *If I have to die today, then it won't be by a bullet.* She plunged in, letting the current sweep her away. Her last glimpse of Talos was of his back as he sheltered behind a tree, shooting towards a higher slope covered in thick brush where someone else was firing at them.

Has everyone gone mad?

Kallie swallowed some water and went under. She lashed out with her arms and legs, fighting to stay afloat. *Jarred said not to fight the current. Pity he didn't mention how to stay above water.* She dragged off her boots and went under again. *I have to save Jane.*

A piece of driftwood came hurtling at her. Kallie ducked, swallowed more water and came up choking. The river churned and tossed her about like a ragdoll in a washing machine. Exhaustion overwhelmed her.

She went under again.

CHAPTER TWENTY-ONE

After securing Bert to a kitchen chair and handcuffing his ankles and wrists, Sam left Nick to guard him and went in search of Jarred and Angus McNeil. He found them in the lounge room. Jarred was pacing, but stopped when Sam entered the room.

"Did Bert say anything?"

Sam shrugged. "Only that the diamond belongs to him and Angus. He insists they found it and he doesn't see why Kallie should have it."

Jarred's eyes narrowed. "So he still denies he's Marzetti."

"Yes."

Jarred turned his attention to Angus. "What exactly did Kallie say to you?"

Angus frowned. "Something about Bert being an underworld boss and that some other underworld bloke was in town showing photos around."

"Why did she think Bert was an underworld boss?"

"Because Donna Ross is in a photo with the man you're all looking for and apparently Bert's been seen with Donna."

Jarred looked at Sam. "Is that true?"

"Yes."

Angus shuffled in his chair. "I told Kallie she was barking up the wrong tree. I've known Bert for years. But she reckons he took advantage of my memory loss."

"What happened then?" asked Jarred.

"We heard a scream in the kitchen and Kallie tried to ring the police, but the line was dead. Then Bert walked in and pulled a gun on Kallie."

"Not you."

"Kallie was blocking me and I'm not much of a threat. I reckon Bert got fed up with the isolation of this place and wanted the diamond so he could get out of here. Kallie agreed to give it to him if he left us alone. I tried to stop her because I don't reckon Bert would have shot us, but Kallie wouldn't listen."

Jarred walked to the end of the room and back. "So she told him where it was, then what happened?"

"He went to get it and Kallie rushed me out to the porch before she ran off to get help. She said you fellas weren't army."

"We're not," Jarred said. "So you don't know where she's headed?"

"No."

Sam stepped closer. "Bert didn't have the diamond, and there are no loose floor boards under her bed."

Angus chuckled. "So Kallie was lying. She sure fooled me."

Jarred's phone rang. "Talos." As he listened, he flinched and his gaze flicked to Sam.

A shiver ran down Sam's spine. *Something's wrong.*

"You're sure." Jarred listened again. "Did you identify the dead shooter?"

Sam waited.

"From the pub?" Jarred's gaze flicked to Sam again. "Get him and Simon on board the chopper and keep your heads down." Jarred hung up and turned to Sam.

"The publican attempted to shoot Kallie, so Talos took him out."

"Who, Bill?" Sam stared at his boss.

"Yes, and there was another shooter on the hill. He hit Simon."

"How bad?"

"The vest saved him, but he might have a cracked rib."

Sam drew in a shaky breath. "And Kallie. Is she all right?"

"Talos thinks she took a bullet."

Heavy dread filled Sam. "What do you mean, he thinks she took a bullet?"

Jarred rubbed his hands over his face. "Talos said she went down near the river and got up clutching her arm, then while they were trying to prevent her being shot, she disappeared."

"Where?" *Not the river. Not Kallie.*

"Into the river."

"No!" Sam ran towards the door.

"Wait," Jarred called. "The boys have searched and they can't find her."

Angus spluttered. "Well they better search some more. Get the SES out there. Call in the army if you have to. Get that helicopter of yours up in the air."

"Calm down, Angus. Do you have Ken Macey's number?"

"It's in the office."

Sam stared at the floor. *This is my fault. If I hadn't checked out the jewel box, she'd still be in town, safe.* His eyes locked with Jarred's.

"I'm going to look for her."

Jarred nodded. "Good luck."

Sam picked up his rifle and strode through the house. The rain continued to hammer the iron roof. He doubted the van would make it back over the bridge, but the CRV might. *The locals will help with the search.*

As Sam neared the barn, Ajax's howls reached him. *Christ, what now?* He flattened himself against the outside wall and scanned the area around him. Nothing moved.

"Ajax." The howling increased. Raising his rifle, Sam edged around the door. A distinct metallic smell hit him. His eyes narrowed. Heavy crashing drew his attention to the tack room at the rear of the barn. *Kallie must have locked Ajax in there.*

Alert to any movement, Sam clipped the safety off and crept forward, keeping his back to the wall. The buzz of flies came from the end stall. Checking the ground, he noticed a large drag mark leading to the tack room. *How'd they get Ajax in there without him ripping them to shreds?*

Reaching the tack room, Sam opened the door and stood back. Ajax, covered in torn netting, hurtled forward. He gave Sam a glance and bounded towards the stall, then sat in the discovery position, waiting.

Who is it? After checking left, right and above, Sam joined Ajax. "Good boy. Hold."

A splattering of blood covered one wall and a woman's body lay crumpled on the floor of the stall. Sam moved closer. Her throat had been cut from ear to ear and she lay in a bed of blood-soaked straw, her vacant eyes staring.

"Fuck." Sam stood his rifle against the wall and pulled out his phone.

"Jarred. While we were raiding the house, somebody threw a net over Ajax and dragged him into the tack room. We've got another body in the barn. It's Donna Ross and her throat's been cut."

"By who?"

"No idea. But Kallie couldn't have dragged Ajax, and there's no way she'd slit Donna's throat. Has anyone seen Roy?"

"I'll check. Watch your back."

Sam ended the call, pocketed his phone and straddled the trail bike. *Please don't let her drown.* Although not a religious man, the whole way to the river, through the heavy downpour, Sam prayed. Kallie's lovely eyes and spontaneous laugh haunted him. For all the torment he'd suffered and horrors he'd witnessed, nothing compared to the pain besieging him. *One night together was never going to be enough. Fuck, a million nights with Kallie wouldn't be enough.* His jaw clenched. *Against all odds, I've found the one woman I want to spend the rest of my life with. I can't lose her.*

Talos was at the river, drenched and in an agitated state, searching the riverbank. The helicopter formed a sweeping pattern in the distance. As Sam approached, Talos shook his head.

"I can't find her, Sam." His voice broke. "She kept running, we tried to cover her and then she just disappeared."

Sam swallowed and cleared his throat. "She has to be here somewhere."

"Ryan's taken the chopper downstream. He's got Simon and Nick spotting for him."

Sam's gaze searched the banks. "Why wouldn't she let us save her? Fuck."

"She yelled at me to leave her alone, and then she told me to go and save Jane. What do you make of that?"

Sam tried to think logically. "Maybe Kallie found something out about Ken, or maybe Jane knows something that could put her at risk."

They continued downstream for several hours, searching the banks and rocks until they rounded a bend and met two boats coming towards them, trawling either side of the river. The occupants wore bright orange overalls.

"Local SES," Talos murmured.

Sam stared, gutted. *If they haven't found her, what hope is there?*

They all searched until the fading light made it impossible. As Sam looked at the now familiar faces etched with exhaustion and desolation, he realised just how important Kallie was to these people. *She left town this morning thinking nobody cared. If only she could have witnessed this.*

Chilled to the bone, Sam and the team returned to the McNeil property by chopper, setting down amongst an assortment of four-wheel drives. Jarred ordered them to collect a dry supply of overalls from the chopper and to get hot showers.

When Sam joined the crowd in the lounge room, he found them organising more search parties to go out as soon as the rain eased. Bert had been interned in his quarters with Nick on guard. Donna's body had been covered and the stall padlocked until the police arrived. Angus sat in his armchair brooding, Jane was inconsolable and Liz kept herself busy making tea and sandwiches for everyone. The atmosphere lay heavy with desolation and shock.

Sam wandered out to the front porch and stood staring into the torrential rain. Ajax sat beside him and small groups of people dotted the porch, talking in low voices.

This is driving me crazy. He was about to go back inside when an approaching vehicle caught his attention. It was Roy's ute.

Sam waited as Roy got out of the ute and ran up the steps. He shook the water off his jacket and ambled along the porch, scratching his head. Silence fell and everyone turned to watch his approach.

"I don't know what's going on, but you better get those vehicles off the lawn or Kallie's going to skin you alive."

Nobody said a word.

Roy's gaze locked with Sam's and his eyes narrowed. "Where's Kallie?"

The screen door flew open and Liz ran out. "Roy, where have you been?"

Roy glanced at Liz. "I took my dog to the vet in Collie and couldn't get back through the water until now. What's happened here?"

Jarred, Ryan and Talos came onto the veranda.

Sam took a deep breath. "Kallie's gone. She..." He swallowed the lump in his throat. "She fell in the river."

The colour leached out of Roy's face. He swayed and reached for the railing. Drawing in a couple of deep breaths, he straightened and focused on Sam.

"You were supposed to be watching her. How the hell did she end up in the river?"

"There was a misunderstanding and she ran from us. Bill Murphy and someone else shot at her. We think she was hit by a bullet before she went into the river."

Roy raised a shaking hand to his mouth, the other hand tightened on the railing. "Where is Bill now?"

"Dead."

"And the other man?"

"We don't know."

"You promised me you would keep her safe." He launched himself towards Sam, hitting him hard and knocking him into the brickwork.

Snarling, Ajax sprang. Jarred grabbed the lead, hauling him back. Ryan rushed forward, caught Roy's arm and attempted to drag him backward.

Ajax leapt forward snarling as Roy lashed out sideways with a vicious kick to Ryan's thigh. Then he twisted, freeing himself to deliver a jabbing elbow to Ryan's solar plexus and sending him sprawling. Sam hardly had time to process the impressive move before Roy was on him again.

Sam took a hit to the chin before Talos overpowered Roy, holding him in an arm and leg lock that took them both crashing to the porch boards. Ajax's teeth gnashed, his bark savage as he fought Jarred to get free.

Sam shouted. "Stand down, Ajax."

The screen door crashed open and Jane hurried forward. "Talos, no, you'll hurt him." She threw her arms around Talos's neck and clung to him.

"Shit." Sam ran forward and attempted to lift Jane off. She wouldn't let go.

"Jane," Liz screamed. "For goodness sake, think of the baby."

Roy stopped struggling and Talos released him to deal with Jane.

Offering his hand, Sam pulled Roy to his feet. The stockman instantly sank into the wicker chair and put his head in his hands. His shoulders shook as grief took hold of him.

Talos helped Jane up then she burst into tears and collapsed against him. He looked around helplessly before picking her up and striding inside.

Ajax whined, his gaze pinned on Sam.

Staring out across the flooded fields, Sam fought to keep his emotions under control. The rain had finally stopped.

Liz shooed everyone except Sam and Jarred inside then sat and rubbed Roy's back. "I'm sorry, Roy. There was a huge misunderstanding. Kallie heard Jane and I arguing. We said things Kallie was never meant to hear. It upset her and she ran away."

Roy sniffed, wiped his sleeve across his eyes and stood. "I want to see Bossy's body."

Sam turned. "We haven't found Kallie yet, Roy. She's still missing."

Roy's head shot up and he blinked several times. "Then how do you know she's gone?"

"We searched the river and banks for hours."

Roy looked from Sam to Liz. "Tell me exactly what was said. I want every detail."

Liz immediately launched into speech, repeating her argument with Jane. Roy cringed when she mentioned the bit about him wanting to leave after the plane crash.

"I was going to take her with me," He turned to Sam.

"I know. Liz told me."

"That explains why she's upset with us, but not you fellas," Roy said.

Sam glanced at Jarred, who nodded.

"What I'm going to tell you can't be repeated to anyone." He glanced at Liz. "It would be better if you didn't hear this, Liz."

Her eyes widened. "I don't understand."

Jarred took her hand and helped her up. "We are in the middle of an investigation and can't afford any leaks."

"Who am I going to tell?" she demanded.

Sam and Jarred remained silent.

Liz stared at them. "Is Ken in some sort of trouble?"

Jarred urged her towards the door. "I'm not at liberty to say, but I really need you to watch for anything unusual and not say anything. A lot of lives depend on it."

She covered her mouth with her hand and nodded.

"Thank you." Jarred opened the door and followed her through.

Sam drew in a breath and as soon as the door closed he turned to Roy and told him about their investigation, the jewel box and the events of yesterday.

Roy remained silent throughout then leaned back in the chair and stared across the fields. After a couple of minutes he sat up.

"Did Jasper come home?"

Sam frowned. "He's not in the barn."

Roy considered that. "And nobody else knows about Donna?"

"No. We locked down the stall and notified the Federal Police."

"Are your mates sure Kallie took a bullet?"

"They saw her go down clutching her arm. Then they were distracted with the shooter and lost sight of her, but if she's alive, we should have found her."

"If she wanted to be found."

"Sorry?"

"It seems to me, she's had a pretty bad day. If that were me, I'd want to go away to lick my wounds and have nothing to do with any of you."

Sam sighed. "Kallie could be wounded and her morale's at rock bottom. It's possible she didn't even try to save herself."

"No way. Kallie's a fighter. I reckon she dragged herself out of the river and when you're least expecting it, she'll turn up with a bloody rifle and shoot you in the arse."

"The current was running strong, Roy, and the river was churning. It would have been hard for an able-bodied man to fight it, let alone a little thing like Kallie."

Roy shrugged. "Maybe. I want you to take me to the place she was last seen and bring that dog of yours. If he's as good as you say, he'll be able to track her."

Sam starred at Roy, a flicker of hope rising within his soul.

Jarred came out of the house with a plate of eggs and bacon. "Here, you'd better eat before you drop."

"No, thanks." Sam explained what Roy wanted and Jarred gave the go ahead for Ryan to take them up in the chopper. He met Sam's gaze.

"I intend to have another go at breaking Bert. It's looking more and more likely that Marzetti has slipped through our fingers, but I want to be sure. Bert could be one hell of an actor but he really appeared shocked when I told him Donna Ross had been murdered. I want that other shooter."

Jarred strolled back inside and a couple of minutes later, Ryan and Talos came out, dressed in dry clothes and ready to go.

Sam jumped aboard the chopper and buckled himself and Ajax in, noting the boys had taken care of Roy.

As they flew over the flooded paddocks, Talos pointed out the rise where their unknown shooter had been stationed. Sam studied the ground. There was a single wheel track leading to a clump of trees and another leading away.

"He was on a bike too."

Talos nodded. "By the time we got in the air, he was gone. But even so, if he kept to the trees, we wouldn't have seen him."

Ryan sat the chopper down on soggy ground and they all walked to the river's edge. Sam and Talos observed Roy as he studied the flattened patch where Kallie went down.

Roy looked up. "There's no blood."

"No," replied Sam. "But it's possible she jumped up so fast and clamped it that there wasn't time for her to bleed much."

Ajax jumped up and scratched at a tree beside the flattened grass. Sam stepped closer. "There's a bullet lodged in it and chunks of bark are missing." Hope flared. He turned to Talos. "How many shots did the shooter get off?"

"Four. One hit Simon. One narrowly missed me and one obviously hit this tree. That leaves one other. It was raining heavily, but the shooter was no novice."

"Fuck." Sam paced to the river's edge. The current was still moving swiftly.

Roy broke off a nearby branch and joined him. "Let's see which way she went." He threw the branch into the water. It bobbed around then shot out into the middle and down stream. Roy jogged along the riverbank keeping pace with the branch. The others followed. Around the bend the branch shot across to the other side, slammed into a large rock and shot back to the middle. Around the next bend the branch did the same thing, shot over to the other side then back to the middle. Roy stared at the other bank for several minutes.

"How far down river did you look?"

"About ten kilometres," replied Talos. "Look, mate, if she was there, we would have found her?"

Roy's jaw clenched. "If Kallie doesn't want to be found then you won't find her." He strode off towards the chopper. "I reckon you were looking in the wrong direction."

Talos shook his head at Sam. "The poor bloke's clutching at straws."

"Maybe." Sam looked around. "What happened to Jasper?"

"After he threw Kallie, he took off. We didn't see him again."

A tiny sliver of hope blossomed in Sam. "Come on, let's check out the other side."

Once in the chopper, Sam caught Roy's eye. "Where did Kallie hide out when she was avoiding Liz's birthday parties?"

"Where the cottage is now. It used to be a little humpy."

"And you think she might be there."

"Kallie's a fighter and there's not one weak bone in her body. I'm hoping she got out of the river then backtracked in an attempt to get away from you bastards."

Ryan set them down on the opposite bank near the spot Roy had focused on. They jumped clear and searched for any sign of disturbance along the bank.

Nothing. Sam pulled a shirt of Kallie's out of his pack. "We still have hope while there's no body." He called Ajax and rubbed his nose with the shirt. "Seek, Ajax."

Ajax began barking then ran back and forth along the riverbank. After a couple of minutes, Sam called him and they checked the other spot. Nothing.

Sam gripped Roy's shoulder. "She didn't come out here either. Let's take the chopper further up stream. It can't hurt to check out the cabin."

As they flew above the winding river, everyone on board studied the riverbanks and churning water below. As Ryan set them down on the helipad near the cottage Sam searched for any sign of Jasper.

Don't give up.

He ran for the cabin, opened the door and entered. Everything looked neat and tidy. Talos and Roy joined him and they checked the other rooms.

Roy's shoulders sagged. "She hasn't been here."

Sam glanced at Ajax running from room to room, wagging his tail and looking for something or someone.

"Maybe, maybe not. If I was dirty, wet and cold, the first thing I'd want is a hot shower and dry clothes." He strode into the bathroom, Talos and Roy followed.

Sam opened the laundry basket. "Empty."

He checked the shower floor. A small puddle lay in one corner. "Hmm." He felt the towel. "Damp." He glanced at Roy. "Did you have a shower here, this morning?"

"No, I've been staying at Bunny's. We came out early this morning to feed the horses then headed into Collie."

Sam returned to the main room. "She must've been starving, after using all that energy. He lifted the garbage lid. An empty frozen dinner pack and several tea bags sat on the bottom. Excitement welled. He touched the kettle. *Warm.*

"Roy, did you make yourselves something to eat or drink this morning?

"Nope."

Sam's gaze fell on Ajax still trotting about the room sniffing.

Talos pointed at the washing machine dryer, sitting alongside the kitchen bench. "Maybe she washed and dried her clothes."

Sam felt the side of the machine. *Warm.*

Sam smiled. "She's alive." His jaw clenched. "But not for long, when I get hold of her." He strode into the lounge. "But, why did she leave here?"

Talos picked up the phone. "The line's dead. She would have been exhausted, maybe she rested while her clothes dried, and then she headed back to check on Angus."

"Fuck." Sam hit his forehead. "Roy, do you have any guns here?"

"Yep." Roy opened a metal locker. "The 303 is missing and only Kallie would know where the spare key is kept."

"She's alive and armed." Sam stared out the window. "What is she planning?"

"Kallie's no killer." Roy said.

Sam scowled. "We can all kill if the need arises. At the moment Kallie doesn't trust anyone. She thinks everyone she cares about has lied to her to either get the diamond, the farm or, in my case, to get Marzetti. She'll also want to check on Angus."

"And Jane," added Talos. "For some reason, Kallie thinks Jane needs protecting."

"Maybe from Ken," murmured Sam.

Talos groaned. "What if Kallie saw Donna's killer and now knows Marzetti's identity? Maybe she's trying to protect the locals or Jane in particular from him."

Sam grimaced. "That's what I'm afraid of." He looked at Roy. "Can you stay here in case Kallie comes back?"

"Yeah, I've got to check on the horses anyway. Give me a call when she turns up, but a word of warning. She won't approach the house with all those people there."

"Thanks, I'll get Jarred to clear the place."

CHAPTER TWENTY-TWO

Kneeling on a bale of hay, Kallie rubbed her sore shoulder as she observed the last vehicle drive away and the helicopter lift off and fly east. *It's about bloody time.* She drew back from her peephole, picked up the rifle, limped to the edge of the loft and climbed down the ladder. An odd smell hung in the air and someone had padlocked Jasper's stall.

Strange.

At the barn doors she hesitated. *It looks deserted, but with all the commotion, I can't be sure.* She waited several minutes but nothing moved, so she hobbled across the yard to the house and plastered herself against the kitchen wall.

Ripping off my heavy boots might have saved my life, but geez, I'm paying for it now.

Holding the rifle tight against her body, Kallie listened intently. The rumble of a male voice came from within. She heeled off her muddy runners, flinching as she knocked a particularly nasty cut and eased the screen door open. It squeaked and Kallie froze.

After several minutes she slid sideways and reached for the door handle. It opened soundlessly. Kallie risked a quick look. The mess on the kitchen floor had been cleaned up, so had the dishes. The voice was clearer. Closing her eyes, Kallie tried to make out what he was saying. She jumped as music blared and a familiar song began.

It's only the radio.

Kallie waited until her heart had calmed and then tiptoed into the kitchen and down the hall. She sneaked a peek into the lounge room. The room was neat and tidy, not a newspaper or cup to be seen. *Somebody has tidied this room.*

Continuing down the hall, Kallie paused at the open doorway of Angus's bedroom. The bed had been made and curtains opened. She frowned. *Where is he?* The hair on the back of her neck bristled.

Glancing over her shoulder, she clicked the safety off and lowered the rifle. "Angus?"

No answer.

Using the muzzle, Kallie pushed the office door wide. Her radio sat on the open windowsill. A DJ announced it was six o'clock and then a newsreader came on. *Something is not right.* Frowning, Kallie lowered the rifle. A floorboard creaked. Kallie gasped and swivelled. Her gaze searched the empty hall.

"Is someone there?" she called.

Silence.

Swallowing, Kallie raised the rifle and took a tentative step, then another. A tremor ran down her spine. Her breath came in shallow gasps.

Don't be silly, there's no one here. Sam and his friends will have taken Bert and be long gone. Kallie edged forward. *But where is Angus?*

She paused at her bedroom door and pushed it open. Someone had taped plastic across a broken pane of glass. A line of bullet holes adorned the far wall. *They shot up my room.*

Her carved jewel box stood on the bedside table with an envelope propped against it. Kallie propped the rifle against the wall, limped over and picked up the envelope. *This is Jane's writing.* She ripped it open and withdrew a single sheet of paper.

Dear Kallie, You are my best friend in the world and what you heard was the ranting's of a child in pain. I swear it didn't last. I love you like a sister and Mum loves you like a daughter. And Roy loves you too. It's true he wanted to leave, but he was intending to take you with him. Please forgive us. We all love you.

Kallie cleared her throat, sniffed and wiped a tear away. "I love you too."

"And what about me?"

Kallie swung around. Sam leaned against the doorframe. He wore black boots, black trousers and a black padded jacket. He looked fierce, intimidating and sexy.

She shivered. "What are you doing here?"

"Waiting for you." His voice was lethal.

"Why? You have your man."

"There's something else I want."

Pain cut through Kallie's heart. "Of course, you want the diamond."

"No. I want you."

Kallie searched his face. His jaw was set and his eyes icy and unblinking as he stared at her. He didn't look like he wanted her.

"I don't believe you. You've done nothing but lie to me. I have no idea who you are."

"I'm the man who loves you, but at the moment I don't know whether to wring your neck for scaring the hell out of me or tear your clothes off and make love to you."

"You're lying." Kallie lunged for the rifle. His arms locked around her waist and pulled her away. Kallie slammed her head back intending to smash his nose. She hit his chest. He lifted her off the floor and threw her onto the bed. Kallie rolled, falling off the other side and landing on her sore hands and knees.

"Ow." Tears filled her eyes as she struggled to her sore feet and hobbled for the door. He stepped across her path, blocking the door. She punched him in the stomach and hurt her hand.

"I hate you." She burst into tears.

"Oh, darlin'." He pulled her into his arms and held her. Kallie collapsed against his chest and sobbed. "People are trying to kill me and I nearly drowned. I hurt all over and nobody is who I thought they were. And the worst thing of all is…I'm in love with you."

"That's not such a bad thing, darlin'. I'm in love with you too."

He rubbed her back soothingly, the gentleness of his touch only adding to Kallie's confusion. A deep longing clawed through her. *Why does he have this effect on me?*

Placing her hands on his chest, Kallie glanced up into his eyes. They'd warmed and he was smiling. He continued to stroke her in soothing caresses. Her heart flipped.

"If you're not part of an army exercise and you're not police then who are you?"

"I'm a highly trained specialist in weapons, martial arts, surveillance and close personal protection techniques."

Kallie swallowed. "What does that mean?"

"It means I can and will protect you."

"But who do you work for?"

"Jarred. He formed our unit two years ago. We were all soldiers in the Australian Special Air Service Regiment, and our clients are anyone who can afford us."

Kallie's heart plummeted. "So you *are* guns for hire and you work for people like Victor Vassello?"

"No, not like Vassello. Our clients are on the right side of the law. Sometimes, as in this case, they are the law, but we work undercover."

Kallie stared into his gorgeous dark eyes. *I want to believe him.*

Raising his hands. Sam gripped her shoulders, pulling her towards him. Kallie flinched.

He frowned. "What's wrong?"

"The river current slammed me into a rock and I hurt my shoulder and knee."

"Is that why you're limping?"

"No, my feet are sore because I took my boots off in the river and I cut my feet on rocks and thorns."

"Let me see." Sam picked her up and placed her on the bed amongst her pillows. He bent to examine her feet.

"Jesus, Kallie, they're a mess."

"I know. I didn't have any tweezers, so I couldn't get the thorns out."

"Stay here. I'll be back in a minute." He pulled off his thick jacket and threw it on the end of the bed before he left the room.

Kallie lay back and stared at the ceiling, confused. The few men she'd allowed close enough to kiss her had never ignited even the smallest spark of desire. Yet Sam ignited an inferno with just the simplest touch. *How can a trained killer be so gentle and caring and exciting, and the only man I've ever wanted?*

Several minutes later Sam paced back into her room, carrying a bowl of water, and the medical kit. He placed everything on her side table and soaked the washer.

"This might sting because I've put a fair amount of antiseptic in the water."

"Okay." Kallie gazed at his hands in fascination as he peeled off her Band-Aids, gently cleaned her muddy feet, pulled thorns out and applied antiseptic and new Band-Aids. When he'd finished he sat back and fixed a steady gaze on her.

"I want you to tell me everything that happened this morning. What you heard, what you saw and then I'll tell you my side of things and what we've discovered. Does that sound fair enough?"

Biting her lip, Kallie nodded. "I guess so." She told him everything from the moment Liz had informed her she'd lost an earring to her terrifying river experience.

By the end of her story, she was lying in Sam's arms and sobbing. He held her gently and told her everything he knew and how the whole town had searched for her.

"They all love you, Kallie."

She sniffed. "I feel so bad now. I should go and apologise to them all. They must be worried sick."

Smiling, Sam brushed her hair off her shoulder. "It's all right. They know you're safe."

"How?" Kallie frowned. "Nobody knows I'm here."

"Roy and I figured you wouldn't approach the house while lots of people were here, so we got everyone to leave, including Angus. He's at Fergie's."

"What about Donna and Bert?"

"Nick has Bert secured in the shearers' quarters until the Federal Police get here tomorrow. Bert swears he's not Marzetti. He also told Jarred he pulled a gun on you because he's convinced you know where the diamond is and he's sick of waiting."

Kallie frowned. "Does Jarred believe him?"

"Jarred never believes anyone without hard evidence to back them up, that's why he's handing Bert over to the police. I'm afraid someone killed Donna shortly after you left her in the barn."

"Donna's dead?"

"Yes, possibly because she told you too much."

Kallie shook her head. "I couldn't understand why Bill was shooting at me, but he must have been protecting Marzetti. Maybe Bill killed Donna. And where's Ken? What if he's part of Marzetti's gang too and only married Liz to get the diamond."

She gasped. "Wait. About fifteen months ago, Andrew came to Willaroi as part of a plan to invest in small communities. It was Ken who introduced us to Andrew. Ken must be part of Marzetti's gang too. Oh my God, Liz is in danger." Kallie struggled to get up.

Sam's arms tightened. "Liz and Jane are safe. Talos is with them. But Liz won't accept that Ken could be involved. She thinks he's either still out searching or watching Vassello." He grimaced. "I'm afraid it's too much of a coincidence to have Ken, Marzetti and Vassello all here in Willaroi. Ken has to be involved. He must be the marksman who got away."

Kallie sighed. "Poor Liz. At least Andrew's in Sydney, so Jane is safe from him, but he's going to be really angry with whoever killed his mother."

Sam sat up and pulled his jacket closer. "That's debatable. If he's anything like his father, it won't bother him in the least." Sam pulled out his phone.

"Who are you ringing?" Kallie scrambled to her knees.

"Jarred. I want to warn him about Andrew."

Nodding, Kallie watched him scroll through his contact list and hit Jarred's name.

"Jarred, it's Sam. I've got Kallie and she's fine. I'll bring her into town tomorrow. I've also got some more intel for you."

Kallie listened as Sam brought Jarred up to date and made plans to track down Andrew. She relaxed at the calm strength in his deep drawl. He made her feel safe and she knew now that Talos would keep Jane and Liz safe.

As Sam spoke, he kept his gaze on her. His eyes darkened and Kallie's heart raced at the open lust in them. Memories of their previous night together flooded her mind and she tingled all over, squirming as a deep-seated need spread throughout her body. By the wicked smile on Sam's face, he knew exactly what she was experiencing. He ended the call, placed his phone on the bedside table and reached for her.

"I'm going to go mad if I don't have you right here and right now, darlin'." Sam toppled Kallie and fell on top of her, pinning her beneath him, her gasp smothered by his lips closing hungrily over hers. Her body softened as he ravished her mouth but it wasn't enough. She wrapped her legs around him and pressed closer. He deepened the kiss. It still wasn't enough. She twisted away.

"Please touch me, Sam. I'll die if you don't."

He chuckled. "Where do you want me to touch you, darlin'?"

"Everywhere. You have to touch me everywhere." She squirmed, trying to get closer.

Sam pushed away and straddled her, his gaze raking her body. Heat flared low in Kallie's stomach, moisture pooled between her thighs, aggravation churned. "Please, Sam."

He leaned forward with both hands and traced a path over her cheeks, along her jaw, down either side of her neck to her collarbone then down over her chest by the edge of her shirt stopping just above the button.

Kallie moaned. "You're driving me crazy on purpose."

"I'm building your anticipation." He gripped the edges of her shirt and tore it open, sending buttons pinging off in all directions. Kallie laughed and tried to reach for his shirt. He gently knocked her hands away and whipped a knife from his boot. Kallie froze.

"What's that for?"

"I want no barriers between us." He inserted a finger under her bra, raised it slightly and sliced through the material. The bra sprang away leaving her breasts exposed.

She gasped. "Sam, that was a new bra. Do you have any idea how much that cost me?"

"I'll buy you a dozen more." He placed the knife beside her and moved his hands to the button on her jeans. "Now for these." He had them and her shirt off in seconds. He picked up the knife again as his gaze lowered.

"No way." Kallie grasped either side of her pants and shoved them down her legs, kicking them off. Sam dropped the knife over the side of the bed, threw back his head and roared with laughter.

Kallie cried out, clasped his black T-shirt and pulled him down, rolling so she ended up on top. She straddled him. "You won't be laughing when I die of frustration."

He stopped laughing but the smile stayed in place. Kallie dragged the T-shirt free of his trousers and up over his massive chest. Only then did he lift his arms and allow her to pull it free. Her gaze feasted on his broad shoulders, powerful arms and sculptured pecs.

"I want you naked too, my handsome protector." She undid his belt and the button then struggled to get the zip down over his impressive bulge.

"Help me, Sam. It's stuck."

He chuckled, lifted her off him and stood. In a matter of seconds his boots, trousers and jocks were off.

Kallie knelt on the bed staring at his body. An excited shiver ran down her spine.

Sam crawled onto the bed, his gaze devouring her as he moved towards her like a circling wolf closing in on its prey, yearning for that first taste.

She fell back on the pillows and grinned. "If you want me, come and get me."

Sam hesitated, his gaze skimming Kallie from head to foot. Her golden skin glowed, her eyes shone with desire. She watched him like a hawk. He gripped her ankles and dragged her towards him, spreading her legs wide. He smiled as comprehension dawned in her eyes.

"It's about time I tasted you, don't you think." Lowering his body he skimmed kisses up the insides of both her legs. Her body jerked as he brushed his lips lightly across her thatch of curls. He pushed her thighs wider and slid his hands under her smooth bottom, lifting her to meet his lips. She shrieked at the touch of his mouth closing over her in intimate possession. Sam thrust his tongue inside her, savouring her flowing juices, exulting as she cried out his name and tangled her fingers in his hair. He sucked hard on her sensitive nub and she screamed, convulsing as her orgasm raced through her.

Sam wiped his mouth and reached over the side of the bed for his trousers and wallet. He removed a condom and quickly put it on then moved over Kallie's gloriously naked body. Her eyes remained closed, her ripe breasts rising and falling with her rapid breathing. Sam smiled. "Open your eyes, sweetheart, we're not finished yet."

As he nudged into her tight sheath, Kallie's eyelids fluttered open, showing passion-dazed eyes. Sam gripped her hips and thrust all the way. She screamed again as another orgasm hit. She tightened around him, almost causing him to explode.

"So sensitive, my love." Sam thrust hard and fast. His own orgasm crashed over him violently. He roared and collapsed on top of her.

She wrapped her arms around his shoulders, smothering his neck in featherlike caresses. Sam wallowed, soaking up each touch like it was his last. Eventually he raised his body, kissed Kallie gently and smiled. "I'll be back in a minute." He strode to the bathroom, disposed of the condom and came back to find her exactly as he'd left her, lying wantonly in the middle of the bed. He leaned over her.

"I've waited my whole life for you."

"So have I." She raised her lips for another kiss before gently touching his cheek. "I'm not like your mother, I love you and I would never cheat on you or hurt a child."

"I know." He rolled to the side and gathered Kallie against him. "That's why I love you. Now I want you to sleep while I make us some dinner. Then, afterwards we are going to have a soak in that huge tub and then I'm going to make love to you again. Slowly this time."

"Okay." She snuggled. "Will you stay with me a little longer?"

"I can do that." Sam kissed her and drew her closer. "I would do anything for you, darlin'."

"Hm." Her eyes fluttered closed.

Sam held Kallie until her breathing evened out, then he eased off the bed, covered her and pulled on his clothes. *I'd better check in with Nick and then see what I can rustle up for dinner.* He picked up his rifle and let himself out of the house.

Alert to any sound or movement, Sam crossed the yard to the shearing quarters where Nick and Ajax were holding Bert. The lights were blazing. Nick and Bert were sitting in easy chairs and the television was on. Bert had been handcuffed and secured to the chair with rope. Sam lightly tapped on the door.

"It's just me, Nick. I've come to see if you two would like something to eat."

"Hang on a sec, I'll let you in," called Nick.

Ajax wagged his tail and gave an excited bark at the sight of Sam.

"So what's for dinner?" asked Nick. "I'm starving."

Strolling into the room, Sam chuckled. "As I can only cook fish, steak or a sticky lime and ginger chicken pasta, they are your only choices."

"I'm over fish and steak, so it will have to be the chicken pasta."

Bert grunted. "I don't care about bloody food. I'm not who you're after and I wasn't going to shoot Kallie. I just wanted to get out of this God forsaken place."

Shrugging, Sam took a seat opposite Bert. "Be that as it may, you still threatened Kallie with a gun, and as Angus gave the diamond to Kallie, it wasn't yours to take. The Federal Police will be here in the morning and they can decide whether you're Dominic Marzetti or if you should be charged for a firearms offence. They'll also need to ask you about Donna."

"That's bloody ridiculous. I never touched her."

Sam held his hands out. "Then why did she come out here in the first place and why were you dragging her towards the house?"

"She wanted me to drive her to Mungindi Airport and I refused because of the flooded roads, so she started screaming at me. I dragged her to the house to see if Angus could talk some sense into her."

Sam stared at Bert. "Kallie told me she heard Donna scream and something smash. What was that about?"

"The bloody woman threw a casserole at me. That was the last straw. I grabbed my gun and went to the office to demand Angus ask Kallie for the diamond so we could clear out. I've no idea what happened to Donna. She was fine when I last saw her."

Nick glanced at Sam. "Bert couldn't have killed Donna Ross. She had to have been alive when we saw Kallie ride off, so Bert didn't have time to get to the barn. It had to be someone else."

Sam studied Bert. "Did you see anyone else about this morning?"

"No, but I did hear a motorbike around the time Donna turned up."

"Did you know Jane's husband, Andrew, was Donna's son?" asked Nick.

"I had no idea. I don't think I've ever talked to the guy and Donna never mentioned it."

"All right." Sam stood and glanced at Nick. "I'll leave Ajax here for now and I'll bring you both some dinner shortly."

His phone vibrated. Sam glanced at the screen. "Jarred?"

"I've had a call from Liz Macey. Roy's girlfriend is worried about him. She said he was on the phone talking to her when a helicopter landed at the cabin. Roy said he'd see who it was and ring her straight back, but that was several hours ago. Can you check it out?"

"I'll have to take Kallie with me. I'm not leaving her in the house on her own."

"Nick's there if she needs him."

"Yeah, okay. Have you found Vassello or Ken Macey?"

"Not yet, the boys are still looking. We could have it wrong and Marzetti is someone else, living on another outlying farm. Let me know how you go at the cabin."

"Sure." Sam ended the call.

"What's up?" asked Nick.

"The boss wants me to check on Roy at the cottage, but Kallie's asleep and I don't like the idea of leaving her on her own."

Nick walked to the door with Sam. "Kallie must be exhausted. Lock the house and let her sleep. I'm here if she needs me."

"All right. I'll be back shortly."

Chapter Twenty-three

A rapid, continuous thumping woke Kallie. Opening her eyes, she blinked into darkness. Yawning, she stretched her sated body and reached for the alarm clock, wincing when her bruised shoulder pulled.

Nine o'clock!

Kallie threw back the comforter, slid off the bed and limped to the window. From behind the barn appeared an intense light. The thumping grew louder.

It's a helicopter. She studied the dark shape as it rose higher then swooped away. *That's not the Black Hawk.* Shrugging she limped to the dresser, extracted clean clothes, dressed and headed for the kitchen.

Kallie's gaze roved the empty room. Other than the chirruping of cicadas and the ticking of the grandfather clock, the house lay in silence.

The shrilling ring of the phone made her jump. Kallie hobbled to the office and picked up the receiver. "Hello, Kallie speaking."

"Jarred Steele, Miss McNeil. Is Nick Flanagan with you?"

"No. He's in the shearers' quarters, guarding Bert."

"He's not answering his phone. Would you mind having a quick look out the window and tell me if anything looks amiss?"

"Sure." Kallie moved to the window and pulled the curtain aside. "That's odd, there are no lights." A shiver ran down her spine. "Jarred, a helicopter lifted off a few minutes ago. Is everything all right?

"Miss McNeil—Kallie. I want you to lock all the doors and windows. Do not go outside. Do not answer the door. Is that clear?"

Kallie swallowed. "Where's Sam?"

"He's fine. Bunny was a little concerned as she was expecting a call from Roy and she can't reach him. With what's going on I asked Sam to check out the cottage. He should be back within the hour. In the meantime, stay in the house."

A cold wave of fear spread through Kallie. "Where's Jane?"

"She's at her mother's along with your grandfather and Les Ferguson."

"Do they know Andrew is Dominic Marzetti's son?"

"No. I'm keeping that quiet for the moment. If Andrew learns his cover's been blown, he'll likely disappear and I have a few questions to ask him."

"Have you found Ken and Victor Vassello?"

"Not yet, but we will. Please, just stay in the house and wait for Sam. Lock the doors."

Kallie exhaled. "Okay."

After replacing the phone in its cradle, Kallie limped through the house, turning off lights and checking each window and door. She stood at the kitchen window peering towards the shearers' quarters. No sign of life showed.

She chewed on her lip. "What would Sam do?"

He'd make sure he had a weapon. Kallie retraced her steps to the office, opened the gun safe and took out her rifle and a box of bullets.

The phone rang again and Kallie jumped.

"Hello."

"So you are there." The voice was hard.

"Bert!" Kallie gasped.

"Yeah it's me. Now listen and listen hard. If you ever want to see Roy again, you'll do as I say."

"Roy!"

"Yeah, Roy."

"How did you get away? Where's Nick?"

"A friend dropped by and took care of him and that bloody dog."

Clasping a shaking hand over her mouth, Kallie squeezed her eyes shut on the escaping tears. "Why?"

"Why do you think? I want the bloody diamond and the money."

"What money?"

"The twenty million we stole from Vassello."

"I don't know where it is."

"Of course you don't. I'm going to tell you where it's hidden."

"You are Marzetti?"

"Stop jabbering and listen. I know about your cabin and the horses you and Roy have been breeding. So once you have the money, you bring it and the diamond straight to me at that cabin."

"You're at the cabin?"

"Pay attention. The money's hidden in a trunk at the back of the storeroom."

Kallie recoiled. "You mean the trunk with Angus's old prospecting gear?"

"Yeah. Only now it's got twenty million bucks in it."

"I'll never lift that trunk on my own."

"You don't have to lift the bloody thing. Drag it into the middle of the barn and use the tractor to pick it up. Come to the cabin and don't tell anyone what you're doing, otherwise, I'll cut Roy's throat. I've got Jane too."

"You're lying. Jane's with Liz in town."

"Not any more, princess."

Struggling not to cry, Kallie willed herself to be calm. "Don't hurt them. I'll bring you the diamond and the money. I promise." She ended the call and sagged against the desk. *This can't be happening.* She glanced out the window at the dark shearing quarters.

"Oh my God, Nick."

Picking up her rifle, Kallie ejected the magazine, filled it with bullets then pulled on a pair of boots and hobbled quickly out of the house.

Trembling she stepped onto the porch of the shearers' quarters and pushed the door wide.

A low growl reached her.

"Ajax?"

The growl turned to a whimper as Kallie switched on the light. The table was on its side, bits of china cups strewn everywhere. Two chairs were smashed to pieces and blood smeared the floor. The whimpering came from the other end of the room.

Kallie's heart pounded as she gingerly stepped forward.

A man in black lay on the floor, Ajax beside him. Kallie ignored her sore feet and ran to them, falling to her knees. Ajax tried to stand, yelped and collapsed to the floor again. Shaking, Kallie rolled Nick onto his back.

He groaned and opened his eyes. "Sam?"

"Sam's at the cabin. Thank God you're alive. I was afraid they'd killed you."

"I won't be alive long if we don't stop the bleeding, Kallie."

Kallie touched his face and shuddered. He was clammy to her touch, perspiration covered his forehead and his skin had a greyish tinge. She ran her hands over him to see where he was hurt. Her fingers felt sticky and she glanced down to see blood. Bile rose in her throat and heat engulfed her as her head spun dizzily. She unzipped his jacket and unbuttoned his shirt. Blood covered his wide chest, seeping from a hole in his shoulder.

"Under other circumstances I'd be thrilled you're undressing me." Nick's voice was breathless.

"That's not funny, Nick. This wound looks really bad."

He closed his eyes again. "The bullet went right through. You need to stem the bleeding and get help. They took my phone."

Ajax whimpered and tried to stand again.

"Stay, Ajax, that's the boy." Kallie ran to the linen press and rummaged through it until she found a couple of pillowcases. Folding them into pads, she ran back to Nick and worked one in around the back of his shoulder and the other she pressed firmly over the front wound. Tearing off her jumper, she tied it tightly around Nick's broad chest and shoulder, holding both pads in place.

Nick's eyes opened. "Thanks, you're an angel."

"How did this happen?"

"Jane's husband dragged her in here with a gun to her head, demanding I release Bert. Ajax went to attack and the bastard shot him, then Jane became hysterical and collapsed with pains. I had no choice but to release Bert. He grabbed the gun and shot me."

Kallie glanced at Ajax. He lay on his side panting, his eyes filled with pain. "It's okay, Ajax." She edged closer. "Can I see where you're hurt?"

He whimpered and lay his head down.

Blinking hard, Kallie choked back a sob. She tentatively ran her hand down his coat over blood-matted hair. Ajax flinched when she reached his hind leg.

Jumping to her feet, Kallie ran back to the cupboard. She pulled out a sheet, ripped it into lengths and knelt beside Ajax. He stared at her from desolate eyes as she padded his wound and wrapped him tightly. "I'm sorry, matey, but we have to stop the bleeding."

Nick wore the same boots as Sam. Kallie leaned forward and felt around the edge of his boots. Her fingers closed over the hilt of the knife and she slid it free. "I'm going for help."

After slipping the knife into her pocket, Kallie hobbled back to the house. She threw the kitchen door open and snatched up the phone, punching in the number instinctively.

"Hello, Liz Macey speaking."

"Liz, it's Kallie."

"Kallie. How are you, love? I'm sorry about…"

"Liz. Andrew's got Jane!

"I know. He picked her up earlier and they're on their way back to Sydney."

"Liz, Andrew is Dominic Marzetti's son and Jane's in danger."

"Kallie, what on earth are you talking about?"

"I don't have much time, Liz. Find Jarred or any of his guys. Tell them Bert *is* Marzetti and he's escaped. Nick and Ajax have been shot and they both need urgent medical attention. Send help as quick as you can."

"Good God!"

"And that's not all." Kallie's voice shook. "It gets worse. Bert and Andrew have Roy and Jane as hostages. They want me to bring them the Kalista Diamond and the twenty million they stole from Victor Vassello."

"I beg your pardon." Liz's voice cracked.

"Liz. I'm trying to save them. Please find Jarred immediately."

A sob sounded in Kallie's ear. "Don't you dare leave the house, Kallie. I'll get help."

The phone line went dead. Kallie sagged against the edge of the table. *How am I going to do this?* Her eyes fell on a faded photo lying on the floor under the kitchen table. It was the picture of Wally holding the Kalista Diamond. She picked it up and studied the roughly shaped gem in his hand. Frowning, she opened the top drawer, reached for the magnifying glass and held it over the photo.

"You've got to be kidding. I thought it was supposed to be pink."

Slipping the photo into her pocket, Kallie limped to her bedroom and picked up her jewel box.

"Desperate circumstances call for desperate measures." She turned each of the six native animals on their heads then lifted the entire frame off its base, revealing the shallow cavities in each corner. They held her black opal necklace, her mother's diamond earrings, a pink sapphire and a purplish gemstone. Her hand hovered over the purple gem. She pulled out the photo and examined it again. *You've got to be kidding me.*

She pocketed both gems. "How do I get help without endangering Roy and Jane?" She scribbled a quick note and then picked up her rifle. *I hope I'm doing the right thing.*

Snatching the keys to the storeroom and tractor, Kallie hobbled across the yard, the pain in her feet nothing compared to the pain in her heart. She switched on lights, opened the storeroom and dragged out fertiliser, sacks of seed and two large cardboard boxes full of farming magazines. The old trunk was at the back under a tarpaulin. Kallie tugged the tarp off and dragged the trunk to the middle of the barn.

Five minutes later she had the trunk in the bucket of the tractor and the rifle under her feet. She glanced up at the starless black sky as she drove past the shearers' quarters. *I can't risk stopping.*

Gritting her teeth, Kallie killed the lights and steered the tractor along the rutted dirt track, grateful for the sliver of moonlight to guide her.

Please don't let anything bad happen to Roy, Jane or Sam.

Chapter Twenty-Four

Satisfied there were no hostiles on watch, Sam crept to the deepest shadows of the stables and squatted, his gaze locked on the small cabin, cloaked in darkness. The blinds had been pulled and other than an occasional wicker from within the stables, all seemed peaceful enough. *Maybe Roy decided to have an early night and left the phone off the hook.*

His phone vibrated. Sam glanced at the screen. "Jarred. I've looked around and I can't see anything out of place. I left Roy here without a car, so he's probably sound asleep."

"You're going to have to check inside. I've just received a frantic call from Liz Macey. She said Kallie phoned and told her Bert Chalmers has escaped and is demanding she bring him the money stolen from Vassello and the diamond. He's holding Roy and Jane hostage."

"Fuck? Where's Nick?"

"Apparently Nick and Ajax have been shot. We're on our way there now.

"Holy shit. How did this happen?"

"I spoke to Kallie earlier when I couldn't reach Nick, and I told her to stay put, but she must have gone to check. It looks like Andrew Rossini may have orchestrated the whole thing. Liz confirmed he pilots his own helicopter and that he picked Jane up earlier."

"Christ. It must have happened after I left. They obviously left in a hurry or they'd have silenced Kallie and taken the money. Any clues as to where they are?"

"No. I can't reach Kallie but I've spoken to Roy's girlfriend. She told me she was on the phone to Roy when a small helicopter landed.

He told Bunny he'd see who it was and ring her back. She hasn't been able to get an answer on the cabin's landline."

"There's no helicopter here but I'll have a closer look. Do me a favour?"

"Sure, what do you want?"

"Find Kallie. You may have to use force, but get her on that chopper and as far away from here as possible."

"No problem. We'll be there shortly."

"Thanks." Sam put his phone away and stood. A low hum had him looking skyward where a small helicopter approached from the west. Sam dived to the ground and rolled under the fence railing. The chopper circled and then descended to the helipad.

Raising his head and shoulders, Sam peered between the rails. Three people climbed out of the chopper, two men and a heavily pregnant woman. Relief surged through Sam. *Thank God, they don't have Kallie.*

The woman cried out when one of the men seized her roughly by the arm and jostled her towards the cabin. They entered without knocking, slamming the door behind them.

Staying low, Sam sprinted behind the stables and around to the helicopter. Cautiously, he opened the pilot's door and checked inside. A man's wallet sat in the console. Opening it, Sam sighted Andrew Rossini's driver's license; he pocketed the wallet and closed the door.

Ducking, Sam ran to the corner of the cabin where he could hear the rumble of male voices. *I'll have to wait for Jarred and Talos. I can't risk Jane's life.* He made his way to the rear of the cabin and tried the back door. It was locked.

An ear-piercing scream shattered the still night. Sam sprinted to the side of the cabin and edged along the wall to a small bedroom window. The blind was down. Through a small gap he could see Jane lying curled up on the furthest bed. He pressed his ear to the glass as a low moan reached him. Sam glanced around the dark yard.

The stallion whinnied and kicked at his stable door. *Perfect.* Sam ran to the stables and unlatched the top half of the doors. Immediately three mares poked their heads out and whickered. The stallion squealed and kicked at his door again. Sam unbolted the stallion's door and made a hasty exit over the fence. The stallion's next kick sent the stable door crashing open. He pranced out, throwing his head around as he whinnied and snorted, pawing at the ground. The cabin's door opened and a man stepped out holding a rifle, his face hidden by shadow. Sam narrowed his eyes. *Something about that fella looks familiar.* The man sauntered to the end of the porch. He walked with the gait of an older man.

Sam stiffened. It was the man with the AK47 from the warehouse. *Who is he?*

The man yelled out a couple of obscenities at the prancing stallion then returned along the porch, passing under the light.

Bert!

The door slammed and Sam's phone vibrated.

"Jarred, I've identified Bert as one of the men from the warehouse raid. He's the one with the AK47 who shot the driver and got away."

"Interesting. We matched the fingerprints from the AK47 to Gus Bowen, Marzetti's right hand man."

"Okay, then who were the other two men in the office who got away?"

"Andrew Rossini would be the younger one with the goatee and the older fellow must have been Marzetti. It's all coming together."

Sam rubbed his chin. "Bert's an asshole, but I didn't see him as the criminal mastermind. How's Nick and Ajax?"

"They've both lost a lot of blood. I'm not sure Ajax will make it."

"Fuck."

"Ryan's going to drop Talos and me a couple of kilometres from you, then fly Nick and Ajax to Collarenabri."

Sam rubbed his hand over his face. "Jane's in labour and needs to get to a hospital as soon as possible. Do you have Kallie?"

"No, but we found a note verifying everything Liz told me. It appears Bert wants Kallie to bring the money and diamond to the cabin."

"She can't. Her feet are in a bad way and she hasn't got a vehicle or a horse." Sam swore. "I know her. One way or another, she'll try to save Jane and Roy."

"Talos had a look around and found fresh tyre tracks leading off in the cabin's direction. It looks like she's taken the tractor."

"Fucking hell."

"Don't do anything without backup, we're on our way."

"Fine. I'm in the shadows beside the stables." Sam sneaked back to the cabin and peered under the blind again. Jane lay facing him, clutching her stomach. No one else was in the room and the door was shut.

Sam tapped lightly on the glass.

Jane sat up awkwardly, got to her feet and knelt on the bed under the window. The blind moved aside and she peered out. Her face was pale and strained. Sam put his fingers to his lips and indicated she should open the window.

With trembling hands, Jane unlocked the window and slid it open. "Sam, help me. My waters have broken and I'm having contractions."

"Try not to panic. Who else is in the cabin?"

"Bert, Andrew and Roy. They've got poor Roy tied up and he's been badly beaten." Tears streamed down her face. "They shot your friend and Ajax. I don't know what's going on, they've gone completely mad and they're threatening to kill Roy if Kallie doesn't bring them the diamond. I'm so scared Kallie's going to do something stupid. She loves Roy but I know she doesn't have the diamond."

Sam squeezed her hand. "Hang in there. Jarred and Talos will be here any minute and we'll sort it out."

"Thank you." Jane wiped her nose.

"How far apart are your contractions."

"A couple of minutes but I've still got four weeks to go."

"Everything will be fine. Try to relax, I'll be back shortly."

"Okay." Jane let the blind drop.

Sam slid the window almost closed and sneaked back to the stables. His phone vibrated.

"Talos, talk to me."

"Nick's been shot in the shoulder and Ajax in the rump. Kallie patched them up but they've both lost a lot of blood and it's vital they get medical attention ASAP."

"Any sign of Kallie?"

"No, we have to assume she's heading to the cabin."

"Shit. Jane told me Kallie doesn't have the diamond. How long before you get here?"

"Not long. We're about a kilometre from you. How's Jane?"

"Not good. I spoke to her through a window. She's definitely in labour."

"Christ, that's all we need."

"You've delivered babies before."

"Not premature ones. I'm passing you to Jarred. He wants a word."

"Sam," Jarred's voice was terse. "Keep an eye out for Vassello and Ken Macey. They're still on the loose and they're the ones that pose a real threat."

Sam ducked behind the stables as the rumble of a vehicle reached him. "There's the tractor now. I won't put Kallie in danger."

"We're almost there, wait for us. That's an order."

Ending the call, Sam clenched his fists. He kept his gaze locked on the approaching tractor. *I'm going to wring her neck when I get hold of her.*

The tractor lumbered to a stop on the other side of the gate. A slim figure climbed down, limped to the gate and unlatched the chain. Sam glanced at the cabin. The door opened and two armed men stepped onto the porch. Raising his rifle, Sam lined them up in the scope. Bert and Andrew stood side by side watching as Kallie swung the gate wide, climbed back into the tractor's cab and slowly trundled up the drive. *That's it, honey, take your time.*

Sam tensed at a soft sound behind him.

"It's us," called Talos softly. "What's happening?"

"Kallie's just arrived and Jane's in the bedroom on the far side of the cabin.

"I'll see if I can get closer." Talos slipped into the darkness again.

Jarred joined Sam. "Let's get closer."

Nodding, Sam led the way around the back of the stables where they dropped to the ground and crawled along the base of the stockyard fence.

Kallie brought the tractor to a stop facing the cabin and lowered the bucket.

"What's she doing?" whispered Jarred.

"I've no idea."

The door of the tractor cab opened and Kallie leaned out. "Here's the trunk and I've got the diamond, so release Roy and Jane."

Bert stomped down the step. "What took you so long?"

Kallie shrugged. "I couldn't get the tractor started." She held out her hand. "This is the Kalista Diamond, but I'm not giving you anything until you release Roy and Jane." She reached inside the cab and the bucket rose.

Sam froze. *Damn it, Kallie, don't antagonise them.*

Andrew stepped off the porch. "You're not in any position to negotiate, Kallie. Lower the bucket and toss me the diamond then you can have Roy. Jane stays."

"No way. Donna told me you're Marzetti's son and that you're planning to take the baby and get rid of Jane. You get nothing until I have both Roy and Jane."

Andrew sneered. "Donna had a big mouth. If she'd kept it shut, she'd still be alive."

"Donna was your mother."

"She was a tramp and I couldn't stand the sight of her."

"It was you who killed Donna?"

A bark of laughter erupted from Bert. "Andrew's never dirtied his hands in his life. He couldn't even take care of that bloody prospector on his own."

"You killed Wally too." Kallie cried.

Andrew shoved Bert. "Shut the fuck up, or I'll shut you up permanently."

Sam nudged Jarred. "Marzetti would never allow anyone to speak to him like that. Not even his son."

"I agree," whispered Jarred. "Bert is not Dominic Marzetti."

"Then who...Oh shit." Sam's jaw clenched. *I didn't see that coming.*

He glanced at Kallie and his lungs seized. She held a rifle in her hands.

"Fuck, she's going to get herself killed."

"I've got the guy with the goatee," muttered Jarred.

Kallie raised the rifle and called out. "If you don't release Roy and Jane, I'll make sure neither of you ever take another breath."

Andrew shook his head. "You don't have the balls to shoot us, Kallie. Throw the diamond to me, then lower the bucket or I'll shoot Roy'. He swung around and pointed his rifle through the cabin's door.

Sam's finger tightened on the trigger.

"Wait," whispered Jarred. "She's lowering the rifle."

"Don't," cried Kallie. She reached inside the cab. The bucket began lowering then she threw a small object at Andrew. He caught it and studied it closely.

Adjusting his position, Jarred whispered. "Bert was in our custody when Donna was killed, so if Andrew Rossini doesn't dirty his hands, it must be Marzetti who topped her."

"I think you're right. They say he's a coldblooded butcher. He certainly had me fooled."

Gravel crunched softly to the right of Sam. He froze and focused on three shadows sneaking along the far side of the stable yard.

"Who the hell are they?" whispered Jarred.

"Vassello and his minders. They haven't seen us. "

The men crept along the fence then changed direction and snuck up behind the tractor, using it to shield their approach.

"I can take the three of them if necessary," whispered Jarred, adjusting his position.

Bert dragged the trunk out of the bucket. "It's locked," he yelled.

"Then shoot the lock, you idiot," yelled Andrew. "We don't have all night. Sam Locke and his SAS buddies will come looking for Kallie once they realise she's missing."

Holding his breath, Sam watched as Kallie climbed down from the cab, stepped away from the tractor and crossed her arms, her expression mutinous.

"What's your real name, Bert? It's obvious you're not Dominic Marzetti."

Sam cringed. "She's too smart for her own good."

Bert snarled. "You won't be so cocky when we've finished with you, princess." He pointed his gun at the lock and fired. The lock shattered and Bert flipped the lid open.

Stepping closer, Andrew chortled. "So that's what twenty million dollars looks like."

Sam's gaze flew to Kallie who'd edged towards the cabin. *Good girl, keep going.* He kept his rifle trained on Bert and his finger on the trigger.

A string of short, sharp bird whistles burst through the night then all was quiet again. The tightness in Sam's shoulders eased. "Talos is in position on the other side of the cottage."

Jarred nodded. "Marzetti has to be close. They'll have some sort of plan to meet up. My guess is it will be here then they'll all fly out together."

Sam hesitated. "I don't want Kallie hurt. How do you want to play this?"

"We split up and take them from all sides."

"All right, what sort of weapons are you and Talos carrying?"

"A couple of gas canisters, our handguns, knives and rifles. What about you."

"My knife, handgun and rifle."

Jarred nodded. "Should be enough, there's only five of them. Here, take a canister."

The three figures stepped away from the tractor, their guns trained on Bert and Andrew who were rifling through the wads of money.

"I believe that belongs to me," called Vassello in a voice as smooth as honey.

Andrew and Bert reached for their guns, but two warning shots at their feet halted them. Kallie screamed.

Sam sighted the back of Victor's head, his finger hovering over the trigger as he concentrated on calming his breathing, his heart pounding as Victor strolled forward, coming to a halt a metre from Kallie.

"Thank you, Miss McNeil. I would not have found this place without you to lead me, although I must admit, it was difficult following you in the dark."

"I honestly didn't know he was following me." Kallie cried.

Vassello turned to Bert. "It's been a long time, Gus. I heard you died in a warehouse fire. Where's Dominic? I know you two are never far apart."

"Screw you," snarled Bert.

Lowering his gun, Victor fired a shot. Bert fell to the ground, clutching his leg and screaming as he writhed in pain.

Sam tracked Kallie as she leapt onto the porch, flattening herself against the wall.

Talos crawled up beside Sam. "She's a gutsy little thing. I've released Roy and helped him to the back of the stables. He's taken a pretty bad beating."

"Jane said as much. How is she?"

"We can't move her. She's fully dilated and ready to deliver."

A loud scream resonated from within the cabin. Kallie dived through the open door and slammed it behind her.

"Shit," muttered Jarred. "Talos, cover the back of the cabin. We'll take care of this lot."

Talos shuffled back and disappeared into the shadows.

"Who else is in the cabin?" demanded Victor.

"My wife," replied Andrew. "She's about to give birth."

"Really?" Victor glanced towards the cabin. "If you want your child delivered safely then I suggest you tell me where Dominic is, otherwise you'll lose both your wife and child."

"I don't know what you're talking about," Andrew snapped.

Victor shook his head. "Thanks to Miss McNeil's little tirade, I know Dominic is your father. I am surprised he never told me about you."

Andrew's face contorted. "I'm not saying anything and I don't give a damn about Jane. She means nothing to me."

Victor laughed. "It seems you really are your father's son. Let's move inside, shall we. I'd like to meet this wife of yours."

"Slow them down," Jarred ordered.

Sam lowered his rifle and squeezed the trigger, sending a volley of bullets into the dirt behind Victor's bodyguards. They threw themselves sideways, hitting the ground hard and rolling for cover. Jarred fired behind Vassello.

The three men scrambled for cover behind the tractor and began shooting randomly into the darkness. Sam and Jarred stayed low, using the lowest fence rail as cover.

Spying Andrew Rossini making for the cabin's door, Sam sent another volley of bullets along the porch floorboards, cutting off his escape. Andrew fell to the boards and crawled to the edge before disappearing round the side of the cabin.

A hail of bullets hit the fence above Sam's head, showering him in chunks of wood.

"Do you want them alive or dead?" Sam muttered, ducking lower.

"I'd prefer alive."

Rapid gunfire burst from the far side of the cabin, throwing Victor and his men into a panic. They hit the ground and crawled under the tractor. The stallion screamed.

Thanks, Talos. Sam fired a couple of shots at the tractor as the sound of the helicopter's engine spluttered into life. "I'm going after Andrew and Bert."

Jarred nodded and pulled out a tear gas cylinder. "I'll be fine." He twisted the can and hurled it towards the tractor. A grey cloud of smoke billowed in all directions and choking sounds reached them as the tear gas engulfed the tractor.

Leaving his rifle, Sam crawled on his belly to the stable yard gate. While Jarred and Talos sent random shots towards the tractor, he unlatched the gate and threw it open. The stallion reared up on his hind legs then galloped through and disappeared into the darkness. Sam slipped through the railings and ran for the helicopter.

The engine still spluttered and coughed. Sam pulled out his Glock. *Looks like Talos also had time to disable the chopper.*

Sam sprinted to the chopper, hauled the door open and dragged Bert out. He smashed his fist into Bert's solar plexus and Bert slid to the ground.

Andrew leapt out the other side and took off at a run.

Sam holstered his gun and sprinted after him.

CHAPTER TWENTY-FIVE

After locking the cabin's front door, Kallie ran into the bedroom. Jane was on her knees, leaning against one of the beds and panting heavily.

"Janie, what can I do to help you?"

"Shit, Kallie. What are you doing here?"

"Saving your butt."

"You bloody idiot. They're planning to kill you and Roy. We have to get out of here, the baby's coming. Oh, Kallie, it hurts so much."

A volley of gunshots sounded, some hitting the outer cabin wall.

"Stay down," Kallie pulled Jane down to the floor.

"We have to get out," Jane cried. "Before the baby comes."

Gunfire boomed right outside the window. Both women screamed.

Above the noise, Kallie heard the helicopter engine. It whined and spluttered. She crawled to the door and cracked it open an inch. "No one's out there. We might have a chance if we slip out the back door now."

Jane began moaning. She'd manoeuvred herself onto all fours, her forehead pressing into the mattress as she rocked back and forth. "It's too late."

The window slid open and someone reached in, gripped the blind and tore it down.

"Watch out, Jane." Kallie pulled the knife out of her back pocket, released the blade and leapt onto the bed.

Jane screamed. "No, Kallie, it's Talos."

"Damn, Talos, I nearly stabbed you." Kallie swung the knife away and jumped off the bed as Talos heaved his big shoulders and body through the window.

"Sorry. I didn't mean to scare you." He shut the window then picked up the mattress and propped it on the bed against the window. He frowned at the knife in Kallie's hand.

"That looks like one of ours?"

"It is. I took it out of Nick's boot. Where's Sam?"

"Outside with Jarred and Roy."

"Thank God." Kallie retracted the blade and slipped the knife back into her pocket.

"How close are the contractions?" Talos knelt beside Jane.

She began panting. "Less than a minute. I can't do this on my own."

"You don't have to. We'll help you." He turned to Kallie. "Is the front door locked?"

"Yes." Biting her lip, Kallie knelt on Jane's other side. "What can I do?"

"I want to examine Jane and I'll need towels and warm water."

"Sure." Kallie ran out of the bedroom and into the kitchen. She gathered everything she thought they'd need and scurried back to the bedroom.

Talos had moved the other mattress onto the floor and taken off his bulletproof vest. Muscles rippled across his broad back as he held Jane's weight. They were both kneeling on the mattress facing each other, Jane's fingers gripping Talos's shoulders, her forehead pressed against his chest as she moaned and rocked.

Kallie dropped the linen on the nearest bed base and placed the bucket on the floor.

"Now what?"

Talos glanced round. "Lay a towel under Jane then soak a towel and rub it with soap. I'll need you to scrub my hands."

"Okay." Kallie did as he asked, washing and drying his hands then she spread the towel under Jane and knelt back.

"It's done."

"Good, now do you have any sterile empty syringes here?"

"Yes, for the horses, why?"

"I might need to clear the baby's airways. Run and get me one and hurry, I'll need you to swap positions with me."

"All right." Kallie jumped to her feet and ran back into the kitchen. She rummaged through the drawers beneath the sink until she found the syringes. She grabbed a pack and ripped it open with her teeth.

The back door crashed open and Andrew ran in, making straight for the bedroom.

"No." Kallie dropped the syringe and threw herself at Andrew, landing a punch on his cheek before he caught her and twisted her into a headlock.

"You little bitch, that hurt." He tightened his hold, cutting off her airway as he dragged her into the kitchen and groped through the cutlery drawer. He pulled out a serrated bread knife. "Let's see how much lover boy cares about you?" He pushed the knife against her chest.

"It won't work," Sam stood in the open doorway and Kallie shivered at the deadly intent in his voice. He stared at them from emotionless orbs of ice, a gun pointed at Andrew. For the first time since meeting Sam, fear raced through Kallie. Fear of what he was capable of doing. Fear of how far he would go to get the job done. This was not the man she loved. This was an emotionless machine.

Andrew's voice wavered. "I'll let her go when I have the money and Jane on board the chopper."

"No fucking way. You're not going anywhere. You release Kallie now and give up Marzetti and you might get a reduced sentence, otherwise I'll kill you with my bare hands."

The knife pressed harder against Kallie's chest. She gasped as the teeth bit into her breast.

"I'm the one with the knife, hero, so I'm the one who makes the deal." Andrew pressed the knife harder.

"Sam." Kallie cried out as the blade bit into her flesh. She choked back a sob at the stinging pain.

"All right. I'm putting the gun down." Sam's cold gaze remained riveted on them as he lowered the Glock to the floor. "Hurt Kallie again and you're dead. As it is, I'm going to make you suffer before I hand you over to the Feds." He kicked the gun across the room.

Dropping the knife, Andrew reached for the gun.

"No." Kallie kicked the gun away and reached into her back pocket for Nick's knife. From the corner of her eye, she glimpsed Sam move as she pressed the release and drove the knife hard into Andrew's thigh.

Bellowing, Andrew loosened his hold on her. Kallie jabbed her elbow into his stomach and went limp, dropping to the floor. Andrew caught her by the hair and yanked her back. Kallie shrieked and reached for his hands to stop him ripping her hair out. He bellowed again and lost his grip on her. Kallie rolled away and clambered to her knees. A heavy thud sounded behind her. She jumped to her feet and ran for Sam.

He caught her with one arm and pulled her tightly against his chest. Kallie glanced back towards Andrew. He lay on the floor moaning, a knife embedded in his thigh and another in his shoulder.

"Why didn't you just shoot him?" Talos called from the bedroom doorway. He held a gun and a knife.

"I needed to hurt him, but I didn't want to piss off the Feds by killing him."

"I've got a baby to deliver." Talos disappeared into the bedroom.

Sam strode across the room and pulled out the two knives. Andrew yowled then his eyes rolled back in his head and he went still.

Tears ran down Kallie's face and she began to shake. "I've never seen you like that. You were so cold and frightening. I thought you were going to kill him."

"No, darlin'." Sam rinsed the knives and placed them on the counter. "I'm sorry if I scared you, but I couldn't show him any sign of weakness. If he knew how much I love you, he'd have had me over a barrel. Both Talos and I were just waiting for a clear shot at him." He walked over and held her. "Did he cut you?"

Pulling out her top, Kallie showed Sam the raw abrasion running across her left breast.

Sam's jaw clenched. "You help Jane while I deal with this piece of garbage."

"I love you, Sam." She stretched up and kissed him.

Sam's arms tightened around her. "I love you too, but I think Jane needs you more at the moment." He nodded towards the bedroom as another groan reached them.

"Be careful." Kallie reluctantly pulled away and hobbled into the bedroom.

Jane was still on her knees, leaning over the bed and moaning.

Talos crouched behind her, encouraging her with his soft drawl. Kallie dropped to her knees on the mattress.

"How's it going, sweetie?"

"Bloody terrible. It feels like I'm shitting out a bus."

Talos chuckled. "You're nearly there. One good push and you'll have your baby."

Another contraction hit and Jane cried out as she strained.

"Here it comes." Talos shuffled closer. "Get a fresh towel, Kallie."

Kallie snatched a towel and leaned in as a small, dark head appeared. Talos held the little head in his hand and eased the shoulders out. Kallie gasped in wonder as the rest of the tiny body slid into Talos's big hands.

"Oh, Jane, it's a girl." Kallie laid out the towel as Talos turned the baby over. Dark little eyes blinked then a frown appeared, making Kallie laugh. The baby dropped her bottom lip and wailed.

"Is she all right?" Jane twisted around.

"She's perfect." Talos laid the baby in the towel, put a couple of cable ties on the umbilical cord and cut it, then he wrapped her and handed the little bundle to Kallie. "Keep her warm while I attend to Jane."

Kallie patted the baby's back gently. "There, there, little one, everything's going to be fine. I'm your Aunty Kallie."

Talos wrapped a blanket round Jane's shoulders and helped her lean back against a couple of pillows. "As soon as the placenta has delivered, we'll get you and the baby to hospital."

Tears ran down Jane's face as she gazed at the baby. "I want to hold her, but I'm shaking so much, I'm afraid I'll drop her."

"No, you won't," Talos soothed. "I'll help you."

Kallie passed the baby back to Talos and he placed the tiny bundle in Jane's arms.

A huge weight lifted as Kallie glanced at the trio on the mattress. Jane's head rested against Talos's shoulder as he supported her. They both gazed at the tiny baby in Jane's arms for a moment then Jane flinched.

"I'm getting another contraction."

Talos handed the baby to Kallie and turned back to Jane. "It's just the afterbirth. Push when you feel the urge."

Kallie glanced across to Sam watching from the door. He smiled and she smiled back, her eyes filling with tears. "It's a little girl."

Stepping forward, Sam helped Kallie to her feet and led her to the door. "Ryan will be here any minute. He's going to fly Jane and the baby to Moree. It has a hospital equipped to cope with premature babies."

Kallie nodded. "What about Bert and Andrew? They need medical attention too."

"They're both okay for now. We've strapped their wounds and once the Feds arrive, they'll take them off our hands."

"And Victor Vassello?"

"He got away, but his two friends surrendered after Jarred and Talos hit them with a couple of teargas canisters. Jarred's locking them in one of the stables and checking on Roy. He might have a couple of broken ribs."

"Where is Roy? I need to check on him."

"He'll be okay but I want you to go to the hospital with him and Jane while we take care of things here."

"Who is Marzetti, Sam? And is Ken involved."

"You let us worry about that." Sam cocked his head to listen. "Sounds like Ryan now. You stay here and I'll check everything's safe to go."

He picked up the two knives, slid one into his boot and the other into Kallie's back pocket. "Keep that with you for now, just in case."

Kallie patted the baby gently as she watched Sam leave. *Why won't Sam tell me who Marzetti is?* She frowned. *Who's left?*

Andrew stirred and then opened his eyes. He tested the rope around his wrists and raised his gaze to the bundle in her arms. "What is it?"

"A little girl."

"I was hoping for a boy. Still, a girl will bring a good price on the adoption market."

Narrowing her eyes, Kallie shook her head. "You're a real prick, Andrew. I hope they throw the book at you."

Skidding tyres sounded and Kallie darted to the kitchen window. Liz was scrambling out of her four-wheel drive. Kallie opened the door and held out the baby. "Hi Liz, meet your granddaughter."

Liz stopped dead in her tracks. "My granddaughter?" Her eyes widened as she stared at the tiny bundle and then Kallie. "Where's Jane?"

Kallie laid the baby in Liz's arms. "She's in the bedroom with Talos. As soon as the placenta is delivered, Ryan's flying Jane and the baby to Moree."

Liz nodded. "I'll go with them. I assume Bert and Andrew have been dealt with."

"Yes." Kallie pointed to Andrew in the corner. "Bert and Vassello's two men are tied up in the stables waiting for the police to arrive. Where are Angus and Fergie?"

"We dropped them at the farm. Poor Angus is in shock over what's happened."

"I'll bet he is. Do you have any idea where Ken might be?"

"No, love, but I swear he's not part of this. I think he's out looking for Victor Vassello."

The bedroom door opened and Talos walked out carrying Jane wrapped in a blanket.

"How's is she?" Jane said.

Liz laid the baby in Jane's arms. "Beautiful. Just like her mother."

Kallie peered in to see the tiny baby sleeping serenely. She smiled and kissed Jane's cheek. "Take care, sweetie, I'll see you both at the hospital."

Kallie stepped back so Talos could carry Jane through the back door. Liz hurried after them and for a couple of minutes Kallie watched their progress towards the big helicopter then she slipped out the front door.

Stepping over the wads of discarded money, Kallie slowly wandered to the tractor, absorbed in recollections she hadn't thought about in years. Her conversation with the friendly visitor she suspected to be her grandfather when she was eight and who gave her the black opal. Her conversation with the heavily bandaged man at Kununurra Hospital, who seemed so frail and who gave her a handful of precious gems, most of which had been spent on funding her breeding program. She thought about the day Bert, a grumpy sour-faced man arrived, informing them he was Angus's friend and carer. *How could I have been so blind?*

She thought about Angus, wheelchair bound after his terrible accident and then the stroke, leaving him with no recollection of his previous life, family or friends.

She shivered as the Black Hawk lifted and flew away. *Please take them safely to hospital.* Climbing the rungs, she reached for her rifle. *Now to deal with Marzetti.*

An arm of steel circled her waist, swung her down and the rifle was pulled out of her hand. "What do you think you're doing?"

"Sam! You shouldn't sneak up on me like that. I could have shot you."

"Unlikely." He released her. "Why didn't you go with Jane to the hospital?"

"Because I don't do helicopters."

Sam's lips twitched. "We're going to have to address your fear of flying. In the meantime, can you help me gather up this money?"

Kallie hesitated. "Shouldn't you be looking for Marzetti?"

"We are. All the roads out of the district are still underwater but as a precaution, Jarred's asked the local police to set up roadblocks. The net is closing around him."

"If you're not SAS any longer then why do you have so much pull with the police?"

Sam smiled. "Don't you know curiosity killed the cat?"

Kallie shrugged. "You may as well tell me. I'm almost part of the team."

"We are no longer full time soldiers in the SAS, however we are still members of the SAS Reserves and occasionally we work closely with the Federal Police, Defence Force and several senior members of Government."

"I see. So obviously your security firm is doing well, seeing as you have a Black Hawk, which I believe are not for sale to the general public or the average millionaire."

A smile spread over Sam's face. "It's all about contacts, honey, and our Black Hawk is an older model." He winked. "Once we have Marzetti, I'm taking you to my place in the Yarramalong Valley. I think you're going to like living there."

Grinning, Kallie began throwing wads of money into the trunk.

As Sam closed the lid, a car engine started and Kallie whipped around. Liz's four-wheel drive was speeding off in the darkness. "Who's that?"

Sam cursed. "It has to be Roy."

Kallie gasped. "Oh no. We have to stop him. I think he's going after Marzetti."

"Let's move," Jarred yelled running from the side of the cottage.

Talos joined them. "I've fixed the small chopper and our rifles are on board."

"Good." Jarred said. "The prisoners are locked up tight and Simon's camouflaged. Let's see if Marzetti takes the bait. Miss McNeil, you had better come with us. "

Kallie backed away. "I'm not going in that thing."

"Sorry, darlin, I'm not leaving you here." Sam hoisted Kallie over his shoulder. "We all have to face our fears sometime, darlin'."

"If you loved me, you wouldn't do this." She thumped Sam's solid back.

"Honey, it's because I love you that I'm doing this. You'll be fine, we're all qualified chopper pilots and flying is safer than being on the roads." He sat her on a rear-seat and slid in beside her.

Talos took a front seat and Jarred climbed into the pilot's seat and slammed the door. "Let's go."

The chopper jerked and lifted off the ground.

Kallie's stomach churned and she began trembling from head to foot. *Oh God, I can't breathe. I can't breathe.*

'I've got you, darlin'." Sam squeezed her hand.

With her eyes closed tight, Kallie clung to Sam, focusing on his steady heartbeat as the whirring blades beat above her.

'There he is," Talos shouted. "Take us lower."

The helicopter dropped and Kallie clenched her teeth as her stomach plummeted. She froze in horror as they swooped towards the bouncing lights of Liz's four-wheel drive, jolting along the soggy track.

Talos slid his window open, aimed his rifle and fired several shots. Kallie screamed as the vehicle fishtailed and slid off the road into a waterlogged ditch. "Are you mad?"

"I was aiming at the tyres, not Roy." Talos pulled his rifle in and closed the window.

Her heart in her throat, Kallie craned her neck and leaned over to see the driver's door open and Roy climb out. She released a shaky breath.

"He's okay."

Sam chuckled. "He's going to be furious though."

Kallie's gaze flew to Jarred's hands as he operated two joysticks. Her heart pounded furiously, her stomach churned but at least they were flying smoothly and relatively close to the ground. Sam's hand covered hers and he squeezed.

"You okay?"

She swallowed. "I can't believe you did this. I trusted you."

He kissed her forehead. "I'd never do anything to endanger you, sweetheart. Leaving you at the cabin is a risk I'm not prepared to take."

Jarred called through from the front. "Miss McNeil, I'm going to put the chopper down behind your barn. Once we've determined the house and surrounding buildings are safe, you may collect anything you need, then you will come with us into Willaroi."

"No thanks, I'm staying at my place."

Nobody answered and Kallie clutched Sam's hand. "Honestly, I'll be fine. I'll lock the door and keep my rifle with me. You do what you have to, but please be careful. I don't want to lose you."

Chapter Twenty-six

As Jarred set the helicopter down, Sam did a quick recon before he opened his door. Talos sprinted ahead to the back wall of the barn then signalled the all clear. After helping Kallie out, Sam grabbed her hand and ran in front, shielding her with his body. The barn's rear doors lay wide. Sam pressed Kallie against the outer wall between himself and Talos. They waited until Jarred had cleared the chopper and joined them.

Talos moved forward. "I'll sweep the barn."

Sam waited another couple of minutes until the tinkling whistle of the Bellbird sounded. Taking Kallie's hand, he towed her into the barn. "I doubt Marzetti's still around but just in case, I want you to stay right behind me."

"Okay."

A short, sharp bird whistle caught Sam's attention and led the way to Jarred. "Anything?"

"Nothing obvious. I've spoken to the Feds and they're setting up their own perimeter around Willaroi and will go door-to-door looking for Marzetti and Ken Macey. After we've checked things here, we're to stake out the cabin in case Marzetti or Vassello show up."

"So we set the trap and then wait. Where's Talos?"

"I've sent him to search the shearing quarters then he'll enter the house from the far side. Switch your head-set on and take the front of the house. I'll cover you and then enter from the rear. If Marzetti's here, he'll have recognised the chopper and be watching. Miss McNeil, you stay with me."

"That's fine with me." Kallie whispered.

As Jarred turned away, Sam caught his arm. "No matter what, if

Marzetti or Vassello pose a threat to Kallie, we take them down."

Jarred nodded and positioned himself by the solid doorframe and studied the house through the gap. "Expect the unexpected. I've got a bad feeling about this."

"You and me both." Sam jogged to the rear of the barn and slipped around the side using the rusty, old water tank for cover. He dropped onto his belly and crawled behind the wooden chook shed. The rooster and his hens had long retired for the night.

Sam studied the house. The porch light beamed over the front steps and lawn. A light shone behind the office curtains. The rest of the house seemed eerily silent.

A short birdcall came from Sam's left. He returned the call, keeping his rifle trained on the house. Talos sprinted across the yard and leapt soundlessly onto the side porch. Five seconds later he disappeared through a French door. Sam waited several seconds then sprinted across the lawn. He plastered his body against the wall and listened.

Nothing moved.

He slid along the wall, ducked under a window and edged to the front door. It stood wide open. *Not a good sign.* The hall lights came on.

Talos's voice sounded in Sam's earpiece. "I'm in and you're clear to enter. Both the shearers' quarters and the house are unoccupied."

Sam swung the screen door open and slipped into the hall. He double-checked each room, ending in the kitchen where Talos met him.

Jarred stuck his head around the back door. "I've found a body in the external laundry. You might want to take a look, but be warned, it's messy."

"Where's Kallie?" Sam said.

"Behind the big tree." Jarred led the way along the porch to the laundry. "Hard to tell, except that it's a male." He hesitated. "And, he's tied to a wheelchair."

The familiar coppery smell of blood hit them. Talos grimaced and glanced at the barn. "If he's in a wheelchair then surely it's Angus McNeil?"

"Not necessarily." Jarred pushed the door open.

"Christ." Sam's stomach roiled. Bile rose in his throat as he stared at the bloody pulp, which was all that was left of the victim's face. "Fuck, what sort of sicko did this?"

Talos grimaced. "The worst kind."

Sam studied the blood soaked corpse from the doorway. "Look at the rope burns around the ankles, wrists and neck. I'd say he didn't die quickly and by the amount of blood, his heart had to have been pumping while he was smashed to pieces. A vicious animal did this."

Jarred closed the door. "Don't forget Marzetti's renowned for his sadistic pleasure in brutalising anyone who crosses him."

Jarred glanced towards the barn. "I don't know if an autopsy will help. By the state of his hands, they won't get fingerprints either. His death is going to rock this little community." He pulled out his phone. "I'll inform the Feds so they can set up a crime scene."

"What about Roy?" Sam said. "He's on the loose and if he comes up against Marzetti, he'll be in deep shit."

"I agree. Let's try and find the murder weapon then we'll collect our little friend. It might be wise not to mention we've found a body."

Sam stepped off the porch. "I agree. The less Kallie knows, the better."

From her position behind the ancient red river gum, Kallie struggled to hear their conversation. She'd picked up enough though to know Roy would be in trouble if he came across Marzetti. Using the tree as a barrier, she skirted the yard and dashed behind the hen house.

She risked another look at the rear of the house. Sam, Jarred and Talos were bent over, searching the garden beds near the porch. *I have to get back to the cottage and warn Roy.*

Once inside the barn, she unclipped Jasper's halter and ran him to the back of the barn. "Good boy." She saddled and bridled him then jumped on her mounting block. "We have to be quick, no sugar lumps tonight. She threw her leg over and nudged Jasper into a walk.

Glancing back, Kallie let out a relieved breath. No one had seen her. She walked Jasper as far as she dared then prodded him into a canter. Galloping was too dangerous. Cantering was risky enough.

When they reached the trees and a well-used trail, Kallie pulled Jasper back to a fast trot and let her mind dwell on everything she'd heard from behind the tree. She clenched her teeth in an effort to hold back the emotion that threatened to overflow. *The body must have been pretty messed up if they can't identify it.* She drew a shaky breath, her head ached, her feet throbbed and her heart pounded so hard it frightened her. Fear of what she might find made her quake. *I wish Liz had just left Angus and Fergie in town.* A small branch whipped her across the face. "Ow."

Crouching over Jasper's neck, she nudged him faster. *Ken must be helping Marzetti. Oh God, I have to get to Roy before they do.*

Once clear of the trees, Kallie soared across the open ground, thankful for the full moon to light her way and the fact these pastures were high enough not to be under water. She shunned the usual route leading to the cabin and took one of the sheep trails, which skirted the stud and wound around the back of a small knoll. Tying Jasper's reins to a small tree, she hobbled to the fence and ducked through.

Pounding hooves and a shrill scream made her dive back through the fence in a hasty retreat. "What the..." Kallie scrambled to her knees and stared through the fence. "Aramis? What is he doing in this paddock?"

The stallion reared and pawed the air. *Good God, what's wrong with him?* Crawling to the fence, Kallie held out her hand. "It's okay, Aramis. Come on, lovely boy. What's got you all fired up?

Aramis snorted, threw his head around and pawed at the ground.

Kallie crouched and jogged along the outside of the fence until she came to the next paddock. Aramis strutted on the other side, snorting loudly. *At least he's obstructing me from any observers.*

She ducked through the next fence and darted to the large water tank where she had a clear view of the cabin and stables. Nothing moved. *Where's Simon? He's supposed to be guarding the prisoners.*

An arm circled her waist at the same time as a rough hand clamped across her mouth. Kallie struck out with both elbows and her boot.

"It's me, Bossy, go easy." The arm and hand fell away.

Whirling, Kallie caught Roy and hugged him. He flinched.

"Shush, not so tight, Bossy. I think I've got broken ribs."

Pulling back, Kallie examined him. His right eye was swollen shut and bruised, his nose off centre. "Bert did this to you, didn't he?"

"Yeah, but he's the least of our worries. Come with me." Holding his ribs, Roy shuffled round the back of the tank, dropped to his knees and crawled underneath.

Kallie followed. "What are we doing under here?" she whispered.

"We're waiting for Marzetti." Another voice came from her right.

"Ken!" Kallie gasped. He looked scruffy, fatigued and more than a little irritated. He also held a rifle. "What's going on? Everyone thinks you're one of Marzetti's men."

"Why would they think that?" He leaned back against a brick pier and closed his eyes. "I've been following Vassello, waiting for the chance to interrogate him."

"Why?" Kallie spread her arms.

"I used to be in the police force. On my last job, we were raiding one of Vassello's warehouses." Ken opened his eyes. "My partner was killed and next thing I know, I'm the main suspect. I've been fighting for years to clear my name."

Kallie frowned. "But how did you end up in Willaroi?"

"I was tipped off that Marzetti was hiding out here. I never met the man but I heard he'd stolen twenty million dollars from Vassello and I knew it was only a matter of time before Vassello got the same info and came looking for him. I just had to wait."

Ken grimaced. "After a few months I figured my info was wrong, but I'd met Liz."

Loud voices sounded from the stables and Kallie glanced out through the lattice. "Who's that?

Roy grunted. "Andrew and Bert haven't stopped arguing since Sam threw them in there and Bert keeps baiting Vassello's men."

Kallie searched the dark for any sign of movement and then turned back to Ken. "If you were following Vassello, where is he?"

"I followed him here, watched the action from the gate, then when I saw Vassello escaping, I jumped into his vehicle and waited. After a couple of kilometres I stuck my rifle in his ear and told him to pull over and turn his lights off."

"Did he confess to setting you up?" Kallie asked.

"No. He confessed my partner was on Marzetti's payroll and would tip them off whenever we were about to launch a raid. Vassello said Marzetti shot my partner because he'd outlived his usefulness then Marzetti disappeared, taking Vassello's money with him."

"Could Vassello be lying?"

"No, it all makes sense. All our other raids on Marzetti's warehouses came up clean. That last warehouse was the only one that belonged to Vassello but was leased by Marzetti."

"So what did you do with Vassello?"

"Let him go. It's Marzetti I need to clear my name and he won't leave without that money or the diamond. The Feds will pick Vassello up."

Kallie bit her lip. "Have either of you seen Fergie or Angus?"

Both men shook their heads.

Drawing in a shaky breath Kallie turned to Roy. "There's a body back at the house and I heard Sam say he'd been murdered."

"Christ," Ken muttered.

Kallie wriggled into a more comfortable position. "Marzetti killed Donna and Wally. My guess is he'll attempt to free Bert and Andrew, then they'll take the money and run."

"At least they don't have your diamond," scoffed Roy. "That was good thinking, giving them the pink sapphire. It certainly fooled those idiots."

"But it won't fool Marzetti. This is what he really wants." Kallie held out the dark gem. "Meet the Kalista Diamond, which although thought to be pink is actually more of a purple."

Ken and Roy stared at the diamond then her. "Wow," they whispered in unison.

∽◦↩

On the hillock overlooking the small horse stud, a man lay on his stomach, amusement pulling at the corners of his mouth.

What kind of soldiers are these cretins? They leave millions of dollars sitting in a trunk on the porch and stick four men in a stable block without taking their phones. Still it's a pity they took Kallie. Now I have to waste time looking for her.

Raising his infrared binoculars, he studied the cabin, stables and surrounding paddocks. The fierce stallion continued to whinny and snort at the corner of the nearest paddock. Movement near the water tank caught his eye.

Well, well, well, I won't have to go searching for my little dove after all.

He studied Kallie as she edged around the tank and ran towards the cabin.

I bet that interfering Aboriginal is here somewhere too. He rotated his sore shoulder. *I might have to shoot him. I shouldn't have wasted so much time on Victor.*

His phone vibrated. "What?"

"Those SAS guys found a body at the farm and now all the roads have been blocked and the town locked down."

"I don't care if they've locked the whole fucking state down, find me a way out. If I go down, so do you."

"What happened to your helicopter?"

"Those SAS idiots took it to the farm, but they'll be back; the clever girl got away from them. Did you find out what sex the baby is?"

"Yeah, a girl and she's at Moree Hospital, but she and the mother are under heavy police guard. You won't get anywhere near them."

"I'd have preferred a boy. I have a few loose ends to tidy up. Buy me some time."

"I can't delay any longer; they'll be coming for the prisoners. Bert's a loose cannon and that son of yours is likely to squeal like a pig if he's questioned."

"Dead pigs don't squeal, but first I need to free Andrew so he can fly us out of here."

"Is your cover still solid if things go belly-up?"

"Of course. You of all people should know I always have a backup plan, and I didn't change my appearance or the way I speak for nothing. You take care of your side of things and I'll deal with the loose ends."

"How long do you need?"

"Twenty minutes."

"All right, I'll ground those SAS men and commandeer the chopper and a pilot. It'll probably take me ten minutes to get there, then we'll dispatch the pilot."

"I'll be waiting with the money and an extra passenger."

"I hope it's the pretty one. I'm on my way."

Dominic Marzetti ended the call and brooded. *I'm going to have to do something about that detective. He's getting too cocky.* He selected another number.

Bert's gruff voice answered. "About time. When are you getting us out of here?"

"I'm on my way. There's been a change of plans. Our detective has managed to get hold of a chopper and it will be here in ten minutes. Andrew can't be trusted to keep his mouth shut but I need him to fly us out of here. Once we're safely on the freighter and well offshore, I want you to feed him to the sharks along with the detective." Dominic ended the call.

Now to deal with Roy and collect Kallie.

Jarred's phone vibrated. He turned it onto loudspeaker. "Anything to report, Simon?"

"Yeah, Marzetti just ordered Gus Bowen to get rid of Andrew and a detective once they're on some freighter. What do you want me to do?"

"Nothing. Our orders were very specific. Where's Marzetti?"

"On the hill behind the cabin. He has infrared binoculars and an AK47. He just received a call and I managed to pick up his side of the conversation on my scanner. There's definitely a mole in the AFP."

"Can you identify him?"

"No."

"What about Roy?" Sam said.

"He's under the water tank and not long ago Kallie turned up on horseback."

"Fuck," Sam slammed the wall. "We've been ordered to stay put. Can you get to her?"

"Not without blowing my cover. Roy whisked her out of sight pretty quick, but then she made a run for the cabin. Probably thought that's where I was hiding."

"Shit. Did Marzetti see her?"

"Yep. He also asked his caller for the whereabouts of the baby and seemed satisfied with the answer. Then he told the caller he wants time to tie up some loose ends."

Talos clenched his fist. "So it's someone with a lot of pull."

"Anything else to report?" asked Jarred.

"Marzetti's got a backup plan. He's arranged a rendezvous in ten minutes and I think he's planning on taking Kallie."

Sweat broke out on Sam's forehead. He grabbed the phone from Jarred. "You're going to have to find a way into the cabin without being seen."

"Relax. If Marzetti heads that way, I'll take him out."

"Make sure you do. We'll be there as fast as we can."

Sam ended the call and passed it back to Jarred. It rang again immediately.

After checking the screen, Jarred pressed speakerphone. "Jarred Steele speaking."

"Colonel Steele, this is Inspector Gibbs. I'm with the AFP Human Trafficking Squad. There's been a sighting of Marzetti in Willaroi, so I can't spare any personnel to relieve you. I have a senior officer on his way to the cabin now. He'll take charge of the prisoners."

"May I ask who sighted Marzetti?"

"Not sure, one of my men took the call. Where are all your men at the moment?"

One of Jarred's eyebrows rose. His gaze locked with Sam's. "I have one in Collarenabri Hospital with a gunshot wound to the shoulder, one enroute from Moree Base Hospital and one out of action with a suspected broken rib. The other two are standing beside me. Why?"

"You didn't leave any men at the cabin?"

"Inspector, we were ordered to the McNeil farm to do a thorough search. The prisoners are locked up tight and I've left the stockman to keep an eye on things. My guess is Vassello and Marzetti are long gone. I don't know what to think of Ken Macey."

"I see, and Kallie McNeil?"

"She took a horse and disappeared while we were searching for the murder weapon."

"Very well. I'll tell my men to keep an eye out for her." He hung up.

Slipping the phone into his inside pocket, Jarred glanced at Sam and Talos. "Well?"

Talos shrugged. "I doubt Gibbs is the mole, but we'd better contact Ryan and check his ETA, he's got to be close. Ring our client and bring him up to date. I'll get Ryan to drop us as close to the cabin as we can."

Roy's stallion whickered nearby.

Sam turned away, anxiety gnawed at him. He'd never felt so helpless in his life. *I can't lose her.*

CHAPTER TWENTY-SEVEN

Kallie peered out the window into the surrounding dark. A light breeze rustled the branches of the big gum by the stables. She couldn't see Simon anywhere.

The phone blared beneath her elbow, startling her. She cleared her throat, "Hello?"

"I am going to kill you when I get my hands on you." Heavy breathing and pounding hooves accompanied the deep voice.

"Sam?"

"Don't speak, just listen. Marzetti is making his way down the hill behind the cabin. He's armed and he knows you're in the cabin."

"I have to warn Roy and...."

"We already have."

"How?"

"Simon's in a tree near the tank. You have about five minutes to get clear. Slip out the front door and hide under the tractor. Marzetti's got infrared binoculars, so stay hidden, and be careful, he's planning on taking you with him."

"Me? But why?"

"Darlin', we don't have time to chat. Go now." He hung up.

"But I know who Marzetti is." Kallie unlocked the gun safe and grabbed the 303 and a box of bullets. She opened the front door and looked at the night sky. *It will be light soon.* After a glance at the gum tree, she hobbled down the steps and crawled under the tractor, positioning herself behind a massive wheel.

Why does Marzetti want me? She loaded the rifle and examined the gum tree. Its branches rustled in the breeze, but for the life of her, she couldn't detect Simon.

After several minutes she saw a shadow moving towards the water tank so she pulled back out of sight and waited, her heart pounding so loudly she feared it would give her away. Curiosity finally got the better of her and she peered round the tyre.

Although shrouded in darkness, she had a perfect view of the cabin and stables. Narrowing her eyes, she studied the water tank.

Where'd he go?

Aramis trumpeted and thundered down the fence line. An answering trumpet sounded, along with pounding hooves. Several mares whickered from within the stables. Kallie let her gaze travel slowly over the building.

A whizzing noise drew her attention to a couple of doors that had been shut before. Kallie searched the shadows; three figures were mounting the fence. The pounding hooves grew louder and closer, so did the sound of an approaching helicopter. Kallie's gaze flew to the paddock.

Aramis soared over the fence and into the yard, snorting and bucking, the whites of his eyes luminous against his black face, rendering him demon-like. The men jumped back against the fence. A small chopper flew in over the yard and landed behind the cabin

The other stallion bellowed from the paddock behind. *That's Roy's stallion?* She wiggled to the other side of the wheel and caught sight of the three men hustling towards the cabin. One was clearly Bert, or Gus, or whatever his real name was. He hobbled along, dragging one leg. She also recognised Andrew. *Prick. Marzetti must have released them.* Narrowing her eyes, Kallie studied the third man. A cap hid his face but there was no denying who he was. She sagged against the tyre as disbelief, horror and pain hit her.

"Hold it, Marzetti," yelled Ken. "I've got a bone to pick with you."

Kallie sat up quickly and sighted the 303 on the three other men.

"What bone would that be?" Marzetti spoke in a smooth, articulate voice. One Kallie had never heard him use before. He and Bert both lowered their rifles.

Ears flattened, nostrils flaring, Aramis pawed the ground and snorted.

Shit, where is Sam and our team? Kallie unclicked the safety.

Ken hesitated. "I can't believe it's you. I'd never have believed it if I hadn't seen you with my own eyes. You deceitful bastard."

"Now you know. What's your gripe with me?"

"Fifteen years ago you killed my partner and left me to take the fall. I've never taken a bribe in my life. You ruined my career and my first marriage."

Marzetti shrugged. "It wasn't personal. Your partner became sloppy and greedy. He had to go and so do you." He pushed Bert towards Ken and raised his rifle.

Kallie pulled the trigger as several other shots rang out. She lowered her rifle, trying to see who was who in the dark shadows. Andrew was scrambling under a fence. Ken clutched at his arm and Bert was struggling to his knees, holding his side. Marzetti backed slowly towards the cabin holding his rifle high.

The small helicopter's engine fired and the blades began whooshing rapidly, and then it lifted above the cabin and swept away to the east. Aramis screamed and charged, rearing and striking out with his hooves. Ken caught a hoof in the back and was sent sprawling. Marzetti took aim but a rapid blast of gunfire sounded and he leapt onto the porch and darted inside the cabin.

Kallie bit her lip and watched as Ken rolled from side to side, struggling to avoid Aramis's thrashing hooves and gnashing teeth. Andrew bolted towards the stables, jumping over what looked like two bodies.

The stallion reared again and a bloodcurdling scream shattered the night as Aramis found his target, bringing more than five hundred kilos of solid horseflesh hammering down on Bert. The stallion reared again, pounding Bert's body into the soggy ground.

Turning away, Kallie covered her ears, trying to block out the carnage.

Oh God, Ken!

Glancing back, she searched the yard. Ken was trapped against the water trough. The stallion's hooves slammed into the dirt, missing him by inches. Aramis reared again, his intent clear. He wouldn't stop until he'd crushed every bone in Ken's body as well.

With tears streaming down her face, Kallie raised her rifle, sighted the magnificent stallion she'd raised since birth and fired.

Aramis jerked sideways and crumpled to the ground.

Kallie dropped the rifle and slumped, sobbing at the brutal death she'd just witnessed, and her heart breaking at the necessary execution of her darling stallion. Today she'd almost lost Roy and Jane, discovered a terrible truth, and shot a magnificent animal.

"This is all Marzetti's fault. I'm going to kill him." She wiped her nose on the back of her hand and reached for her rifle.

A large hand covered hers. "No, darlin'. Killing another human is something you never want to do."

"Sam." Kallie threw herself into his arms and sobbed. "I had to shoot my beautiful Aramis. I didn't have a choice, he would have killed Ken."

"Shush." His arms tightened round her. "Aramis is fine. You're a terrible shot."

"What!" Kallie pulled away and stared at Sam. "But I saw him go down?"

"Roy shot the horse with a tranquiliser, but he'll be fine in a couple of hours, and with some tender loving care he shouldn't have any ill effects."

Tears spilled down Kallie's cheeks. "Is Ken all right?"

"Except for a few nasty bruises and a bullet graze, he'll be all right."

"Oh no, Marzetti *did* shoot him."

"No darlin', you did."

"What? I was aiming at Marzetti."

"As I said. You're a terrible shot, but don't worry, I won't tell Ken."

"Huh." She swiped him. "Tell me everything, where is our team?"

His lips twitched. "It looks like Marzetti shot Vassello's thugs. Bert is dead, thanks to your stallion and Marzetti's holed up inside the cabin with a detective the Feds want to get their hands on. I told the chopper pilot to get the hell out of here."

Kallie bit her lip. "Can you and Simon handle Marzetti on your own?"

"We're not alone." He kissed her. "Stay here and stay quiet."

"Sam, wait. I know who Marzetti is." She gulped and took a deep breath. "And I'm pretty sure the body back at the farm is Fergie."

"No, It's not Fergie. Marzetti thinks we're a bunch of idiots and that we're all back at the farm or injured, which is what we want him to think. Now please stay under here where I know you're safe and let us do what we do best."

"So, the whole team is here?"

"All except Nick, but he's going to be fine. Give me your word you'll stay here?"

Kallie nodded and hugged him. "I love you."

"And I love you." He wormed backwards and disappeared into the night.

Gripping the rifle, Kallie crawled to the front of the tractor and shuffled into a sitting position. To either side she had a clear view of the yard, stables, Aramis's great hulk and anyone who may approach. The cabin stood behind her. She stared into the darkness, nursing the 303, and leaned against the cold steel bucket. *What could be safer than steel?*

Sam pulled his glove back and checked the time. He lowered his night vision goggles and scanned the dark yard. After a minute, he located Simon concealed in the large gum tree where he could cover Kallie's position. Sam's gaze moved to the top of the water tank silhouetted against the night sky, where Ryan lay flattened amongst rolls of fencing wire, the muzzle of his rifle the only thing visible. Talos and Jarred should be amongst the tall grass at the rear and far side of the cabin. Sam didn't even try to locate them. He glanced to the hilltop behind the cabin. *Roy and Ken should be up there with Fergie by now.* Sam's lips quirked. *Nick will be surprised to learn Jarred's hired a sniper.*

After one final scan over the tractor, Sam unclipped his gas cylinder, lifted his lip mike and whispered. "Ready whenever you are, Colonel."

Jarred's voice came through, cool and precise. "Let's get this party started, Lieutenant, and try not to kill either of them or shoot up the money."

"Does that mean we're all getting a large bonus?"

"You should know better than that. It's tainted money. Now stop jabbering and launch those fucking canisters."

"Understood." Sam raised his rifle butt, smashed the lounge window and tossed in the gas cylinder and then ducked back, plastering himself against the wall. Simultaneously the kitchen, bedroom and bathroom windows shattered.

Two short bursts of gunfire rang out from inside, then hacking coughing could be heard.

"Get ready. Simon, if they come out the front door, force them back."

"Got it."

Edging to the corner of the cabin, Sam peeked round as the front door opened. Simon unloaded a round of bullets into the wooden boards at their feet. The door slammed.

Sam jogged along the side of the cabin, ducked under the lounge window and continued to the back corner. He held his breath and waited.

The continual coughing gave away the position of the two men. Sam released his breath as he heard furniture being dragged about.

"Now they're coming your way, Fergie. Let them get clear of the cabin. Talos, watch the detective doesn't kill Marzetti to save his own skin and Simon, keep an eye on Andrew."

"He's still in the stable," answered Simon."

The unknown detective hunched and darted towards the hill. Dominic Marzetti shadowed him. Both carried AK47's and both glanced around furtively. Sam tracked their progress through his night vision goggles. "Marzetti's no fool. He's staying behind because he doesn't trust the other guy either."

"There's no honour amongst thieves," Jarred muttered. "Let's separate them."

The night erupted into gunfire. Muzzle flashes coming from six different directions, dirt and small stones hitting the two men's bodies. They both ran one way then another and another as the bullets bombarded the ground in front of them. The detective ran for the open field. Marzetti dived into the thick undergrowth bordering the helipad and came up firing. Behind, him, Jarred stepped from the cover of a she-oak and delivered a powerful roundhouse kick, sending Marzetti face first into the tussocks. Jarred straddled him, digging his knee in hard and twisting Marzetti's arms behind him until he cried out in agony.

Satisfied, Sam turned his attention to the detective. He'd changed direction and was heading towards the side of the cabin. "Shit." Sam went after him. "Simon, incoming."

"Got him."

A burst of gunfire spewed out of the tree. The detective lunged sideways, returning fire. A couple of small branches plummeted to the ground. The mole rolled, scrambled to his feet and sprinted towards the tractor.

"Head him off," Sam roared, throwing his goggles down and racing after the man.

Bullets sprayed the ground from three different directions. The detective dived.

Sam bellowed. "Kallie, get out of there."

Shit, she doesn't have time. He raised the rifle and fired a bullet into the man's lower leg, but the guy still managed to crawl behind a wheel. A shot rang out from under the tractor.

"Fuck." With his heart in his mouth, Sam leapt into the cab, gunned the engine and lifted the bucket high. *I have to get Kallie out and give the boys a clear shot at the bastard.*

The light from the porch revealed their target crawling out from under the tractor and then he raised his hands. Blood gushed from wounds to his lower leg and buttock. Sam ignored the man and leapt out of the tractor, dropped to his knees and stared at the unmoving body, lying prostrate in the dirt.

Kallie lay deadly still. *No, no, no.* He began examining her frantically. *Where's the fucking blood.* His body iced over as his world plummeted into nothingness. The sunlight in his heart over the last weeks turned to dense fog. His shoulders sagged and he collapsed on his heels, staring at his beautiful angel.

"Sam, wake the fuck up," Talos yelled. "Kallie knocked herself out trying to shoot this piece of shit." He kicked the AK47 across the yard and away from the detective.

"What?" The ice around Sam's heart began to thaw.

Talos indicated the rifle beside Kallie. "I saw her fire that ancient piece of shit and the kickback threw her against the bucket."

Sam slid his hand over Kallie's head. His lungs expanded. "I can feel a lump."

Kallie moaned and opened her eyes. "Did I get him?"

Sam pulled her into his arms. "Yes, darlin', you got him." He blinked the moisture out of his eyes, cleared his throat and then studied the man sprawled at Simon and Talos's feet.

"Who is he?"

Flipping open a brown leather wallet, Simon read. "Detective Greenwood."

Ryan strode over from the stables dragging Andrew behind him. "I caught this piece of shit trying to escape." He shoved Andrew onto the ground beside the unconscious man. "I'll get the chopper and bring it closer."

Jarred appeared from the side of the cabin pushing a handcuffed Marzetti ahead of him. He ripped Marzetti's cap off his head and threw him down to join the other two.

Sam glanced at Kallie to see her staring in stony silence at Dominic Marzetti. The man she'd believed to be Angus, her crippled grandfather, whom she'd taken into her home and cared for over the last eleven years.

Shit. Sam took Kallie's hand. "I'm taking you home."

"Wait." Kallie stared down at the man on his knees. "How could you do this? I loved you. What happened to my real grandfather and the real Bert Chalmers?

Marzetti looked around the circle of men aiming high-powered rifles at him and shrugged. "Maybe they met with an accident on their way to this Godforsaken place."

Kallie gasped.

Fury burned in Sam's soul. "What did you do to them?"

"I don't know what you're talking about." Marzetti looked up at Kallie. "Think carefully before you testify against me, girl. I'd hate to see you disappear into an Asian brothel."

Blinded by rage, Sam drove his fist into Marzetti's face, knocking him backwards.

Andrew snarled. "You have no idea who you're messing with. My father only has to give the word and everyone you hold dear will be gone, like that." He clicked his fingers.

"You arsehole." Talos planted his size thirteen boot in Andrew's face, breaking his nose and knocking him head over turkey. He hauled Andrew off the ground and pressed a switchblade against his throat, scoring the skin. "Marzetti or you give any such order and I'll skin you both alive, strip by tiny strip. That's a promise."

Blood seeped from the corner of Andrew's mouth and nose.

"Do we understand each other?" Talos asked coldly.

Jarred placed a restraining hand on Talos's arm. "The AFP will move Jane and Kallie into protective custody. If Marzetti and this piece of shit ever get out of jail, they'll never be able to find them."

Talos dropped Andrew and grimaced at Sam. "I'd better say goodbye then." He turned to Ryan. "Can you give me lift to the hospital?"

"No worries."

Drawing Kallie out of hearing distance, Sam lowered his voice. "Once Jane and the baby are given the all clear, they can stay at my place until the trial's over."

She sank against him. "Oh, thank God. I was afraid they were going to separate us."

As Jarred joined them Sam nodded towards the bloodied men. "What about them?"

"Inspector Gibbs and his men are on their way. Take Kallie to visit Jane then collect your truck and go home. Simon and I will wait for Gibbs." He grimaced. "And don't forget the money. That will need to be passed on to the right people"

"I won't."

Kallie gazed into Sam's eyes. "What about Fergie and Roy? Where are they?"

"Here." A crusty voice called from behind Sam.

"Fergie, you're alive." Kallie hugged him. "I thought it was you in the laundry."

"Nah, that was Victor Vassello. I got out of there just in the nick of time. And guess what? I'm moving to Sydney. Jarred's offered me a job."

"Oh, Fergie." Kallie hugged him as Roy ambled over, his face all swollen, his lip cut and his arm in a sling.

Kallie hugged him gently. "You look terrible. We need to get you to the hospital and have you checked out."

"Soon. I've got a few things to take care of here first." He walked over to Ken.

Sam turned to Jarred. "Did you hear what's happening with the young Asian girls Marzetti brought into the country?"

"The AFP intercepted the freighter and after interviewing the girls returned them to Vietnam. They thought they were coming to Australia to work as tailors and manicurists. They had very little English and no idea they were headed for Marzetti's sweat shops and brothels. They couldn't read the contracts they'd signed."

Car lights beamed across the valley and the Black Hawk came swooping in over the cabin and landed close to the tractor. Sam took Kallie's hand and nodded to Jarred. "We've got to go. I'll give you a call later."

"No worries. Take care of her, Sam. She's the best thing that's ever happened to you."

"I will. Thanks." He turned to Kallie. "Come on, darlin'. Let's go?"

She drew a deep breath and smiled. "Okay, but how?"

Sam winked at her. "Talos, Simon, you fellas ready?"

"Ready," they chorused, picking up the trunk and trudging towards the Black Hawke.

Kallie's eyes widened. "Oh no."

Sam bent and hoisted Kallie over his shoulder. Kallie spluttered. "Put me down, Samuel Locke. I absolutely refuse to go in that thing."

"It gets easier the more you do it and don't call me Samuel."

"I really will never speak to you again." She punched his back.

Roy chuckled from close behind. "Don't worry about a thing, Bossy. I'll put the farm on the market and take care of things here once I get these ribs checked out. Just get busy and build some yards so I can freight the horses to you. I might even come down and give you a hand to build the stables."

"Not if you don't stop them putting me on the helicopter." Kallie cried.

Sam patted her bottom. "Roy's not going to help you. He knows I've got your best interests at heart. You ready, Talos?"

"Yep, just securing the trunk so it doesn't go anywhere. Okay, give her here."

Kallie squirmed. "I mean it, Samuel Locke. If you don't...Oh."

Sam had tossed her to Talos, climbed in and held out his arms. "Come here, darlin'."

"No, I..."

Talos lowered her onto the seat beside Sam, helped Roy in then shut the door and climbed into the cockpit with Ryan. Roy closed his eyes and leaned back in the seat.

Kallie wrapped her arms around Sam tightly and he could feel her heart hammering against his chest. He kissed her forehead. "It's not far to Moree Hospital and Jane will be the happier for seeing you and Roy safe."

Kallie shivered. "Don't let go of me."

"Never."

As they lifted off, Sam took Kallie's hand. "Yarramalong is a beautiful valley surrounded by hills and the Wyong River runs along the back of my place. You're going to be very happy there with me, your horses, Ajax, and our babies."

"Don't try to sweet talk me, Samuel Locke."

Taking her chin, Sam lowered his head and kissed her sweet lips tenderly.

Kallie groaned and melted against him, her hand coming to rest on his chest as she parted her lips and returned his kisses. After a minute she drew back and met his gaze. "I really do love you, Sam."

He raised her hand and kissed the palm softly. "I love you too, Kallie, and I want to spend the rest of my life with you. Will you marry me?"

"Yes, my darling." She smiled at him, her eyes brimming with love and happiness.

Elation filled Sam's soul as he lowered his head again and took possession of Kallie's lovely lips, which parted under his as she returned his kisses with fervour.

"Where does a fella find a special woman like that?" Ryan said.

Reaching for his headphones, Talos grinned. "Let's get this bird flying a little faster. I've got a special woman at Moree Hospital that I need to check on."

I hope you enjoyed Sam and Kallie's story. Book Two of the Steele Ops Series is **Precious Gems** and set in both Australia and Vietnam. The Team is hired to hunt down a human trafficking ring. Matters become complicated when they are assigned to safeguard the only person who can identify the ring members—a beautiful young woman who is on the Ring's hit list.

Here is the back cover blurb.

He's a trained commando who has been enticed by a pair of green eyes.

Former SAS Captain James Talarico (Talos) is on a mission to locate a ring of people traffickers before they succeed in killing the person who can identify them. Talos saved the life of this beautiful young woman and delivered her baby on a previous mission. Unable to stop thinking about Jane, Talos tracks her down and ends up saving her life again. Now he won't trust anyone else to keep her safe. Nor can he ignore his growing attraction to her. Yet the perfect solution will place her and the baby in much greater danger.

She's never met a man like him.

Jane Rossini didn't know she was married to a mobster's son until she walked out of her short-lived marriage and ended up as a hostage in the middle of a gun battle. She owes her life to a handsome giant who makes her heart race wildly. Yet she refuses to commit to another man unless she can be sure he truly loves her. Under the constant threat of death and with the police insisting she be relocated and given a new identity, Jane decides to take control. She demands Talos and his Special Ops friends take her with them to Vietnam, so she can identify the ring members before they succeed in killing her. Little does she know what awaits them.

About the Author

 **Erin Moira O'Hara** grew up in the Blue Mountains of Australia, with a garden backing onto native bushland, hidden caves and fabulous lookouts. Weekends were spent exploring, climbing trees and creating secret bases. Her love of reading began with visits to the local library, where she became absorbed in a world of intrigue, fantasy and action-packed adventures. The moment Erin read her first romance; she recognised the importance of finding the right man to share her life. She now lives with him close to the largest saltwater lake in Australia. Their home overlooks bushland and is surrounded by an abundance of bird life and an ever-growing garden.

Erin's writing encompasses everything she loves—intrigue, suspense, passion and romance.

If you would like to know more, please visit:
http://www.erinmoiraohara.com

ALSO BY ERIN MOIRA O'HARA

The Knight of Castle Kildare

Conspiracy in Emilia Romagna

Beat of the Jungle

Steele Ops Series

The Kalista Diamond

Precious Gems

Jewel of the Kimberley

The Amethyst Code

Bindarra Creek

Tempting Fate

Date with Destiny

A Twist of Fate